T5-AQQ-378

More praise for
Treasures of the Heart...

"*Treasures of the Heart* is an often lighthearted and always heartwarming story about people learning to accept their differences and discover their similarities through love and compassion . . . Ms. Runge has an incredible talent for creating characters the reader falls in love with."
—*The Romance Reviewer*

"Tina Runge makes her debut with a warm and charming Americana romance that your heart will treasure."
—*BookBug on the Web*

"Ms. Runge has created a gem of a quilt treasure for you to savor."
—*The Belles & Beaux of Romance*

"The sparkling talent of Tina Runge shines in her intriguing storyline and appealing characters."
—*Romance Communications*

Autographed Copy

Treasures of the Heart

TINA RUNGE

For Frank.
Thanks for all of
your help, and support!
Enjoy!
Tina Runge

JOVE BOOKS, NEW YORK

This is a work of fiction. Names, characters, places, and incidents are
either the products of the author's imagination or are used fictitiously, and
any resemblance to actual persons, living or dead, business establishments,
events or locales is entirely coincidental.

A QUILTING ROMANCE is a trademark of Penguin Putnam Inc.

TREASURES OF THE HEART

A Jove Book / published by arrangement with
the author

PRINTING HISTORY
Jove edition / November 1999

All rights reserved.
Copyright © 1999 by Tina Runge.
Cover illustration by Griesbach/Martucci.
This book may not be reproduced in whole or part,
by mimeograph or any other means, without permission.
For information address: The Berkley Publishing Group,
a division of Penguin Putnam Inc.,
375 Hudson Street, New York, New York 10014.

The Penguin Putnam Inc. World Wide Web site address is
http://www.penguinputnam.com

ISBN: 0-515-12680-2

A JOVE BOOK®
Jove Books are published by The Berkley Publishing Group,
a division of Penguin Putnam Inc.,
375 Hudson Street, New York, New York 10014.
JOVE and the "J" design
are trademarks belonging to Penguin Putnam Inc.

PRINTED IN THE UNITED STATES OF AMERICA

10 9 8 7 6 5 4 3 2 1

I'd like to express my gratitude to a few very special people:

Jenni, Judith, and Liz: GMTA forever! You're the best!

Tazz, my shoulder to cry on: thanks for always making time for me and my whining.

My family: your support means everything!

Pesha Rubenstein: many, many thanks!

To Jordan, Joshua, and Jeremy: my own three heroes, thank you for being patient with such a crazy mom! I love you guys.

And lastly, this book is dedicated to my husband, Ray. Your undying support, encouragement, and faith helped me to realize this dream. You are the treasure of my heart! I love you.

Prologue

FANNY STAYED CROUCHED IN the prickly brush, wishing the moon would disappear behind the clouds again. Nausea squeezed her stomach. Fighting the urge to vomit, she peeked.

"Eli, what have you done?" she whispered from her hiding place. She bit her bottom lip to keep from crying aloud.

Having left in such a hurry, she hadn't grabbed her bonnet or shawl. She shivered uncontrollably now as the night air reached into the brush and blew its frost at her. Hair slapped across her face with stinging force. It stuck to her moist lips and tear-dampened cheeks.

As she peeled the locks from her face, she realized how comfortable it felt to have her hair loose. Had the circumstances been different, she knew she would have enjoyed the small sense of rebellious freedom. She wondered if that was the attraction that had lured Eli to do the awful thing he had done.

Peering out again, Fanny's eyes widened and her jaw

dropped. Eli had pulled a gunnysack from his ragged black jacket. He smiled, a sardonic smile she didn't recognize, teeth glimmering eerily in the moonlight that filtered down through the ancient limbs. Like a hungry child, he scooped his share of the gold pieces and then dumped them into the sack. Her heart sank. An even stronger wave of nausea swept through her. There was no excuse for what Eli and the other man had done.

A wicked chuckle wafted through the quietness, the sound curling around her heart like a clammy hand. Had that come from her brother? There obviously were many things she and her family didn't know about him. For him to do such a thing. . . .

Eli parted from the man, keeping to the trees. Fanny crawled through thicket. The underbrush seemed an enemy, taunting her, hindering her movement by pulling at her thin nightdress and mercilessly cutting into her hands and knees.

Tears blurred her vision again, but it wasn't from any of her own pain. Her heart ached. Somehow her brother had gone astray. It would kill her parents to learn what he'd done. He'd be shunned and probably out of their lives forever. Gulping back a sob, she tried to think. She couldn't lose him. She loved him too much.

When the bristly copse ended, she stayed where she was, watching and waiting. Where was Eli?

"Oh, please," she mumbled. "Blessed are they that put their trust in him. Blessed are they that put their trust in him." The familiar mantra helped steel her nerves. "Help me to help Eli."

A ray of silvery moonlight slashed through the obscurity of the oaks like a beacon from heaven. Fanny saw Eli, darting in and around the trees. He came to the clearing and looked over both shoulders, then stepped out to the trail that led home.

The gunnysack was gone, but she knew it was probably just hidden on his person. She waited, breath raw in her throat, as he meandered around the bend of pines like he had not a care in the world. She ran then, to the end of the same grove of pines. Pushing aside an aromatic, needle-covered bough, she peeped at the trail. Eli was on their property already. He'd just passed the huge fieldstone their brothers and sisters liked to play on.

Closing her eyes, Fanny forced herself to wait. A careless mistake would spoil everything. Slowly she counted to five. Then, taking a deep breath, she dashed to the rock. It felt cold and damp; but at the same time, soothing to the abrasions on her hands. The guilt she had felt about spying on her brother had vanished long ago. She was glad she had stayed awake and followed him this time. She was the only one who could save him from himself. And save him she would, for the answer had come to her.

Like a creature of the night, Fanny peered around the side of the earthy-smelling boulder, catching just a glimpse of Eli as he disappeared into their small barn. She started after him, running as fast as she could in her too-small boots. She slid to a stop upon reaching the back side of the barn. Horses nickered inside, but her brother's muffled voice calmed them. What was Eli doing?

Fanny's gaze flitted across the timbers of the structure. Then she saw it in the far corner when the moon again generously answered her pleas for help.

Dropping to her stomach, she slithered to the gap in the barn wall. Moisture soaked her garment. She felt so cold, bones like brittle icicles ready to snap. Gritting her teeth to stop their chattering, she willed herself to be strong. Raising up on her elbows, her eyes were level with the break. It didn't matter; it was nearly impossible to see through the blanket of blackness. A fleeting moment of despair filled her. She heard Eli whispering to the old dobbin. A pause, then the unmistakable rustle of straw being tossed with a pitchfork.

Fanny's heart slammed into her chest. A few minutes slipped by before there was a muffled thud as Eli dropped the log back into place on the latch of the barn door. Moments later, he crept into their Spartan four-room house. When the door closed behind him, Fanny made her way into the barn.

The gold was easier to find than she'd anticipated. She slung the bag of it over her shoulder, grabbed the shovel with the dried-on manure and headed for the grassy hills.

The coldness she felt lessened as she concentrated on Eli's salvation.

One mile. Two. Little white puffs shot into the crisp autumn air with each of her labored breaths. From the top of the last grassy hill she saw the crooked place, the place where the tiny forest of different hardwoods all tipped to the north as if curtsying to some unforeseen royalty. An unexpected tornado two years back had been responsible for the odd-looking alteration. Being early in the season, some reluctant leaves still clung to their branches with the hopes of fooling mother earth. They stirred in the wind, whispering to her, telling her she was almost to the spot.

As she loped down the hill, rich, loamy-scented air greeted her, causing a mixture of excitement and relief to course through her body. The slight but fast-moving creek that twisted through the oaks, elms and maples gurgled its encouragement. She puffed like a bellows, but still sprinted to the clump of the smooth-surfaced birches that splayed straight into the air like a human hand, strangely unaffected by the twister. At the base, the area she thought of as being like a wrist, she dropped the gunnysack and began to dig.

Once the gold was buried, Fanny rested her hands and chin on the end of the shovel. Eli certainly wouldn't go to law over something that was stolen from him that he'd stole in the first place. And she knew he'd never tell their parents or the bishop. She had solved his problem.

It was almost dawn when she crawled into bed. Her body shook as she wearily clutched a half-finished quilt against her breast. "I know what my design will be. Please," she prayed in a tone softer than a whisper, "let someone in need acquire this quilt. Help them decipher my map and let goodness be the result of this evil mess."

Exhaustion overtook her. Fanny fell asleep, smiling, thinking how wonderful a mass of daffodils would look planted on the spot.

1

AMANDA GLOSSER CAREFULLY CUT pieces from the skirt of the mauve sateen gown. Once completed, this would be the tenth quilt she'd made since her mother's death eight years ago.

With a sigh, she laid the scissors down on the smooth surface of the walnut counter and gazed wistfully at the quilts displayed about the general store. Six were those her mother had made. The other five adorning the papered walls were those Amanda had created from bits and pieces of her mother's dresses and gowns. Though her father called her loony, said the store looked like a shrine, she didn't care. The quilts gave her comfort. She missed her mother, missed the family that had been.

The vibrant colors of the hanging quilts were suddenly masked as a hulking shadow fell across the windowed door, blocking the brilliant spring sun.

Amanda turned toward the door, and though her heart stepped up a beat, she chewed her bottom lip to keep from smiling. The top of the black straw hat and the navy homespun trousers told her it was Amishman Josiah Miller. He fumbled with the doorknob, his loglike arms full of so many quilts she wondered how he could see.

Glancing back to the fabric in front of her, she wondered if he had seen that she'd noticed him. The clapper of the brass bell that hung on the lintel above the door swung precariously. She could almost hear its resounding tinkle, just a formality now, announcing his arrival.

From the corner of her eye, she saw him adjust his armful, then try again to open the door. She knew she should help, but she was enjoying the watching far too much.

Finally the bell rang, and he stepped across the threshold followed by Ophelia, her fat tabby cat. With a grunt—of either agitation or frustration, Amanda didn't know which—he slammed the door with a bump of his hip.

"Josiah," she said cheerfully, "is that you behind that pile of quilts? What can I do for you?"

"I would like to set these down."

"Goodness sakes. 'Course you would. They must be awfully heavy."

"Awkward." Two narrowed eyes peered at her from the side of the quilts.

"Goodness me. Just a moment. I was right in the middle of something." Amanda smiled and made a big production of picking up the fabric pieces she'd cut. Josiah said nothing, but his mouth crimped in annoyance before his head disappeared back behind the mound of cloth.

Amanda's smile grew. She loved to tease Josiah. Out of all the men in Prosper, he seemed the only one immune to her playfulness. Though she'd seen him smile only a handful of times in the many years she'd known him, that had been enough to etch the memory of his devastating dimples firmly in her brain. Then there were his eyes. He had eyes like she'd never seen before. They weren't blue, and they weren't gray, but more the color of silver. A liquid, fiery silver. Like today, they were almost always piercing and intense, as if a storm raged somewhere inside him. Truth be known, she thought him the most handsome man in all of Prosper, especially more handsome than Leon Violette.

"I'm trying to hurry. Truly I am," Amanda fibbed as

her gaze shamelessly roamed Josiah's physique. His powerful-looking legs were slightly bent at the knees and his back arched a small degree to accommodate the load he carried. It registered once again to her how nicely he filled out his worn, navy trousers.

"Since you are working there, perhaps there is another spot where I could put these?" Impatience laced his tone.

"No. No, I'm done now," Amanda said quickly. "They can go right here on my counter." She patted the surface.

Josiah craned his neck as he stepped forward. She smiled at him again. Suddenly his eyes widened. He stumbled, and a heart-stopping, shrill meow broke the silence. Amanda's mouth dropped, but before she could utter a word, the mountain of quilts avalanched at her. Flapping her arms, she tried to elude them. It was useless. One musty-smelling coverlet after another tumbled upon her.

Reeling blindly backward, Amanda and her large bustle knocked into the tobacco plugs and cigars she always prided herself on keeping so orderly. The display crashed to the wooden floor, she right along with it, crunching her bustle and landing spread eagle.

"Amanda? Amanda?"

The concerned voice sounded so far away. Amanda fought to free herself from the layered shroud, the stays in her corset mercilessly cutting into her tender flesh. "I need your help," she shouted, certain she heard the sound of tearing fabric.

"I am very sorry."

His voice had grown louder. She felt his nearness, felt the load upon her lightening. As Josiah plucked the last quilt from her head, Amanda gulped the fresh, sweet air.

He wasn't more than two feet from her, his spicy, woodsy scent filling her senses. From his kneeling position, he sat back on his feet. Thick tawny lashes framed his silvery eyes, and for the first time since she'd met him all those years ago, they danced with an intriguing blend of humor and mischief. Her heart tripped over itself.

Remembering propriety, Amanda shifted awkwardly so she could cover her ankles properly. All while she cursed the torturous corset and its reason for being: the fashionable hourglass figure. She knew she probably couldn't even get up by herself and would embarrassingly have to rely on Josiah for assistance. Then it struck her that maybe things wouldn't turn out so badly after all.

"Whew," was all she could think of to say. Sticking out her bottom lip, she blew a puff of air upon her sweaty forehead.

"That is not necessary," Josiah said with a grin, those deep dimples peeking out at her. "It is already sticking up quite far into the air."

Her hands snapped to her head, instantly feeling a slew of fine locks standing at attention. A groan rumbled in the back of her throat as she tried to push them back into place, little crackles of static vying for victory. Heat surged across her face. Ignoring the fact that the display case was jabbing the middle of her back, she rested her head against the striped pattern on the papered wall and closed her eyes in embarrassment.

Amanda heard Josiah as he tried to stifle his chuckling. Her eyes flew back open. His broad shoulders shook and the lines and angles of his face had softened. He looked even more handsome. "All right," she said as petulantly as she could, "laugh if you must. I suppose I am a sight, hair looking like dandelion seeds and sprawled on the floor like this. . . ." She found it impossible not to return his infectious smile, and a smile of her own tugged at the edges of her mouth. "It's not my fault, you know. If you hadn't thrown these quilts at me—"

"I would not have dumped the quilts on you had your cat not crossed my path."

"Poor Ophelia. She may very well be superstitious of crossing the paths of people from now on. And she's such a slip of a cat. You didn't crush her, did you?"

Leaning back farther on his legs, Josiah glanced around the corner of the counter. "I believe the portly Ophelia is fine. She washes her face in the sunlight." He rested his hands—the largest Amanda had ever seen—on the tight, worn fabric covering his thighs. "Enough of the jesting. I am sorry that I caused you to fall. I hope you are not hurt."

The humor faded from his eyes right before her own.

She felt disappointed somehow that he felt it necessary to end the teasing so soon.

"I'm fine. Truly I am, though I don't think I can get up by myself. My corset threatens to pierce something vital should I twist too far to either side. And, well, this bustle has about hampered all hopes of me jumping to my feet."

Pushing easily to his own feet, Josiah stretched out his hands. As Amanda took them, a ribbon of sensation unfurled in her midsection. He let loose of her hands almost the instant her feet touched the ground, and the strange sense of disappointment returned. She could count the times on one hand—skipping her thumb and forefinger—that she'd actually heard him laugh. Determination coursed through her. She didn't care if it was shyness, rudeness or cultural differences; she considered him a friend and she wasn't about to be slighted by the handsome Amishman again.

Coquettishly cocking her head, Amanda smoothed her skirt and offered a small, almost shy-type of smile. She purposefully locked her gaze with Josiah's in an unspoken challenge. At first his lips curled ever so slightly, but then his eyes darkened and all emotion seemed to drain from his face. If was as if he'd suddenly remembered something sorrowful. A sadness emanated from him, sobering Amanda's sportive mood and tugging on her heartstrings.

Stupefied, she bent awkwardly in her now-misshapen bustle and picked up one of the quilts. Every fiber in her body told her the quilts had everything to do with Josiah's melancholy. "Why did you bring in all of these?" she asked finally.

He cringed slightly at her question—or had she only imagined it? She wasn't sure, but felt more certain than ever that something was going on. Something important. Studying his face, waiting for an answer, she folded the quilt. His back stiffened under her watchful eye, and she saw the deep breath he took. Then his chin raised proudly.

"You have quilts throughout the store," he said softly, gaze sweeping the walls. "I wondered if perhaps these, too, could be sold here."

Frowning, Amanda walked the few steps to the counter

and laid down the pumpkin-colored, plain-weave cotton percale quilt. With her back still to Josiah, she fingered the bars pattern, pondering what her father would say if she bought the coverlets. With spring in full swing and the warm, summer weather close behind, she knew they truly didn't have a need for the quilts. They'd never sell. How was Josiah to know those displayed were just that, for display?

She glanced over her shoulder, watching some more, feeling that familiar ache in her heart as he busily refolded those quilts still on the floor. Though she didn't know all that much about the Amish as a whole, she knew Josiah was a proud man, always paid with cash and never put anything on credit.

Amanda chewed her bottom lip, thinking about her father and how he always said that they were the ones responsible for her mother's death. He believed the Amish had killed her by giving her cholera. Amanda knew how her mother had died, but she refused to believe the Amish people had knowingly infected her. The husband of the woman her mother was midwifing had had early symptoms of the disease but was unaware of them. Her mother's contraction of it was a terrible tragedy, but no one's fault. Amanda felt it an injustice to hold such a prejudicial grudge against an entire group of people. Maybe now was her opportunity to make up for her father's ill manners. Josiah was here, obviously needing monetary help. Her father wasn't. It couldn't be more simple.

"This one here is nice," Amanda said, turning back to the quilt. "The stitching is neat, thirteen or fourteen per inch. Someone is handy with a needle."

"I do not know much about quilting," Josiah replied, handing Amanda another. "Most of these are newer, made by my mother and others in our community. One is very old, made by my grandmother as a girl. I am told the quality is poor as she was young, but it still provides warmth on a cold night."

Amanda pretended to examine the quilts as Josiah laid them one by one upon the counter. Her thoughts were on how much to offer without seeming too generous. She didn't want to arouse his suspicions and make him feel like he was being given a handout, for she guessed he'd just as soon take them all away if that's what he thought.

"Well, I'll try to be fair here, Josiah, but some of these designs are little drab." Pursing her lips, she tapped her pencil.

"I am not one to judge. Whatever you feel fair is acceptable to me. This is the last one, the one I was telling you about." He laid it in front of her almost hesitantly.

A musty, closed-up attic type of smell bombarded Amanda's nostrils. Her nose twitched and she sniffed, fighting off a sneeze. "Yup," she said with a smile when the sneezy feeling had dissipated, "I can tell it's old, all right."

A brief appraisal told her the faded, plain-weave indigo-blue quilt had been constructed from two separate panels. The back—a brownish-red color Amanda guessed to have come from logwood—appeared to be from two large panels as well, though the weave was looser and coarser than that of the front. The thread used was a coarse, faded yellowish-brown hand-spun cotton of some sort.

Grabbing her pad, Amanda scrawled some figures. "I'll take them all . . . ," she raked her teeth across her lip, "for say . . . this." She circled the tally, but before she had a chance to push the pad across to him, Josiah stepped closer. Flattening one palm on the counter next to her, he looked over her shoulder. His warm breath fanned her cheek as he studied the paper. He smelled faintly of sassafras, and she knew all the pots of tea she'd ever brewed had never smelled so good.

He didn't speak, didn't move. The heat radiating from his body made her own feel like a lump of butter melting in the sun. His arm was so close, all she'd have to do was lean just a tad . . .

"How about preserves?" Josiah asked suddenly, interrupting Amanda's reverie.

"What?"

A crazed, almost desperate look glazed Josiah's eyes. "Is there anything else I could sell to you that you might have need of here at your store? Candles? Soap?"

"No. No, I'm afraid not."

"Are you sure? There must be—"

"Josiah, I said no. What's going on?"

Pushing back his hat, Josiah shoved his hands into his pockets. "I am sorry," he said, bowing his head. "You have been more than generous."

Seconds turned into minutes. The silence grew deafening. Amanda finally realized the stubborn Josiah wasn't going to offer further explanation. She opened the cashbox, counted and handed him his money. She tried hard to ignore the tingling in her hand as his fingers brushed her palm. "If you'd tell me what's going on, maybe I could help."

He tensed again at her question. "No. Thank you."

"All the times you've been in here, I considered us friends. Friends help friends," she said, shaking her head disapprovingly. She smiled then, wishing she could somehow absorb the pain that etched his features.

"Is that what we are, friends?"

Heat burned in Amanda's cheeks. "I'd—I'd like to think so."

Josiah's mouth curved into an unconscious smile, and for an instant the pain disappeared. "Good day, *my friend*. Thank you for buying my quilts." Stopping momentarily to scratch the sunbathing Ophelia, he left the store without a backward glance.

Amanda sighed as a pleasant confusion that had everything to do with Josiah muddled her senses. She headed to the storeroom, remembering the exact tone of his voice when he'd called her his friend. Humming happily, she returned to the counter, two wooden crates in tow.

As she folded the coverlets and began to pack them into the crates, Ophelia padded over and sprang to the last quilt covering the countertop. She pushed against Amanda's hand, begging more attention.

"You silly cat," Amanda whispered, stroking the velvety fur. "What's going on with Josiah? We need to find out. Must be pretty big for him to be selling their family quilts."

After indulging the cat one last scratch behind the ears, Amanda scooped her pet into her arms and set the animal on the floor. She stuffed the last quilt, the old one made by Josiah's grandmother, into the crate. "Seven. Goodness me, seven of these things." She chewed her bottom lip. "What in heaven's name am I going to do with more quilts?" she asked the tabby beside her. The corpulent feline ignored her, preferring to rub her chin on the corner of the wooden box.

The store bell rang. Amanda rose and, with her back still to the door, smoothed her skirt, hoping she looked presentable enough.

"Amanda Glosser, that Amish boy twist your arm?"

"Widow Marly." Amanda spun around with a guilty start. "I don't know what you mean."

The widow smiled a knowing smile. "He's mighty handsome. Strong as an ox, too."

"I wouldn't know. Never noticed," Amanda replied as she bent down and hefted one crate with a grunt, then plodded to the empty space along the far wall and set the box out of the way.

The widow stared at her. "That so?" Pulling off a kidskin glove and dropping it onto the counter, she reached up a gnarled finger and adjusted a smoky curl that had fallen near her temple. "Dear, dear, dear, Amanda. Say what you will, but I know what I see. It's written all over your face. I was across the street at the bank. Saw Josiah come in with coverlets piled to the sky. You bought them, didn't you?"

Amanda grimaced and lifted her shoulders in a noncommittal type of shrug.

"Ah, ah, ah. What's your father going to say when he finds out what you've done?"

Rolling her eyes, Amanda planted her hands on her hips. "Guess I don't really care. We've more than enough money, and Josiah seemed, well, sort of desperate."

"Reckon he is." The widow had muttered so softly Amanda wasn't certain she'd heard correctly. "You've got a kind heart," Widow Marly continued, "Newlin should be proud, but the old coot can't see nothin' past the nose on his face."

Amanda smiled. The eccentric, buckskin-clad widow

with her cluster of gray curls was like a surrogate mother, always looking after her. Not a day went by that Amanda didn't thank the Lord for bringing Widow Marly to her life. She didn't know how she would have survived the lonely, heart-wrenching time after her mother's passing if it hadn't been for the old woman. Her door was always open, had been from the first time they'd met. As she'd progressed from the fanciful whims of a twelve-year-old child to the hopes and dreams of a grown young woman, Amanda had loved the fact that Widow Marly always listened, never judged or criticized.

"Do tell," Widow Marly said, breaking the reflective moment, "what's the grin for?" She rested her hip and elbow against the counter.

"Why, it's for you." Amanda walked over and kissed the woman's leathery cheek, the scent of camphor inching up her nose. "Don't know what I'd do without you, is all."

"Pshaw!" Though the widow flipped her hand dismissively, the look on her face revealed how touched she was by the words.

"Widow," Amanda said, leaning close again, "you seem to know a lot about him. Tell me, why is Josiah Miller so *desperate*?"

"Simple. Needs money."

Folding her arms across her bosom, Amanda cocked her head, narrowed her eyes and gazed speculatively at the old woman. "I figured that much. You're doing this purposely. Are you going to make me drag every detail from your mouth?" Grinning, she slowly shook her head. The grin faded when she saw the remoteness glazing her friend's eyes.

"Hopelessness and guilt can turn a person crazy," the widow said eerily. "Don't think that's happened to the boy. Yet."

Though a sheer black fright swept through Amanda, curling around her heart, she refused to believe any wickedness of Josiah. "Tell me," she insisted, ready to argue his defense. "What's he done?"

Gazing off into space, Widow Marly continued on as if she hadn't even heard Amanda. "Will be a sad, sad thing, if it gets him. Poor fella. He's caught in a trap of the worse kind.''

"Stop. You're not making any sense. Widow, please. Just tell me what's going on with Josiah.''

Amanda had no sooner spoken her appeal when someone cleared his throat. Her gaze flew to the door, her jaw dropped and her body glazed with shock. Josiah stood in the doorway.

2

BLOOD POUNDED AMANDA'S TEMPLE and a blush scorched her cheeks. She felt like a child who'd gotten caught cheating on a spelling test.

"Excuse me," Josiah said, tipping his head more toward the widow than Amanda. "My mind is full today, and I almost forgot the iodine my mother is in need of."

His words were clear and crisp. He'd heard. Amanda felt even more heat flood her face, and in between gulps of air, she tried her best to recover a friendly, businesslike atmosphere. Finally finding her tongue, she stammered, "I-iodine. O-oh, yes. Of—of course." Groaning inwardly, she unconsciously fumbled with the folds of her skirts, wishing she could turn back the hands of time. She'd done it now, her blasted curiosity humiliating her in front of the person she realized she wanted so badly to impress.

Chancing a glance of mute appeal in the widow's direction, Amanda instantly knew she'd receive no assistance from her friend. The old woman's preoccupation appeared to be gone and the wrinkled edges of her mouth were curled in amusement. She was enjoying this! Amanda's eyes narrowed, but her friend just winked and pointed one crooked finger toward the back of the store. "I believe you keep the medicinal supplies that way, dear girl."

"Yes. Yes, you're right, widow," Amanda said through marble lips. She'd never known it possible to be both excited and so aggravated at the same time. "How many bottles"—she licked her sandpaper lips—"would you like, Josiah?"

"Three."

He didn't add his usual *please*. That made Amanda feel even worse. As she made her way to the back of the store, she heard Widow Marly asking, "How's your folks doing? And Elam and Lena?" A new surge of determination coursed through Amanda's veins. It didn't matter that she'd embarrassed herself by begging information about him. If Josiah was truly angry with her and not flattered, she'd find a way to fix that somehow. More important was this secret, the secret involving him and his family. She wanted to help him, and she would. She just needed to find out what was going on.

A tiny voice in her head shouted, "Busybody!" With a wrinkle of her nose, she shut off that voice. If simply wanting to help a family made her a nosy meddler, then that's just what she was.

Not wanting to miss even the slightest bit of their conversation, Amanda quickly grabbed a small box containing six brown bottles of iodine and hurried back toward the front of the store. Her heart skittered when she saw that Josiah had relaxed some and was now leaning casually against the counter, arms folded against his broad chest. He was grinning at something the widow had said. Finally he turned his gaze on Amanda and she felt herself drawn to him like a bee to sweet nectar.

Reminding herself she couldn't be distracted by romantic notions—she had a job to do—Amanda swallowed hard and smiled. "Josiah," she said, setting the box down on the counter next to his sun-bronzed forearm, "you can only believe half of what Widow Marly tells you. She's got more stories in her than Mark Twain."

"Ha!" The old woman elbowed Josiah. "Dear girl knows me too well, she does. You're wrong this time, though, dear. Josiah and I weren't discussing antics penned by anyone.''

"How much do I owe?" Josiah asked, smile disappearing, aloofness returning.

Amanda wondered what persuasive charms the widow possessed that she didn't. After all, the old woman wasn't innocent, either. Josiah had to have heard her passing on the gossip.

Sighing, Amanda forced a smile. She was being unfair to the widow. After all, she had pressed her friend for the information. It just seemed to Amanda that Josiah made her act crazier than a loon.

"Did you not hear me? How much?" he asked again.

"Nothing really. Fact is," Amanda added quickly, "I was thinking I probably owe you."

Josiah's honey-colored brows rumpled into a frown, and his eyes turned a darker shade of silver as he stared at her.

"Well," she said, feeling increasingly uncomfortable under his scrutiny, "the quality of one of the quilts was better than I originally thought." The excuse sounded as weak as her knees felt, but she continued on in a light, almost humorous tone. "I don't want to be accused of cheating anyone. Take the iodine for free and we'll call it even."

"Take her offer, boy," the widow said with a grunt. "She knows her quilts. She says she owes you, then she does."

"I thank you," Josiah replied softly, skepticism lacing his tone. Still, he picked up the bottles. "Good day to you both," he said as he turned and ambled toward the door.

"Watch out for Ophelia," Amanda said, grasping at one last chance to warm the air between herself and Josiah. "She's lurking around here somewhere. We know how she loves to tangle your feet."

A flash of humor crossed Josiah's features. If he had been miffed at her, it appeared he no longer was. Triumph washed over Amanda. She sighed as the bell above the door tinkled with his departure.

"Nice, nice fella," Widow Marly mused.

"Nice fella!" Amanda shrieked. "That was embarrassing. You knew it, and you didn't do anything to help me out of that mess.''

''You didn't need my help until the end there.'' Widow Marly shook her head, curls dancing. ''Then, my dear girl, you almost messed it up with that *free* nonsense.''

Resting her elbows on the countertop, Amanda cradled her face in her hands. A throaty groan sounded deep in her throat. ''Do you think he heard everything?''

''Do you think he did?''

Amanda nodded.

''Reckon he probably did, then.''

''Now that we got caught,'' Amanda said, lifting her head and rolling her eyes, ''you can finish your story. And don't leave any of the details out.''

''Details. What were we talking about? Oh, oh yes, of course. The accident. Now mind you, this didn't come from Josiah himself. Doc Rollins told me. The doc should know, though, seeing as how he was there.'' The widow fiddled with her gloves. ''Seems the oldest Miller boy, that's Elam—he's married to Lena Yoder. Let's see . . . they got married oh—''

''Not those details, widow. The stuff going on with his family. You said Josiah felt guilty. What did he do?''

''Yes. Yes, all right. There was a freak accident 'bout six, seven weeks ago. Elam lost a leg just above the knee. Doc says Josiah feels responsible and is trying to raise money to take his brother to a big city where some specially-schooled doctor can make him a leg that'll work like the old one did.''

''How terrible,'' Amanda whispered, clutching the edge of the counter. A painful knot of emotion shoved up into her throat.

''Yes. Yes, mighty terrible.'' The widow dug into the reticule hanging from her wrist and pulled out a small jar of ointment. She dabbed some of it onto her hand, sending a fresh, powerful wave of camphor into the air. After replacing the lid, she dropped the jar back into her bag. Rubbing her crooked fingers, she clucked her tongue. ''Doc says it'd be quite an expense to make something other than a peg leg. Poor Josiah. Family's having conniptions over it all, too. They want him to leave well enough alone. Josiah keeps it up, reckon the entire group'll shun him.''

''Shun him?'' Amanda frowned. ''What do you mean?''

''Excommunicate him. Ostracize him.''

Eyes widening, Amanda exclaimed, ''But why? He's trying to do something good.''

''Good maybe, but worldly. Worldly is against their beliefs. Take your fancy dresses and bonnets and notions—items like that would never be accepted in their culture.''

''How do you know so much about the Amish?'' Doubt laced Amanda's tone. ''Josiah and some of the others have been coming in here for years, and I don't know all that much about them.''

''Well, when Hollis and I traveled the East—oh, years and years ago,'' she said, flapping a hand, ''we ran into a few of their settlements. They live simply. Nothing frivolous. Never. Most of them speak Pennsylvania German when they're not around us 'English.' Their beliefs are based on some Anabaptist biblical interpretation.''

''Well, being a Christian is good,'' Amanda said with a wan smile. ''I sometimes think Papa and I need a bit more religion in our lives. Maybe we wouldn't have all the problems we do. Maybe an Amishman would make a good husband for me.''

''Oh, no, no, no, no, no, Amanda!'' The widow shook her head again, loosening another curl from the cluster at the back of her neck. ''Don't make light of this. The Amish live a very different lifestyle. For them, religion and custom mix to form this life. They're strict—very, very strict. And particular. They must follow the rules that have been passed down. Young Josiah, he must marry someone who is Amish. Not by a jugful could you and he get friendly.''

''You mean it's against their rules?''

''Oh!'' The old woman clamped her hand to her mouth. ''Great shakes, yes. That boy'd have that group in even more of a pucker if he cavorted with a young woman who wasn't Amish. Has to be Amish with Amish.''

Amanda suddenly felt very deflated.

''You know,'' the widow continued, ''it's kind of like

us English. Your pa has all of Prosper thinking you and Leon'll be tying the knot someday.''

Rolling her eyes, Amanda shook her head. ''I know what Papa wants, but that doesn't mean it's going to happen. I'm marrying for love, not because he owns horses.''

''Good for you, dear. Don't let any man push you into anything.'' Clucking her tongue again, the widow pointed to a small glass-encased counter. ''I almost forgot the reason I came. I need me some more buckshot.''

''Widow Marly,'' Amanda chided, humor returning to her voice, ''you aren't going to shoot that gun again, are you?''

''Reckon so. A gal's got to fend for herself, especially when that meat supply gets low.''

Reaching in the case, Amanda grabbed a pouch of the buckshot. ''I suppose nothing I say will change your mind?''

''Don't waste your breath,'' her friend replied, fishing in her reticule again.

''Well,'' Amanda hesitated before handing over the pouch, ''promise me you'll be careful?''

''Careful? I can outshoot any man in this town, Amanda dear. You should learn, too. I'll teach you,'' the widow coaxed, flipping a couple of gold dollars on the counter. ''You just say the word.''

Amanda laughed, envisioning herself with her father's rifle slung over her shoulder, traipsing through the woods and fields hunting for squirrel and pheasant with the widow. ''I'll let you know when I'm ready to learn.'' She handed over the ammunition and the change and walked the widow outside.

The sweet scent of lilacs greeted them. Amanda rubbed her arms against the spring chill. Her humor faded, replaced by a dolefulness she knew had everything to do with Josiah. ''Widow, do you really think Josiah's family would *shun* him for what he's doing?''

''Yup,'' the old lady snorted. ''No doubt in my mind.''

''That's sad.'' That achy knot returned and pushed up into Amanda's throat. ''I wish I would have given him more money now. More iodine, anyway.''

"Don't know how much you gave him, but he'd known if it was more than fair. He's a suspicious one, that Josiah. They're a proud people. Reckon Josiah's as honorable as they come. Got to go, Amanda dear."

The widow's pattens clomped on the planked sidewalk as she returned to her buggy. With a quick wave, she snapped the team to movement and disappeared down the road.

Amanda trudged back into the store. She spotted Ophelia atop the stacked crates containing the quilts. The cat was bent in half, hind legs stretched, bathing. "You may just as well have that one," she told the tabby. "No one will buy it, and it's so . . . old and unattractive, I can't hang it. Come on, kitty." Swooping the protesting animal awkwardly into one arm, she grabbed the poorly crafted quilt with the other.

As Amanda started across the floor toward the large, oval wickerwork basket by the front windows, Ophelia squirmed, meowing her displeasure at the unexpected manhandling. "Oh, just a minute, you spoiled thing," cooed Amanda. "I want to put the quilt in your basket."

A deep, guttural sound came from Ophelia's throat, and before Amanda could stop her, the disgruntled cat clawed her way up the quilt and leaped from Amanda's arms. The feline landed on the floor with a thud and scurried to the back of the store, disappearing behind the cans of Maxwell House and Chase and Sanborn coffee.

"Oh, just be that way." Amanda turned, ready to dump the old quilt back in the crate with the rest, when the light pouring in through windows caught it at an odd angle. The honey-colored stitches glittered, almost sparkled like gold flecks in the sun, piquing Amanda's interest.

"What in the world?" With a snap of her arms, the quilt rose into the air. It floated gracefully to the wooden floor like a kite on a dying breeze.

Amanda frowned, chewing her bottom lip as she bent over the quilt. She recognized the heroic attempt at a basic pumpkin-seed border along the straight line of the binding, which consisted of nothing more than the back piece folded over and stitched to the top piece. There were also four small, mediocre feathered hearts in each corner. She couldn't identify the other quilting.

"How strange," she mumbled, walking a quarter of the way around the coverlet. "I wonder what Josiah's grandmother was doing."

Ophelia scampered across the floor and strutted onto the laid-out quilt, curiosity apparently having gotten the better of her. She walked and sniffed and finally plopped to her side in the sun-kissed middle of the coverlet, drawing Amanda's attention.

"Flowers. Now those have got to be flowers." Amanda approached the cat who looked as though she were now about to doze. "Move, Ophelia. Come on, girl," Amanda said, nudging her. "I want to see what's under there."

No longer caring about etiquette, Amanda hiked her skirt and dropped to her knees. She wiggled her fingers patiently, finally spurring the cat's playfulness. With a pounce, Ophelia left the spot and darted after Amanda's hand.

"Either you're makin' quilts or you're playin' with that blasted cat. This how you mind the store when I'm gone?"

"Papa," Amanda said, scrambling to her feet, "I didn't hear you come in."

"Because you were playin'. What if I'd been a customer? Look at you."

Straightening her skirt, Amanda took a deep breath. "The customers wouldn't care. They all love Ophelia."

"That ain't the point. This is a business." He stomped to the quilt and yanked it out from under the cat. Bunching it in his arms, he continued, "Don't appreciate comin' in here and seein' one of these things spread out in the middle of the floor for . . . *her majesty*."

"You know, Papa," Amanda said, hands on her hips, suddenly tired of the all-too-familiar speech, "it'd do you good to play more. Life's passing you by and you won't grab the simple pleasures it has to offer."

"Aww, jiminy. Don't need none of your riddles. Just like your mother, you are. She always talked in circles and said next to nothin'."

"And you loved her so."

"Now don't go tryin' to get me sidetracked. Point is

this." Newlin fumbled, but finally lifted the quilt by the corners until it was level with his chin. "This here—" He grimaced suddenly, as if seeing the quilt for the first time. "Mercy, this is an ugly thing." Dropping his chin against his chest, he peered upside-down at the quilt, then craned his neck to view it sideways. "This ain't your work. Your mother's, either. I'd a remembered this one. Where'd it come from?"

Amanda's throat closed like a plugged-up chimney. "Um . . ." She swallowed hard. "I—I bought it."

"Huh? This thing?" Newlin's eyebrows folded into a straight line. "From who?"

"The Amish," Amanda squeaked.

A jagged vein stood livid at her father's temple. "Confounded Amish! You actually gave them money for this? What for? Your cat?"

"Not exactly. I bought them because I thought, um . . . maybe they could be . . . brightened up. I wasn't trying to be a spendthrift, just trying to make you some money. I can sort of . . . refurbish them. And much more quickly than I could make seven from scratch," she added purposefully, hoping she'd said enough to appeal to her father's love of moneymaking. "Come fall, we could sell them here in the store."

"Seven? You bought seven of these blasted things?"

Taking a deep breath, Amanda lifted her chin and boldly met her father's gaze. "I got this truly great deal. A steal, really," she lied. She paused to wipe her palms on the front of her dress, hating the fact that although she knew she'd done the right thing, her father could still make doubts and regrets surface.

"Think them confounded Amish got the steal!" Newlin shook the faded old quilt angrily, scattering the motes of dust that had been lazily hovering in the air. The mysterious gold stitching glinted and beckoned to Amanda as the sunlight bounced around with her father's movement. She no longer heard his harsh mutterings, and could only concentrate on the quilt.

Though some of it was missing, there was no mistaking the subtle pointing arrow that had been stitched into the material. It seemed to start in the bottom right corner and went clockwise from picture to picture. Near the top of the quilt it stopped, but Amanda somehow knew it would have continued along the same path, ending with the strange design of flowers and the other things in the center.

"Are you listenin' to me?" Newlin stepped toward Amanda, breaking the spell the quilt had cast upon her. "Looks more like a map than any blasted quilt I've ever seen. Ought to be hanging in the town hall. Jiminy," he mumbled, "get 'em outta here."

"Yes, Papa." *Quilt! Map!* Head swimming with intriguing thoughts and ideas, Amanda eagerly took the quilt. "If you're done in the back barn and can mind the store, I'll just take them all home right now. And I won't bring them back until they're done and proper-looking enough for you to sell."

Grunting, Newlin waved off all other talk with a peremptory gesture. Any other time his abrupt dismissal would have bothered Amanda, but now all she could think of was the quilt, and she hurried behind the counter. Draping the old musty coverlet over her arm, she lifted the top crate of quilts. Biting her bottom lip, she tried to adjust the awkward load. It would be much easier just to pull each of the quilts from the crates and throw them into the back of the wagon. Pride and defensiveness stopped her. She didn't want to hear another word from her father about how ugly the quilts were, or how Josiah had gotten the better of her. She'd rather leave the quilts folded in the crates and struggle a bit to keep the designs hidden from her father's probing gaze.

"Aww, jiminy." Newlin raked his hands through his hair. "Go ask Rogers to get the buckboard ready. I'll carry the blasted things out for you."

"No. I can get them."

"And you'll end up breaking your neck. Don't be so confounded stubborn. I'll carry them out. *Please* let me get them," he said in a tone that had softened considerably.

Shocked, Amanda stared wordlessly, and her father took the crate from her arms. Orders, always orders, but at least this time he'd said *please* and used a pleasant tone. Who was she kidding? It didn't mean anything. If only her mother were alive, things would be different. They'd be a normal family. Amanda envied those who had a normal family.

Rising on tiptoe, she grabbed her caped-collar overcoat from the wooden peg, slung it over the quilt still on her arm and hurried out the back door.

The sun smiled down on her and the spring breeze lifted the hair off her shoulders, cooling her body and her temper. She'd work harder on her relationship with her father. He'd kept himself closed off for so long, it was no wonder he was lacking in the area of feelings and sensitivity. She'd make it work. She wasn't a quitter. In the meantime, she'd go home, study the old quilt and see if she couldn't prove her father wrong by actually beginning a refurbishing project on one of the other quilts.

The odor of manure crept up her nostrils as she stepped into the barn. As if a hood had been thrown over her head, her vision blackened. She blinked and it finally cleared as her eyes adjusted to the dimly lit interior. "Leon? Rogers? Oh, Rogers, there you are," she said when she spied the man in one of the stalls brushing the lather from a glistening palomino.

"Ma'am." He dropped the brush and removed his beaver-pelt top hat.

"Rogers! For goodness sake, we've known each other too long for this formality. Put your hat back on." Amanda smiled at him as she always did, but he, as usual, had already lowered his gaze to his dirty, brown boots.

Having yet to make a difference, she skipped the don't-be-so-meek lecture. "I need my father's buckboard readied as soon as you can manage it."

"Yes, ma'am," he replied, crushing his top hat against his chest and dipping his head as he scooted past her.

Fingering the edge of the mysterious quilt, Amanda watched the people-shy Rogers harness Goodwin, the biscuit-colored hackney. The horse anxiously stomped its one socked foot as if in anticipation of the ride. Rogers patted the animal's neck and soothed him with some soft-spoken nonsensical words.

Pursing her lips, Amanda's thoughts floated back to·Josiah. Suddenly she smiled. "Rogers is proof that people aren't always what they seem," she murmured happily. "Maybe Josiah Miller isn't what he seems to be, either."

That thought unexpectedly seemed even more intriguing than the odd quilt she held. The mustiness from the quilt appeared to have evaporated, for all she noticed now was the faint scent of woodsmoke, horses . . . and man. Closing her eyes, Amanda breathed deeply of the heady scents. How different could the Amish culture be? She never remembered her mother mentioning any differences, and she'd delivered four babies in their community. Widow Marly was old. Maybe she was wrong. Maybe she'd been remembering another group from another voyage. Amanda felt certain that that was the case.

Hugging the quilt close, she pictured in vivid detail the liquid silver of Josiah's eyes, the dimples that peeked at her when he barely smiled. Though she'd known him for some time, it was as if she'd seen him in a new light. It appeared there was much she'd failed to notice, all of which she liked.

Within minutes Amanda had cast away Widow Marly's opinion of the Amish culture. She climbed into the buckboard and waited for her father to load the quilts. She wouldn't be doing anything wrong by visiting the Amish, she defended herself silently. No matter what her father thought about them, she believed they were good people. At least, Josiah was good. Who better to ask about the map on the quilt than the family of the woman who'd made it?

"Here's the last one," her father said, dumping the crate into the buckboard. "Oh, and the widow left this." He pulled a kidskin glove from his back pocket. "Just found it on the counter."

Amanda didn't think it possible, but her spirits soared higher. Widow Marly lived northeast of the town! Not only did Amanda now have an excuse to travel by the Amish community, but she didn't have to lie to get it.

"I'll take it to her."

"Good. Don't want the old gal gettin' upset."

"Have a good day, Papa. And, I'm sorry about the quilts.

I'll put in more hours at the store to help pay them off.''

"Now, don't make me feel like some confounded ogre. I just . . . worry 'bout you bein' taken advantage of. And them people'll do it. The money you spent don't mean nothin'.''

It was times like this when Amanda's heart swelled—the very few times when her father, in his own gruff way, expressed his love. "Oh, Papa," she said with a sigh, "we so need to—''

"There you go 'gain. Don't be gettin' all soft like your mother. Can't stand it.'' Spinning on his heels, Newlin stalked back toward the store.

The rebuff felt like a slap. Pain squeezed her heart, but Amanda forced back her tears of disappointment. "I'm going to have a family someday,'' she muttered, not caring that he was already out of earshot. "I want someone to talk to, someone who'll talk to me. I deserve that much. Why can't you be like you were before?''

A hot tear rolled down her cheek. Swiping it away, Amanda prodded the hackney to movement. She needed to get her mind off the problems with her father, if only for a short time. Josiah and the mysterious quilt were just what she needed.

3

JOSIAH PRODDED THE HORSE to a faster gait. He'd taken too much time at Doc Rollins's office. Again.

The thick, leather-bound book haunted his thoughts and caused him to scowl. He wished he understood the medical terminology that lay between its covers. It frustrated him, stumbling over the long words, not being able to pronounce them, let alone know their meanings. He didn't want to act ungrateful, for he felt it a blessing Doc Rollins even allowed him to come in and go through the volume he did have on prosthesises, but Josiah just wished the doctor had time to explain the things in the book.

Shifting his weight, he ignored the dismay coursing through his body. Though he'd raised seventy-five dollars in a few short weeks, what he did understand from the reading sessions made him realize that Doc Rollins spoke the truth when he talked about it probably being nearly impossible to raise the amount of money needed for Elam to travel and be fitted for a fully functional limb.

Gritting his teeth, Josiah focused on the positive. The money already made had been from the sale of what he considered worthless items found around the homestead.

Once the fields were planted—his family's and Elam's—
he'd plant others, for a fee. He'd do odd jobs, repairs, whatever it took to raise that money. He wouldn't settle for
anything less than the best for his brother.

Stress and anxiety pinched the muscles of his neck and
shoulders. It happened a lot lately, especially when he
thought about Elam and the task ahead.

Loosening his grip on the reins, Josiah dropped his chin
and began slow circles with his head. He felt some relief,
but his back still pained him. Hips facing forward on the
wooden seat of the wagon, he inhaled deeply, straightening
his back, then twisted his torso until he had a clear view
over his left shoulder. His eyes widened. He was being
followed, his pursuer none other than Amanda Glosser in
her buckboard.

Cocooned in some dark-colored cloak, Amanda's long
locks looked almost alabaster trailing behind her. They
danced with the wind like graceful strands of silk. Josiah
had touched silk once and wondered if her hair felt the
same. Almost all of the women he knew were Amish, and
he couldn't remember ever catching a glimpse of one with
her hair loose, the way Amanda wore hers. Even after
washing, his mother and sisters all pulled theirs into knots
on the back of their heads and instantly replaced their caps.

Strange—he'd never thought about such things before,
never noticed the smoothness of a woman's skin, or how
expressive a woman's eyes could be, especially eyes the
color of cornflowers.

Like Amanda's eyes.

He'd been so close to her at the store, closer than ever
before. Kneeling on the ground next to her, he'd even
caught a glimpse of her fancy apple-red stockings and the
shapely ankles and calves they hugged. She smelled like
spring and wildflowers. His belly tightened all over again
at the memory. He knew she'd been embarrassed about
falling, but she'd quickly recovered. She'd been kind, as
usual, and he liked the way her eyes softened and glinted
with compassion. Not pity—just compassion. She always
seemed cheerful, bright and knew probably as much, maybe

more, about quilts and quilting as his mother. For some reason that thought pleased him.

He glanced over his shoulder again. She still followed. Though he'd been living close to the English all his life, he'd yet to understand them. It wasn't up to him to question them, either. He didn't know why Amanda trailed behind, and he knew he should probably be worried, but somehow he didn't think she'd renege on their quilt deal.

A slight smile turned the edges of Josiah's mouth. He'd never forget the look on her face when she finally noticed that he'd returned to the store. She and the widow had been talking about him. Amanda hadn't even heard the bell, she'd been so engrossed in their conversation. He tried to ignore it, but the spark returned every time he thought about forbidden Amanda being interested in him, a simple Amishman. Odd, the more he thought about her, the less he thought about Elam. The monetary problems seemed sinfully insignificant now. Nothing seemed to matter except the gnawing fire in his belly.

It confused him. All of it did. It was like he had lost his mind the moment he stepped in the store this morning. The constraint he'd used so many times in the past just couldn't be summoned today. He wanted to touch Amanda's upturned nose and smooth the disheveled hair from her forehead. And her lips, always smiling, always moist like roses bathed in early-morning dew, always drawing his gaze. He'd never felt such attraction for a woman before. And this was an *English* woman. It wasn't right. The feelings weren't right.

Shifting again on the hard seat of the spring wagon, Josiah stretched his legs, another scowl twisting his lips. He had allowed his mind to idly wander to frivolous matters. He was later than late, had many things to do. A flowery-smelling woman with hair and lips like an angel's from heaven was a distraction that couldn't be allowed again. With a snap of the leather reins, he prodded the team into a faster gait and shoved all of the perplexing thoughts of Amanda from his mind.

It wasn't an easy thing to do, knowing she followed.

∞

AMANDA DIDN'T KNOW HOW it happened that Josiah
was just now traveling back to his community, and she truly
didn't care. The excitement racing through her body confirmed what a wonderful idea the visit was—and now, not
just solely for the sake of the mysterious, old quilt.

Josiah disappeared from sight as her hackney slowly
climbed the side of a hill furrowed from the spring thaw.
As the wagon topped it, two rabbits unexpectedly bounded
into the path, startling the horse. Amanda pulled hard on
the reins, trying to regain control and calm the animal. She
breathed a sigh of relief when the beast reluctantly stopped
and the furry critters scampered to safety on the opposite
side of the road.

Jerking its head and stomping its front foot in a seemingly anxious protest to get going again, the horse whinnied.

"Whoa, baby. Hang on. Whoa. Whoa," Amanda cooed,
pulling as tightly as she dared. From her high point on the
hill, she was content to sit for a moment and gaze in awe
at the sight before her while the skittish horse relaxed.

White house after white house and unfinished barn after
barn spread out across the straw-colored, green-tipped
spring grass. Each of the homes and outbuildings all looked
so similar it made her think of a gathering of birds. Large
white ones, weathered brown and sun-faded gray ones, all
planning their migration south.

Many plots of black earth near different homes had been
freshly plowed and readied for planting. Though yet too far
away, Amanda could imagine the rich earthy scent floating
through the air near those fields. Splashing color throughout
that area were daffodils as yellow as lemons and tulips
more vibrant than all the hues of any rainbow.

She'd never ventured near the Amish community because, until now, she'd never had reason. It was far different than she had anticipated. It was beautiful. Her thoughts
returned to Josiah and what Widow Marly had said. Amish
or English, excommunication or lack of communication,

Amanda didn't see that much of a difference. Even though she lived with her father, she'd felt a sickening emptiness and a stabbing ache in her own heart too many times to count. She hoped Josiah never had to experience it with his family. It was hell.

With a sigh, she relaxed her taut hold on the reins and allowed the horse to start down the hill. She'd talk to Josiah about the quilt and learn what she could. She didn't want to get into that nosy-body stuff again, but if things went well, she decided she'd mention his honorable quest. Between the both of them, hopefully they'd stumble upon some new money-raising ideas that would be acceptable to his culture.

The sound of axes biting into wood echoed more loudly through the air as the horse carefully picked its way down the rutted hillside. Amanda saw men dragging fallen timber from a grove of maple and oak trees. Others worked together on the foundation of some type of structure. Like their neat homes and property, the men of the community all looked similar in their wide-brimmed black hats, dark-colored homespun shirts and trousers. Though not a single man wore a mustache, the majority had beards that hung long and untrimmed, reminding her of the ones described in the Book of Leviticus.

Several women worked around their homes, using tools or their hands, clearing old flowerbeds and what Amanda assumed were old vegetable gardens. Though she'd seen a few Amish women in the store on separate occasions, it didn't surprise her to see that when together they, too, were copies of each other. Like a string of cutout paper dolls, they all wore drab-colored dresses and aprons. They all wore their hair pulled severely away from their faces, and a white starched cap with trailing lace on each side covered their heads. In all the magazines Amanda had browsed through she'd never seen anything like those hats except on the Amish. It seemed strange that the garments these women wore were dark, yet their head coverings were as white as the sugar they bought from the store.

The horse slowed to a stop as they reached the bottom of the hill. Amanda had yet to catch a glimpse of Josiah and wasn't sure which way to go. She wished she'd seen into which barn he'd driven his buggy.

Feeling curious gazes upon her, she coaxed the horse down a narrow, unpopulated lane. Black and brown and faded gray clothing stretched across a clothesline, basking in the sun and occasionally flapping in the light breeze as if coming alive and waving a welcome. There were dresses and aprons and too many diapers to count. And trousers! Amanda had never seen so many. She wondered if any belonged to Josiah. An image of him without pants flashed in her mind. Her midsection twisted in response and a heat that had nothing to do with the sun pervaded her body.

Taking a deep breath, she shrugged out of her coat and pushed the hair back off her forehead, thankful it wasn't possible for people to read minds. What a story hers would tell.

As the hackney continued its slow, easy gait between the generously spaced homes, Amanda kept a watchful gaze out for Josiah and the man who sometimes accompanied him to the store, the man she assumed was his father. Her bravado slipped with each cloud of dust the horse's hooves raised. She was normally sociable, and always the one to sing or recite poetry without trepidation when asked, but now, nerves and uneasiness fluttered around in her stomach. This wasn't the same. She most definitely was out of her element. Had she made a mistake by coming?

"Are you here to return the quilts?"

Amanda spun around on the wooden wagon seat. Her eyes widened. Lounging almost indolently, one shoulder propped against a weathered barn, stood Josiah. His arms were crossed familiarly against his broad chest, and his left leg crossed his right at the ankle, the toe of his worn work-boot sticking into the ground. A lazy half smile curled the corners of his lips and a long piece of grass dangled there as he chewed.

It took Amanda a moment to realize she hadn't stopped the buckboard. Turning from Josiah, she tugged on the reins and shouted in her most authoritative voice, "Whoa!" She felt his gaze upon her, guessed his smirk had probably grown into a full-fledged smile. At least it seemed he was no longer angry about her gossiping. Still, a flush crept up her neck and across her cheeks.

"Goodness me," she muttered, hearing the crunch of stones and hardened dirt beneath Josiah's boots as he approached. Raking her top teeth across her bottom lip, she prayed she wouldn't say anything loony that she'd regret later. Never before, in front of anyone, had she ever felt such nervousness.

Straightening her shoulders with a deep breath, Amanda found that smile of poise and self-confidence she used so often and pasted it on her face as she waited for Josiah to come around and help her from the wagon.

Suddenly, and most unexpectedly, a slim, smiling, young-looking Amish woman appeared before her. Amanda felt her own smile fade. She had always been impulsive, but this time she wondered if her impetuousness would only serve to embarrass her. Maybe this young girl was Josiah's sweetheart, or worse—his wife!

Arranging that smile again, Amanda willed her shaking knees to quiet as she fidgeted with the reins lying in her lap. The young woman continued to smile, the sincerity of it sucking all coherent words from Amanda's brain. Her pulse roared in her ears as she saw Josiah in her peripheral vision. Clearing her throat, willing the threadiness to disappear, she pushed to her feet, hoping her legs wouldn't buckle.

Josiah nodded slightly. "Amanda, this is my sister Mary. Mary, this is Amanda Glosser, the merchant's daughter."

Merchant's daughter. That's what Amanda was and she was normally proud of it, but the words sounded stern, almost cold, coming from Josiah. For some reason his demeanor had changed again, and she now felt very out of place towering over them from the buckboard.

Ignoring Josiah's hardened jaw and probing expression, Amanda concentrated on the delicate-looking Mary, who smiled as if she were about to burst with delight. "It's a pleasure to meet you, Mary."

Mary nodded vigorously, her white cap bobbing atop her head, like a worm on the end of a fishing line.

"Does she speak English?" Amanda asked Josiah, remembering the different language spoken by most of the Amish that came into the store.

Josiah tucked his hands under his armpits, face expressionless. "Mary is standing here, yet you ask me. Why?"

Heat flooded Amanda's cheeks and spread to the tips of her ears. Was it her imagination, or was Josiah purposefully embarrassing her?

Running her tongue across her quickly drying lips, she struggled for composure. It didn't help matters that his silvery eyes seemed to follow her every move.

"Stop teasing her, Josiah." Mary elbowed him in the ribs. "Yes, Amanda, I do speak your English."

Anxiety coursed through Amanda's veins; she wished the ground would consume her. "I didn't mean to offend you. I'm sorry," she squeaked. "I just didn't know—"

"Most of us do speak English. Some not so well. It is our Pennsylvania German that the elders prefer." Josiah's expression softened, and Amanda thought she noticed another smile trying to form.

"Do you speak it?" he asked Amanda, his eyes sparkling with that mischief she now recognized.

"Yes, I do. Fluently."

Josiah stared, obviously taken aback by her words. Amanda's breath quickened. She wanted to hear his laughter again, wanted to see the smile that she knew could light up his eyes and bring out those dimples.

"Surprised?" She laughed at the astonishment on his face. As if in agreement, her horse neighed and tossed his head. "Truth be told," Amanda said, "I speak your dialect as fluently as my hackney's." Throwing back her head, she gave her best impression of a horse's whinny.

Mary's laughter filled the air, and Josiah couldn't seem to stop himself from joining in.

Amanda loved the warm, bubbly feeling his laughter caused. He needed to laugh more, and she felt a raw determination to see that he did.

"Mr. Miller," she said coquettishly, "I realize there are differences in our cultures, but certainly, you do help your ladies down from buggies, don't you?"

The flush crept up Josiah's face this time.

Mary snickered and held out her hand. "I shall help you, Amanda."

"Mary, go help Ma." Josiah stepped in front of his sister, forcing her to move away from the buckboard.

"But Amanda's come for a visit. I want her to meet everyone."

"Go," Josiah insisted. "I will bring her over."

As Mary trudged back down the path toward one of the white houses, Josiah leveled his gaze on Amanda and held up his hands. His cheeks had reddened even more, and she felt a deep, heartrending tenderness.

For propriety's sake, she knew she should simply place her hands in his and take the big step from the buckboard. But to the devil with propriety! Amanda wanted more than anything to feel his hands around her waist. "Thank you," she said as she bypassed his hands and placed her own on his shoulders.

Josiah tensed at her touch. His eyes darkened and shadows grew, masking all emotion, but she was not to be dissuaded. "I can swoop like an eagle from its perch and risk twisting my ankle." She tightened the hold on his shoulders, "Or you could put your hands around my waist and lower me to safety."

"Is it safe here on the ground? I am not so certain."

His words were a whisper, spoken only for her ears. They muddled her mind and sent a tremor through her body. One thick blond eyebrow rose and disappeared into the shock of golden hair that fell across his forehead. His eyes were smoldering as his viselike fingers encircled her waist. She felt herself being pulled, almost roughly, against him. Softness melding with hardness. Time seemed to stand still as they shared an intense physical awareness. . . .

Before Amanda knew what was happening, she was set solidly on her heels.

Josiah's eyes danced with that mischief, and his hands lingered momentarily at her waistline. "Safe," he muttered, releasing her.

Was that a question or a statement? Amanda wasn't sure.

He wore a blank expression again, as if his last few moments of emotion had never been.

Feeling she had lost the controlling position, she backed away from his closeness. Josiah's gaze didn't waver, but when that hint of humor returned to his eyes, she knew she had almost let him beat her at her own game.

"See there," she pointed out, not about to be the loser in this round. "Our cultures aren't so different after all, are they? We both appreciate *nice* things."

A lopsided grin slanted his mouth. "I appreciate *practical* things."

"Practical?" Amanda rubbed the frown creases in her forehead. "I'm a *practical* thing?"

He shrugged. "I do not know if that is true. I was referring to the quilts. You brought them back, did you not? Is that not what this visit is about?"

"Why, yes. It is."

Shoving his right hand deeply into the pocket of his trousers, Josiah withdrew some money. "It is all here," he said, outstretching his hand.

"Oh, no. No, wait. I don't want to return them. I just wanted to talk to you about the old one. The one your grandmother made."

"I do not understand."

"Put the money away, and I'll show you." Amanda dashed to the buckboard and pulled the old quilt from the crate. She draped it across the back of the wagon, smiling. "What do you see?"

Josiah stared at it, then at Amanda. Shaking his head, he threw his hands into the air. "I see a quilt. A faded blue quilt."

"You're not looking hard enough. Start here," she explained, pointing to the bottom right corner where the large sunlike object had been stitched. "Follow the pictures all the way around to here."

"I see shapes that I cannot make out. The objects do not look like anything. I see a poorly crafted quilt made by a young girl."

"I think your grandmother stitched a map of some sort on this quilt. That's why I'm here. I hoped maybe you or your mother or father could tell me more about it. And her."

Josiah cocked his head, an I-don't-believe-it expression on his face. "That is not a map. It makes no sense."

"I know." Amanda scratched her head. "It's . . . it's probably just because we don't understand it yet. Won't you help me?" She rubbed her hands together, the excitement in her escalating. "It'll be fun. We'll—"

Stopping her with a raised hand, Josiah said, "It is nonsense. That stitching does not mean anything. It is a design thought up by a young girl. That is all."

"I don't think so. Tell me about your grandmother. Um . . ." Amanda paced a few yards away from Josiah, hands clasped behind her back. Suddenly she spun around and retraced her few steps. "Where did your grandmother grow up?" she demanded, pointing her index finger. "What did she like as a young girl?" A second finger pointed at Josiah as Amanda continued her interrogation. "What was the town like? What was the time period like?"

Josiah shook his head in utter disbelief. "I do not know the answers to your questions. And I do not think there is anything to solve. This is child's play."

Amanda sighed and pushed her lip out in a trained endearing pout, but even this most pitiful look of appeal didn't seem to move Josiah. "You can disbelieve if you want," she said hotly, "but I still think this quilt is a map."

"I have work to do," he replied, arms akimbo.

"Go. I'm not trying to stop you. I'll talk to Mary. I'll bet she won't be so rude."

"Mary has work as well. Take your map home."

Crossing her arms over her bosom, eyes narrowing in challenge, Amanda quipped, "Mary has work? Good. I'll help her. We'll talk as we work. I'll prove to you this is a map."

Josiah pushed back his hat and ran the back of his hand across the tiny beads of sweat on his forehead. "I do not understand what it is you want. So you prove this is a map. What happens then? Will you travel to Sommerville, the hometown of my grandmother as a girl? Will you search to find the place this . . . this map tells about?"

Amanda shrugged impatiently. "I'm not sure."

"A treasure map. Perhaps," Josiah said softly, leaning toward her, "it *is* where my grandmother hid a secret. A big secret. A forbidden hair ribbon, or a diary, or a favorite cornhusk doll." His mouth quirked with humor. "Would that be your plan? Find this childhood item from nearly fifty years ago?"

Exhaling with a whoosh of agitation, Amanda snapped, "I—I don't know." It annoyed her, the way Josiah's clear silvery eyes sparkled with amusement. Maybe she had gone a little overboard with the map bit. But that didn't mean it was right for him to poke fun at her aspirations, either. "What if it's a map to a treasure and there's lots of gold or jewels here at the end by this X?" She stabbed her finger at the honey-colored X. "Huh? What about . . . oh, what's his name?" She snapped her fingers. "Your brother. You know," she said, arms akimbo like Josiah's had been, "the accident. You're trying to raise money. You want to help him. What if there was enough money for you to take him to a big city and get fitted with that prosthesis thing you want him to have? You wouldn't think I was being loony then, would you?"

The humor quickly drained from Josiah's face. His startled hurt turned into white-hot anger. Taking a step away from him, Amanda swallowed hard, wondering if her temper had overruled good sense. She'd never seen Josiah in such a state. It appeared she'd pushed him a mite too hard.

4

A VEIN THROBBED AT Josiah's temple. He didn't know why, but Amanda's words had pierced his heart like the prongs of a pitchfork sinking into hay. He stared at her as she backed away, now wide-eyed and meek as a field mouse.

"I do not know what *loony* means," he said, finally finding his tongue. "Is it the same as rudeness?" Insinuation laced his words. She just seemed to bring out the worst in him.

Amanda stopped moving and blinked owlishly. Except for the dark scarlet flush on her cheeks, she looked as innocent as a babe. "Rudeness? I was maybe a mite outspoken, but I don't think that classifies me as being rude." She sniffed and rocked back on her heels. "Actually, you weren't all that polite, either. Shouldn't mock a person's aspirations. Especially," she said, stepping back to Josiah and poking her finger at his shoulder, "if that someone is just trying to help you. That's what I was trying to do, you know."

Her eyes were bright with intelligence and interest. Her sweet, flowery scent burrowed into Josiah's senses, dissolving his hurt and anger. "I do not need your help," he said in a softer, friendlier tone. "You have done enough already by buying those quilts."

"Well," her head cocked slightly to the right, and her hands went to her hips, stirring the embers of Josiah's fire, "if I didn't want to help you, I wouldn't offer."

An amiable silence descended around them. "I—I'm sorry about what I said, too." Amanda rolled her eyes. "It didn't come out like I planned. Happens to me a lot. My father says my tongue flaps faster than my brain can think."

Her mouth curved into a smile, and Josiah felt his breath catch in his throat. Never had any woman affected him so. He was older than most who took a wife, and he had often times wondered when he'd meet that perfect mate, the woman he would want to share his life and his farm with. He knew Amanda, worldly Amanda, could not possibly be the one, and yet he couldn't imagine experiencing stronger feelings of desire than he did now. Shifting his weight, Josiah knew he needed space from her nearness.

"Cat got your tongue? Come on. Say something," she prodded, her smile growing, lighting her entire face and making it harder for him to ignore the ache in his groin.

For some odd reason, he longed to please her. If she wanted him to talk, then he'd talk. "What does your word *loony* mean?" It seemed a simple and safe enough question to satisfy her.

When Amanda laughed, a full-hearted, contagious sound, with her head thrown back and her golden hair swaying on the light breeze like rich strands of thread, Josiah moaned inwardly. He'd only made more trouble for himself.

"Loony is what I am," she said, wrapping her arms around herself in a type of hug. "Loony is crazy and," she shrugged, "I suppose foolish at times. Father says so. Says I'm too much of a dreamer. Like with the treasure map and that quilt. You were right. I was being foolish. *Loony*," she said matter-of-factly.

An immense defensiveness rocked Josiah's mind and body. He found he wanted to argue on her behalf, support the insane notion he had just moments ago disregarded, his grandmother stitching a map to some kind of treasure. He especially wanted to defend Amanda to her seemingly apathetic father, explain to the English merchant that if she appeared foolish, it was that somehow her good intentions and kindness had just gotten out of control.

"Anyway," Amanda continued, "I won't mention this old quilt to you again. Unless, of course, you bring it up."

"Of course," Josiah replied, wondering what she would think of him if she knew how the accident had happened. How his moment of laziness had cost Elam a leg. Would she still smile that loving-life smile? He didn't think so.

"Josiah!" Mary's voice saved him, snapping him back to the present and away from the unwanted memories that threatened to surface.

"Amanda is company," Mary scolded. "Where are your manners?"

"Forgotten," Josiah said with quiet emphasis. Bowing his head to Amanda, he swallowed hard. "I must return to the fields. The work cannot wait."

Mary wrinkled her nose. "Yes, yes, we know. Go and do the work of the men. Come." She took Amanda's hand and led her away.

Amanda looked back at him once, just when he was about to enter the shed for the hoe. Josiah pretended he didn't see. He needed to concentrate on readying Elam's garden and fields and then formulate the next money-making project. It wasn't proper to remember so vividly the feel of the red-and-white checked fabric that made up Amanda's dress. And it wasn't proper the way the sun filtered through the material and the bustle, silhouetting her willowy legs as she walked away with his sister. His thoughts of late were anything but decorous. He somehow needed to push Amanda from a mind that no longer seemed his own.

"Elam. Elam. Elam," he muttered. He traipsed to the far end of the garden plot, conjuring the horrible memories of the fated accident, hoping they would serve as a reminder of the necessary priority in his life.

Working the thin, flat blade of the hoe with a vengeance through the hardened weeds leftover from last season, Josiah recalled the exact words Elam had spoken that day.

That horrible day. *"I think it would be best to get the new chain. This one is too old to hold so much weight. I will steady the timber. You go, Josiah. Get the new one."*

The quarter-mile round trip hike hadn't appealed to Josiah. He'd argued against his brother's judgment until Elam had finally relented.

A chill traveled the length of Josiah's spine, and his skin grew clammy. He shuddered but forced himself to visualize the snapping of the old chain, the puff of rust bits that had scattered into the air a split second before the logs had avalanched at Elam. The logs had pressed upon his brother's limbs like a merciless steamroller.

The hoe slipped through Josiah's fingers as he put his hands to his ears. He'd never, even in death, forget Elam's cries of anguish.

⚭

MARY TOOK AMANDA TO a clearing not far from the house. Early grass was greening and promised lushness. Earthy-smelling smoke floated through the air, carrying an occasional ember on its wake. Birds chirped from some nearby, hidden place and the sprinklings of daffodils caught Amanda's gaze. The Amish settlement was a beautiful place.

"That is Mama," Mary said, increasing their pace. "Perhaps you have seen her in your store." She waved to the plump woman who sat on a wooden stool before a large cast-iron kettle that hung over a fire.

"What is she making?" Amanda asked as the woman stirred the contents of the kettle with a big stick.

"Candles. Mama," Mary called, "this is—"

"The merchant's daughter." Mrs. Miller stopped stirring and gazed at Amanda. "I have been in your store a few times."

Mrs. Miller's tone held no emotion. Amanda couldn't even tell if she was welcome. She felt a cursed flush of guilt creep up her neck and cheeks. She didn't even remember Mrs. Miller.

Hoping to warm the woman's heart, Amanda pinned on a smile. It was ironic, really. For the first time in her life, she wished she could be just plain Amanda Glosser, not Newlin's doted-upon daughter. She pictured the shock and agitation she'd see on her father's face if she ever told him of the stigma that now seemed to be attached to the phrase *merchant's daughter*.

Mrs. Miller eyed Amanda skeptically, and Amanda felt she needed to explain her visit. "I came to see Josiah," she blurted without thinking.

"And have you?"

"Yes. Yes, we talked."

"Mary," Mrs. Miller said as she started the stirring again, "give Amanda a glass of goat's milk before she goes. Then I need your help with the candles."

Goat's milk! A spasm of nausea tickled Amanda's insides. Mrs. Miller was trying to be polite, and Amanda didn't want to offend the woman further, but she didn't think she could swallow a glass of sweet, thick goat's milk, either. "Oh, no thank you," she said quickly. "I don't care for anything. Truly."

Stepping closer, Amanda peered into the bubbling kettle. "You said candles. Are you making candles? I could stay and help Mary."

"Could she, Mama?" Mary's face brightened, as if coming back to life. "I will show her."

Mrs. Miller lifted the stick and rested it on the side of the kettle. "Do you not have to return to your father's store?"

"No," Amanda replied before her conscience could jump in and answer for her. "I'm free for the rest of the day."

It was a lie, plain and simple, but she just wasn't ready to leave. She'd always wanted to be part of a big family. And today, if for just a while, she could be. She'd bide her time and then ask about the old quilt. It would be perfect, and such fun. The circumstances couldn't be better, either. The way she and the widow were when they were together, Amanda knew she had plenty of time before her father would wonder what was taking so long.

"The wicks are in the bin. Daniel and Sarah have already gathered and stacked the sticks next to it." Rising to her feet, Mrs. Miller smoothed the front of her black skirt. "Thank you for helping, Amanda." With a fleeting smile she waddled toward the house.

As Mary hurried over to the bin, Amanda watched Mrs. Miller, consciously appraising the woman's pear-shaped body. What wonders could be done for the woman with a different style of dress. And Mary, too. Amanda gazed at the girl as she pulled the long braids of cotton from the bin. Her drab brown dress hung lifelessly on her thin body. Smiling, Amanda knew just what to do. She'd make Mary her special project, share all her fashion sense with her. They could be like sisters!

∞

JOSIAH STOPPED SPLITTING WOOD for a minute and wiped the sweat from his brow. He saw Amanda and Mary in the clearing, leaning over the kettle, dipping the wicks into the hot tallow. Their laughter drifted through the air, and he couldn't stop a grin from turning the edges of his mouth.

He knew he shouldn't look, should ignore the pair instead, but he couldn't. He told himself he'd look just one more time. The visible differences between the two cultures astounded him. Though both girls had shed their coats, Amanda's sun-kissed hair blanketed the back of her patterned dress like the cloak of a queen. She moved gracefully and unhurried, like sap from a maple.

Mary's dress, though clean, was the color of muddy water. She looked as though she had very little hair, and the starched bonnet made her neck look long and fragile. Josiah's brows drew into a straight line. He'd seldom noticed, never before cared, what any woman wore or what she looked like.

Suddenly Amanda bent to pick up a wick she had dropped. Josiah's gaze wandered to her waistline again. She was tiny—he had felt it helping her down from the wagon—but unlike Mary, possessed curves and roundness he had never . . . What was he doing? Here they were again, those feelings. Was it wrong to care about such things?

Shoving his hat further down on his head and thus hiding the sight of the girls, Josiah grabbed another log. Then another. This time he'd work off the ache that knotted his insides.

∞

MARY PULLED THE LAST candle from the kettle of tallow.

"So many. These must last for hours," Amanda exclaimed, picking up a fat, squatty one.

"They do not last as long as you think." Mary pushed a wisp of auburn hair that had escaped from her bonnet back out of her eyes. "The men use these in the barns before and after the sun sets. Mama and I and the other women have to make many. Sometimes each week. During the winter it is hardest to get them done."

"Gas lighting is truly wonderful, but this was fun." Amanda bent and set the candle on the ground with the others. Time had slipped away from her, more than she'd planned. The many candles lying about her feet were proof. "I really have to go. My father will wonder what's happened to me."

Rising, she pulled on her coat and smiled at Mary who was again pushing that strand of fiery hair from her eyes. "Do you always wear that bonnet?" Amanda asked.

A frown pleated Mary's brow. "No, I have others."

Fastening her coat, Amanda shook her head. "Don't you and the other ladies ever take them off and let your hair down?"

"No," Mary said softly. "Our caps show reverence to the Lord."

"But I don't think the Lord would mind if you let your hair loose once in a while. Mine's down all the time and I respect the Lord."

Mary's thin shoulders rose in a shrug.

"I know." Amanda clasped her hands together as an idea took hold. "If it's all right, tomorrow I'll come back, and I'll bring a surprise."

"Tomorrow we are making soap."

"Good. I'll help."

"You want to make soap? Why?" Mary asked, folding her arms quizzically against her slender form.

"Why not?" Amanda countered. "I like to do domestic things. I like to cook. And I quilt, too."

Gawking in disbelief, Mary said, "You do?"

"Sure. I make a terrific cobbler and I've stitched five quilts. Have you ever been in my father's store? I like to hang them there."

Mary smiled broadly and, for the first time, Amanda saw that she, too, possessed dimples like Josiah. "Since you quilt, perhaps, then, you would like to attend a quilting bee. The next one to be held in our home is in three weeks."

"That would be such fun. Oh, Mary," Amanda said, grabbing the girl's arm, "I just know we're going to be good friends. The best, maybe. I have to go, but I'll see you tomorrow."

As Amanda walked back toward the buckboard, the steady sound of the axes prodded her thoughts to order. She envisioned the emerald crepe her father had bought for her last year. She saw Mary wearing it. With her slimness, Amanda knew the girl wouldn't even need to bother with a corset. Mary's pale, porcelainlike skin and blazing head of hair would be the perfect compliment for the dress.

More chopping, more ideas. Amanda smiled. She had many other old dresses and frocks and even gowns that she just simply didn't wear anymore. She'd bring all the garments she didn't need and share them with Mary and any of the other Amish women who wanted them.

So deep in thought, Amanda didn't see the little girl until she almost ran into her. "Goodness, me. I'm sorry. I didn't hurt you, did I?"

The child said nothing, just shook her head as she clutched a handful of wild oats. Amanda opened her coat so that she was able to squat comfortably to the child's level. She ignored her pinching corset and asked, "Did you pick those?"

The little girl nodded.

"They're beautiful. I'm Amanda," Amanda said, extending her hand. "I'm a friend of Josiah and Mary Miller. Do you know them?"

Again, the girl nodded. She smiled slightly, gaze traveling to her bare feet.

"Can you tell me your name?"

"Sarah," the child whispered.

"Well, Sarah, it's very nice to meet you."

Sarah's smile grew, revealing a missing bottom tooth. She held the weeds out to Amanda.

"My!" Amanda said, throwing her hands into the air in an exaggerated gesture. "Are those for me?"

"Yes," Sarah answered, raking her tiny top teeth across her lip.

Mindless of the wet, muddy clumps hanging from the roots of the plant, Amanda took them and cradled them against her bosom.

Shoulders raised in shyness, Sarah smiled.

"Look at the green leaves," Amanda exclaimed, enjoying the encounter, hoping to prolong it for just a bit. "Did you see the little hairs all over them? Come here, Sarah."

The girl backed away.

"Oh, it's all right. Don't be scared. I just thought you might like to touch them." Amanda ran her fingers across the leaves. "They feel almost like . . . whiskers. Probably like your daddy's whiskers."

Sarah stepped closer. Her small, dirty hand reached out and stroked the leaves. Her smile returned, and Amanda laughed. "You like candy? I'm coming back tomorrow, and I'll bring you a piece. We could play leapfrog if you'd like."

Wiping her hands on her dress, Sarah inched away. Amanda didn't know if the child understood, but she hoped that come tomorrow she'd have made another friend.

The weeds clutched in one hand, Amanda stood and waved to Sarah with the other. Amanda had always wanted to be part of a large family. She'd even gone so far as to harbor hopes that her father would remarry and she'd eventually have a brother or sister. It had never happened.

When Sarah stopped and waved again before disappearing around the corner of one of the houses, Amanda's suppressed yearning to feel a sense of belonging in a real family surfaced. She so badly wanted to feel accepted. She wanted a home filled with laughter and closeness, and most of all love. That was the one thing in the world that had no price. Her father couldn't buy it for her, could only give it. And it seemed the harder she tried to help him, the harder it was for him to give. An empty sadness filled her, but she wasn't about to give up. God willing, someday she'd have that family and sense of belonging she so desperately craved.

"The hillside has many more of those weeds. If you would clear the rest, my job would be easier."

Amanda's breath caught in her throat at the sound of the husky voice. Once again she had been wrapped in her dreams. She glanced over her shoulder at Josiah and when she saw the small crooked smile that tipped his mouth, a tingle of awareness fluttered in her belly.

She took a deep breath and counted to three, hoping her voice wouldn't tremble when she spoke. "These aren't just weeds. They're special," she said as she turned to face him. "They're a gift from a girl named Sarah."

Josiah's eyes widened, and though he did his best to avert it, his gaze seemed drawn to her bosom. Amanda looked down. Crusted mud flecked the front of her coat and a mushy glop the size of an egg sat on the front of her dress. Moisture had seeped not only into the checked material, but also through the shift she wore beneath it. The bodice of the garment was more transparent than was appropriate.

"Goodness," she squeaked out through her closing throat. Flicking what she could of the mud from her dress, Amanda pulled her coat more tightly to cover herself.

Josiah had looked away and now scuffed at the ground with the toe of his boot. Though it was an innocent occurrence and Amanda felt some embarrassment, she disregarded it. In fact, when she saw the deep scarlet color that had flooded Josiah's cheeks, her own embarrassment dissolved and laughter bubbled inside.

Repressing her amusement for a moment, Amanda said in her most serious tone, "In my family, an intimate incident like this calls for . . . rather desperate measures. We must marry.''

Josiah's head snapped up. He opened his mouth, then clamped it shut again. Amanda bit her lip to keep from spoiling the ruse. Emotion after emotion flitted across his face. She knew she'd rendered him speechless. Then, the mask of blankness and coldness returned, and Josiah retreated behind it. In spite of herself, Amanda found she was responding to his harsh features.

''Josiah,'' she said, laughing, ''I'm teasing.'' Clucking her tongue, she continued, ''You don't make a person feel very good about themselves. If it were a true . . . *custom* in my family, would it really have been such a horrible fate?''

''I must return to my work,'' he said sharply.

''Wait. Now wait a minute.'' She dropped the wild oats she still held in her hand and grabbed at his arm to stop him. Her eyes met two pools of silver—bottomless and emotion-free. ''I was kidding. It was a joke. I—I was just trying to make us both feel better.''

''I must get back to work.'' Shrugging off her arm, Josiah started to walk away.

''What are you so mad about? Josiah!'' Amanda hurried after him. ''I know you're embarrassed,'' she said, trying to keep up with the long strides he was taking. ''And I shouldn't have teased you. I'm sorry about that.''

He kept on walking, and it infuriated her. How could he just shut off his feelings so?

''Oh! Now, come on!'' Irritation edged her voice. ''You're supposed to at least stop your . . . your blasted walking and apologize back. Any decent man would. And . . . and especially after I just helped Mary make your candles!''

Josiah stopped and faced her, one eyebrow cocked at her announcement. His cheeks were still slightly flushed and Amanda's heart stepped up a beat. She couldn't help smiling at him.

''Marriage and love are not to be taken lightly. That is God's union. I do not joke about such things.''

Shaking her head, Amanda rubbed her arms against the sudden chill she felt. ''I know that now.'' She struggled to maintain an even, conciliatory tone. "Seems everything I do is wrong in your eyes. I know someone who is a lot like you. I'm going to tell you what I tell him. You're too serious. You're letting the fun and the simple pleasures in life pass you by. I think that's sad."

She spun on her heel and started for her horse. Stopping to retrieve the wild oats Sarah had given her, she tossed a backward glance in Josiah's direction. "I also think if you wouldn't try so hard not to, you'd find you might even like me." Hiking her skirt, she climbed to the buckboard and slapped the hackney into motion.

5

WATCHING AMANDA'S BUCKBOARD AS it shrank
further into the horizon, Josiah knew he should never have
gone back near her. He should have just let her leave.

Clenching his teeth tighter, he remembered how his heart
had stopped when she had teased him about marrying her.
She was so different than any woman he had met before.
She spoke her mind, seemed to do as she pleased. She liked
to laugh and make light of things that most folks wouldn't.
And that teasing . . . Not that it was bad, or that he didn't
like it—he just wasn't used to it. He wasn't used to having
someone gaze at him the way she did. Just a smile or a
look from her could set his blood to boiling and his body
on fire.

She had already done it to him twice. He suspected she
knew it, too.

The dot that had been Amanda finally disappeared. Josiah's gaze turned to the two young women from his community who had stopped to talk to Mary. Though he
couldn't hear their words, he guessed they were talking
about Amanda. It wasn't every day an English woman paid
their village a visit and helped make candles. Mary was

talking, her thin arms moving in exaggerated gestures, and
Rachel Yoder and Elnora Borntrager seemed to be en-
tranced by her words. He figured wherever Amanda went,
she caused quite a stir.

Josiah took off his hat and raked a hand through his hair.
He forced himself to appraise Rachel Yoder as he had never
before—as a woman. The intentional leering wasn't proper
and made him feel like a pervert of sorts. But still, the need
to prove Amanda Glosser wasn't the only attractive woman
in Prosper impelled him to continue.

The color of Rachel's loose, no-form dress made Josiah
think of sparrows. The grayish-brown garment would have
nearly hung to the ground, covering her black stockings,
had it not been for her apron. His gaze roamed upward,
skipping her breasts with a blink and traveling to her face.
He supposed most men considered her attractive: her face
a perfect oval, her lips like a tiny bow. "Too tiny," he
remarked, startled that he'd spoken the thought aloud.

Drumming his fingers on the brim of his hat still held in
one hand, he turned his gaze on Elnora Borntrager. Though
he wanted the self-imposed study completed, to be fair, he
reminded himself of all the good things he'd heard about
her. Like the special gift she had with animals; all men
admired that in her. And her pie-making abilities. She made
a crust that melted in a person's mouth. Unlike his sister
and Rachel, Elnora's mottled work dress hugged just about
every inch of her five-foot frame. Josiah concluded she
liked to sample pies as well as bake them. But all that didn't
matter. There was just something about the way the corners
of her mouth turned downward more than upward. Even
when she smiled, like she was doing now, she didn't look
happy.

Amanda smiled more often than not. Even when she
wasn't smiling and was perplexed about something, her
face radiated with enthusiasm and a love of life. And she,
too, had a special way. It didn't matter to Josiah that it
wasn't in dealing with a horse about to foal or some sickly
or injured farm animal, but that it was with her own fat,
spoiled tabby cat.

Josiah's mind whirled with Amanda's attributes. From

her silky, golden hair and dancing blue eyes to her buying the quilts and befriending his little sister, Sarah, he realized he didn't want any other woman to measure up to her.

He exhaled with a whoosh, nostrils flaring. "Why can I not get her out of my mind?" Glancing back to Rachel and Elnora, he grumbled, "What is wrong with me? Both would make a fine wife." His stomach lurched at the thought. It wasn't their fault, he silently defended, that they didn't have the worldly independence Amanda did. Josiah stiffened. Where had that thought of independence come from? Is that what emphasized the difference between the Amish women and Amanda? Is that what he was attracted to? Guilt twisted his gut. "Perhaps I am loony, too," he said in a soft, strangled voice. "Too loony for my own good. 'Be ye not conformed to this world,' " he mumbled quickly, " 'but be ye transformed by the renewing of your mind, that ye may prove what is that good and acceptable and perfect will of God.' "

The verse didn't make up for his thoughts but served as another reminder of what was important and what could never be. Stuffing his hat back on his head, Josiah almost wished he hadn't taken the quilts to the general store. He had a feeling nothing would ever be the same.

AS THE BUCKBOARD BOUNCED and creaked across the rough terrain, Amanda tried not to think of how angry her father would be when she told him where she had been and where she hadn't.

She snorted, wondering how time had gotten so away from her at the Amish village. Though she had had every intention of stopping by Widow Marly's to deliver the glove, Amanda knew it was too late now. Supper needed to be fixed, and truth be told, she wanted to spend some time alone studying the quilt again. She needed to think, needed to come up with just the right questions for the Amish women to get the answers that would uncover the mystery behind the old quilt.

The grove of maple and elm trees birthing the tiniest

starts of new leaves indicated the five-minute mark to town. Amanda always wondered who had come up with the five-minute idea. Did it mean five minutes by horse, buggy or foot? Right now all it meant was she was closer than ever to receiving her father's probable wrath over her tardiness.

She purposely bypassed the main street, not wanting to make herself any later by upholding etiquette and having to stop and speak to a friend or neighbor should she meet one. Instead, she decided to return the way she'd left, down the narrow lane that led to the back of the store.

Since the alley appeared empty, Amanda laid down the reins, turned around in her seat and adjusted her bustle so that she could stretch to reach the old quilt made by Josiah's grandmother. The backside of the tiny redbrick library passed her peripheral vision just as she got a fingertip on the coverlet. The horse clomped slowly down the lane, and feeling safe enough, she leaned further into the back of the buckboard, her rump sticking into the air.

"Got it," she said with a grunt, awkwardly snatching up the quilt like an inexperienced, overanxious fisherman. As the wagon moseyed past the rear of the newly built train station that would soon be accommodating Prosper's first passenger trains, Amanda righted herself. To her dismay, she saw that Leon Violette had witnessed her entire escapade from the doorway of the stable.

She groaned as she laid down the quilt and quickly adjusted her bustle and skirt.

"Hellooo, Amanda," Leon said, a devilish grin showing the nub of a blackened tooth. "Sure is nice to see you. Got anything else back there you need to fetch?"

His meaning was not lost on her, but she ignored his remark. "Afternoon, Leon," she said flatly, having to force politeness. Rogers, Leon's worker, was such a nice, quiet man. Why couldn't it have been Rogers out here instead of Leon?

"Wish I would've had a camera to photograph that picture. Mmm, mmm, mmm."

"Stop it." Amanda spit out the words with contempt. She found that of late, the horseman tried her patience more and more. If only her father could witness the man's crude

behavior, maybe then he'd understand why she wasn't interested in any type of proposal Leon had to offer.

"Don't go bein' all huffed," he said as he approached
and took the reins from her. "I was funnin'. I'd have to be
a Nancy-boy to not appreciate your fine arse."

"Leon!" Amanda's voice rose an octave and she glow-
ered. "Keep talk like that away from my ears."

"Oh, jeez. Most women would be gigglin' over such a
compliment, but not you." He led the horse and buckboard
to the barn. "Your pa's havin' conniptions. Where have
you been anyhow?"

"I was running an errand. No. No, don't unhitch the
horse," she said quickly. "I'm not staying here long. Just
want to tell Papa I'm back, then I'm heading on home."

Leon tethered the horse loosely to one of the weather-
beaten pillars that held up the small overhang of the barn.
From a nearby location, the clang-clang of the smithy forg-
ing metal rang through the air. "Where'd you go, anyhow?" he asked loudly over the clamor. "Been gone a long
time." He stretched out his arms to help her from the buckboard.

"I told you," Amanda replied, grabbing Widow Marly's
glove from off the seat. "Errands." With a sigh, she reluctantly placed her hands on Leon's broad shoulders.

He captured her about the waist, his hands sliding to the
underside of her breasts as her feet hit the ground. He didn't
release her and even through her coat, Amanda felt his
groping fingers. Her skin crawled.

"Get your hands off me, Leon." She pushed against his
chest, the sweaty, horsey smell of him turning her stomach.
"I'll scream. I swear I will."

"Who's gonna hear you? Reckon Smithy's makin' too
much noise." He chuckled as if he'd made some joke. A
chill Amanda had never experienced before slithered up her
spine.

"If you don't get your hands off me, I'll tell my pa. I'll
keep telling him until he believes me. You'll wish you'd
never touched me."

"Tarnation, Amanda!" Leon dropped his hold but didn't
move away from her. "I can't be around you and see you

as much as I do and not get . . . *feelings*. Someday you're gonna be my wife.''

Gritting her teeth, Amanda stepped away, silently counting to ten. "We've talked about this before. You'd best get rid of those *feelings*, Leon, because I'm not interested. You *know* that. We're friends. That's it. Don't do anything like that ever again."

"Don't go being all sassy," Leon said, again closing the distance between Amanda and himself. "Just because you live in a fancy house and your pa owns the store don't mean you're any better than me. I own all them horses, and someday I'll own that barn, too. And a house, bigger than yours. No. You shouldn't act like you're better than me." He stepped even closer so that their noses were almost touching.

Amanda knew that thanks to her father almost everyone in town expected her and Leon to marry. Though she'd never given him any encouragement, right now his demeanor seemed different, and she didn't think an argument would help any. "I'm sorry if it seems I act like that," she said slowly, trying hard to keep her voice and breathing even. "If I do, I don't mean to. I certainly don't think that way." She pushed a bit harder against Leon's solid chest, hoping she'd been successful in placating some of his irrational anger.

Before she knew what was happening, quicker than she could even anticipate, Leon captured her wrist. "You need to be friendlier to me. I saw the way you let the Amishman touch you. I was watchin'. You didn't know because you were so busy makin' those cute little eyes at him. Can't be a teasin' like you do. One day it's gonna blow up."

Leon's tone was almost a growl. Amanda felt as though her feet had rooted to the earth. She smelled the onions on his breath and the grime from his work on his body, but it was his threatening insinuation that convulsed her stomach now.

Suddenly he tilted his face. Amanda felt his lips smash into hers, felt his wet, spongy tongue invade every inch of her mouth. She wanted to vomit. The fear and intimidation vanished. Raising her knee, she connected forcefully with his groin.

"Aaahhhwww!" Leon's eyes clamped shut as he released her and doubled over.

Amanda's face contorted with something akin to guilt and even a bit of sympathy as she stared at the top of his oily head. "I'm . . . I'm sorry, Leon, but . . . but you deserved that. I know I'm no better than anybody else in Prosper. I resent you talking that way about me, and I resent your threats even more. I . . . I thought we were friends."

She drew the back of her hand roughly across her mouth, wishing she could erase the kiss. "Let's . . . let's just forget any of this ever happened. I won't tell a soul."

Leon straightened as much as he could, hands clutching his privates and eyebrows still furrowed deeply. "Forget? Sure," he spat through gnashed teeth.

His reddened face, the white lines around his mouth and the crazed look in his eyes made Amanda almost regret what she'd done. Swallowing hard, she touched his shoulder. "You going to be all right?"

"Just go. Get outta here!"

"I'm sorry. I'm . . ." Heart racing, Amanda hurried from the barn. She expected a scene with her father—*that* she could handle—but she hadn't been prepared for Leon and such unpleasantness.

She fled the short distance to the back door of the store, stopped and leaned heavily against it, willing her heart to still. The muscles in the left side of her face twitched, and she had the horrible sensation of a trapdoor opening in her belly. The messes she got herself into!

Closing her eyes, she took several deep breaths. She had to get Leon out of her mind. Her father would sense her anxiety, and they'd end up having the same old "Leon argument." Her father wore blinders when it came to the man. She knew, somehow, even if she told her father about the advance, he'd pass it off as an adoring suitor's friskiness.

All thoughts evaporated as the door opened, and Amanda fell backward, landing in her father's arms.

"There you are! Where in the blazes you been?" Newlin

set her to her feet. "I been worried sick about you." His gaze softened, and he drew her roughly into his embrace. "Jiminy, Amanda."

Amanda knew she had truly worried her father, for he seldom demonstrated any affections. To be hugged . . . "I'm sorry, Papa. But you had nothing to worry about."

Gathering more courage, she pushed from his arms, wondering when his gaze would land on the glove of Widow Marly's that she still held in her hand. "Funny, isn't it, how different things make people react in ways they never dreamed of?"

"You're babbling. Must be the crazy old widow's influence. What stories did she feed you this time?"

"Well," Amanda said, turning away from him so that he could help her shrug out of her coat, "it wasn't the widow." She retrieved the garment from her father's hand and took another deep breath to calm herself as she headed to the front of the store, her father at her heels.

"Who, then?" Newlin persisted.

Knowing this would probably take longer than she had anticipated, Amanda reached to hang her coat on the wooden peg behind the counter. The widow's glove slipped through her fingers and plopped to the floor. Though the odor of camphor had already been released, Newlin picked it up and smelled it anyway. He glared at her, his mouth quirking in annoyance.

"This is the widow's. Must not've been at her place since you still got her glove. Where in the blazes were you all afternoon?"

Stomach knotting, Amanda licked her lips. "I went to the Amish settlement. Remember that old, old quilt? I had a few questions about it and thought they could help me."

"You what?" Newlin bellowed.

"You heard me." She met his angry glare, but unconsciously wiped her palms on the front of her skirt.

"You went out to God knows where to see *those people*?"

Wanting to stamp her foot in frustration at the derogatory way he had said *people*, but knowing she didn't dare, Amanda bit her lip, fists clenched at her sides. "You're not being fair. They may be different but, Papa, they're people just like us.''

"They ain't like us. Not a bit like us. They're . . . they're unfriendly. And self-righteous, 'specially that big fella. The one that cheated you with them confounded old quilts. They ain't people to be gettin' friendly with, I tell you! You shouldn't go out there again!''

Amanda gasped. "You can't be serious. What do you mean, unfriendly? Have you ever started a conversation with Josiah?''

"Josiah? Josiah, is it now? What'd you and them people do all the hours you were there?''

"Talked. I met Josiah's sisters, Mary and Sarah—''

"Enough," Newlin shouted with a flip of his hand.

She'd seen that reaction too many times from her father and this time she wasn't going to let him dismiss her. "I had fun. I don't know about all the Amish, but I know the Millers are good people. You're so stubborn, you're just not letting yourself see the goodness.''

"Don't you be talkin' to me like that!''

"I'm sorry, but you're wrong this time. You should see their community. You'd have been impressed, Papa. The men were all working together, the houses and plots of land were all neat and trim. And self-righteous," she threw her hands into the air, "where'd you get that? There are women and children. Lots of children. Look!'' Amanda yanked her coat from the peg. "Look at these," she said, pulling the wilted wild oats from her pocket. "The sweetest little girl gave these to me. How can you say they're people not to be friends with?''

Newlin's face pinched tight. "That where you got all that mud on your dress? From the blasted weeds?''

Ignoring his sarcasm, she answered, "Yes. And this here," she bent and pointed to a shiny, hardened spot near the hem of her skirt, "this is where the hot tallow dripped on my dress.'' Rising, she smiled at her father. "I made candles today. Me! Can you believe it? It was fun. Josiah's sister Mary—''

"Don't care who you met. I don't care to hear 'bout them Amish no more.''

Amanda felt her face growing hot. Her nostrils flared as angry puffs of air burst from her nose. "Papa—"

"I don't want you out there with 'em. None of 'em."

"They're no different than we are. No! No, you know what?" she said, shaking a finger. "They *are* different. They have real loving families."

"Confound it! You just stay away."

Eyes widening, Amanda bunched the material of her skirt. "If Mama were alive, you wouldn't be like this."

"Enough, I said!"

"It's true. I was old enough. I remember how it used to be, Papa. You buried your heart the day we buried Mama!"

"Enough, blast it all! I've had enough!"

The vein in her father's neck had swelled and now pulsed dangerously. Amanda could only stare. She hadn't meant to speak that thought aloud. Even Ophelia seemed to sense the dissension, for the cat wove around her legs.

"I'm sorry," Amanda gulped, hot tears trickling down her cheeks, "but that's how it seems to me."

"I got work to do. Just go on home. And take that damn cat with you."

As Newlin stalked to the back of the store, a strange sense of relief washed over Amanda. The realization had been dredged from someplace deep inside, and she felt as though a mental weight had been lifted. Wiping her face with the back of her hand, she sighed, sorry to have hurt her father so. "He'll come around," she whispered, hugging Sarah's weeds. "He just needs more time."

∞

AMANDA LICKED HER THUMB and index finger, then pressed them to the wicks of the still-burning candles on the dining table. They sizzled and the odor of smoke filled her nostrils. She liked candlelight. It made her feel cozy inside. The venison steaks, potatoes and corn bread had long ago turned cold, just like the night air after the sun slid down to the horizon.

Grabbing her cup from the table, she walked to the stove and poured the last of the tea. She sipped the still hot, soothing liquid, steam kissing the tip of her nose. The smell of sassafras filled her senses and made her think of Josiah. She wished Josiah were here now. Lowering the cup from her lips, she crept through the darkened hallway, unconcerned with the liquid that sloshed over the rim and puddled the floor.

Shadows danced across the walls of the sitting room, silhouetted by the generous moonbeams that spilled into the room. The quilt, folded neatly and draped along the back of the sofa, beckoned to her. Amanda set her tea down on the marble-topped console table, next to her favorite photograph. She wiped her hands on her skirt and picked up the coverlet. It certainly had helped to pass the lonely hours of the evening. Her gaze darted to the sketches she'd made of the different stitches and designs on the quilt. She'd have to remember to take the drawings to her room before her father saw them. She couldn't tell him any of her speculations. He'd think her loonier than ever. And Josiah. She didn't know if she'd even tell him, disbelieving her theory the way he did.

A heavy sigh wracked Amanda's body. Now wasn't the time to be thinking about the quilt. The quilt and Josiah were what had started the argument with her father. As she laid the coverlet back on the sofa, she told herself she'd be better off remembering that fact.

Where was her father? He'd never been this late before. She could no longer control the spasmodic trembling inside. She grabbed the photo from off the table. Rigidly holding her tears in check, she clutched the picture to her heart and paced the hardwood floor.

"Papa, where are you? What have I done?" Stopping in front of the window so she could see more clearly, she blinked back tears of anxiety. She lifted the picture and gazed with reverence at the two people who smiled up at her.

"Mama, where is he?" Amanda whispered, running a finger over the picture, wishing she could feel the softness of the sausage curls tumbling around her mother's face, remember the true color of her hair. And the roses. Mama had always smelled like roses.

"I feel so alone at times. I don't know what to do. And Papa, he's miserable. I know he is. He buys me things, but I just want him. And when I try to make him happy, all I seem to do is irritate him. Today was the worst. Oh. I got him so huffed. . . ."

Amanda's vision blurred, and she swiped the back of her hand across her eyes. "Just bring him home safely. Please, Mama. I can't lose him, too. Won't you help me?"

6

THE HORSE'S WHINNY SOUNDED so real. Amanda curled up tighter against the chill, drowsily wondering why her room felt so cold. A door slammed and she bolted upright, nearly falling from the low-back sofa.

Blinking, she sifted through the fog that cloaked her brain. Slowly, rational thoughts filtered to the forefront. Josiah and the quilt . . . Leon Violette . . . the fight with her father.

Her father.

Jumping to her feet, Amanda rushed through the sitting room to the darkened hallway and the door. She could barely see the crumpled form that lay in front of the door, but there was no mistaking the stench of whiskey and vomit.

"Papa?"

Silence eerily greeted her.

With her hands out in front of her, she felt her way to the kitchen. She lit the gas chandelier, blinking against the light that instantly spilled into the room. Taking a shaky breath, she gripped the edge of the table and gathered her bearings. Though she felt relief, she also felt fear. She had never before seen her father so vulnerable. He never got drunk; barely even indulged. For him to do so, she knew he had to have been pushed past his limit.

Guilt flooded her. She had done the pushing.

Amanda grabbed the matches lying next to the kerosene lamp on the walnut sideboard. Though her fingers were shaking and fumbling, she managed to get the thing lit. Staring at the smoky flame trickling up the glass chimney, she unconsciously wrung her hands, fighting the rising panic. "What have I done? Oh, goodness. Oh, goodness, I shouldn't have said those things."

Holding back tears, she pumped some water into a basin. Picking up a cloth and the lamp, she rushed back to her father.

His top hat sat crookedly on his head, and the distinguished look he usually had when he wore it was gone. His face, his double-breasted waistcoat, and even his watch and fob were soiled. He looked pitiful, and guilt stabbed at Amanda without mercy.

"Papa?" Dropping to her knees, she lifted his head into her lap. Tears she could no longer contain streamed down her cheeks as she wiped his face with the rag. "Papa, wake up. Come on. We have to get you to bed."

His head turned at the sound of her voice. His eyes fluttered open. "Olivia?"

Amanda froze. "Oh, Papa, no. It's me."

"Olivia. Where you been?"

A huge lump pushed up into Amanda's throat. Shaking her head, she cried, "No! Look at me. It's Amanda, not Mama. Mama's gone."

A chuckle rumbled from inside Newlin's chest.

"You look like her," he slurred. "Sound like her, too. You're so much like her, not a day goes by without me thinkin' 'bout her. Ain't never been a woman like her. Ain't never gonna be 'gain."

Amanda didn't want to move. She was afraid to breathe. She didn't want her father to stop talking. She wanted to hear it all, wanted to know every thought her father had. It didn't even matter that the whiskey had prompted it.

"You loved her a lot, didn't you?" she coaxed.

Newlin licked his lips and the odor of stale whiskey floated through the air again. "I ain't no good with words. Shoulda told her."

"I know," Amanda said soothingly, "but I'll bet Mama knew how much you—"

"Said she didn't miss the city. Didn't mind travelin'. Just wanted her to be happy. Wanted to be able . . ." His voice trailed off.

"Be able to what?" Amanda prodded.

"Give her what she was used to. Give you . . . stuff. Everythin' you wanted."

A frown pleated Amanda's brows. Things hadn't always been easy for them. She knew what most in the town thought, but few knew the real story, the story of the penniless traveling peddler, with his wagon of wares and the woman who had loved him enough to give up her wealthy family.

When Amanda contemplated her childhood, she realized it was like living in two different eras. She vividly remembered the hours upon hours of traveling, bumping around in the wagon, bruises forming with each mile. One town blended into the next, and after a while, to a child, they all looked the same. It had been optimistic Mama, the cutting of fabric scraps and the simple needlework that had kept Amanda content. Those were the early days, the days where she knew her passion for quilting had originated.

The second portion of her childhood had started out well. They'd settled in Prosper simply because Mama had fallen in love with the name. The rundown old store that her father acquired quickly turned into a prolific success. Wonderful, prosperous things had begun to happen. Until . . .

With a shudder, Amanda stopped the thoughts before the pain came. She knew the things she wanted in life couldn't be bought with money.

Her father focused a glassy gaze on her. He seemed to be waiting for her to say something. Amanda touched his cheek in reassurance and forced a smile.

"Papa," she mused, stroking his cheek, "what's happened to us? We had such fun times. You remember, don't you? I remember one night so very long ago. We were out in the middle of nowhere, a tarp as our shelter from the night. It was beautiful. Just the three of us. We made those hats out of leaves. . . . An—and you picked me up and we all danced around the fire. We made paper dolls, long strings of them. You always made yours talk with those funny voices."

Swallowing hard at the persistent lump in her throat, Amanda cradled her father's head more closely, lovingly, against her body. "Remember the marbles, Papa? You have to remember the marbles. That old box . . . there was every color imaginable. You always said someday Mama and I would own a dress of each of those colors. And we did. You bought them for us. Mama loved you. I love you. We had *good* times then. Why can't we now?"

Amanda gulped. She hadn't meant to voice that last part. She didn't want her father any more upset than he already was. It didn't seem to matter, though, for Newlin's eyes blinked and then shut again.

"Miss'er," he mumbled. "Mis . . ."

"Papa?" Amanda gently shook his shoulders.

It was useless. The whiskey had won.

She sat for the longest time, wrapped in the old quilt she'd bought from Josiah, watching her father sleep. She'd always thought of him as a person that never surrendered to regrets. As she studied his face, the stern lines softened by his inebriated sleep, she realized there was much more to Newlin Glosser than anyone knew.

Amanda gently eased his head from her lap and pushed to her feet. Grabbing the kerosene lamp, she ascended the staircase, gingerly skipping the creaky fourth and seventh steps. With a weary sigh she entered her father's bedroom, the flickering light casting elongated shadows across the dark-papered walls. "Ophelia!" she scolded, when she saw the cat on her father's bed, arching its back in a sleepy stretch. "Thank heavens for you it's me and not Papa who's found you here. Bad kitty!"

Scooping up the cat with her free hand, Amanda set her on the floor. She pulled a pillow and a feather tick from the bed, a smile forming as the ever-forgiving Ophelia rubbed contentedly against her ankles.

Arms full, Amanda slowly started toward the staircase. The cat bounded past and down the stairs at lightning speed, skidding to a stop at Newlin's still form.

"No. Ophelia, come here," Amanda demanded in a harsh whisper from the top of the stairs. She clucked her tongue, hoping to draw the cat's interest away from her father. Much to her dismay, the feline ignored her, sniffed and stepped warily onto Newlin's body. Ophelia sniffed some more and then made her way up to his face. Amanda's eyes widened in horror when the cat settled herself on one shoulder and began cleaning his soiled neck.

The staircase had never looked so long. Amanda knew she needed to keep her attention on the lamp and the flammable tick, but she just couldn't imagine what would happen should her father open his eyes and find the one animal he seemed to hate most licking his face.

She started as quickly as she dared down the stairs, anxiety spurting through her body. Anxiousness caused forgetfulness. Her foot landed on the seventh step and the tired old wood screeched like a banshee. Amanda froze. Newlin groaned, mumbling something incoherent, and Ophelia, pausing momentarily, resumed Newlin's bath.

Pulse racing like erratic floodwaters, Amanda darted down the rest of the stairs. "Ophelia!" she snapped barely louder than a whisper.

"Huh? Huh?" Newlin muttered. "Wha—what's goin' on? Huh? Ophelia? That you, Ophelia? Whatcha . . . whatcha doin'?"

Backing with deliberate slowness around the banister and further away from her father, Amanda held her breath, waiting. She wasn't quite certain what to do. Her father didn't seem angry at the cat. He was blinking a lot; maybe he'd fall quickly back to sleep without realizing what was happening, or at least think it a dream. Then she'd snatch the obstinate, poorly mannered animal and give her a good swat.

"Ophelia. Kitty, kitty. Good kitty," Newlin said thickly as he awkwardly patted the cat's head. "This . . . this'll be our lil' secret. Ain't so bad, are ya? 'Manda, she loves ya.

So do I.'' With a heavy sigh, he laid his arm across Ophelia's back and closed his eyes.

The even rise and fall of his chest told Amanda he indeed
had slipped back into his slumber. She crept from her hiding place with a knowing smile. For fear of disturbing him,
she didn't put the pillow beneath his head. But she did
cover both him and Ophelia.

Mood suddenly buoyant, Amanda knew she wouldn't be
able to sleep. Before retiring to her room, she strolled back
to the sitting room and plucked the quilt from the sofa and
the sketches from the table.

Long into the wee hours of the morning, she studied the
quilt. She believed one portion of the design represented a
town or village of some sort, and another area had something to do with a grove of trees or a forest. The last picture
in the sequence—at least the order of succession she felt
represented the sequence of the map—she knew was a
grouping of flowers. There at the flowers was the special
something. Amanda felt it, knew it as well as she knew
how to thread a needle. Somewhere, in some town, was the
original area this quilt design replicated.

That was her last thought as she drifted into a peaceful
sleep.

DISREGARDING THE LACK-OF-SLEEP, gritty feeling
beneath her eyelids, Amanda cracked the last egg on the side
of the bowl, watching as it slid onto the rest of the ingredi-
ents. She dropped the shell pieces, picked up the wooden
spoon and absently stirred the flapjack batter. Though her
body felt weary, her mind craved answers—especially
about the young woman who had held the needle and
stitched those pictures on that piece of fabric so many years
ago.

The kitchen floor creaked behind her, drawing her
thoughts from the intriguing quilt-maker. ''Morning,'' she
said cheerfully over her shoulder.

Newlin grunted.

''I have hot water in the bath,'' Amanda continued on

quickly, knowing how much her father enjoyed a hot soak. "Was just coming to wake you. By the time you finish, I'll have flapjacks, mince pie and tea waiting."

"Don't bother. Ain't hungry," he replied, as if the answer should have been obvious.

Amanda stopped stirring, set the wooden spoon down and turned to face her father. Gone were his top hat and waistcoat, but he still wore the same wrinkled white shirt and rumpled trousers. Red etched the whites of his eyes, and dusky stubble dotted his chin. He looked a mess, but she smiled at him anyway.

"You have to eat. You didn't have supper last night."

"Because I was off getting corned. Ain't that what you mean?"

His tone was sharp, and a thoughtful sigh escaped Amanda. When she thought of his embarrassment and how his head must feel, a smile of sympathy returned. "Papa, stop it now. It's all—"

"Me getting drunk didn't bother you?" Newlin interrupted. "You hate my cussing, seem to hate the way I pass judgment on folks. Can't believe you took a liking to my drinking."

Amanda's smile faded as she tucked a strand of hair behind her ear. "Didn't say I liked it. I . . . I understand," she explained softly.

"Understand?" He stomped and stood before her. "What in blazes do you understand?" he demanded, throwing his hands up in disgusted resignation.

Amanda's eyes widened at the unprovoked outburst, but she held her tongue.

"You think you understand every confounded thing. Just like your ma, you are."

Though shocked and hurt by his words, she couldn't deny the evidence any longer. They had reached a point in their relationship where something had to be resolved. Amanda drew her bottom lip between her teeth. She couldn't go on living like this. She needed him to give of himself.

Taking a deep breath, she searched for the right words to say. Her mind seemed empty, except for the truth. "I understand why you went off drinking. I know I remind you of Mama, and I know it hurts you."

"Jiminy. You don't know nothin'!"

Though her father's fists clenched, Amanda wasn't afraid. When unexpected tears welled in his eyes, she saw into his very soul. Her resolve grew. "You called me Olivia. Do you remember anything you said last night, Papa?"

"Whatever I babbled about was strictly because of the whiskey."

Amanda stood her ground. "I don't think so. I think you miss Mama. You miss her a lot. And for some reason, you feel guilty about her death."

"You don't know nothin'. Nothin', I say!"

"Yes, I do." Meeting his gaze with an unwavering one of her own, she closed the short distance between them. She wrapped her arms around his rigid body and held him tight. "I know you think you aren't good with words, so I'm going to say them. You miss her. You're sad and still hurting inside about her. It's all right to feel those things. But you need to let yourself heal. Her death wasn't your fault. I'm here. We can help each oth—"

Newlin shoved from her embrace, but Amanda wasn't about to be dissuaded. "I know I'm right. I am going to help you. We are going to be a family, you and me. Go have that bath," she whispered. "We'll talk later."

The floor immediately squeaked again, confirming Newlin's speedy retreat. Amanda prayed she would be able to break through his granite exterior. Refusing herself tears, she lifted her apron and dabbed her eyes. In the last eight hours, progress had been made. Definite progress.

∞

OTHER THAN THE SOUND of silverware scraping against china, silence reigned at the breakfast table. Her father avoided looking at her, and Amanda figured idle chit-chat wouldn't get them anywhere. She thoughtfully plowed a forkful of her flapjacks through the maple syrup, watching the path disappear as the thick amber syrup spread back across the plate's flowered surface.

Her head throbbed, just like his, she supposed. She was beginning to think even his sharp tongue was better than the deafening silence. Clearing her throat, she gathered her courage and decided now was as good a time as any to tell him she planned to go back to the Millers and see Mary.

"I'd like to use the buckboard. I'm going to take Widow Marly her glove this morning," Amanda said brightly.

"Should've done it yesterday like you said you were," Newlin retorted without looking up.

The fork slipped through Amanda's fingers and clattered onto the china before she could stop it. Her father looked up and triumph filled her; she'd finally snared his attention. "I know," she said, careful to keep her tone even, "but I think the widow will forgive me." Pushing her plate to the side, she drummed the table with her fingertips. "Papa, it's so strained between us. Can't you feel it?"

She stopped the drumming and folded her hands as if in prayer. "You're going to make yourself crazy. You need to let go or you'll never get over Mama."

"Aw, jiminy! Don't go ruining my breakfast with your nonsense."

"Nonsense?" An edge of impatience crept into Amanda's voice. "I'm trying to talk to you. I care about you."

"I—I don't want to talk. Just . . . just shush now."

Her father suddenly looked old, old and tired, and it had nothing to do with his binging the previous night. She stared, as if noticing for the first time the wrinkles across his forehead, the shadows beneath his haunted eyes. Amanda's heart ached, ached for his release from his ghosts of the past, and it also ached to hear him say the words she'd just spoken, that he cared, that he loved her. She needed desperately to hear them.

Tossing her linen napkin to the table, Amanda slid her chair back. "Widow Marly's isn't the only stop I plan to make today. I just wanted you to know I won't be in the store at all."

Nothing. Not a response, not a glance. Amanda felt her throat constrict. She licked her lips and swallowed hard. "I hope you have a good day, Papa. I'll clean all this up in a bit when you're finished. I've got some sorting and straightening to do upstairs now." Not allowing her chin to sink dejectedly to her chest, she held it high and strolled leisurely from the room as if she had not a care in the world.

It didn't take long for Amanda to weed the seldom-used outfits from her closet. Having heard the slamming of the door shortly after she'd left the kitchen, she knew her father had left for the store. Guilt peppered her conscience, but she told herself she wasn't just trying to retaliate. The fact was, she'd made a promise. And she wasn't going to break it. As it stood, she suspected he knew exactly where she planned to go in addition to the widow's place.

Once the kitchen was cleaned and the dishes put back in the coffee-brown, walnut cabinets, Amanda dragged the heavy trunk out of her room and to the staircase. Chewing her lip, she pondered the best way to get it down the stairs without ruining the sleek finish or breaking her back. Suddenly an idea took hold, and she dashed down the steps.

The piece of rope she'd taken from the smokehouse was the perfect length to reach all the way around the banister, back to the top of the stairs and still encompass the big trunk of dresses. She went to work assembling the simple device that would enable her to get clothing down the long staircase and to the Amish settlement.

With her pulley system in place, Amanda took a deep breath, braced her feet against the corner of the wall and pulled. With a thud that came more quickly than she'd expected the trunk dropped a step. Though happy her plan worked, she prayed she hadn't marred the portion of the stair not covered by the carpet runner.

Ophelia appeared almost instantaneously and rubbed her chin against the laces of Amanda's high shoes. "Oh, no," Amanda groaned. She hadn't thought of the cat and her insatiable curiosity. She prayed even harder that Ophelia would stay with her at the top of the stairs and not go snooping about the unstable-looking trunk.

Jiggling her foot as much as she dared, hoping the cat would continue to bat at the laces, Amanda pulled again. Another clonk. Another. Then another.

Beads of perspiration popped out along her hairline. She

huffed and puffed like the trains at the station in town, the rope now cutting mercilessly into her fingers like razor-sharp teeth. She felt at any moment she'd be jerked around the wall she'd braced herself behind and yanked down the stairs. At least Ophelia seemed content.

Another step.

When she made it to the halfway mark, Amanda directed one of her father's favorite curses at herself for her own stupidity in thinking she was strong enough to carry out this plan. Her back burned from the strain, and her fingers felt as if they were about to be severed. How could clothing be so darned heavy?

"Amanda? Amanda dear, where you hiding?"

Ophelia meowed at the voice, and without thinking, Amanda shouted happily, "Widow Marly! Come quick." Her relief was short-lived. She couldn't ask the arthritic old woman to help with something like this. Amanda knew her friend would try, and Amanda didn't even want to think about the widow getting hurt.

"I need to get this blasted thing down there now," she said through gritted teeth. No longer concerned with damaging her father's house, Amanda began to unwind the rope from her hands. Ophelia, an apparent friskiness taking hold, pounced at the hem of Amanda's skirt and bounced onto the staircase just as Amanda uncoiled the last loop from her hand, releasing the trunk.

"No!" she screamed. "Ophelia!"

7

A SOB ROSE IN Amanda's throat. She hiked her skirt and rushed down the stairs. Ophelia lay sprawled on her side, next to the trunk, her once-mischievous yellow-green eyes now flat and lifeless.

Grief and despair tore at Amanda's heart. "Oh, God," she cried, dropping to her knees, mindless of her bustle and the stays stabbing into her flesh. "Ophelia. I'm so sorry." She lovingly stroked the tabby's silky, bridled coat. "What have I done?"

Ophelia's eyes slowly closed. Amanda shook her head in disbelief, weeping.

"Oh!" gasped Widow Marly, as she came upon the scene.

Through her tears, Amanda saw the old woman's hands fly to her face in horror.

"Dear, dear, dear! What happened?" the woman asked, her moss-colored eyes like two huge buttons.

Gulping hard against the convulsive sobs that threatened her body, Amanda cradled her head in her trembling hands. "I—I killed her. I killed Ophelia." A fresh batch of tears blinded her again. She leaned closer to the cat, flung her arms out and circled the still form.

With a grunt and a deep groan, Widow Marly squatted stiffly beside Amanda. "There, there, dear," she cooed, rubbing Amanda's back. "This was an accident, that's all it was. An unfortunate accident. Goodness. Goodness me! Amanda," the widow said suddenly, "reckon Ophelia hasn't used up them nine lives, yet. Look, dear, she's still breathing."

Amanda popped erect, staring at the cat's body. Ophelia's side erratically rose and fell with short, labored pants. A cry of relief broke through Amanda's lips. "Thank God. Oh, thank God!" She clutched the widow's arm, now hopeful. "Heavens . . . oh, my, I—I need to get her to Doc Rollins. Surely he can help."

"Child," Widow Marly said, her eyes taking on a wounded look as she pushed a clump of wet hair from Amanda's face, "the doctor's gone. Remember? He's in South Pierce, speakin' against bloodletting. Won't be back for two, three days."

Tenderly petting Ophelia's head, Amanda bit her bottom lip. "What can we do? You seem to know everything, Widow. There has to be something. She's not bleeding. Maybe we should pick her up, get her off the cold floor, and you could take a look?"

Shaking her head, the widow frowned. "Don't rightly know if that'd be a good thing, me poking around. Poor critter could be hurt inside. She's robust, that one, but to get in the way of that trunk . . ."

A crazy combination of fear and hope whirled Amanda's mind. "Ophelia? Ophelia," she whispered, willing her pet to open her eyes again.

A throaty moan rumbled inside the feline. "Good girl. Come on, kitty," Amanda coaxed, "open your eyes."

"I know!" Widow Marly shouted, making Amanda jump. "That Amish woman. Let's get her to the Amish healer."

"Wh-what are you talking about? What healer?"

"Don't know her by name, only that she lives in Josiah Miller's community. Leon knows of her. Yes, yes! Why

didn't I think of her sooner. This old mind . . ." The old
gal shook her head again, smoky curls dangling against her
buckskin jacket like diamonds against flannel. "This girl,
seems she's got a gift or somethin' with animals. It's who
the Amish call on when they're needin' help."

"We have to go," Amanda exclaimed, pushing awk-
wardly to her feet. "We have to find this girl. She'll help
Ophelia. I know she will." A huge smile spread across
Amanda's face as she quickly mounted the stairs.

"Where are you going, dear? Amanda?"

Moments later, Amanda rushed back down, carrying the
old quilt. "I wanted to wrap her in something, keep her
warm enough. Can you mind the horses and buckboard,
Widow, so I can hold her while we ride?"

"Great shakes, yes. Let's get a move on, dear. Come,
come, come."

With a prayer on her lips, Amanda carefully picked up
Ophelia, wrapped her limp form in the coverlet and hurried
after Widow Marly.

∞

JOSIAH STOPPED THE DOBBIN and plow at the end
of the row. Taking a deep breath, the rich, loamy scented
air filling his senses, he ran his forearm across his brow,
wiping away the sweat. He had one more of Elam's fields
to complete before he would be free to help his father and
other brothers with the family land. There was so much he
needed to accomplish, he wished the Lord had put more
hours into each day.

He watched a sparrow for a moment, a smile forming on
his lips as the small bird chirped and flapped its wings,
rolling in the freshly turned earth. If only life could be that
simple.

Mary's voice, calling his name, wafted through the gentle
midmorning breeze. Josiah's smile faded. He wasn't thirsty,
didn't want the refreshments he knew his mother and sisters
had made. No one seemed to understand that his working
Elam's fields alone was a retribution of sorts for the accident he'd caused his brother. A cool drink and fresh bread

with preserves was a reward he didn't deserve.

Mary's voice grew louder, and Josiah clucked the work-horse to movement.

"Josiah. Josiah, stop!" Mary tottered through the uneven ridges of the dark soil, her arms occasionally extending for balance. "I know you hear me, stop plowing," she said, wagging her finger.

"Whoa. Whoa," Josiah relented, stopping the horse once again. "What is it, Mary?" he asked through clenched teeth. "I have much work to do."

"I know, but I hoped you could come help with Elam for a moment. Lena and Mama are washing clothes, and I thought I would help by bathing him, but he refuses. Please, it would only take me a bit if you convinced him to co-operate."

Guilt rose on a wave of acid in Josiah's belly. He'd bathe his brother. That was the least he could do.

Grabbing Mary's arm, Josiah helped her through the field and toward Elam's tiny house. Josiah's chest felt so heavy, his head throbbed. He knew his brother's leg was gone, knew his sister-in-law and his mother and Mary helped to keep Elam washed and the bandages on the stump changed daily. Still, Josiah had not seen the mess since that fated day.

A dull, empty ache gnawed at his soul. It was about time he did see exactly what his laziness had caused. He made a mental note, too, to tell his sister-in-law that from this point on he'd bathe his brother until he was on crutches and could bathe himself.

"Elam," Josiah said, entering his brother's bedroom, Mary on his heels. "We've come to bathe you."

"And wash your leg with iodine," Mary piped cheer-fully.

"I do not want a bath today," Elam snapped. "I want to be left alone. Mary," he said harshly, "you and Lena need to listen. I am still a man with my own wishes."

The stench of blood and decay and everything evil hov-ered in the room. Elam's mood seemed to match, and Jo-siah's heart shriveled a little. "Mary, go help Lena. I will take care of Elam. Go."

Mary's gaze darted between her brothers. Josiah forced
a thin-lipped smile and with a tip of his head, motioned to
the door beside him.

"Iodine's in the basket with the clean bandages. The
water in the basin is probably cold. I could go and—"

"Thank you, Mary," Josiah said, dismissing her. "We
will be fine."

Wincing, Elam scooted up further on his elbows. "What
are you doing?"

"Doing?" Picking up the small square rag, Josiah sunk
it into the basin of water sitting on the maple bureau. "I
am going to.give you your bath."

"Why can I not do my own bathing? Lena and Mother,
and even Mary, they treat me like a child. I know I cannot
stand by myself very well yet, but there are still things I
would like to try to do for myself. The women, they will
not even let me try." Crossing his arms over his chest, a
smile slanted Elam's lips. "Are you going to be like the
women, Josiah?"

Lifting the basin, Josiah walked slowly over to the bedside. He'd been wrong about Elam's mood, and he even
thought he understood his brother's frustration, but he
couldn't return his brother's smile. The painful memories
and the soul-snatching guilt wouldn't allow it. Setting the
basin on the floor, Josiah rubbed the thin bar of lye soap
against the rag until suds formed. He squeezed the excess
from the rag and handed it to his brother.

Elam's smile grew as he shifted his weight and threw
back the quilt and thin linens covering his body.

Josiah blanched when he saw the wrapped stump. He
didn't think anything could have prepared him for seeing
his brother, minus a leg from the thigh down. His heart
ached as he sat in the straight-backed wooden chair next to
the bed. "I am so sorry this happened. Because of me you
will never be able to do the things you love."

Holding out the rag for more soap, Elam frowned.
"What do you have to be sorry for? This was not your
fault. This was God's will."

Josiah soaped the rag again and handed it back, shaking
his head. "Is that your true feeling? Inside here?" he asked,

firmly slapping his own hand over his heart. "If I had used the new chain . . ."

"I do not think it would have been different. God's will. No one blames you, Josiah, but you. It is now time to stop the blame. Lena and I both know it was not meant for me to walk on two legs behind the plow. Nor will I carry our children. God has other plans for me. I will use the crutches, and I will accept these new plans."

"But what if," Josiah said, removing his hat and raking his hand through his hair, "there was a way for you to still do those things you spoke of? Would you not want to try that way?"

Elam fell back into the flat pillow. "Forget your *worldly* notion. I hoped you already had. It will not work, and it would do you and our family good to forget it."

Pushing to his feet, Josiah clenched his fists. "Why?" He clamped his eyes shut and took a deep breath. Opening them again, he whispered, "Why would you not want to try? I do not understand, Elam. I know what Mother and Father say, but why would it be so wrong to make the trip to the big city and see one of those doctors? Tell me why you would prefer to give up and have to use a crutch than walk on a limb made by the *English*?"

"It is not our way," Elam replied matter-of-factly.

"Our way. Our way!" Throwing his hands up into the air, Josiah paced around the tiny bedroom. "Many times I do not know what I think of *our way*. I am confused. I do not see the wrong that our parents see in the worldly. I love the land like you and father and grandfather, but I do not know if it is enough for me. Elam," Josiah stopped and sat on the edge of the bed, "if I could raise the money for a new, useful leg, would you be willing to go to the city?"

"Oh, Josiah—"

"Do not think of Father and Mother and *unserer weg*, our way. Listen to what is in here." Placing his hands on his brother's chest this time, Josiah whispered, "Listen to your heart."

A sorrowful smile turned the corners of Elam's lips. "I would like to hold my future children upon my shoulders. I would like to lift them high like Father used to do with

us, so that they could try to pick the clouds from the sky
as we did.'' Elam's eyes turned downcast. ''I would like a
new leg. In my heart, it is true.''

''Then I will get the money so you can have it.''

''But how? That much money would surely take a miracle.''

Josiah smiled and tossed him a towel. '' 'Faith is the
substance of things hoped for, the evidence of things not
seen.' I think the Good Lord will help me. You will see,
Elam. I will raise the money for your leg.''

∞

JOSIAH FELT A SURGE of elation as he closed the door
to the house and stepped off the stoop. Now that he knew
Elam's true feelings, he was more determined than ever to
succeed in his quest. It didn't matter if his parents and the
elders continued to oppose—he'd never give up.

Suddenly the ground shook and the sound of hammering
horses' hooves filled the air. Turning toward the sound,
Josiah saw a buckboard rounding the bend. He raised his
hand to block the sun, and a tumble of confused feelings
assailed him. It was Widow Marly and Amanda Glosser.

As the old woman yanked the wagon to an abrupt stop,
Amanda lifted her skirts, revealing stockings that were the
same pale green as her dress.

''Josiah. Oh, Josiah,'' Amanda said, running to him,
clenching his arm as she huffed to fill her lungs with air.
''You have to help me. I almost killed Ophelia. I need to
take her to that . . . that healing woman.''

Amanda's voice was choked. A glazed look of desperation etched her face. Josiah's heart went out to her. ''What
are you talking about? What woman?''

''Josiah, dear, dear boy,'' Widow Marly said, waving a
gnarled hand. She stepped slowly from the buckboard,
speaking over her shoulder, ''I heard about the Amish
woman who attends all your animals.'' The old woman
grunted as both her feet hit the ground. ''Heard she's got
a special way. Amanda's beside herself 'bout the accident

with poor, poor Ophelia. Can't you help us?'' she asked, stopping beside Josiah.

"Healer?" Josiah rubbed his chin. "You must be speaking of Elnora Borntrager. Yes, she does have a way with animals."

"Take me to her. Please," Amanda said, squeezing his arm even more tightly.

"Yes. It is not far. Where is the cat?"

"On the wagon seat. Oh, Josiah." Amanda hurried alongside him, her expression pained. "She got hit with a trunk. I dropped a trunk on her."

Questions filled Josiah's mind, but he asked none of them. Though he thought it odd that the English women had chosen to come to his community for help, the determined set of Amanda's jaw and the hope and trust shining in her eyes tugged sharply at his heartstrings. He prayed Elnora Borntrager could help Ophelia.

As though it were an infant, Josiah gently scooped the quilt and lifeless body of the feline into his arms. "I will not be long."

"No. No, wait! I'm coming with you."

"I think it would be best if you and Mrs. Marly stayed here."

"No. It's my cat. I'm going."

Josiah didn't want to upset Amanda further, but Ishmal Borntrager, Elnora's father, was Old Order of the strictest. Josiah wasn't even certain Amanda would be welcome in their home. With staid calmness, he replied, "I must insist you wait here. Elnora's family is not like mine."

Amanda's lips formed an indignant O, but she quickly composed herself. "I understand," she replied, thinking of her father and his irrational prejudices. Amanda wouldn't take the chance of the Amish healer not tending to Ophelia because her owner was English. "Just go," she said. "Please hurry."

Josiah disappeared down the lane, and Amanda paced the yard. All seemed quiet around the Millers' house. There was no sign of Mary or Sarah or even Josiah's mother. Glancing in the direction of the fields, Amanda saw men and boys working. She supposed that was what Mary was doing, too. Circling a lilac bush that buzzed with zealous bumblebees, Amanda noticed the widow had made herself comfortable. The old woman leaned thoughtfully against a sturdy maple whose new, tender leaves were unfurling like tiny supple, green flags.

"Widow," Amanda said, strolling toward her, "I want to thank you for helping me. I don't know what I would have done if you hadn't shown up." A shudder ran through Amanda's body.

"I'm glad I was there, too, dear, but that doesn't mean Ophelia's gonna make it."

Exhaling with agitation, Amanda rolled her eyes. "What is taking so long?"

"Hasn't been all that long. Tell me," the widow said, thoughtfully fingering her bottom lip, "What were you doing with that trunk? I assume it was full of clothing?"

"Running away," Amanda replied off-handedly. She saw her friend's eyes narrow.

"Don't you be joshing an old woman. What were you planning on doing?"

"What do you think, Widow? I think twenty is old enough to be away from Papa."

"Reckon it is, dear. But your pa, he isn't ready for that. Not one little hooter. No, no, no, he isn't."

Amanda laughed, for the widow had shaken two curls loose. The habit the woman had of shaking her head to get a point across, coupled with her outdoor activities, made Amanda wonder why her friend persisted in wearing the fussy style. "Don't worry," Amanda said, nudging the widow affectionately, "I'm not leaving home."

"Well then, do tell. What didos were you cuttin' up, trying to take your belongings from the house?"

"You're a snoop, Cordelia Marly!" Amanda blinked owlishly with feigned shock.

"And you, Amanda Glosser, were up to no good. *Again*."

"Uncle already," Amanda said laughing. "If you must know, my plan was to bring them here. I thought I'd help Josiah's sister with her fashions."

"Oh!" The old woman clutched at her heart. "You're talkin' like you've done gone and had a conniption. A caution, dear—these people don't want help. They wear homespuns. Not ready-mades from mail orders or the cities. The blacks and browns, the simplicity, it's their way. I thought I set you straight on this yesterday. Don't go pokin' that little nose of yours where it don't belong."

Cocking her head, Amanda gave it a shake. "You could be wrong. Maybe they just don't have the money."

The widow's tongue clucked faster than Amanda'd ever heard before. "I know what's going on. I wasn't born in the woods to be skeer'd by an owl! These carryings-on got to stop," she said firmly, sticking her face near Amanda's. "Got to get Josiah Miller out of that mind of yours."

"What?" Amanda tried to keep the defensiveness from her voice. "I don't know what you mean."

"You're fawning. Not today, maybe, but yesterday I'd bet my shotgun you were. It won't work. Can't work."

A sigh of exasperation escaped Amanda. "Isn't it possible that you're wrong? Aren't you ever wrong?"

"About what, dear? My knowledge of the Amish, or your fawning after one?"

"Why does everything I do seem to backfire?" Amanda's spirits sank again. "Why is it wrong to do something nice?"

"Not wrong. Humble, even." Suddenly the old woman reached out. Amanda found her nose smashed against the widow's soft buckskin jacket. The smell of camphor soothed her ragged nerves, and Amanda realized that like her father, she needed comfort, too. She hugged the widow back, never wanting the safe feeling to end.

"If I am wrong," Widow Marly said softly, "I hope it's about Josiah and the Amish."

The crunching of gravel beneath boots snapped Amanda from the comfort of the widow's motherly hug. Josiah approached, shoulders hunched forward, hands shoved in his pockets, the bulky quilt draped over one arm.

Amanda couldn't bear the sight of his empty hands. She flung hers out in simple despair. Josiah's eyes were unreadable, but she thought she noticed him nod. What did that nod mean? The breath came raw in her throat. Her heart pumped spastically. Swallowing hard, she bit back the tears. She suspected the answer.

8

"ELNORA DOES NOT KNOW if Ophelia will live. She would like to keep the cat at her home."

Amanda's heart soared. "At least she's still alive. If she's hung on this long . . ." Her lips twitched with a smile. "Yes, of course I'll leave her there."

"You must realize," Josiah said, his eyes brimming with compassion, "there are no guarantees. The cat could pass at any time. Elnora does not know if her herbs and prayers will be enough."

"I think they will be. They have to be. She can't die."

"Sakes alive, Amanda, you are a stubborn one." The widow smiled kindly. "What do you think, Josiah? That fat cat must be, too. However it turns out, thank you for helping us, dear boy." She laid a gnarled hand on his arm. "Might we thank the healer, Elnora?"

"Yes," Amanda chimed in. "I want to talk to her. Thank her personally, and, perhaps, see Ophelia before we leave."

"I do not think that is possible. But I will relay your gratitude." Josiah bowed his head slightly, and Amanda felt as if she and the widow had just been politely dismissed.

"Why can't I see my cat?"

"Amanda dear," Widow Marly said in a singsong voice, "maybe it's best if you wait a few days. See how everything goes."

"But it's my cat," Amanda protested. "My pet. I think I should be able to see her if I want."

Josiah looked at his boots, avoiding Amanda's eyes, and it suddenly became clear to her. "The English-Amish thing." She threw her hands into the air. "Your Amish people have prejudices, too?" she asked, wonderment tinging her tone.

"I am not always proud of—"

"Oh, no. No," Amanda gestured furiously. "You don't even have to say it. People are people. Amish or English," she said sighing heavily, "we're all the same. It's ironic, really, because the ones that are so set on the differences between us are really the ones that are the most similar."

The widow chuckled at the analogy, and Amanda's breath left her in a rush when a lopsided smile slowly tipped Josiah's mouth.

"I won't press visiting Ophelia—not today, anyway. But you have to promise you'll keep me posted of her progress. Good, bad, everything. Deal?" Amanda asked, holding out her hand.

"You have a deal."

Josiah pulled his hands from his pockets, the faint scent of soap swirling about with the movement. His gaze was as soft as a caress, and Amanda reminded herself to breathe as he stepped closer. When he took her outstretched hand in his warm grasp, she had to fight the overwhelming need to be close to him. Something in the pit of her stomach tingled. She wanted to throw her arms around him, thank him with all of the emotion she felt inside. But as quickly as it happened, the handshake was over.

"Here is your quilt. Or should I have said *map*?" Josiah held it out to her, another teasing smile pulling at the corner of his mouth.

Amanda took it, her fingers brushing against his again, billowing a ribbon of sensation up her arm that spread like wildfire throughout her body. Her insides now felt like hot cornmeal mush, and her heart beat faster than the gait of a galloping horse. Her body just seemed to have a mind of its own when Josiah was near.

"Amanda? Dear girl, you look peaked. Are you all right?"

"Yes. I'm . . . I'm fine. I think all the excitement's finally gotten to me." Amanda turned her gaze from the widow to Josiah. His silver-gray eyes clung to hers. They sparkled with mischief and seemed to be analyzing her every reaction. Feeling vaguely disconcerted, she pointedly looked down at the quilt in her arms. Fingering the reddish-brown binding, she swallowed hard and licked her quickly drying lips. "Well," she said, trying her best to concentrate on the quilt, "I shouldn't even be sharing this with you, Josiah, nonbeliever that you are, but I happen to know there is a treasure of some sort—coins, jewels," she shrugged, "just some round, valuable item. It's buried in some special spot your grandmother knew of."

Crossing her arms over her chest, Amanda sighed and smiled. Her composure had returned, and she even felt a bit smug over the chance to reveal her latest discovery about the quilt.

"The quilt told you all that?" Josiah asked.

"Yes. There's much, much more. I'm sure of it."

"Hmm." He thoughtfully fingered his bottom lip. "Something round, in a location we do not know."

"Valuable. Don't forget valuable. Why else would she stitch the map onto the quilt?"

"Valuable. Yes, you are right."

"By the horn spoons! What are you dears talking about?"

"This old quilt," Amanda explained, hugging it tightly. "Josiah's grandmother stitched a treasure map on it."

"A what?" the widow asked, her silver brows shooting up her forehead like two upside-down U's.

"You heard me. A treasure map. Don't you be a doubting Thomas, too. I know what I know," Amanda said firmly.

"Ah-ha!" Josiah exclaimed suddenly, pointing his finger. "I know what that treasure is. I should have thought of it sooner."

"What?" Excitement raced through Amanda. "Tell me."

"It all makes sense. It is manure. Dried chips of horse manure. Grandmother must have hidden some in case the firewood ran out. Your mystery is solved," he said, a trace of laughter in his voice.

Amanda's lips puckered with irritation. Not only was Josiah still mocking her, but Widow Marly, her surrogate mother and confidant, rocked with the laughter of revelers.

"Laugh if you must," Amanda snapped. "I'll prove to you both this is what I believe it to be. I'll find out more information, and I'll piece it all together. We'll see who's laughing in the end."

"Oh, child," the old woman said, apparently trying to gather her bearings. "I don't mean to poke fun. No, no, no, I don't. That manure bit just tickled my old funny bone. Come on, dear," she said, giving Amanda's shoulders a squeeze, "we'd best be traveling back. I reckon Josiah needs to get himself back to work."

"That I do," Josiah replied with a nod.

"I hope," Amanda said, a glint of her own humor returning, "you have oodles and oodles of manure to shovel. It'd serve you right." She took hold of the widow's arm and they started toward the buckboard. "Don't forget about our deal," she called over her shoulder to Josiah. "You said you'd keep me posted on any news about Ophelia."

"And I will."

"Thanks. Oh, and tell Mary I'll try to come back later to help make that soap. I don't want to miss it." Slowing her pace, she glanced back at Josiah. She saw his perplexed expression before he could mask it. She was just about to comment, when Widow Marly pulled her the last few paces to the buckboard. Without looking back at him, Amanda waved falteringly. What was going through Josiah's mind now?

∞

ON THE WAY BACK to the ranch, the widow chitchatted about the weather, the crops that would soon be planted

and her plans to check her traps later that day. Amanda
fondled the quilt in her lap and made herself listen to the
old woman, forced herself not to dwell on Ophelia or Josiah. She even murmured, "uh-huhs" and "oh, my good-
nesses" in the appropriate places. Still, she wasn't able to
rid herself of the nagging sensation that she shouldn't have
left without seeing Ophelia.

When they arrived, Amanda thanked the widow and returned her glove, knowing the woman would probably need
it for her trapping excursion. Amanda walked hesitantly
back into the foyer, the quietness of the big house envel-
oping her like a shroud. She wished her friend could have
come in for just a bit before heading out to check her traps.

The trunk lay on the stairs where Amanda had left it.
Looking at it sent a shiver up her spine and memories to
the forefront of her mind. At Josiah's she'd felt so hopeful,
so certain the Amish girl Elnora would heal Ophelia. Now,
back at the scene, Amanda couldn't seem to conjure even
a tiny bit of optimism that her pet would live.

"Ophelia will be all right," she told herself as she hurried to the trunk. She dropped the old quilt she still held,
and then sank awkwardly to her knees beside it and the ill-
fated chest. Flinging back the cover, she yanked clothing
from it. One piece after another. Tears burned her eyes, and
though she could no longer see, she continued to pull garments from the trunk.

"Please be all right. Please be all right." Amanda
gulped, wringing her hands, the mantra making her feel all
the more empty and hopeless. The trunk was too large and
too heavy. How could she ever have thought the poor cat
could be hit by such a force and still survive.

"I shouldn't have left her." Crumpling against the trunk,
Amanda buried her face in her arms. "Please, please don't
die."

"A-Amanda? Honey, you okay?"

Bolting upright, Amanda swiped the back of her hands
across her eyes. Her father stood less than an arm's length
away.

"I didn't hear you come in. I"—she wiped her face on
the sleeve of her dress—"I was just going to pick up this
mess."

Newlin cleared his throat and wrinkled his face with a big sniff. "I ran into the widow outside. She told me what happened. Some of it, anyhow. Sorry 'bout that ca . . . 'bout Ophelia."

Pushing to her feet, Amanda blinked away her tears. "Papa," she said, arms akimbo, "Ophelia can't die. She just can't."

Suddenly—and unexpectedly—her father's arms reached for her. He wrapped her in a snug embrace, causing a fresh batch of tears to brew. She pressed her face closer against the softness of his linen shirt, gaining consolation in the metronomic sound of his strong heartbeat. He smelled of spices and sweet tobacco and everything comforting. She never wanted the moment to end.

"What in blazes were you trying to do?" Newlin asked gently, his voice ragged with emotion.

"I was . . . sorting out dresses and skirts that I don't wear. I was going to take them to the Amish settlement." Amanda felt her father stiffen, then his arms slackened.

"See." His voice had turned gruff. "See what follows them people? Nothin' but trouble." He backed away from Amanda, features scrunched with disgust. "Don't seem to do no good to tell you to stay away from them. I ain't gonna say it no more." He grunted, shifting his weight from one leg to the other. "I'm . . . ah . . . sorry 'bout breakfast this morning. That's what I came home to tell you."

Opening his waistcoat, Newlin pulled out a small handkerchief-wrapped package. "These were your mother's," he said, studying the weave of the handkerchief, avoiding Amanda's gaze. "She wore them twice. Don't know if you remember them. Just thought they'd look real nice in your hair . . . the way you wear it loose like you do." Without looking at her, he held out the package. When Amanda took it, her father spun on his heels and started for the door. "I am sorry 'bout that cat, too," he said as he walked. "Don't feel too good to lose something you love so much."

He disappeared into the foyer, and Amanda heard the barely audible click of the door closing behind him. Wiping her eyes on her sleeve, she took a deep breath. She still felt the warmth of his arms. What a surprise that unexpected embrace had been. Seemed he was full of surprises today.

Hands trembling, she slowly peeled the fabric, revealing a pair of jeweled combs. She ran her fingertips down the smooth golden teeth, then across the rough cut of the stones. A lump shoved up into her throat as she pictured an image of her mother, honey-colored hair cloaking her shoulders like a glorious shawl, held away from her face by the beautiful combs. That was the sole time Amanda remembered her mother wearing the hair ornaments. Clutching them tightly against her breast, Amanda realized how difficult it must have been for her father to give her the combs. And the vulnerability he showed where Ophelia was concerned—that also had to have been so very hard for him.

Sighing, she closed her eyes, willing herself to be patient. She knew, for the time being, she had to disregard the aspersion directed at Josiah and his family. She'd take what little bits of himself her father chose to give. The rest—the stubborn bitterness that festered inside him and rolled off his tongue like venom—she'd forgive.

By the noon hour, Amanda had picked up the clothing she'd thrown about. The trunk had been lugged back up the stairs and stashed in her closet. To be safe, she'd heeded her friend's advice and put back many of the outfits she'd originally planned to take to Mary. With a discerning and selective eye, she'd chosen only a few dresses and packed them into her valise. Topping the lot was the small bag of rock candy she'd promised little Sarah.

While the corn bread for her father's lunch baked, Amanda nibbled on a cold turkey leg. Gone was the pessimistic Amanda, and in her place was a stronger, more positive one. She knew what had caused the mood change. She wiped her hand against the linen napkin in her lap, then touched one of the combs nestled snugly in her hair. She felt doubly beholden to her father.

Crooking her finger around the handle of the china teacup, Amanda brought it to her lips. She inhaled deeply—knowing she'd always think of Josiah when she smelled sassafras—and swallowed the last drops of the smooth, earthy-tasting tea she'd sweetened with honey from the widow's hives. Excitement filled every inch of her body. Not only did she want to see Ophelia and Josiah, but she couldn't wait to see Mary's face when the dresses were pulled from the valise. Widow Marly had to be wrong about the Amish wanting to wear the drab homespuns, and after this visit, Amanda would politely tell her so.

She left a note next to her father's place setting on the table. In it she explained her whereabouts, and though she knew he'd probably still be angry, she hoped he'd at least appreciate her honesty.

Warm, moist air puffed out at Amanda as she opened the oven door. The aroma of corn and spices floated through the air as she removed the pan of corn bread. She placed it on a board on the kitchen table and covered it with a clean towel. Hands on her hips, she surveyed the room, wanting to make certain everything her father could possibly want for his meal was available. Satisfied, she took off her apron, grabbed her coat and the valise and headed for the door.

Hoping her father wouldn't mind her using the hackney again, she hitched it to buckboard. With a loud grunt, she lifted the valise and swung it to the platform next to the bench seat. Stepping up next to it, she clucked her tongue and prodded the horse to movement.

With each mile, Amanda bumped up and down on the hard seat of the buckboard, certain she'd have bruises to show for the day's travels. Still, eagerness consumed her. She was excited about seeing Ophelia, and she couldn't wait to see Mary's face when she pulled the dresses from the valise.

A hawk circled overhead in the distance, searching for food, screeching like a soul-taking demon. Such a contrast to the pleasant singing of the other birds she'd heard along the way. The fight for survival could be cruel. Amanda felt sorry for the unsuspecting critter that would no doubt end up as the majestic bird's meal.

The sun climbed higher to its throne in the sky, supplying generous amounts of springtime warmth. Shedding her coat, Amanda lifted the hair off her neck, relishing the feel of the warm, spring breeze against her skin. Finally the Amish houses came into view.

She stopped the buckboard down the narrow lane near Josiah and Mary's home. Amish men were out in the fields again and several women were nearby, some hanging clothes and others tending to chores around their homes. Amanda didn't see any of the Millers. Still, she stepped from the wagon and slid the valise to the edge where she could grab it. Grunting, she yanked the bag from the platform, the force causing the hard-sided piece of luggage to slam into her shins. She dropped it, muttering one of her father's favorite curses under her breath.

"You should have asked for help."

Amanda spun guiltily on the toe of her high shoe at the sound of Mary's voice, hoping her friend hadn't heard the curse. "I didn't think it would be that awkward to get down."

"Do your legs need to be packed in herbs for healing?" Mary asked, the edges of her mouth lifting with humor.

"Don't think anything will stop those bruises." Amanda puffed her cheeks and exhaled. "Did I look as foolish I think?"

Eyes twinkling, Mary nodded.

Amanda wagged her head. "I'm not too late to make that soap, am I?"

"You are not. We have just finished devotions. The soap will be made soon." Mary's gaze returned to the discarded valise.

Amanda knew the girl's curiosity was piqued. "Is there someplace we could go?" she asked, glancing about. "Your room, maybe? I've got something I want to show you."

"Yes, we must hurry. I share the room with my sisters. Once they find us, they will never leave us alone."

The girls each took hold of the leather strap, and Mary quickly lead the way into the white stucco house.

Amanda found herself in a kitchen, the large open area of a fieldstone fireplace taking up more than a quarter of the room. The rough timber floor was spotless, as was the brown oilskin covering the long, wooden table. Benches surrounded the table, providing seats for twelve people. The walls were a bluish color, stark and bare, and the very mood of the house was somber, almost dismal. Except for the two colorfully embroidered, white linen tea towels folded neatly on the wooden sideboard, the room was empty of adornment.

"Come," Mary said, opening one of the doors in the kitchen, revealing a staircase, "before Sarah sees your wagon."

Amanda hesitated. She didn't know what she'd expected an Amish house to look like, but it wasn't this.

"What is it?" Mary asked.

"Nothing. It—it's nothing."

"Yes, there is something." Suddenly Mary smiled a knowing smile. "What is it you want to ask me?"

Swallowing hard, a gulp coming from deep within her throat, Amanda smiled sheepishly. "I'm sorry. I don't want to offend you, truly I don't—"

"But . . . ," Mary prompted her.

"There's nothing here. No photographs of your family, and you've got a big one. There are no curtains or pictures. . . ."

"The *Ordnung* says we must be practical. And as for photographs, they are graven images."

"Practical?" Amanda cocked her head, confusion muddying her mind. "What about beauty and color? You know—decorations, trinkets and knickknacks. And, good heavens, what's a graven image? Sounds horrible."

"If a photograph focuses on a person, it encourages pridefulness. That for us is not good." Mary shrugged. "We do not have knickknacks, either. But now beauty, Mama's dishes provide us with beauty. So do the tea towels. Did you not notice the birds and flowers on them? The thread used is purple and red. Very colorful but also practical, since we do use them. That is not against the *Ordnung*."

"What's this *Ordnung*?"

Frowning slightly, Mary sighed. "It is hard to explain. It is the set of rules our settlement follows."

"You mean this list tells you you can't hang a photograph of your family?"

Mary's frown grew. "No, that is not really how it is."
Scratching her cheek, she seemed to be searching for the
right words. Finally she said, "It is not actually written,
but it is what conveys the spirit of our faith. *Unserer weg.*
Our way."

"I don't know if I'd like someone else making all the
rules and deciding things for me."

"I do not know any other way. Come," Mary said,
grasping the handle again, a smile now on her face, "soon
the children will bother us."

Amanda trailed up the narrow, uneven stairs behind
Mary, the valise pitching awkwardly between them. They
reached a small landing with a door on the right and one
on the left. Mary turned the knob on the door to the right
and shoved her shoulder against it.

"Josiah and the boys sleep across the hall. Rebecca,
Sarah and I share this room," Mary said, nearly pulling
Amanda across the threshold.

Just the mere mention of Josiah's bed had stopped
Amanda in her tracks and caused the breath to catch in her
throat. "How many brothers do you have?" she squeaked,
feeling as though she had to say something.

"Four," Mary said, rolling her eyes. "Elam, Daniel,
Samuel and of course, Josiah."

"All in the same room?"

"No, not Elam. He and Lena have taken up housekeep-
ing in their own home now that they are married. But the
other boys, yes, they all share. Like this room," Mary said,
throwing her arms wide, "there is enough space for all their
beds."

Amanda finally took notice of her surroundings. Three
beds covered with exquisitely appliquéd quilts were lined
side by side along one wall. Had Mary actually been serious
when she spoke of enough space? To Amanda, there looked
to be barely enough room to scoot between the beds to get
into them, let alone try to make them or change the linens.
A small dresser holding a lantern sat diagonally in one of
the corners, and a black curtain serving as a closet door

hung along the partially cutout wall shared between the girls' and the boys' rooms.

"Goodness," was all Amanda could think to say.

Sitting on the bed first in line, Mary folded her hands in her lap and looked up at Amanda. "You are shocked at my home," she said softly.

"No." Amanda shifted her weight from one foot to the other. "No, I just—"

"It is not so bad. I sometimes wish Sarah were older, but next year when I come of age, I will have the *Kammerli* all to myself as my bedroom. It is much bigger, and Papa says he and Josiah will make me a dresser and a chair."

Amanda didn't know what Mary was talking about, but she sensed her coming of age was an event she looked forward to. Amanda sat on the bed beside her. "We're just different," she said finally. "But different can be very good. It doesn't matter when you're friends," she whispered, wishing she could have thought of something more profound to say. "Does it matter to you that we're different?"

Smiling, Mary shook her head.

The excitement returned, and Amanda adjusted her bustle so that she could kneel on the small braided rug alongside the bed. She couldn't wait to see Mary's face. Unfastening the valise, she sang, "Ta-da."

Mary's eyes widened and her jaw dropped open. "What are those?"

"Dresses, silly." Pulling a lacy, leg-of-mutton sleeve blouse and a skirt from the valise, Amanda stood, held them against her body and twirled. "I always liked this outfit. There's nothing like lace against your skin. Here," she offered the garments to Mary. "We're almost the same size. I want you to have these."

Mary gasped, then coughed as if she were choking.

"Are you all right? Mary, what's the matter?"

Smiling, Mary wiped the tears that spilled from the outer corners of her eyes, her body shaking.

"Are you laughing? What is so funny?"

"Papa's face," she said at last, gathering her composure. "I am sorry, but I can imagine his beard turning white before my very eyes if I were to wear that." Mary fell back on the bed, laughing some more.

"What?" Amanda plopped on the edge of the bed, her stays cutting into her sides. "What is wrong with this?"

"Nothing, except for everything! Amanda, do you not see how different we are? Look at my home. The brightest thing here are prayer caps and white church shirts. I am not allowed to wear worldly colors like orange or pink. Colors like that are allowed only in our quilts. And then that is only on occasion."

"Good heavens. The widow was right, as usual." Falling to her back beside Mary, Amanda giggled. "I'm glad I didn't bring a corset and bustle for your mother. I can't even get you to try anything on? I know." Amanda bolted upright. "How about we swap? I'll dress like you and you can dress like me, just for a few minutes to see what it's like."

Mary pushed to her elbows. "I could not."

"But why? No one's around. No one would ever know."

"It would not be right."

Sighing, Amanda knelt beside the valise again. "This is the one I thought would look beautiful on you." She pulled out the emerald crepe, and Mary's eyes widened. "With your auburn hair, it's the perfect color."

Tossing it to the bed, Amanda watched as Mary reached out her hand almost reluctantly and ran her fingers across the lightweight fabric.

"It is the color of God's trees." Mary looked up. "I do love this color."

"Isaac's Mary!"

Mary's face instantly paled, and Amanda slowly turned her head toward the door.

9

MRS. MILLER STOOD IN the doorway, hands on her
wide hips, her jaw set in what Amanda guessed to be anger
and disbelief. The woman glared at her daughter. Amanda
recognized the guilt in Mary's eyes—guilt she had caused
her friend to feel.

"Hello, Mrs. Miller," Amanda said quickly. "I hope you
don't mind, but when I was here yesterday, I kind of invited
myself back for the soap-making. Mary's too kind and said
yes."

Smiling brightly, Amanda pushed as gracefully as she
could to her feet. "Thought some of the material in these
old dresses of mine could be put to use. This one here is
Mary's favorite," Amanda said, taking the emerald dress
from Mary's hands, noticing Mary's eyes had widened even
further.

Gripping the garment firmly in both hands, Amanda
pulled. The sound of ripping fabric cut through the air.
Mary gasped.

"Oh, goodness. I am such a loon. Scissors." Amanda
clucked her tongue. "Scissors would be best to cut this old
thing, wouldn't they? Why, I think there's enough material

here for anyone who wants to use some. And some of these fabrics might even work for the braided rugs, don't you think, Mrs. Miller?''

Mrs. Miller's face softened. ''Yes, they probably would. Thank you, Amanda. Mary,'' she said, pulling an egg from the folds of her apron, ''it is time to start the fire. Do not forget your job.''

''Yes, Mama,'' Mary replied, taking the egg. ''We will be right there.''

Mrs. Miller turned and disappeared back down the stairs.

Mary exhaled with a whoosh and crumpled back onto the bed. ''I cannot believe this.''

''What? I don't think your mother's mad anymore.''

''Your dress.'' Rolling her head from side to side, prayer cap shifting back and forth, Mary closed her eyes. ''Your beautiful dress, ruined. I am sorry.''

''It's all right. Truly it is, Mary.'' Amanda sat back down on the bed. ''It's my fault you were almost in trouble anyway. And I'm sorry I suggested you put the dresses on. That was wrong. Can you forgive me?''

''There is nothing to forgive.'' Mary sat upright. ''You are full of kindness. That does not need forgiving. We must go before Mama calls again.'' She paused momentarily, gazing at the torn green gown. With a smile, she snatched it up and stuffed it under her pillow. ''God's trees. I will use pieces of this when I make my quilt. Come,'' she said, holding up the egg. ''It is time to check the lye.''

''Lie? Whose lie? And what's the egg for?''

Laughing, Mary said, ''You will see.''

Amanda followed her friend as they retraced their steps to the kitchen and out a back door. An iron kettle similar to the one that had been used for the candle-making the previous day, hung on a three-legged stand. Twigs and branches had been neatly arranged underneath.

''This is the fat pot,'' Mary explained. ''I have to gather logs yet, but that can be done once the kindling takes.''

''You cook your soap?''

Mary lifted one shoulder in a shrug. ''You could say that. It has a long way to go before it is truly soap. First, we must see if this egg floats.''

"What are you talking about?"

"Follow me, and I will show you." With a spring in her step, Mary headed toward an odd-looking contraption. This is the ash hopper."

"The what?" Amanda had never felt so ignorant in all her life.

"The ash hopper. Papa and Josiah made it. It's lined with straw. My brothers shovel in ashes and pack them down as tightly as they can."

Frowning, Amanda shook her head, wondering if maybe her brain had fallen asleep, for she still didn't understand. "You make soap out of ashes?"

"No. It is what comes from the ash. I add water every day. Right here." Mary pointed to a hollow place in the middle of the hopper. "The water soaks through the ashes and lye is what runs off. This," she said, gesturing to a large stone jar, "is what holds the lye. If a fresh egg floats close to the top, the lye is strong enough. If it sinks, it is not ready."

Amanda stepped closer as Mary put the brown egg into the crock. It bobbed around, over half of the egg staying above the liquid. "It's floating! It's really floating. It's strong enough, right? Now we make it into soap?"

"Now we make soap," Mary agreed with a grin.

The girls dragged the crock over to the iron kettle, careful not to spill any of the lye. As Mary stooped to light the kindling, Amanda peeked into the pot. "Oh!" She jumped back, hands flying to her face. "What is in that pot? It smells horrible."

Laughing some more, Mary fanned the tiny flames with her hands until they jumped and danced, consuming all the twigs and brush under the kettle. "That is the fat pot. Poured-off grease and fats and cracklings are kept in there. All we have to do is add the lye and keep the fire going until it boils to the right thickness."

"This is so amazing," Amanda said as she helped pour the jar of lye into the smelly kettle. "Where do you keep the firewood? I'll go get some, so you can stay with your pot."

Picking up a large stick that had been resting against the

kettle, Mary stirred the mixture. ''There are some smaller pieces stacked on the back side of that barn.'' She motioned vaguely with her hand. ''An armful will be good for now.''

Amanda reached the barn and had just grabbed one split log, when she thought she heard Josiah's voice from inside the structure. Though her conscience screamed, ''Eavesdropping nosy body,'' her curiosity overruled. Setting the wood back down on the pile, she glanced over both shoulders. An odd elation filled her. No one was around, and she definitely was out of Mary's sight. Amanda crept closer to the side wall and the large gap she spied between the timbers. The softest of murmurs floated gently on the light breeze. She'd been right. It was Josiah's voice.

''We should not be doing this,'' she heard him say. ''I have much work to do. But you have been neglected, and I am sorry for that. Does that feel good? I can tell by your eyes that it does.'' There was the sound of the rustling straw, and Amanda's own eyes widened. Who was Josiah whispering to? And what in heaven's name were they doing together, in a barn, in broad daylight?

She had to find out.

Her gaze swept the area again. She knew she had to hurry, for Mary would expect her any time now.

''How about here?'' wafted Josiah's voice. ''I know you like it there.'' More straw rustled. ''Hold still,'' he continued, ''and we will finish more quickly.''

Amanda felt a curious swooping tug at her insides. Her body obscenely tingled in all the inappropriate places. The worst of it, Josiah's endearments weren't even for her ears!

Heart hammering wildly against her ribs, she lifted her skirt and adjusted her bustle so that she could squat and peer through the hole. Knees bending, she started her descent. Lower and lower she slowly crouched, gathering more and more of her skirt, wondering why it suddenly seemed so voluminous and why the blasted gap in the wall didn't seem so close to the ground before. Holding her breath, she wavered slightly in the awkward position, heels shifting in the dirt to recapture her balance. Silence topped all in importance, Amanda knew, for if discovered, how would she ever explain her peeping notion and not sound like a madwoman?

A smacking sound assaulted her ears. Kissing! Loud kissing! She didn't know why, but she felt desolate and even furious with Josiah, like he had somehow betrayed her. She had to see them together, see exactly what kind of woman it took to seize his attention. Caution to the wind, Amanda clenched her teeth and moved quickly for the hole.

Balance disrupted, she felt herself wobbling toward the barn. Dropping her skirts, she slapped both palms against the timbered wall. Silence surrounded her. Time seemed to have stopped. The noise hadn't been that loud. And Josiah was . . . *occupied*. Swallowing hard, she waited to see if she'd been discovered.

"I must leave you now," came Josiah's voice. "We will meet later."

Exhaling audibly with relief that she hadn't been caught, Amanda bent her elbows and moved her face to the hole.

Blackness. She couldn't see a thing. She moved closer still, her eyelash batting against fibers of timber. Suddenly an eye peered back at her. "Aaaah!!" she screamed, reeling backward, tumbling to the ground.

Skirt bunched around her thighs, Amanda gasped when Josiah rounded the corner of the barn, a devilish, devastating smile curling his lips.

"You brute," she said in a broken whisper as she tugged frantically her clothing. "If you had any decency—"

"I would not be peeping?"

Josiah's voice, deep and sensual, sent a new ripple of awareness through Amanda. "No," she snapped, wishing she didn't find herself so extremely conscious of his virile appeal.

He rubbed his bottom lip in that all-too-familiar way as he strutted toward her. "I understand. It is proper for you to peep, but not for me."

Her lips thinned with irritation, and she flashed him her best lofty expression. "I was doing no such thing." She looked away with a sneer, wiggling her backside a bit more, finally loosening enough material to cover her legs to the bottoms of her knees.

Josiah's dusty boots came to a stop only inches from her thighs. She refused to look at him, his nearness both disturbing and exciting her.

"Truth," he said softly.

Truth? Truce? Amanda wasn't even certain which he'd said. When his hand appeared next to her face, she relented her prior refusal and gazed up at him. The mischieviousness vanished from Josiah's eyes and an unquenchable warmth replaced it.

" 'Great is Truth,' " he said matter-of-factly, " 'and mighty above all things.' "

She wanted to continue being angry with him—that seemed easiest—but she found her anger evaporating like puddles after a summer rain. His hand remained outstretched, and finally she took it, imposing what she hoped was an iron control on her emotions.

"You win," she said, allowing him to pull her to her feet. "Your sermon on truth warrants a confession."

"That," he pointed his finger, "was not my intention."

Rolling her eyes, Amanda dusted off her clothes. "I don't believe that," she retorted, adjusting her bustle as best she could. "You said it expecting a confession. Here goes. I was peeping. Trying to peep," she amended. "I'm not accustomed to people getting sweet with each other in a barn in the middle of the day." Her voice no longer sounded her own, but she continued on. "And by the way, what in heaven's name have you done with the poor girl? I hope there's a back door that I didn't notice. Or is she still stuck in the barn?"

"Girl?" Josiah's brows shot up under the brim of his hat. A glint of humor returned to his eyes. "The girl. Yes, she is still in the barn. She has hair the color of autumn leaves and creamy buttermilk. She is insatiable for sweetness . . . and having her belly rubbed."

"Oh!" Amanda fanned the air in a show of disgust. "Will you please stop?"

"I must admit," Josiah said, ignoring her request, "she does have a few undesirable habits. Like the licking. I do not always like that. And at times," he said, lowering his voice to a whisper, "she bites."

Eyes narrowing, Amanda shook her head. "I've heard enough. I'm going to go help Mary. Which," she said, backing away, "is what I should have been doing in the first place."

"But wait. You must want to see her. I *want* you to see her."

"No. No, that's fine." She held up her hands as if warding off an attacker. "I don't want to."

"I insist. You went through all the trouble of . . . *almost peeping*. Come," Josiah said, grabbing Amanda's hand.

She felt his fingers, warm and strong, lace through hers. Helpless to deny him anything, she trailed a step behind, feeling much like one of the wooden mannequins from her father's store. Her chest felt so heavy she expected it to collapse. She knew that it shouldn't matter, but yet it tore at her insides even thinking about the woman whose lips had been on Josiah's.

As he pulled her into the barn, the odor of manure and horses filled her nostrils. Josiah stopped walking, and Amanda fought the urge to shut her eyes. She realized how foolish she'd been in thinking Josiah wouldn't have noticed her outside. Sunlight filtered in through many cracks and crevices, and any person outside walking past would be seen.

Chewing her lip, she looked about the barn. "Where is she? Still in the straw somewhere, waiting for your return?"

"She is there," Josiah said, inclining his head in the direction of the closest stall.

"But that's . . ." Amanda's jaw dropped and a surge of heat rushed to her face.

"That is Cinnamon." He walked over to the sorrel who instantly nuzzled his neck and shoulder, and then dropped her head to sniff around the pocket of his trousers. Laughing, Josiah pulled something from his pocket and fed it to the horse. "You see, she is insatiable for sweets. She will do anything for her favorite: sugar beets."

Amusement flickered in his eyes, and Amanda couldn't stop the smile that played at her lips. "She's beautiful, really beautiful." Moving alongside Josiah, purposefully avoiding his gaze, she stroked the horse's tawny forelock. "Well, I must admit, I do think she's your type."

"What is my type?" he asked, in a voice huskier than she'd ever heard.

His breathing grew labored, and her senses leaped to life. He was so close, she felt the heat from his body. All she'd have to do was lean, just a bit. . . .

"Did you not hear me?"

Amanda hesitantly dragged her gaze from the beast to Josiah, wondering if he truly expected an answer to the question. His compelling, probing eyes riveted to hers, confirming he did want an answer. The passionate challenge was hard to resist, and a sinfully delicious shudder ran through her body. "Your type," Amanda whispered, running her tongue across her quickly drying lips, "is—"

"There you are, Amanda." Mary stood in the door of the barn. "The kindling is almost gone. I thought perhaps you could not find the wood."

"I was showing Amanda Cinnamon," Josiah explained quickly. He shoved his hands deeply into his pockets. "If you want, I will carry the wood for your fire."

Apparently in no hurry, Mary joined them next to the horse. Amanda managed a wan smile, hoping her eyes didn't divulge the wanton sensations that were coursing through her. It scared her to think of what she would have said or done next, had her friend not appeared.

"Josiah worked long and hard for five years to buy Cinnamon," Mary said. Josiah grunted and tossed his sister an icy glare, but she ignored him and smiled proudly, running her hand down the sleek hindquarters of the animal. "The horse is useful, and therefore acceptable," she said, as if reading Amanda's mind.

"I was just saying how beautiful she is." Amanda rubbed her palm against the horse's velvety nose, her thoughts turning to Ophelia and how the cat, too, liked her nose rubbed.

"I must return to the fat pot," Mary said, affectionately slapping Cinnamon's backside as she strolled toward the door. "Don't keep Amanda too long, Josiah," she called loudly from the outside of the barn. "I am teaching her to make soap."

Josiah rested a shoulder against the support beam of the stall wall. His eyebrows rose inquiringly. "You came back today to make soap with my sister?"

"I told you earlier that I wanted to come back. She's my friend." Amanda shrugged, knowing she should heed proprieties and leave to find Mary, but the reluctance she felt was overpowering. "Besides," she reached up and fingered one of the combs holding back her hair, "there's something here I want." The words sounded horribly insinuating. She realized she'd meant them to. Her gaze locked with Josiah's. She wanted him to desire her as much as she did him.

For a moment, his silvery, stormy eyes drank up every inch of her, then they changed. He changed. Amanda's heart sunk as a silent sadness etched his face. Closing her eyes, she shook her head. What was wrong with her? Why did she do such crazy, amoral things around Josiah Miller?

"Mary needs the wood," he said abruptly, pushing off the beam. "We must go."

"I want my cat. Josiah," Amanda said, grabbing his arm, stopping him in his tracks. "I just want to see Ophelia. I should never have left this morning without seeing her. I can't do it again. I won't." She realized she still held his arm. It felt so strong and muscular, she couldn't imagine there being anything that Josiah couldn't accomplish. If ever there was a perfect specimen of life, it was him.

Removing her hand from his arm, Amanda wrinkled her nose. "I don't always say or do the right thing, so I understand if I shouldn't go to this Amish home where that Elnora lives . . . but it is my cat."

Compassion shone in Josiah's eyes. "I know how it feels in your heart to love an animal. Let me get the wood for Mary, then I will go see Elnora."

"Good, I'll come with you."

"No, you will stay with Mary. Please. It must be done this way, for Elnora."

Though polite enough, his tone left no room for argument. He started walking again, and Amanda quickly took up his pace. The silence that fell between them bothered her, and she was glad for the crunch of the stones beneath his feet.

"So tell me," she said finally. "Why does Elnora's family hate the English?"

"I did not say *hate*."

"Dislike, then," she replied as they rounded the corner, approaching the woodpile.

"I did not say *dislike*, either."

Sighing, Amanda picked up a split log and placed it in Josiah's outstretched arms. Then she stacked another. And another. "You know," she said as she continued to add to the pile, "it really doesn't matter to me what a person is. We're all the same, just people. Take Elnora, for instance. I won't make trouble for her. She's going to make Ophelia well. That's all that's important."

"Enough wood," Josiah said so sharply that Amanda flinched. A stricken look glazed his eyes, and he shook his head.

"You do not hear. Ophelia is not well. She still sleeps the sleep of those who have passed. You count on Elnora, but you should not."

Amanda felt the blood drain from her face. "Do you think she'll die?"

"That is up to the Almighty."

Though her stomach contracted into a tight ball, Amanda forced a smile. "I understand," she said, voice crackling. "I am sorry."

"I know you are. Ju-just bring her to me when it's over. I want to bury Ophelia at my home." Without waiting for Josiah, Amanda hurried off in the direction of Mary and the fat pot. With each step she took, she pushed Ophelia further and further from her mind. She'd found out when her mother died that she coped more easily if she didn't dwell on what ifs and could have beens.

She found Mary back at the kettle, stirring. "I'm sorry I was gone so long," Amanda said. "Josiah's coming with the wood."

"You do not have to apologize." Mary winked conspiratorially at her as the crunching of Josiah's boots came within earshot. "I know how my brother dotes on Cinnamon," she said loudly. "You poor thing, Amanda. You were cornered, and he would not let you get away."

"That is right," Josiah retorted, squatting next to the meager fire and emptying the wood from his arms. "I was trying to save our guest from having to help with your chores again, Mary."

A scarlet flush crept up Mary's neck and traveled to the roots of her auburn hair. She gasped, then her eyes widened. "Josiah is right. Twice now I make you work. That is not right of me."

Amanda felt her mood lightening with the sibling banter. "He's teasing, Mary. I wanted to come back. I wanted to help you and check on Ophelia." The thought spilled from her tongue before she could stop it.

A look of suspicious bewilderment crossed Mary's features. "Josiah, did you not tell her the cat still sleeps?"

"Oh, he did," Amanda said quickly in his defense. "It just took me a while to hear."

Setting her spoon down, Mary's brows furrowed deeply. "We are sorry. If there is anything that can be done, Elnora—"

Amanda said quickly, "It's all right. Don't even say it." She swallowed hard, refusing to get her hopes up again. "Let's get your soap made," she said, pushing her lips into that familiar tight smile she'd used only minutes ago on Josiah.

Mary returned the smile, picked up the spoon and stirred. "Off with you, Josiah." She shooed at him with her free hand. "You do not want to be labeled a gossipmonger."

"Who would label me as such?"

"My dear brother, I do not know." Mary's eyes crinkled mirthfully. "But I think it could happen were you to stay with us and make soap."

Josiah cocked one eyebrow and his mouth quirked with humor. "I will leave because I have work to do, not because of your idle threat, *my dear sister*."

Mary brought her free hand to her mouth, and Amanda knew she was trying to stifle laughter. "Go now, gossipmonger," Mary squeaked out.

Shaking his head, Josiah walked away with an elaborate nonchalance that made Amanda's heart trip over itself.

"You stare at the gossipmonger," Mary said matter-of-factly, yanking Amanda from the unexpected daydream beginning to form.

Curling her toes in her shoes, Amanda shrugged. "He's just different from most men I know."

"Yes," Mary agreed, wagging her head, her bonnet shifting lower on her forehead with the movement. "Josiah is not like any other Amish man I know, either. Grandmother used to call Josiah a *fresh* Amish. She encouraged him to explore what she called his 'uniqueness.' Papa says Josiah acquired several of grandmother's negative traits." A sigh escaped her. "There were many things Grandmother did that Papa will not talk about. But Grandmother was good, and so is Josiah." Smiling, she rested the spoon against the side of the kettle. "His heart is so big and full of love. I know what Papa says, but I do not see how that can be negative."

The love Mary felt for her brother was obvious and touched Amanda deeply. As far as she could see, Josiah was as close to perfect as a man could be. "Mary," she said, voice quivering, excitement surging through her, "is this rebellious grandmother, by chance, the grandmother that made the odd quilt?"

10

A HUGE FROWN PLEATED Mary's brows. "How do you know of Grandmother Miller's quilt?"

"I own it. Josiah sold it, and others, to me to raise some money for your brother."

Dropping her chin to her chest, Mary exhaled with a loud whoosh. "I did not know he had gone through with it," she said softly. "What else did he sell you?"

"Nothing. The quilts were all. Here," Amanda said, taking the spoon from Mary's hand, "let me stir a bit." She studied her friend's pinched face, recognizing the anxiety etched there. "Why are you so upset?"

"It is not right. Josiah knows it."

"What's not right?" Amanda asked, as Widow Marly's words regarding ostracism chose that moment to haunt her.

"Josiah should not be trying to raise that money for Elam. It is against the wishes of the elders and my parents." Pacing a small area, Mary fiddled with the hem of her white apron. "That is what I mean when I say Josiah's heart is so big. He will needlessly risk his future for our brother. He will never, never raise the money that is needed. What happened is God's will and should be left alone. I do not want to lose Josiah."

"He only wants your brother to walk again. Why is everyone in your community so against that? I think it's honorable and selfless. He should be commended, not condemned," Amanda replied flatly.

"You can say that because you do not know how it is." Deeper worry lines furrowing her face, Mary marched back to the boiling pot and Amanda. "The elders and bishop will shun Josiah." Unconsciously twisting her hands, she whispered, "I fear my father and mother will, too."

"What if he is able to raise the money? You all are assuming he can't do it. What if he does?"

"It is your world we speak of." Mary rubbed her arms as if the very thought sent a chill through her body. "Surely you must have some idea of the expense. Josiah could work five lifetimes and probably not save enough."

"What if he were to find a treasure, a treasure worth more than what was needed for Elam?"

Mary laughed cynically. "Treasures like that do not exist. God provides for us."

Amanda inclined her head in compliance and put down the spoon. "But what if," she said, pointing her index finger, "God provides the treasure? How do you know this treasure is not God's will as well?"

"You talk nonsense that makes my head hurt." Grabbing the discarded spoon, Mary stirred again with a vengeance.

Silence descended upon them, and Amanda debated whether or not to pursue the treasure map issue with Mary. Chewing her lip, Amanda watched the glutinous, sandy-colored contents of the fat pot roll slowly to a boil. Mary continued to stir, and the soft *plop-plop* of the soap bubbling broke the awkward silence.

"Where is this treasure you speak of?" Mary asked suddenly.

"Well, before you say anything, let me finish telling you everything."

"All right," Mary replied. "I am listening."

"I don't know where it's buried. But your grandmother

Miller did. The odd design on that old quilt of hers is a map to a treasure.''

Gentle laughter rippled through the air. ''Surely you tease me.'' Mary wiped her tearing eyes with the back of her free hand. ''My grandmother would never have buried a treasure. Where would she have gotten one? I am sorry,'' she said, laughing again.

''That quilt was made almost fifty years ago, right?'' Amanda asked, determination lacing her tone.

''Yes, that is probably right. I guess.''

''So how old would your grandmother have been then?''

Face scrunching comically, Mary mused, ''I believe she would have been fifteen or sixteen.''

''I don't know how she got it, but I truly believe she had a treasure and buried it. There's a sun on the quilt at what I think is the starting point. I'm thinking maybe it stands for a season or a town.''

Mary's expression stilled, and she grew very serious. ''Grandmother was born and lived in Sommerville until she and Grandpapa moved here. Perhaps,'' Mary said, blinking with incredulity, ''that is what the sun is telling you.''

''I have questions, loads of questions, and I just need some answers,'' Amanda said, feeling euphoric over the information Mary had given her. ''I've been quilting since I was about ten. Before my mother died, she showed me and taught me everything she knew. I've seen many stitches and designs. The one on your grandmother's quilt is very different. I truly believe it's a message.''

''The quilting bee!'' Mary shrieked. ''Some of the women who attend are my grandmother's age. There are a few families in our community who are from the old town of Sommerville. Perhaps they can give you the answers you seek.''

''I think you could be right. Hmm,'' Amanda mused, planting her hands on her hips. ''I don't know if you should mention this to your parents. I don't want to get Josiah or you into more trouble.''

Mary's hand flew to her lips. ''I will not utter a word. This is your secret,'' she said with a smile.

Excitement poured through Amanda's veins like rainwater down a windowpane. She returned her friend's smile twofold. "A treasure for Elam, Mary," she said, squeezing the girl's arm, "how could that not be God's will?"

Amanda and Mary finished the soap and said their good-byes as storm clouds gathered overhead.

"I wish you would stay," Mary said as Amanda climbed up into the buckboard. "You will be caught in the storm."

"I'll hurry," Amanda replied, secretly wanting to stay, wishing she could see Josiah once more. Waving to her doubtful-looking friend, she reluctantly started the hackney down the road for home.

Amanda hadn't gone far when the sooty, inky clouds overtook the last of the defiant white puffs. A bleak breeze pressed down upon the earth, and she pulled her coat more tightly about her body. The hardwood trees around her swayed to and fro in the wind, their sprouting leaves flapping wildly about on skeletonlike limbs. They reminded her, oddly enough, of the one very peculiar crooked area on the quilt.

Just then thunder clapped in the distance with such force that Amanda jumped. She pulled her drifting thoughts together, knowing she needed to concentrate on handling the horse should it become skittish with the rapidly approaching storm. The air now hung heavy as if it had been absorbing the moisture all along, trying to protect her from a downpour. Prompting the beast to a faster gait, she wished she had stayed at the Millers.

She had yet to reach the five-mile mark when the beating rains fell. The horse increased its pace, visible breath shooting from its nostrils as it huffed through the torrential waters, hooves slipping and sliding on the soft, squishy trail. Amanda bounced around on the seat, barely able to hang on, mud and rain pelting her face and clothing. "Whoa!" she shouted, pulling hard on the reins. She tried unsuccessfully to slow the spooked horse.

Prayers flew from her tongue, and as if her petitions had been miraculously answered, a godsend in a slicker appeared in the distance. The rider quickly closed the distance and approached her side.

Leon. She didn't know if she was up to coping with him.

He drew his horse in close and hollered something to her that she still couldn't hear. Suddenly he jumped from his horse's back to the buckboard, knocking Amanda to the platform where her feet had been moments ago.

"What in blazes you doin'?" he shouted without even looking at her. "Tryin' to get yourself killed?"

Knowing an argument was not what either of them needed now, Amanda swallowed the defensive retort that threatened to roll from her mouth. She focused on staying in the wagon, clutching at the seat, even at Leon's legs, anything her fingers could grab. Minutes seemed to fly past as Leon wrestled with the frightened animal's reins. Finally, with an expertise that didn't surprise her, he regained control of the wagon and brought it to a creaking halt.

His horse had doubled back and now stood pawing at the mire alongside the wagon. Jumping from the platform, he roughly pulled Amanda down into his arms. "We need shelter," he hollered to her, the wind taking his voice and whipping it to a raspy whisper.

Amanda felt herself sliding down the length of Leon, felt his thigh between her legs. He set her to her feet, the mud oozing over and into her high shoes.

Leon dashed for the saddlebags on his horse. Amanda couldn't imagine what he was rummaging for, but she knew more than anything she wanted to be away from him and back at Josiah's home.

Leaning into the wind, carrying what looked like a tarp of some sort, Leon squelched through the mud back to Amanda's side. "We'll set it up yonder." He pointed in the direction of an open area where several big fieldstones dotted the landscape.

"But what about the trees?" Amanda yelled back. "Won't we be drier near the trees?"

"It's no good to be sittin' under trees in a storm like this. If lightning struck, we'd never make it. Come on," he ordered, hurtling her along like a pony.

"Stop." Wrenching her arm free, Amanda shoved her wet hair away from her eyes and glared at him. "Stop manhandling me. I'm not one of your horses. You're pulling and shoving me all over. I don't like it. I can walk by myself.''

"Sakes alive! I'm savin' your arse and you're gettin' all huffed because I'm not treatin' ya like a lady? Get the hell over here,'' he said through gnashed teeth, "or I'll just leave you!''

Amanda's hackles rose, but her options were limited. She swallowed dryly, and her leadened feet sloshed her forward.

"Good girl.'' Seizing her by the arms, Leon gave her a little shake and flashed her a grin that made her stomach feel as though a trapdoor had suddenly opened. He hurried for an area of big rocks, pulling her awkwardly along behind.

"Sit,'' he commanded, tossing her a slicker that had been folded inside the tarp.

Anxiety clutching her, Amanda disregarded the slicker. She didn't want to be more indebted to Leon in any way. She took a seat on one of the cold, wet fieldstones and hugged her knees tightly to her body. As a glorious streak of lightning zigzagged across the sky, she wondered what was the lesser of the two evils present.

Much to her surprise, Leon efficiently erected a lean-to of sorts from the tarp and two long oak branches. He crawled beneath the covering and sat next to her on the rock.

"Why didn't you put the slicker on like I said?''

Amanda ignored his question. "Wh-what about the horses?'' she asked, her own voice sounding stifled and unnatural. "My father's hackney is still hitched to the wagon.''

"The horses are fine. Farin' better than we are, I reckon.'' He wiggled closer so that their thighs touched. "This here is mighty cozy, wouldn't you say?''

The heat from his body and the hot, sour breath that swept across her face caused bile to rise. "No,'' she spat, "this isn't what I call *cozy*. How'd you find me, anyway?''

"Your pa's madder 'n a hornet. Said you shouldn't be poking 'round them Aim-ish. Asked me to come get you.''

"They're Amish, not 'Aim-ish.' ''

Leon grinned and indolently lifted one shoulder. He pre-

tended to stretch, and then casually moved his arm around
Amanda. Shrugging it off, she turned an icy gaze on him.
"Don't touch me. We've had this discussion before. Re-
member yesterday?"

"Dammit. You should be actin' a bit grateful, don't you
think? I saw your face. You were scared, then you saw me.
The fear disappeared cuz ol' Leon was there to save pretty
Miss Amanda. Smiling, he reached out and ran his finger
along her bottom lip.

Slapping his hand away, Amanda bristled. "I mean it,
Leon. Don't you touch me."

"Who you gonna complain to? Ain't no one here but us.
How about a little smooch?" He leaned closer.

Bridling, Amanda scooted to the edge of the rock. "Listen," she struggled to maintain an even, conciliatory tone,
"I'm not interested in you that way. I—I think you're a
wonderful man," she nearly choked on the words, "but
I'm not the one for you."

His eyes raked boldly across her soaking, huddled form.
Amanda squeezed her knees more tightly against her chest,
unable to shake the sensation that he could see right through
her clothing.

"How do you know we're not right for each other?"
Like a predator stalking its prey, he inched closer until she
had nowhere to go but out into the fury of the storm.
"You've never given me a fair chance. Never. Reckon this
is it."

Before Amanda had time to think, Leon threaded his
hand tightly through her hair, painfully capturing her head.
The position she was in greatly hindered her movement.
His mouth lowered and covered hers, and his other arm
rigidly immobilized her. The kiss was angry, punishing. His
tongue seemed to be everywhere, thrusting and invading
every hidden recess of her mouth. She tried to push it out
with her own, but only succeeded in making matters worse,
for the tastes of whiskey and tobacco and some sort of
cheese were stronger than ever. Panic like she'd never
known before welled in her throat. An all-consuming nausea churned in her stomach. She thought she'd surely suf-
focate. Wiggling her hands free, she shoved at Leon's chest

with all the strength she could muster. The nausea worsened, creeping further and further . . . until she vomited.

"Christ Almighty!" Leon moved away from Amanda like she was poison. He scrambled on all fours, like a dog, to the opening of the tarp. Then, pushing to his feet, he ran into the rain, cursing and spitting and wiping at his face.

Gulping the air that never seemed fresher or sweeter, Amanda closed her eyes. She didn't feel guilty, nor did she care if Leon left her there. That's just what she wanted— to be left alone.

"What in the devil are you doin' here?" It was Leon's voice, and he seemed angry again.

Wiping her mouth on her coat sleeve, Amanda took another deep breath, punctuated with several even gasps. She straightened her stiff legs, not able to imagine who else would have ventured out on such an afternoon.

"I am here to make certain Amanda Glosser gets home safely," came Josiah's deep, baritone reply.

Amanda felt such soothing relief that tears sprang to her eyes. Josiah spoke again, his voice comforting her frazzled nerves. "That is her horse and wagon. Where is she?"

"She's safe. She's with me."

"Josiah. Josiah, I'm here," Amanda said as she hunched over and waddled to the opening of the shelter. She straightened then and hurried to his side, giddy with joy. The heartrending tenderness of Josiah's gaze was not lost on her. Though lightning danced across the now-slate-colored sky, Amanda blinked past the raindrops and found she couldn't stop smiling. Each time she saw Josiah, the confusing magnetic pull seemed stronger.

"You must get back under the tarp." Josiah took her elbow and steered her toward the lean-to.

"Hold on just a confounded minute there, *Mr. Aim-ish*. Amanda's with me." Leon scowled and grabbed Amanda's other arm.

A protest quickly died on her lips, for suddenly thunder cracked and a lightning bolt speared the ground not more than twenty feet from them. A yellowish-green smoke wafted through the air and along with it came the acrid odor of sulfur. Amanda felt both Leon and Josiah pulling her toward the makeshift shelter.

They crawled underneath, the unrelenting heavens bombarding them with water. While Josiah crouched in the mud, holding stationary the one side of the tarp that had come loose in the wind, Leon sat Amanda roughly back on the rock. Joining her, he glared at Josiah.

Amanda didn't know if she'd ever seen Leon more furious. The expression he wore was more devilish than that of yesterday when she had kneed him in the privates. "Leon," she began, only to be silenced with a keep-your-mouth-shut look.

"There ain't no room under here for you. Can't you see, mister? Hop on your horse and ride back to your own kind."

"Stop," Amanda hissed. She lifted her chin and met Leon's icy glare. "No one's going anywhere until this storm's over." Feeling safe with Josiah there, she scooted closer to Leon, then patted the empty space next to her. "Sit down," she said to Josiah. "It could be a while before this blows over."

"Josiah, is it? My, my, my. How'd you two get to be so blasted friendly?" Leon ran his tongue over his teeth, a smacking sound filling the tiny space under the tarp. "Must be them dark clothes that you've taken such a fancy to, huh, Amanda? Funeral clothes, ain't they?"

"I am Josiah Miller," Josiah said, his silver eyes flashing Amanda a silent warning. He extended his hand as if he hadn't heard any of Leon's derogatory comments. "Amanda is a friend of my sister's."

"That so?" A satisfied light came into Leon's eyes, but he ignored Josiah's outstretched hand. "Just don't be tryin' nothin'. Her pa sent me to fetch her and bring her home. That's what I aim to do."

Josiah nodded, and Amanda fought the urge to roll her eyes. She felt Leon's curious gaze, scrutinizing her and Josiah. At least for the time being, Leon appeared placated, probably assuming she and Josiah were merely acquaintances. She certainly didn't want to spoil that.

Time slowly crawled by. Amanda had no idea how long

they'd been sitting there; she could only tell by the stiffness of her body that it had been too long a time. The rain seemed endless, plop-plopping against the tarp and rolling to the earth, adding to the puddles already there. While Josiah remained crouched, his large hands firmly holding the flap of the shelter in place so that the water did not blow in, Leon sat more comfortably on the rock, his jaw working a chew of tobacco. Every so often he'd spit out the side of his mouth, and Amanda had to bite her tongue to keep from voicing her repugnance aloud.

The two men were so different. Leon needed a bath, clothes included, and a toothbrush; not to mention lessons on chivalry and respect. Amanda shuddered, remembering the horrible kiss and the vile taste that had filled her mouth.

Josiah, on the other hand, was a gentleman, sensitive and caring. He'd yet to forget his manners in her presence. She wondered what it would be like to be kissed by him, and realized she actually ached inside to find out. She shifted on the hard rock, her insides tingling as her gaze strayed to his thighs, his muscles there staining against the home-spun material. His appeal simply devastated her, and Amanda felt her emotions sliding out of control.

Raising her eyes, she found Josiah watching her. A warning voice whispered to her that she'd best mind her manners and stop the ogling before she got them into more trouble. She felt her cheeks color under the heat of his gaze, but she couldn't make herself look away. His silvery eyes flickered momentarily with what she thought was desire, then the spark faded and slowly died. Josiah looked away, awkwardly shifting in his crouched position, back ramrod straight.

Once her pulse quieted, Amanda heaved an affronted sigh and cleared her throat. "Leon," she said to him, laying her hand on the arm of his stiff, wet slicker, "maybe you'd better check on Papa's horse. You know how he loves that animal."

Casting her a sidelong glance, the ball of chew poking his cheek out like a stored walnut, Leon grunted. "Maybe Mr. Miller there can do that, seein' as how he wants to help."

Taking a gulp of air, Amanda leaned in toward Leon so that their heads were almost touching. "I'm not sure," she whispered, "that he's as good with horses as you are. But if you think—"

"You're right." Leon crawled to the opening, a smug smile stretching his lips. "I'm gonna check our horses, Miller. Keep the shelter together. Can you do that?"

One of Josiah's eyebrows cocked, but a nod was the only answer he gave. Amanda sensed that he was working to keep his features deceptively composed.

Leon disappeared and Amanda moved toward Josiah. "I just said that to get rid of him for a minute. Thank you for coming after me," she said, feeling the need to explain, wondering what was going on behind the mask Josiah insisted upon wearing. "Leon is . . . is just—"

"In love with you."

Was that an observation? A statement? Amanda didn't know which. "No. Oh, goodness, no." She spoke quietly but with a desperate firmness. "He . . . he just—"

"Wants you," Josiah finished bluntly.

Startled by his conjecture, Amanda couldn't object. The only thing she cared about was that Josiah was there, that he cared enough to brave the weather to search for her. He brought her untried senses to life, and nothing else mattered. Not Leon's crazy fantasies, not her father's anger, nothing.

It was as if the world suddenly silenced just for them. The rain lessened until it sounded like a gentle serenade. Amanda reached deep inside and gathered her courage. "What do you want?" she asked Josiah as she slowly reached out and brazenly caressed the back of his hand, the hand now holding tightly to the tarp as though it were a lifeline. She closed her fingers over his bunching knuckles, loving the feel of his strength and his cool skin beneath her own cold fingers.

Josiah didn't speak, but his broad shoulders heaved as he breathed. Amanda knew she affected him at least a little, and the thought thrilled her. She felt almost drugged by him, consumed with the yearning to wrap her arms around his waist and hold him close. Her earnest gaze sought his.

Stroking his hand, she willed him to look at her. Finally he did.

His eyes more than betrayed the passion he felt.

"Hey, Miller!" Leon slapped the side of the lean-to, making Amanda jump and pull her hand away from Josiah's. She felt the tenuous bond that was just beginning to develop between them shatter. "Rain's 'bout stopped," Leon called, grating her nerves. "No need for you to stay any longer."

Josiah instantly straightened to his full height, knocking the tarp over as he did so.

"What the hell did you do that for?" Leon's eyes narrowed with contempt.

"You said the rain stopped. There is no longer need for your shelter," Josiah replied. "Amanda can now continue to her home." Water droplets dribbled off the sides and back of his black hat. There was a type of contentment on Josiah's face, and coupled with his ruggedness, Amanda couldn't help but smile.

"He's right, Leon," she said, throwing strands of wet hair over her shoulder. "We all can go now."

"I'm escortin' you. Your pa wants it like that."

"My father made the same request of me," Josiah said, "to ensure Amanda's safety."

Leon's face pinched with annoyance. "I can take care of her. You don't need to come along."

Folding his arms across his chest, his massive shoulders filling the old coat he wore, Josiah shrugged. "I do not doubt your capabilities, but I must go as well." He tipped his head to Leon as if in dismissal, and approached Amanda's horse, murmuring quiet, easy words to the frightened animal.

Slamming his fist into this hand, Leon stalked to his mount, but said nothing further.

What irony, Amanda thought happily. She swallowed an unseemly giggle and scurried through the mud after Josiah. With an escort on each side, she clucked the horse and wagon to motion, admiring the fiery, rosy hues now swirling across the heavens. Josiah had come for her. Everything suddenly seemed fresh and promising.

11

THE SKY SEEMED TO brighten with each mile they covered. Crimson and gold now bathed the heavens in one last attempt to recapture some of the late afternoon glory that had been prematurely stolen by the spring storm. Leon rode to Amanda's left and Josiah to her right. Though she worked diligently to keep her head forward, her gaze slid to Josiah more times than not.

He sat straight and proud atop Cinnamon's bare back, the set of his chin suggesting a stubborn streak she'd never noticed before but knew she liked. And his thighs—they hugged the sorrel's midsection with an intimacy she envied.

Suddenly Josiah glanced over at her and, just like back at the shelter, their gazes held. The light breeze rumpled the swath of drying hair that poked out from under the brim of his hat. Amanda could all but smell his fresh, musky scent wafting through the air. When his lips lifted ever so slightly with a conspiratorial smile, her heart tripped over itself. She couldn't help wondering what it was she wanted or expected from him.

Leon sniffed and spat, fracturing the moment and drawing Amanda's gaze. "Yup," he said to her, "be to your house in just a bit. Miller can go on home now. Hear that?'' he said loudly. "I got things under control."

"Yes, I can see that you do," Josiah replied, making no move to stop or turn his horse.

"You deaf?" Leon asked, his eyes narrowing to two tiny slits.

"Leon," Amanda interjected, not able to ignore the anxiety that stabbed at her gut at the thought of Josiah leaving her alone with Leon again. "Bet you and Rogers hate storms like that one that just passed. What work, cleaning all the mud from the underside of the horses. Whew," she exclaimed, "I don't know how you do it." She knew she was rambling, about nothing really, but hoped her tone revealed enough admiration to appease Leon's ego for another couple of miles. Just to make certain, she continued on, "I've never ever seen a speck of dirt on any of my father's horses. It's amazing how well you do your job."

Nodding his head, Leon shifted, sitting up straighter, the leather of his saddle squeaking with the movement. "Reckon I am one of the best grooms."

"Oh, I agree," Amanda goaded with a bright smile. "Folks are always commenting."

"They are?"

"Truly." She smiled again, silently asking for forgiveness for the little white lies she'd just told.

"Isn't that somethin'," he mused, rubbing his nose with the end of his thumb, chest puffing out like that of a strutting turkey. Leaning forward to see past Amanda, he cast Josiah a sidelong look. "Speakin' of horses, how'd you get that one, Miller? Never seen none of your people with one like that before."

Josiah's mouth crimped in what Amanda knew was annoyance. "I got it the same way *you people* get yours," he retorted. "I bought it."

Amanda's own lips twitched slightly with amusement at his unusual use of sarcasm, but she didn't dare smile. Animosity again flowed from Leon, and she felt it as though it were a tangible force.

"Sure you paid—"

"Leon," she interrupted again, a protectiveness for Josiah washing over her, "let's . . . sing."

A frown rumpled Leon's dirt-smudged forehead. "What the hell do you want to do that for?"

"Well . . . ," Amanda shot Josiah a look of mute appeal, "it'll be fun. Help pass the time while we ride. You start us off. What's that song you always sing when you're brushing out a horse?"

" 'Little Brown Jug?' You want me to sing 'Little Brown Jug'?"

"Yes, any tune. Just sing," she urged. "You have such a fine voice."

Amanda didn't think it possible, but Leon straightened even more in the saddle under her feigned praise. She wasn't ordinarily a liar, but the little untruths had rolled so easily from her lips, she wondered if she was becoming one. She quickly pushed the notion aside, reminding herself it was Leon's lascivious actions that had prompted it all anyway.

With each song that they sang, Amanda sensed Leon's anger dissipating. It helped, too, she supposed, that Josiah didn't join in but rode along in silence. Whatever the case, she only knew she felt immense relief that Josiah was still there and Leon seemed calm.

They had just finished the refrain of "Johnny Get Your Gun" when her house came into view. Lights peered out through the windows like eyes, and she guessed that from some room, her father watched. The sky had darkened to indigo with only scant traces of gold outlining the horizon like misplaced halos. The awkwardness she'd felt the last few hours would soon be over, like the day, and she realized her biggest regret would be if she wasn't able to have a few moments alone with Josiah.

"Here we are," Amanda said as they passed the old oak that used to hold her wooden swing in its sturdy branches. "Safe and sound." Pulling back on the reins of the hackney, she stopped the buckboard. Much to her dismay, both Leon and Josiah stopped their horses, dismounted and came to the side of her wagon. Though she wanted to stand and reach for Josiah, feel his arms wrap around her body as he lowered her to the ground, she didn't want Leon to make any trouble. And she guessed that he would, for his face was pinched with an eerie possessiveness that made the hairs on the back of her neck stir.

"Well, well. What have we here?"

"Papa," Amanda said, raising from the buckboard seat and spinning around to face him. Newlin's icy gaze froze on Josiah.

"Seems I worried a lot of people today." Amanda sighed and threw her hands out to her sides. "Josiah only wanted to make certain I got home safely. Like the way you sent Leon." Turning away from her father and back toward Josiah, she smiled, imploring him to understand.

Josiah didn't return the smile, and the probing query that shone in his eyes tugged on Amanda's heartstrings.

"It is getting late," he said tersely. "I must go."

"'Bout time," Leon said. "This fella ain't got a lick a sense in him, Newlin. Been tellin' him to go home right along, but he's deaf or dumb or somethin'."

Nostrils flaring, Amanda dug her nails into her palms. "Josiah," she said sweetly, unclenching her fists and outstretching her arms, "you're a gentleman. Will you please give me a hand before you leave?"

A strangled choking sound came from Leon, but Amanda didn't care. She only cared about Josiah and what he was feeling. Though he stepped up to the wagon and reached for her as she'd asked, he wore a mask of stone.

"Thank you," Amanda whispered as he lowered her from the wagon. He set her gently to her feet as his strong fingers slid away from her body. For an instant a wistfulness stole into his expression, and a greater reluctance filled her. She still held onto his shoulders. She wanted to hang on, forever if she could. Her heart shouted to her, and she listened. It didn't matter that her father was standing nearby, or that Leon watched, his furor probably mounting. All that mattered was the moment. Rising on tiptoe, she pressed her lips to Josiah's warm cheek. "Josiah," she murmured against his face, "oh, Josiah, thank you."

"Reckon it is time you took your leave, Miller."

The sharp edge of her father's tone was unmistakable

and when he walked around the wagon to stand beside her, as though she were a little girl that needed looking after, Amanda's lips pursed with fury. "Yes, Josiah, you probably should leave. All you'll get here now is rudeness." From lowered lids, she threw a scorching look at her father, then lifted her chin into the air and grabbed Josiah's arm. "Come, I'll walk you to your horse."

"Newlin," Leon protested, stepping closer, "say some—"

"Shut up, Leon," Amanda's father interrupted. "Just shut up."

Looking up at Josiah, Amanda's mouth creased into a slight, sheepish smile. "I apologize for my father's behavior," she said softly.

"An apology is not necessary. You are his daughter."

"Yes," Amanda agreed as they reached Cinnamon, "but that doesn't give him the right to treat other people the way he does."

Josiah stroked the sorrel's neck before finally turning his gaze on Amanda. "It is not up to me to judge your father or the other man." He fingered his chin with his thumb and index finger. "I almost forgot that tonight. I must not forget again."

In one fluid movement, he swung up on the horse's bare back. Blankness again covered his face. He touched the brim of his hat and nodded in what Amanda considered a half-hearted farewell. She knew a protest would be useless, and she watched with a heavy heart as he rode off into the night.

"He's trouble, I'm tellin' you." Leon's voice cut through the hushed stillness with all the intensity of a steam engine.

Amanda whirled around, ready for battle.

"You should have seen—"

"Told you to shut up once, Leon. Ain't gonna tell you again." A spasm of irritation crossed Newlin's face. "Get the buckboard taken care of. That horse needs a good brushin'. What am I paying you for? Not to sit and gossip like a confounded woman. Go!"

Leon sulked off toward the buckboard, kicking at the

ground with each step. Amanda could only imagine the choice words he was muttering under his breath at her father.

"When that's done," Newlin called out, "go on home. I'll see you in the morning. Thanks for your help."

Swallowing at the lump in her throat, Amanda prepared herself for the tongue-lashing she'd no doubt receive from her father. She stood and waited, but when Leon and the wagon disappeared into the barn, her father shoved his hands into his trouser pockets and simply said, "I'm goin' in. You comin'?" There was no monstrous glare, no withering stare, nothing.

Amanda's eyebrows rose in surprise. "Yes, let's go in."

Picking her way around puddles, she walked alongside him, wondering about his unusual mood. When they reached the front stoop, her father opened the door, spilling light onto them and into the twilight. Though she'd thought him calm and collected, something brewed beneath the surface. Stepping across the threshold, glancing at his face in the glow of the kerosene lantern, she felt certain of it. His jaw shifted and his eyes gleamed like crystal rocks in the sun.

The door closed with a click, and Amanda vigorously wiped the bottoms of her soggy high shoes against the braided rug.

"Looks like they're ruined." Newlin sat with a grunt on the oak deacon's bench next to the door. Tugging on his own muddy leather oxfords, he said, "I'll get you a new pair."

Wrinkling her nose, Amanda shook her head. "I think they just need be cleaned and set to dry."

Pulling off his wet black socks, Newlin stretched his legs and wiggled his toes. "I offer to buy you a pair of shoes and you're turnin' me down? You sick?"

"No, I don't need them."

"But you love shoes. And hats. We'll replace those."

"Papa, you're not listening." Amanda shrugged out of her wet coat, finding it hard to believe her father was talking about shoes and not lecturing her about Josiah and the Amish. "I don't want a new pair," she said, snapping the coat, sending water droplets flying. "I want these."

"All right, then, keep 'em." He leaned back and steepled his fingers against his chest, studying her. "So tell me. What did you do all day with them Amish?"

"Didn't you read the note I left you?"

"I read your note. Can't figure what'd possess you to go there to help make soap. Why can't them people buy it like normal folks do?"

"Oh, and are we the normal folks?" She planted a hand on her hip. "I'm not so sure about what's normal anymore."

"Makin' soap and candles sure as the blazes ain't. Not when a person can buy that stuff. That's time-wasting, in my book."

"I disagree," Amanda said with a sigh as she took the seat on the bench next to her father and laid her coat across her lap. "When members of a family are together, for whatever the reason, it's not a waste of time." She cast him a sidelong glance, enjoying the gentle sparring and praying it wouldn't end in an argument. "Maybe," she wagged her finger, "we should make our own soap. And candles, too."

"Blast that. We got inventory coming up soon at the store again. We'll be together 'nough then. I reckon you'll be mighty tired of me by the time we're finished."

There was a trace of laughter in her father's voice, and it warmed Amanda's soul. Drawing a deep breath, she acted on her emotions and laced her arm through his. She felt him stiffen slightly, then he relaxed. "This is nice," she murmured, hoping he felt the same.

"Yup. Nice." A long, slow whistle sounded through his lips. "Nice is that horse Miller had. Wonder where in the dickens he got the money to buy a beast like that?"

Amanda felt a rush of heat to her face. Her father's musings made everything else click into place. The wonderful conversation and the warmth and kindness had just been pretense. She'd guessed that from the moment he'd seen it, his mind had been occupied not by her safe return, but by Josiah's sorrel.

Shoving aside her own hurt, she pulled her drifting thoughts together. "I think Josiah stole it. Think that's how he got the other five that are back in his barn, too.''

Newlin's mouth gaped at her words. Tossing her head in dismay, Amanda pulled her arm free and gave an irritable tug at her sleeve. Pushing herself to a standing position, she draped the coat over her arm and gazed down at her father. ''Oh, close your mouth. Josiah didn't steal that horse. He bought it. And at least in his barn, there aren't any more like it.'' She rolled her eyes. ''I only said that stuff to get your attention. To prove, I guess, you were more concerned with that horse than whether or not I'd gotten hurt, or just what had happened during the storm.''

''There you go 'gain, talkin' nonsense and makin' me out to be the bad guy when you were the one out gallivanting all day with them people. I *was* concerned. I knew you was still upset 'bout that cat, too. Why else do you think I sent Leon to fetch you?''

Amanda's stomach contracted like a fist. Taking a deep breath, she fiddled with the buttons on her coat, mixed emotions swirling like a fast-running brook. How could her father be so kindhearted about Ophelia, and so black-hearted about Josiah? She breathed again, willing her voice to be steady and calm. ''First of all,'' she said slowly, ''I appreciate your sympathy with Ophelia. Secondly, I wasn't gallivanting. You know that. And I wish to heaven you'd have come for me yourself. Leon was the last person I needed or wanted help from.''

''But it was mighty fine gettin' help from the Amishman, wasn't it?''

Impatience rushed Newlin's words, and Amanda found her own muscles tensing. ''At least I trust Josiah,'' she said before she could stop herself.

Jumping from his seat as if propelled by some explosive force, Newlin stood in front of her, staring intently. ''What in the devil is that supposed to mean? Why do you dislike Leon so?''

Amanda's breath quickened. Now was the time to tell him. ''Papa, he's made two improper advances now. Both times were when we were alone. The last time was just this afternoon during the storm.''

Newlin chuckled softly. ''Blasted oaf. He's just so smitten with you, honey. He don't mean no harm.''

A shudder ran through Amanda. Her father wasn't upset in the least. Reaching up, she massaged one of her aching temples. "I am not interested in that man. I know you like his horses and you think he's a dandy, but I don't. I've seen his evil. I don't want to be near him alone anymore.''

"But the Amishman, Miller, he's different?"

"Josiah and I are friends.''

"That supposed to make me feel better? I don't like him. Never will.''

"That's a horrible thing to say. If you'd only give him a chance. He's kind and hardworking—''

"Jiminy, will you stop already,'' Newlin said, waving his hand. "The fella's a saint in your eyes, but not mine. I admire that sorrel he owns, but that's where it ends.'' Leaning toward her, his eyes narrowed. "If I had my way, I'd lock you up so you couldn't go near them people.''

"Thanks for your good intentions today,'' Amanda said, ignoring his last ridiculous comments. "I'm going to take a hot bath, then I'll fix your supper.'' Spinning on her squishy heels, she headed for the staircase.

"Don't worry 'bout me. Already ate. Hey! You ain't gonna come home sometime wearing one of them black dresses, are you?"

Gritting her teeth, Amanda dashed up the stairs to the sanctuary of her room.

She flung open the door, the gaslight in the hall casting a meager but warm glow across her bed. The old quilt lay there like a faithful friend, its odd gold stitching glinting in the light like flecks of the true precious metal.

Tossing her coat to the back of a wing chair, Amanda removed her misshapen bustle and wet petticoats. She flopped onto her stomach on the bed. Resting her chin atop her folded hands, she stared at the quilt until the room around her blurred.

"Sommerville. Sommerville,'' she murmured again, remembering Mary's words. "The answer starts in Sommerville. I know it does.''

Though she still wore her damp clothing, the chill that possessed her had disappeared, and she felt only invigoration and enthusiasm. Rolling to her back, she bolted upright, turned on the light in her room and quietly closed her bedroom door. After spreading out the quilt, she grabbed her pad and pencil, and sat back down. Her gaze swept over and over the quilt, desperately trying to locate a hint or clue that could be added as a piece of the puzzle.

Chewing the end of her pencil, Amanda concentrated on the stitched trees in the upper right-hand corner of the coverlet. They were indeed lopsided, similar to the way the trees had looked during the storm. All the other times she'd gazed at the area, she'd thought Josiah's grandmother had simply lacked skill with her needle. Now, Amanda wasn't so certain that was the case. The pine trees and the other area of trees on the quilt had all been stitched as straight as a book edge. Why would the maker intentionally take crooked stitches?

Eyes widening, Amanda exclaimed, "It's another piece to my puzzle." She rubbed her hands together. "Somewhere there's a place where all the trees lean to the right. That's it! It has to be. Just think, Ophelia—"

Amanda froze, and a huge lump shoved up into her throat. For the last several minutes she'd been so immersed in the quilt she'd forgotten about the accident. She struggled to catch her breath. The memories were so pure and clear her heart ached. She missed her friend, missed how the tabby would follow her and push against her hand, begging to be petted. And the purring . . . that chubby body beneath the sleek mottled fur, rumbling with contentment over a rub behind the ears. Ophelia's love was unconditional.

Amanda's entire body suddenly felt engulfed in waves of weariness and despair. She wrapped herself in the quilt the way Ophelia had been earlier, deep sobs racking her insides.

12

LEANING AGAINST THE COUNTER of the store, Amanda sightlessly turned the pages of the May edition of *Godey's Lady's Book*. She usually loved to keep up with the latest apparel and notions, and the fashion plates in the magazine provided her with the latest styles, but today she couldn't seem to concentrate on them. Her mind kept drifting back to Josiah and the storm and the unbidden memories that caused her blood to boil.

Seven days had already passed, and though she hadn't seen him since, the feelings she felt for him grew stronger each day. The delightful shiver of wanting that ran through her body just thinking of Josiah confirmed it once again.

Closing the magazine with a sigh, Amanda rested her elbows on the cool surface and propped her chin in her hands. How did he feel about her? At times she thought she knew, but then something would happen and doubts would taint her optimism. She even considered just simply asking him, but she didn't know if her heart could handle his rejection. She wished Widow Marly was back from her visit south. Her old friend would be able to make sense out of all of this.

Sighing again, Amanda flattened her palms on the counter. Though things were so very uncertain, she preferred them this way than to knowing Josiah didn't return her feelings.

"Back to work," she said, grabbing a pencil and the inventory list from the counter. She threaded her way through the crowded store to the staples section in the back, reluctantly forcing the thoughts of Josiah to the back of her mind.

The huge barrels containing the flour and sugar and cornmeal were almost empty. She had bagged the products into ten-pound sacks four days ago, and there wasn't enough of any one of the products to bag again. She hoped the train delivering the supplies wouldn't be late a second time.

After tallying and straightening the sacks, she cocked her head and closed one eye as she looked down the aisle. She prided herself on tidiness and smiled when she saw that each sack was perfectly aligned with the one next to it. Grabbing the three-legged stool that stood next to the shelves, she moved to the canned goods area.

∞

THE SUN CLIMBED HIGHER into the cloudless blue sky. Josiah inhaled deeply, filling his lungs with the still-dewy, loamy-scented air. The trail to town was still a bit muddy and the draft horse's legs and underside were now speckled because of it. Josiah took it slow, enjoying the lush richness of the land that spread out before him. A large wild turkey with grand reddish-brown plumage strutted across the trail as if he owned it. It struck Josiah, as it had so many times before, that Prosper and all it offered was a gift from above.

Suddenly Amanda's smiling face crept into his thoughts. Was she part of that gift?

Sarah squealed from the back of the spring wagon, and Josiah turned, grateful for the distraction. She and nine-year-old Daniel had been tossing a rag ball back and forth. Josiah smiled when he saw his brother. Daniel's head was tipped back and he balanced the homemade ball on his forehead. Even with the jostling of the wagon, the boy was able to shift and keep the ball from falling. Sarah giggled some more. Josiah was glad his mother had allowed the two to accompany him to town. He knew Sarah would enjoy seeing Amanda again.

Amanda. Again she slipped back into his thoughts, where she shouldn't be. Scowling, Josiah turned away from the children and back to the trail. It wasn't anyone's fault that the old yoke had rotted. And he couldn't help it that his father had asked him to make the trip this morning to purchase it along with another new chain. But what he could control, and he was determined to do it, was the flutter in his belly when he saw Amanda, the pounding of his own pulse in his ears when she smiled and the heat, the heat that unfurled in his belly like wildfire.

The spring wagon creaked and jingled as it descended the last sloping ridge before Prosper. When they rolled past Doc Rollins's office and closer to the store, Josiah told himself Amanda was a complication, one he didn't want or need. He thought of the storm last week and all the other times he'd been weak and fallen under her charms; but that wouldn't happen again. Today he'd prove to himself that she no longer had any effect on him.

Pulling back on the reins, he brought the team to a stop a few doors down from the store.

"Josiah!" Daniel shouted from the back of the wagon. "You made me drop it."

Jumping from his seat, Josiah approached his brother, sitting at the back of the wagon. "I made you, did I? Oh, Daniel, my boy," he said, grabbing the youth and tickling him. "I am so sorry."

Giggles, snorts and laughter filled the air. "Me next!" Sarah cried as she scrambled over to her brothers. "Tickle me, Josiah. Please," she said, pulling his arm.

Josiah released Daniel and grabbed Sarah in one fluid movement. She squealed with glee, tears trickling down her cheeks, her little black bonnet askew from all her squirming.

The happy sound touched a chord deep inside Josiah.

There was nothing in the world like the sound of children's laughter.

"You two," he said, letting go of the children and picking up the rag ball, "have to be good while I am in the store. Sarah," he continued as he tossed the ball back to her, "see if the top of Daniel's head is as flat as his forehead."

Daniel groaned and stuck his tongue out.

Winking at his brother, Josiah headed toward the store. He felt his heartbeat increase as he reached the door. He saw Amanda through the window, standing on a three-legged stool, her back to him, apparently counting the canned goods on the shelf.

Josiah's mouth went dry. The determination he had felt such a short time ago vanished, and he couldn't remember what it was he had been so resolute about doing. He shook his head, trying to clear out the feeling that he had been knocked senseless. All that seemed to matter was the vision of the English girl in front of him. He stared at Amanda, knowing without even seeing them that her blue eyes would be flecked with the same azure color of her flounced skirt. He couldn't even tell what soft material her garments were made from, only that he envied the fabric caressing her skin.

Slowly and carefully, so as not to disturb the clapper of the brass bell hanging above the entrance, he pushed open the door. "Hmm," he heard Amanda murmur as she raised on tiptoe and reached even farther to the top shelf. The tiniest bit of her slender ankles showed, and the cursed heat started. Josiah couldn't quench it. His manhood stiffened as his eyes shamelessly drank in the sight of her.

A breeze caught the telltale bell clapper, and Amanda turned abruptly toward the door. With the shift of her weight, the stool tottered. She shrieked, and Josiah ran to her, grabbing her about the hips and swinging her into his arms.

The astonished look on Amanda's face quickly dissolved and he was treated to the brightest smile he'd ever seen.

"Josiah! Oh," Amanda exclaimed without giving him a chance to reply, "thank goodness you were here and caught me. I'd surely have injured myself otherwise."

The tip of her pink tongue darted across her lips and Josiah's eyes followed it. When she smiled again, he knew he wanted to kiss those lips.

He couldn't seem to move, let alone speak. All he wanted to do was bask in her company, memorize every detail of her face and how it felt to hold her.

"Is the ground moving beneath your feet?" she asked in a hushed tone.

Josiah shook his head, suddenly wishing he had not only had more experience with women, but also more of a formal education so that he could think of something profound to say in response.

"I suppose, then," she continued on, "it's safe for you to put me down."

Heat burned Josiah's cheeks, and the tips of his ears felt as though they had caught fire. With as much grace as he could manage, he set Amanda upon her feet.

As she cleared her throat, her slender fingers traveled across the tight bodice and then down the front of her dress, smoothing it back into place. She chewed her lip for a moment in that way he found so endearing. "I spotted an old tin on that top shelf." She shrugged her shoulders and her feathered eyebrows rose to meet a few wayward wisps of hair. "Wondered what was in it, is all. Not awful smart, standing on such a wobbly thing and reaching like that."

For the first time since he'd met her, Amanda seemed self-conscious. If he hadn't seen the situation unfold with his own eyes, he knew he would have wondered at the coincidence of it. His heart swelled, and he allowed himself to smile back finally. Without uttering a word, he stepped to the shelf, rose on tiptoe and outstretched an arm, easily seizing the tin Amanda had referred to.

"The cause of your problems," he replied, handing it to her.

"Problem? I didn't say *problem*." She blew the dust off the tin, apparently having recovered from her discomfiture. "Maybe," she whispered, leaning toward him, "it was fate."

"Fate?"

"You know, like destiny. I chose that rickety old stool because some great force made me. Like you coming here. You were made to come in at the precise moment and save me from a fall."

"I came to buy a yoke and a chain."

"See there!" she said, touching his arm. "You need supplies. That's destiny. You can't avoid it. It's already predetermined. What's going to happen to you . . . and me, we can't change it."

Josiah was only half listening to her chatter. He couldn't seem to concentrate on anything except the way her eyes shone like sparkling stream water. And he couldn't seem to get enough of the flowery scent surrounding her. He had fallen into the worst kind of quicksand.

"What do you think is in here?" she asked, eyebrows arching again. "Josiah?"

With another quick shake of his head, he willed himself to snap out of the strange mood. Amanda's playful, earnest expression did nothing to help his struggle. He wanted to keep the banter going. He wanted to kiss her. Plain and simple, he wanted to make love to her.

Amanda turned the tin over and over in her hands, the contents rattling and clattering against the container, she tipped her head and smiled again. "Well? You guess first."

Had she no idea what she was doing to him? Josiah drew a ragged breath, feeling as though the air had been punched from his lungs. "No," he said more sharply than he had intended. He steeled himself against the wounded look that came to her eyes. "I do not have time for your fun and games."

A frown momentarily pleated her brows. She recovered and replied, " 'Course not. Fun is a terrible thing, isn't it, *Mr. Miller*?"

Amanda spoke his name as though it were a distasteful word. Ignoring the regret that coursed through him, he watched as she marched across the floor and around behind the counter, her hips swaying all the while in feminine anger. Slamming the tin upon the walnut surface, she looked up at him.

"So you need a yoke and some chains. They're out back

in the barn. Across the alley. You know where. My father's
not here now, but you're big, probably can carry what you
need all by yourself. Back door's the same place it's been
for years.'' She pointed with one hand and grabbed a magazine with the other.

Josiah knew he'd been discharged from her company,
and rightly so. His coat hung heavily on his body and his
suspenders suddenly felt too tight. He meandered past the
counter, and though Amanda pretended nonchalance, he felt
her hostility. He knew she watched and wondered why his
disposition had changed so abruptly. He wished he had it
in him to stop and try to explain the foreign feelings rushing
through his body. But even if that kind of boldness was
miraculously bestowed upon him, it still didn't make the
attraction he felt for her proper.

Amanda was English. He was Amish.

He opened the back door, welcoming the cool spring air
that splayed across his face. It just wasn't enough, though,
to blow the thoughts of her from his head.

Her prattle about destiny stuck in his mind as he crossed
the back road to the so-called storage barn. What was it
she had said about not being able to avoid it? His Amish
upbringing had taught him the cultivation of humility. He
believed in the will of God, had been taught to fear pagan
philosophies. Did destiny and fate classify as one of those?
Or was God's will the force Amanda had referred to? He'd
never known such confusion.

The interior of the structure was moderately bright. A
flap of oilskin that barely reached the halfway point hung
over the doorway and more light flooded the lean-to from
the countless crevices and gaps where new boards had been
randomly replaced. At least the ground inside was fairly
dry and the implements had been somewhat protected from
the weather.

Overgrown grass from last season clung to everything on
the ground, trying its hardest to hide the merchandise and
hinder the growth of the new. Josiah absently fingered a
wooden mold board on one of the plows. He needed distance from Amanda, needed to sort and understand the feelings she evoked.

He half-heartedly continued his search through the menagerie of farm supplies. He found the iron chains, grabbed one, then coiled an extra around his right shoulder, pushing away the thoughts of Elam that tried to sneak into his mind. Finally he spotted a yoke similar to the one they used to have. With a grunt he hefted it across both shoulders then headed back to the store and Amanda.

"That was quick," she said as he awkwardly maneuvered his way past the pickle and vinegar barrels.

"I knew what I wanted," Josiah replied, stopping at the counter.

"And what you didn't," she retorted flatly.

Though her eyes were still shadowed with hurt, a definite spark of defiance burned. Josiah couldn't stop the slow, easy smile that spread across his face.

"What I did not want was to waste your time. The Lord gives us only so many productive hours in a day. We must make the most of them. It was not my intent to anger you, either."

Pursing her lips, Amanda thoughtfully regarded Josiah. "Your moods change quicker than the weather." She tapped her fingertips on the counter. "Well, I was a mite huffed . . . but I'm not anymore. Do you ever have any fun? Don't you ever just frolic and tease? I saw the children in your community playing. What about the adults?"

Disregarding his protesting shoulders, Josiah stood straighter as he pondered her question. "Yes, of course, we have fun."

"Doing what?"

"Ah . . . ah . . . there are many things I do for fun."

"So you say." Amanda stopped the tapping, propped her elbows on the counter and rested her chin in her hands. Gazing at him, she challenged, "Like what?"

She looked so innocent and eager for his answer that Josiah smiled again. "The Lord's time is wasting. I must get back with the yoke."

"Josiah Miller!" Amanda exclaimed, slapping her palms flat. "You are such a tease!"

No one had ever called Josiah a tease before. He didn't

know what to say, but he knew he liked the sound of it coming from Amanda's lips.

He pulled a handful of bills from his pocket and laid them on the counter. Sighing, Amanda pulled out a worn piece of parchment. She ran her index finger down the column, silently adding as she came to the prices of Josiah's items. Counting the correct amount from the pile, she placed it in a strongbox and pushed what was left back to Josiah.

"One of these times I'll get you to talk, and I won't let you clam up." She wagged her finger at him. "You'll see. Oh, wait," she said suddenly, "I wanted to show you what was in the tin." She disappeared below the counter for a moment. When she popped back up, her heart-stopping smile was back in place. "They're marbles. Old marbles. I used to play with them when I was a child." She moved the tin in a slow circular motion, the marbles clattering together and against the sides. "I haven't seen these in years. Forgot about them, really." A frown erased her smile. "Papa's more sentimental than I thought."

Amanda's eyes seemed to darken for a moment, and then more cheerfully, she said, "Whenever you and Mary are up to a game of marbles, you know who to come see."

Josiah groaned inwardly at the thoughts tumbling through his head. He'd play marbles, he'd quilt, he'd help her scrub the laundry if it meant spending more time with her.

He gazed at her smiling face and knew he had to get out of there. "I must—"

"I know. I know. You *must* go." She strolled around the counter. "At least let me get the door for you."

Swallowing hard, Josiah clumsily stuffed the rest of the money into the pocket of his homespun trousers. He followed as close behind Amanda as he dared, hoping his legs held out until he reached the spring wagon.

As they neared the door he'd left ajar, children's laughter floated into the store.

"Whatcha gonna do now?" someone called out.

"Dummy!"

Josiah's gaze flew from Amanda's backside to the windows. The malicious tone twisted his insides, but from the store, he couldn't even see to where he had parked the wagon.

Amanda ran the last few steps to the door and yanked it open. Josiah saw that a group of five school-aged boys had gathered around the back of the spring wagon. Someone had taken Daniel's hat and Sarah's bonnet. The hat lay crushed on the road.

"Yer clothes stink and so do you!" a boy shouted as he dropped Sarah's black bonnet into a puddle and stomped on it. "Why don't ya go back where ya came from?" The other children laughed and flung a handful of pebbles at the wagon.

Rage surged through Josiah. The fist of his free hand clenched until he felt pain. Quickly he appraised his brother and sister. Though Daniel's head hung to his chest, his hair covering most of his face, his arms were wrapped tightly around Sarah. Sarah's eyes looked to be as round as the rag ball she had been playing with. Tears streamed down her face and her hair was mussed, but from what Josiah could tell, neither she nor Daniel appeared to have been physically harmed.

"Do something!" Amanda cried. Disbelief and repugnance were etched on her face. "For heavens sake, Josiah!"

" 'Blessings are upon the head of the just,' " he mumbled, " 'but violence covereth the mouth of the wicked.' "

"What? Now's not the time to be reciting some verse. Do something!" she shouted again, tugging roughly on his arm. He realized he wanted nothing more than to answer her pleas and dunk the tall freckle-faced boy's head in the puddle and give all the kids a whipping.

Sinful thoughts again. Where did they keep coming from? Somehow right had blended with wrong, and revenge was foremost on his mind. Both went against everything his disciplined community believed in. With mixed emotions he forced himself to remain motionless. He recited the biblical verse again, and he prayed.

"What is wrong with you?" Amanda glared at him, hiked her skirts and hurried through the mud. "Charlie

Thompson," she scolded the boy, "you put those rocks down now!"

"Chrissake, Amanda. They're just havin' some fun."

Josiah whirled toward the voice. Leon Violette cockily ambled toward them.

"Leon," Amanda said, hands on her hips, "don't you encourage this behavior. Make them stop."

"What's it worth to you?" Leon chuckled.

Ignoring him, Amanda wagged her finger at Charlie. "Picking on people again. I'll make certain your parents hear about this and that my father doesn't sell you any of that taffy you love for the next month. Maybe even two! Or three!"

Charlie Thompson opened his fist and the rocks he held plunked into the puddle, splattering more mud on his already-dirty trousers.

"And the rest of you," Amanda continued. "Get on back to school. I'm telling the schoolmarm you don't deserve recess for the rest of the week."

As the children ran down the street and disappeared around the corner buildings, Josiah went to the wagon. "Daniel, Sarah," he said, setting down the yoke and then sliding the chains from his arm. "I am sorry. Are you all right?"

Though Daniel nodded, the bewilderment in his eyes and the tremble of his lower lip told Josiah the pain his brother felt was worse than anything physical. Sarah sniffed and wiped her hand across her eyes, smearing the tears on her cheeks. "They didn't get my ball, Josiah. I hid it," she said, pulling it from under her coat.

Josiah's heart ached. "I have what we came for," he said brokenly. "It is time to go back."

Leon roared with laughter. "Are you some kind of half-wit, hidin' behind a lady's skirt? Aren't much of a man, are you?"

"Stop it," Amanda demanded.

Leon stepped around the wagon toward Josiah, his lips curled in a hateful grin. "Coward," he taunted.

Turbulent feelings rocked Josiah. Amanda had come up with a nonviolent solution. He admired that. But Leon now stood only inches away, his sneer daring a reaction. The chains were so close.... It'd be so easy to grab one.... "No!" shouted a voice inside, reminding him that he wasn't supposed to judge other human beings, wasn't supposed to take up arms. But a different, stronger voice, countered that it might already be too late.

Amanda ducked between the two men. Placing her hand on Josiah's chest, she said, "Just go. Go back to your settlement."

Drawing a labored breath, Josiah backed away and returned to the wagon. He climbed aboard and chanced one quick look back at Amanda as he snapped the horses to movement. Sadness and confusion flashed in her eyes. He'd never forget the look on her face when she had screamed at him to help Sarah and Daniel, and he hadn't. And he'd never forget how sick that made him feel.

"You're a blasted coward!" Leon shouted behind him.

Remorse knifed Josiah's heart. He had unwillingly upheld his Amish faith, but that made him a hypocrite of the worst kind.

13

AMANDA STARED AS JOSIAH and the spring wagon bounced over the gently rolling hills in retreat. It wasn't really a retreat, she decided, but more of a heated withdrawal. The tension between Josiah and Leon had been thick, thicker than the ice that glazed the town during the storm not more than three months ago.

But that had thawed.

Stooping, Amanda pulled Sarah's little black bonnet from the puddle. She shook the dripping hat, splaying droplets of mud in all directions. Leon, whom she had almost forgotten, scoffed at her side.

"I swear, he's a half-wit. Blasted fool ain't got the gumption even to fight for his kin. Did you see him?"

"Shut up," she snapped defensively, though she wondered the same thing. Why hadn't Josiah stuck up for his brother and sister? Nausea swelled in her belly. She'd never forget the look on Sarah's face. The child had been frightened, and her gaze begged for help. Anger had emanated from Josiah, yet he had made no move to stop the cruel children and their heartless monkeyshines. Amanda didn't understand it—any of it.

"A real man doesn't walk away from a fight." Leon's impudent tone irritated her even further. "Yup, he just ain't a man."

"And you are?" Chest heaving with short, angry bursts of air, Amanda glared at him. "You." Her voice shook. "You're no better. You laughed and encouraged those kids. Then, you tried to pick a fight with an innocent man whose brother and sister were already getting picked on by a bunch of bullies. You call that a man, Leon? I don't." Giving the bonnet one last vigorous shake, she stalked toward the store.

"Hey! Don't you be talkin' to me that way."

Before she knew what was happening, Leon grabbed her arm and spun her roughly against his chest.

"No, no, no," he growled, his nose almost touching hers, the stench of him shoving another wave of sickness across the pit of her stomach. "You have to get rid of that cussed high-falutin' attitude, Amanda. Doesn't become you."

Amanda knew that to the passersby on the street, Leon looked to have wrapped her in a passionate embrace. Just that thought caused the bile to rise in her throat. Not wanting a scene, she swallowed hard and forced a calm smile. "See what I mean? Is this another of your *manly actions*?"

"You pokin' fun at me?" A blush crept up Leon's face and his fingers bit more tightly into her arm. He returned her smile with a huge, almost evil one of his own, showing the blackened nub of a tooth halfway to the back of his mouth. "If I didn't know better, I'd say you're comparin' me to that half-wit again. I ain't nothin' like him."

"For once we agree," Amanda replied, derisive humor lacing her tone. Now, let me go." She lifted a foot and slammed the heel of her high shoe into Leon's instep.

With a yelp of pain, he released her. She sidled around the puddles and hurried the rest of the way to the store. Closing the door, she leaned heavily against it and caught her breath. She was no longer so certain she could handle Leon. His ill temper seemed to show more times than not, and she never knew what he'd do next. Somehow she had to make her father see the real Leon.

Turning, Amanda peered at him through the window in

the door. He still stood near the street where she'd left him. Their gazes met, and Leon blew her a kiss, but the fire shooting from his eyes and his contorted facial features revealed a different story.

A clammy shiver swept her spine. A little voice in her head told her Leon was not a man to reckon with, and she'd best take care not to be caught alone with him. On shaky legs, Amanda backed away from the door. She stopped only when she was at the counter and out of Leon's sight.

Setting down the bonnet, she placed her palms flat, dropped her chin to her chest and closed her eyes. "I'm not going to worry about him. There's nothing to worry about." She repeated the two sentences over and over until finally her resolve grew. Then, straightening herself with a deep breath, Amanda picked up the hat and headed through the store to the back door where the rain barrel stood. She'd wash it and as soon as it dried, she'd travel to the Millers, return it and apologize again for the schoolchildren's lack of manners.

Scrubbed and looking almost as good as new, Amanda perched the bonnet on the end of the broom handle to dry. She went back to the inventory, tallying the results, wishing she could shove the incident with Josiah from her mind. It nagged at her until she thought she'd burst from the unanswered questions flowing inside her head. Why hadn't he even uttered an admonishment to the mean children?

Whistling sounded from the back door, and she looked up from the list she'd sightlessly been staring at. Newlin treated her to one of his rare smiles as he crossed the threshold and approached the counter.

"Doc Rollins bought me two cups of coffee. Can you believe that? Two cups."

Shrugging, Amanda made a halfhearted attempt to return the smile. "The way you teased him before, probably felt as if he had to."

"Teased him? Oh, pshaw! He's always after me about somethin' he needs that we don't have here. Got to pay him back."

Pay him back. Her father's words bounced around in Amanda's head like a trapped toad. Was Josiah a vengeful person, someone who would look for vindication? She didn't think so, but now she suspected Leon was. Thrice now, and in a very short period, she'd infuriated Leon. She couldn't ignore the coldness that crept up her spine again. She didn't want to know what Leon's payback would be.

"Jiminy! Amanda!"

Her father's bellow commanded her attention, and all other thoughts disappeared.

"We aren't selling *those* in here now, are we? Tell me we're not."

His questioning eyes regarded her as his thumb pointed in the direction of Sarah's black bonnet.

Defensiveness pumped back through Amanda's veins. "What if we were selling them?" she retorted. "Why would that be so bad? You allow the townspeople to buy the Stetsons and top hats and the other notions they want."

Newlin grunted and his eyes narrowed as he glanced back at the small bonnet. "That's a child's. Whose is it? What's it doin' hangin' in our store?"

A glimmer of hoped surfaced. Her father wasn't an ogre. Surely he'd side with Josiah and his siblings when she told him what had happened.

"You're right. It is a child's." Amanda closed her eyes for a moment again and rolled her shoulders, trying to loosen the stiffness that seemed to have worsened. "Josiah Miller came a while ago. To buy a yoke and some chains."

Newlin exhaled audibly, and Amanda's eyes popped open. "Now don't go doing that already," she chided. "Please. You don't even know what I'm going to say."

"Better not be that you bartered some of my hard-to-come-by merchandise for that blasted hat."

With a loud cluck of her tongue, Amanda folded her arms across her bosom and glared. "I can't even talk to you. You won't even let me finish without butting in. And no, I have better sense than to barter your precious merchandise for a bonnet. *They* have money. And they *always* pay. Better than some of your other customers."

"All right. You're right." Newlin threw up his hands. "Don't go gettin' huffed. I'm . . . I'm sorry. Go ahead and finish your story."

Though she was a bit reluctant to learn what her father's reaction would be, Amanda told him exactly what had happened, except for the details afterward with Leon. She wasn't in the mood to have to defend her actions against her father's protégé.

The lines and angles of Newlin's face softened. His eyes held an inkling of compassion. "Them young'uns get hurt?"

"I don't think so," Amanda replied, "not physically, anyway. I think the parents need to be told what happened. Especially the Thompsons. Charlie—that boy is always picking on someone."

"He's just a kid. Reckon he don't mean no harm."

"That *just a kid* will grow up to be a man someday." Amanda's voice rose an octave. "What's he going to be like then?"

Again Newlin raised his hands into the air, only this time Amanda didn't know what the gesture meant. Then the rigidity returned.

"Young'uns need looking out for. Miller's a coward," he said gruffly through clenched teeth.

"Not you, too? Charlie and the kids were wrong. Leon was wrong, not Josiah."

"The Amishman did nothing. Nothing. That's a coward in my book."

Josiah's face flashed in her mind. Amanda remembered the hurt and fury etched all over it, remembered it so vividly she ached inside. He wanted to do something, she believed that with her heart and soul. But he hadn't. He had the will and the strength to resist, even though Leon jeered and goaded.

"Maybe it's the coward that gives in," she mused aloud.

"What's that?"

Gazing at her father, Amanda accepted the revelation she had stumbled upon. "Cowardice," she said softly. "Maybe it's the coward that can't walk away. It took more will and more courage for Josiah to do nothing."

A long, slow whistle of amazement sounded from her father. "Got things a mite mixed up there. A coward is afraid. Don't want to face danger. The man's a milksop, I tell you."

Amanda lifted her chin a notch. "I disagree. The coward fights because he's afraid not to. Josiah Miller is no coward."

"We obviously disagree on this subject. Ain't gonna do no good to keep talkin' 'bout it."

With a lift of her eyebrows and a compliant nod, Amanda agreed. She chewed her bottom lip as she pushed the inventory list across the counter to her father. "It's done. All of it. I'd really like to return Sarah's bonnet."

Newlin leaned lazily against counter. "You askin' me or tellin' me?"

There was a shimmer in his eyes. His good mood hadn't been diminished by their debate on cowards, and Amanda realized she was being teased. "I'm telling you, I guess. But I also hope for your blessing."

"Go on. Return that hat. Won't get another lick of work outta you if you're sittin' and thinkin' 'bout some little girl."

"Thank you, Papa." Amanda came round the counter and kissed his cheek. "Um . . . you know that same little girl loves rock candy. . . ." She trailed off the words with a hopeful lilt. By the way her father rolled his eyes, she knew he hadn't missed it.

"Go on," he said. "What do I care if you're the cause of their teeth rottin'?"

"You can be such a sweet man." Amanda smiled and hugged him close. "Thanks for this," she whispered in his ear.

❀

JOSIAH STOPPED FOR A moment to wipe the sweat from his brow. He glanced toward the sky, estimating that an hour or so had passed since the other men had left the fields for lunch. Then there'd be devotions, probably already started. He couldn't do either of it, lunch or the devotions. He wanted to be by himself, alone with the pain in his gut that worsened every time he thought of the in-

cident in town. Daniel and Sarah had said nothing upon
their return, not even made a remote complaint. That bothered him the most. It was like a forbidden secret. A sordid
piece of information not meant to be shared with anyone.
He hadn't asked the children not to say anything—they just
simply didn't.

The question he kept asking himself was: Why? Why
didn't Daniel and Sarah tell their mother? They'd been
frightened, their hats stolen and ruined, and yet nothing was
said. As far as Josiah was concerned, that wasn't normal.
It wasn't normal, moral or right that he'd just stood there,
either.

Drawing his forearm across his brows once again, he
closed his eyes. The rich, earthy scent of the freshly turned
ground usually soothed him, but not today. There was nothing that could erase reality and what had happened.

He and his family and the rest of the Amish were out-
casts to Newlin Glosser and to some of the others in Prosper. He didn't know why. It angered him. And it hurt. He
insanely wondered what the outcome would have been today if he had fought back. How he'd wanted to. It had taken
all his restraint, all of his will to remain emotionless.

Though the situation was over, the rage and frustration
continued to gnaw at him like acid eating tender flesh. He
felt ready to explode. Finally, with a groan of pent-up rage,
Josiah threw the hoe he had been using. It twirled awkwardly through the air and landed with a dull thud several
feet away.

"Do you feel better now?"

Whirling around, Josiah staggered, almost falling over
the mounds of earth. "Mary. What are you doing here?"

She held a small crate that contained a handkerchief-
covered pail and a jug. "I brought you lunch. Ma and Pa
and everyone else wondered why you never came in."

"It is time to get the fields ready. Time to fertilize. I
want to make certain Elam's are the best."

"Ahhh, yes. And you must starve yourself to do it properly."

Josiah ignored Mary's retort, adjusted a drooping sus-
pender and walked stiffly to retrieve his hoe. "There are

things to be done, trees to fall and land to clear so that Elam and Lena can have a bigger home. And yes," he snapped, "am I the only one that remembers the dates and predictions of the almanac? These fields are dry enough now that they need to be readied again. That last storm set us back. The planting cannot wait."

Mary set the crate down and pulled out the pail and jug. She flipped over the wooden-slatted box and took a seat. "*The Experienced Farmer*. Or what is that French name?" Her face wrinkled in thought. "Yes, *L'Anabaptiste ou Le Cultivateur Par Experience*. I do not believe there is anything in either translation that says you must skip meals to work God's land and be a good farmer."

"You win," Josiah said, sorry for his ill temper. He dropped to his knees beside Mary and the pail. "I will eat only so that you will stop bothering me."

Smiling, Mary pulled a fork and tin of sausage balls from the pail. "I am sure they are cold now, but that is your fault."

Josiah felt some of the tension leave his body, and he settled himself cross-legged before taking the plate Mary offered. "Why are you not at devotions?" he asked as he brought a forkful of the meat to his mouth.

"I told Papa I'd come out here and bother you instead."

"That I believe." Josiah chewed, then grinned and grabbed a corn-bread cake from the pail.

"And I told him I'd try to find out what happened in town this morning."

A coldness that had nothing to do with the spring breeze washed over Josiah. He couldn't explain how he felt. No one would understand. He wasn't even certain he did.

"Daniel and Sarah's hats are both gone," Mary prodded. "They said they are still in the 'muddy' town and the other children have them."

"They said *muddy*?" Josiah flipped a crumb from his trousers. "It is a muddy town. A dirty town. We are lucky to be on higher ground. So lucky. I would not want to live any nearer to that . . ." He was rambling, and he knew it. Tossing the half-eaten cornbread cake onto the tin, he pushed to his feet. He kicked at a clod of dirt as he gathered his thoughts. "Mary," he said, barely louder than a whisper, "do you ever wonder what it would be like to . . . to *not* be Amish?"

He heard her quick intake of breath, but that was the only reaction she let escape. Her eyes sparkled with tolerance and compassion.

"For us, well," she said thoughtfully, "there is no 'not Amish.' It is what we are. It is in our hearts. It *is* our soul."

"I do not know if that is true for me." Dropping back to his knees, Josiah absently sifted the moist soil through his fingers. Finally he wiped his hands on his thighs, removed his hat and shoved a hand through his hair. "Did the children tell you what happened?"

"I had hoped the story came from their imaginations," Mary said softly.

"It did not. We are not Amish to the people of Prosper. We are still the outsiders, the people who for some reason cannot be trusted."

"We were the newcomers. The English were here first. Things will change," she replied, the note of hope in her voice striking a chord in Josiah's heart.

How he loved and respected his sister. Optimistic, trusting Mary. He brought his hat to his chest and gazed toward the flawless blue sky, realizing how much he worried about disappointing her. Of all the people in their community, he needed Mary's understanding and acceptance.

"Amish have been here for years, Mary. I think we are foolish to believe it will change with us. There were others before us. It is because of the cholera that they were never fully accepted." Looking toward heaven, he shook his head. "If two decades have not changed the feelings of some of the English, no amount of time will. Mary," he stared at his sister, wishing he could make her understand, "I felt the hatred in the schoolchildren. I saw the willingness to hurt. I did nothing." Josiah wasn't able to control the angry tremble of his words, or shove away the shadow of guilt.

Touching his arm, Mary replied, "There was nothing you could do."

"Do? I wanted to punish those children for what they

were doing to Daniel and Sarah. I wanted to punch the man who confronted me. I wanted to punch him and wrap the chain around him until he could not get up, could not move. That is what I wanted to do.''

Mary swallowed hard. "It was a difficult situation. But you did do the *right* thing. The Lord has already forgiven your wayward thoughts.''

"You do not understand. I do not think the thoughts were wrong!'' Josiah winced as if in pain and rose to his feet. "I do not think like an Amishman. I am different. I am different than Papa. Than Milo Wickersham and Sanford Guengerich, and all the rest. Do you understand what I am saying, Mary?''

He gazed at the flock of geese flying overhead, returning to their northern summer home. They honked as if they, too, disapproved of his words. When he looked back at his sister, he saw that, though she nodded, the color had drained from her face.

The shadow of guilt darkened, pressing heavily upon his shoulders. Was there no way to get rid of it? "I am done with the food. Go back for devotions, Mary.''

With misty eyes, she stood and stared at Josiah. "You are my brother. I will love you no matter what thoughts you have.'' She hugged him, grabbed the pail and crate, but left the jug of water behind.

Josiah threw himself into his work, swinging at the earth, chopping the soil, hoping to block off all thoughts and feelings of his family, his heritage and Amanda. He saw the other men return to their work, many helping each other with the same plot of soil. Josiah was glad to be alone. He wanted and needed solitude. The muscles in his shoulders and arms burned with exertion, but something deep inside drove him on.

Suddenly a shadow landed across his path. He knew without even looking who it was.

Inhaling deeply, Josiah turned. "Papa.'' He jabbed the hoe once more into the ground and rested his hands on the end. "What is it you want?''

"Peace for my son.''

Josiah felt his stomach contract like a fist. "You spoke to Mary," he said flatly.

Isaac Miller nodded, staring toward the hardwood forest about a quarter-mile away. "Look at that," he said in his broken English. "Trees older than your ma and me. Oaks and maples and even sycamores. Different, but they are all the Lord's trees. All living together."

Knowing a point was coming, Josiah kept quiet.

"Salvation is free. It is all around you as you live your life. It is a gift given by God's grace. Do not forget *Nachfolge Christi*. That maple will not change into a sycamore. Nor will the oaks. We, too, must be right with God."

"What if one does not know what the right is?"

"Search your soul, Josiah. The answer is there, but only you can find it."

Josiah gazed at his father. "What if that answer is not what you expect?"

Fingering his peppered beard, Isaac Miller closed the short distance between himself and his son. Josiah felt a lump shove up into his throat as his father faced him and placed a hand on each shoulder.

"I love the soil," his father whispered, "and the stewardship that goes with it. I live to care for creation, need to care for you and your brothers and sisters and your mother. The elders. That is my fulfillment." Giving Josiah's shoulders a shake, he said, "You and only you can decide what yours must be." Sliding his hands from Josiah's shoulders, Isaac shrugged. "It may be that Prosper is not the place where you will achieve your fulfillment. Still, you are my Amish son."

His father smiled, but the smile never reached his eyes, and Josiah saw through it. Sadness and desolation filled the man. He tucked his hands in his pockets and trudged back through the field, his body drooping and his head no longer held at that proud angle. Josiah's heart beat crazily against his rib cage, guilt swallowing him whole.

He wasn't English, but at the moment didn't feel worthy enough to be called an Amishman, either.

14

JOSIAH THOUGHT LONG AND hard about what his
father had said. His head seemed to spin with thoughts,
each making him feel worse than the one before it. He was
Amish. *He was Amish.* Why didn't his feelings match what
he was?

"I must try harder," he said, bending to pick up a stone
that had found its way to the surface of the soil. "I must
be a man like my father and grandfather. I must be true"—
he whipped the stone across the field—"to my heritage."

"Josiah! Josiah, come! Hurry!" Mary stood at the corner
of the barn, motioning to him. When he picked up the hoe
and started through the fields, she disappeared. The small
hairs on the back of his neck stirred, and his stride turned
into a run.

"Mary, what is it?" he asked as he darted into the structure, straw crunching beneath his boots and the scents of
manure and animals swirling all around.

"Over here. Come."

Excitement laced her tone, and Josiah felt relief. He
headed in the direction of the bonnet poking out from behind the wheelbarrow. "I have got much work to do," he

said impatiently. "I do not have time for—" The rest of his words stuck in his throat. There, on the floor in a wooden box licking her fur in her finicky way, was Ophelia.

"Is it not wonderful?" Mary asked, clasping her hands in simple glee. "Elnora stopped by a few minutes ago. She said she thought her patient will be just fine now." Rubbing Ophelia behind the ears, Mary said, "You must take the cat to Amanda."

"No." Josiah's tone was sharper than he'd intended it to be. He couldn't do it. There was no way he could see Amanda after what had happened in town. He'd seen the look of disgust in her eyes, had felt the agony in his own heart.

Suddenly it dawned on him. This would be different. These circumstances would help her to forget the incident in town. She'd be excited, ecstatic, probably throw her arms around him, hold him close and kiss him. Her softness would be pressed into his hard, yearning body. Her full, dewy lips would be pressed to his face. No, he wanted them against his own lips, wanted to feel them against his neck, against . . .

Mary thankfully interrupted his dogged thoughts with a loud cluck of her tongue. "What is the matter with you?" she asked, shifting on the dirt floor, tucking her legs beneath her. She folded her arms across her bosom like he'd seen Amanda do so many times. "Amanda loves this cat. Josiah, you made a promise to her. If you are still concerned with the incident in town, do not be. It is over. You need to . . . just remember yourself."

"Remember myself? Remember me?" He slapped his palms against his chest. "Are you saying to keep in mind who I am? If that is the case, you tell me, Mary. Who am I? I do not know."

"I—I thought," Mary said, looking down to stroke the silky fur beneath Ophelia's chin, "that Papa had come to talk to you."

"He did. He spoke the same words as you. I must be right with the world. Seek my fulfillment, my *Amish* fulfillment."

Mary's eyes widened. "You are cynical today. It does not become you, Josiah."

Setting the hoe against one of the wheelbarrow handles, Josiah sank to the ground beside his sister. Drawing a ragged breath, he rubbed his hands across his eyes and his face. How could he tell Mary that the English merchant's daughter, after all these years, had finally gotten under his skin like no Amish woman ever had? Or that the importance of earning money to help Elam was more significant than the Zooks' barn raising, or the daily devotions? How could he even begin to explain?

"Mary, oh Mary," he said softly. "I do not know what is wrong with me. I only know my feelings in here," he placed a fist on the area of his chest covering his heart, "are not the feelings of an Amishman. As hard as I try, I cannot change what is there."

"Why now? Why all of a sudden is your heart telling you something different?" Her brows drew together in an agonized expression.

Josiah felt as though he could explode. He needed Mary to understand. Reaching a shaky hand to his sister's face, he smoothed the deep furrows from between her brows. "My heart has been telling me things for years. I just did not listen. I think I have to listen now. It is time."

Silence fell around them. Swallowing hard, Mary squared her shoulders. "I told you before," she said finally, "I will love you no matter what. 'A merry heart maketh a cheerful countenance: but by sorrow of the heart the spirit is broken.' " A thoughtful, accepting smile curved her mouth. "Follow your heart, Josiah. Listen closely to it, for there will be no turning back."

Ophelia chose that moment to arch her back in a big stretch. She climbed from the box and cautiously crept onto Josiah's lap.

Mary's smile turned to a chuckle. "There is still the matter of Amanda's cat. I think *you* should return Ophelia," she said, pushing to her feet. "She seems to like you best."

As she strolled from the barn, laughing, Josiah felt his spirits lifting. Mary stopped at the door and glanced at him

from over her shoulder. "You are a good man, Josiah—
Amish or . . . not."

His lips twisted into a sour grin. "I do not believe Papa
or the elders will agree with your thinking."

Her shoulders lifted in a small shrug. "Then you must
make them see."

∞

AMANDA DIRECTED THE HORSE down the narrow
lane that would lead to Josiah's home. She relaxed her grip
on the animal's reins and loosely held them in one hand.
The fingers of her free hand reached for the bonnet on the
seat next to her. Absently she caressed the stiff brim of
little Sarah's organdy bonnet, wondering how she could
possibly apologize for the cruelty and thoughtlessness of
the other children.

The higher hills of the Amish community were dry, and
stones and pebbles crunched under the iron wheels of the
buggy. Amanda did her best to ignore the creaky moaning
that occurred with each revolution. A grassy, almost earthy
scent wafted on the warm breeze, the occasional fragrance
of lilacs sweetening the air even more. After what had happened in town, she felt confident the rest of the day could
only be brighter.

She had almost reached the Millers' property when she
saw Mary enter a tiny coop with chickens that were scattered about and pecking at the ground. Stopping the horse
with a tug of the reins, Amanda stepped from the buggy
and hurried after her friend, bonnet and rock candy in hand.

"Hi," she said as she entered the structure, sidestepping
a chicken, the hat and candy hidden behind her skirt.

Mary spun around, the few eggs she'd gathered in her
basket knocking into each other. "Amanda," she said, her
hand flying to her chest, "you startled me. What are you
doing here?"

"I brought a gift for the children. And this." Amanda
pulled out the candy and bonnet. "I tried to clean it, but
there's still one stubborn stain that I couldn't get out."

Shrugging slightly, she said, "I wanted to say, too, how sorry I am about what happened."

"It is a difficult thing, but children are children."

"That's not true." Amanda fiddled with the long ties on the bonnet, finding it hard to believe Mary, in her subtle way, was defending the bullying schoolchildren. "Children need to be taught manners. Those obviously need more teaching."

"The JOY motto is what we are taught as children. It helps us to remember to yield to family and community. *Jesus* first, *you* are last, and *others* are in between. JOY."

"I like that. Yes, that's what the children need." Amanda's face broke into a wide smile. "All children should be taught the Amish JOY."

Mary managed a small tentative smile of her own as she took the bonnet and sack from Amanda's hands. "JOY alone will not always work. *Gelassenheit* must be practiced along with it."

"What?"

"*Gelassenheit.* Submission. Obedience."

A frown creased Amanda's brow. "Submission. Huh. I'm not trying to be a nosy body," she drew her top teeth across her bottom lip, "but can I ask you a question?"

"Yes. Ask."

"Is this *Glassenhat* thing why Josiah didn't defend your brother and Sarah?"

"Personal conflict, force, fighting—they are not acceptable," Mary replied matter-of-factly.

"Oh. I see."

"Do you? It is like a very thin line of difference. My grandfather, my father and the others in the community are not afraid to take a stand, but they always obey God rather than . . . mere men."

Nodding, Amanda said, "I do understand, but it's so different than how I was raised. I'm not saying it's wrong, either," she added quickly, "just different. You see, my father'd push up his sleeves and fight another man in an instant if that's what he thought it would take to protect me or his store."

Mary wagged her head for a moment, then resumed her

egg-gathering. "It can get very complicated if your heart tells you something different."

"Yes," Amanda replied wistfully, somehow knowing Mary was referring to Josiah.

"Enough about my community." Mary smiled a conspiratorial smile. "Do you remember the barn where Josiah's Cinnamon and the other horses are kept?"

"Yes. Why?"

"There is something of yours there." Mary's mouth twitched with humor. "You must go get it. When you walk in, go to the left. It is over by the wheelbarrow."

Gazing at her friend with a critical squint, Amanda said, "You come with me."

"I cannot. I must gather the eggs."

"I'll help you, then we'll both go."

"No," Mary replied, shaking her head. "It will not wait. You must go now. Shoo." She waved the bonnet as though she were warding off a swarm of oncoming bees. "Shoo, I say!"

Amanda backed from the chicken coop, laughing. "It's a good thing I trust you, Mary Miller," she called out. "I wouldn't be doing this otherwise." She hurried toward the barn, not able to think of a single thing she'd left at the Millers. She wondered if this was some kind of game or prank, but then decided it couldn't be, for how could her friend have known that she'd be making a visit to return the bonnet?

Taking a deep breath, Amanda entered the building, her gaze immediately traveling to the left as she'd been instructed. She spotted the wheelbarrow . . . and a black straw hat. Josiah's hat. Swallowing hard, she was all too aware that her pulse leaped with excitement.

Whatever Josiah had over there on the ground, he seemed fully immersed in it for he hardly moved. Amanda guessed he hadn't heard her or expected her arrival. "Well," she said, smiling when he started at the sound of her voice, "you're not mine, so I know Mary couldn't have been talking about you when she said there was something I needed to get in the barn."

"It is not always wise to assume." Josiah's voice was

soft but composed, and sent Amanda's heart into an erratic rhythm.

"Close your eyes," he demanded in a velvet murmur. "I'll bring *it* to you."

"I don't know. Can I trust you?"

He chuckled, low and throaty. "Close your eyes, Amanda."

He had yet even to turn and look at her, but Amanda tingled anyway. She loved the sound of her name when he said it. Closing her eyes, she knew she was helpless to do anything other than what he asked. "They're closed," she replied hoarsely.

"Good. Then I will give it to you. Remember, do not peek."

Josiah's clothing rustled ever so slightly. Amanda guessed he had risen to his feet. She'd been correct, for she heard his footsteps, heard the straw crackling beneath his boots. Closer and closer he came. Her body suddenly felt heavy and warm as she realized exactly what it was she wanted from him. It was mad. Maybe she'd finally gone loony.

Silence descended, and Amanda could all but feel the heat from Josiah's body as he stood at her side. "Open your eyes," he whispered against her hair, his breath stirring her locks, stoking the already-blazing fire in her body.

Taking several uneven breaths, she squeezed her lids more tightly, hoping to still her pounding heart and rekindle her sanity before she looked at him.

"Did you not hear? I said you could open."

"I—I know. I think I've got something in my eye," she fibbed, rubbing her fist against her face, praying that when she did open her eyes, he wouldn't be able to know her thoughts by reading them there. She rubbed some more, reminding herself to breathe.

"Let me see. Perhaps I can help." His leg innocently bumped against hers as he moved closer still.

Amanda thought she'd surely swoon. Her clothing felt too constricting. She couldn't breathe. She needed distance between them. Eyelids still clamped, she took two steps backward, hoping there wasn't anything behind her that she'd trip on and make a fool out of herself. "There. I think I've got it now." Blinking a couple of times more for good measure, she opened her eyes and turned her gaze to Josiah. Her jaw dropped; for cradled lovingly in his arms was Ophelia.

"I . . . I . . ." She couldn't seem to make her tongue work and she blinked again, this time with incredulity. "Ophelia," she said in a broken whisper. "Josiah, I don't believe it. Oh! Oh, goodness!"

Amanda reached for Ophelia at the same time Josiah tried to hand her over. Their arms tangled and Amanda's fingers brushed against his broad chest. It didn't matter that the homespun cloth separated her hand from his skin. She could imagine how wonderful it would feel. She giggled, suddenly feeling very nervous and self-conscious, and moved her arms to grab Ophelia from a different angle. This time she ended up stroking Josiah's forearm. His shirt-sleeves had been rolled to his elbows and she was treated to unyielding muscle and skin. She again had to remind herself to breathe. The golden hair on his forearms felt downy soft, and she wondered if he had hair on his chest to match.

"You are too anxious," he said chuckling. "We do not want to drop poor Ophelia after what she has been through. Hold still, and I will give her to you."

The tenderness in Josiah's expression caused a billowing of emotion inside Amanda. With a long sigh of what she assumed was contentment, he gently placed Ophelia into her arms. The tabby's now-slender body vibrated with new life. Tears stung Amanda's eyes. Her body was consumed with a bottomless gratitude that she knew she'd never rightly be able to repay.

"I don't know how to thank you. I thought . . . I just figured after so many days . . . Oh!" Without thinking, Amanda rose on tiptoe and pressed her lips against Josiah's. He stood there, frozen for a moment, but then suddenly, to her surprise, he yielded to reckless abandon. Josiah's lips feather-touched hers with such tantalizing persuasion that she eagerly parted her mouth. A shock wave tore through her body. She hadn't been prepared for such delicious sensations.

The desire to be closer to him was so great she forgot everything else. As she leaned into him, and a shrill meow cut through the stillness.

Immediately, Amanda and Josiah stepped away from each other. An awkwardness floated between them.

"I . . . I apologize for that," Amanda said, finally able to speak. She rolled her eyes. "Here you saved Ophelia, and now I almost squashed her . . . between us." Glancing down at her shoes, then up again, Amanda sighed. "I just wanted to thank you. And I was excited that she was still alive." She swallowed hard. "I shouldn't have . . . kissed you like that. I'm sorry." Tears welled in her eyes, and with a nervous laugh, she wiped the back of her hand across her face.

Josiah straightened his shoulders with a deep breath. "I did nothing. Elnora and the Lord healed Ophelia. I am happy you two are back together." Eyeing her curiously, he suddenly closed the distance between them again. His expression became unreadable. "Tears? Why?"

"Happy tears," Amanda choked out.

"Hmm . . ." he cocked his head and studied her face. Finally a lopsided grin tugged at the edge of his mouth. "Tears of happiness are still tears. Do you know what my culture believes?" he whispered huskily, wiping her tears away with the thumbs from both hands.

Amanda felt mesmerized. Was it happening again? She didn't know if she could trust herself so soon. A soft moan escaped her, and she dumbly nodded her head.

"When a man causes a woman to cry happy tears, the Amish way says he must marry her." Humor laced his tone and amusement shone in his eyes.

Amanda's cheeks still burned, but she was no longer sure if it was from Josiah's touch, the embarrassment she'd caused herself again, or both.

"You are not laughing," he said, his gaze seizing hers. "That was a jest."

Forcing a smile, Amanda shook her head. "That's funny, too, because we both know you have to marry an Amish woman from your community." Moistening her dry lips, she said, "That really is funny. Us marrying. I couldn't even imagine that." She laughed then, for she knew if she didn't she'd probably cry. The hollow, wooden sound grated on her nerves.

The silence returned.

"Why did you come here today?" Josiah asked, rubbing Ophelia between the ears.

"I brought Sarah's bonnet back. It was filthy." As soon as the words rolled from her tongue, Amanda regretted them. Josiah's entire body seemed to slump in defeat. He stopped petting Ophelia and shoved his hand into his pockets.

"That was kind of you." His voice instantly hardened and his eyes narrowed. "I am certain you are busy at your father's store. You now have your cat and can be on your way."

"What?" Amanda's brows shot up in surprise. "Are you asking me—no, telling me—to leave?"

Shrugging, Josiah said, "I have work to do."

"Well go, then. Don't let me stop you, Mr. Miller, man of many moods."

One of his eyebrows raised in amusement, but he said nothing.

"Come on, Ophelia." Amanda sniffed, gave Josiah a curt nod of farewell and walked to the door with as much dignity as she could muster. "I want you to know," she said, stopping but not turning to face him, "I understand why you didn't defend your brother and sister this morning. I think what you did was . . . honorable. And as for the kiss, which you neglected to comment on, it was the first time I've ever initiated one. It wasn't my first, but I don't mind being honest—it was the most enjoyable I've ever had. I'm withdrawing my apology for kissing you." With that said, Amanda sauntered from the barn.

Once outside, she forgot her poise and hurried to the buggy as quickly as she dared without bouncing Ophelia around too much.

"Amanda," Mary's voice called from somewhere.

Amanda bit her bottom lip, disregarded her manners, and

pretended not to hear. She didn't want to be delayed for she didn't know what she'd say to Josiah if she saw him again so soon. Just as she was about to step up into the buggy, she saw Mary running across the green-tipped grass two houses away.

Waving her arms, Mary shouted, "Amanda! Amanda, wait!"

Waving back, Amanda pasted on a smile, then glanced over her shoulder, fully expecting Josiah to be standing there with a biting retort ready to roll from his tongue. She shuddered, wondering why in the world she'd said that last part about the kiss. It was the shock factor, she decided. She wanted to make him notice her. After all, he'd completely ignored the kiss, like he seemed to do with everything else he didn't want to deal with.

It was the marriage thing that really got her. She knew she'd opened that Pandora's box weeks ago when she'd teased him about them marrying as an English custom. For some reason it wasn't funny any longer.

Pushing all thoughts that had anything to do with Josiah from her mind, Amanda instead concentrated on Ophelia. She stroked the cat's fur, reveling in the fact that she was alive and appeared well. That was because of Josiah and his friend Elnora. Amanda wrinkled her nose. It seemed that no matter what, Josiah always snaked into her thoughts.

"I am glad I caught you," Mary said, huffing like a steam engine. She wiped the beads of sweat from her brow and shoved back the several strands of auburn hair that had escaped and now curled and bobbed around the brim of her white hat.

"Goodness, Mary," Amanda said, grabbing her arm, "catch your breath."

"Yes. Yes, I am." Exhaling with a whoosh, she smiled and took a couple of normal breaths. "I see you did find Ophelia," she remarked, trailing a finger down the cat's velvety nose.

"Yes. That was truly a miracle." The edges of Amanda's lips tipped with a smile. "I'm afraid Ophelia is spoiled. I need to get her home and back to her normal routine of laziness and attention."

Mary laughed. "Yes, Elnora said she has never seen an animal that craves attention like your Ophelia."

"I hope she was no bother."

"I do not think so. Elnora loves all animals."

"I'd like to thank her. Pay her."

Shaking her head, loosening more fiery locks, Mary said, "Oh, no. Payment is not expected. Elnora has a gift and her desire is to share it with those in need. She would be offended."

"I don't want to offend her, but—"

"There are no *buts*." Mary's smile returned, larger than before. "I wanted to remind you of the quilting bee tomorrow. You are attending, are you not?"

"Yes. I wouldn't miss it. Mary," Amanda said, tipping her head closer to her friend's, "I've studied that quilt, and I know in my heart it's a map. I've come up with questions that I need to have answered in order to find the starting point. I may need your help."

"Oh, I do not know." A worried looked creased Mary's forehead. "What is it I must do?"

"Don't worry. I would never ask you to do something that would compromise your customs. I just don't know to whom I can ask these questions. Or how to get on the subject in the first place."

"That I believe I can help you with. Leave it to me. Tomorrow, Amanda, if there are answers, you will have them."

The same mischievousness that Amanda had seen so often in Josiah's eyes now sparked in Mary's. If unfurled a tumultuous ribbon of excitement inside her. She believed in that map and that treasure. After tomorrow, she'd make her plans. With or without Josiah, she was searching for that treasure.

15

WHILE OPHELIA SLEPT CURLED on Amanda's lap, thoughts of Josiah were very much alive in her head. She passed the five-minute mark to her home and still hadn't decided what to make of her feelings.

It seemed strange, awkward even, to have feelings shift into something other than the customer/friend-from-store relationship. She didn't have the answer to the whys and whats her logical mind kept asking about. All Amanda knew was her body ached for Josiah's touch.

Stopping the buggy outside the front walk, she scooped Ophelia into her arms. "I know someone who'll be surprised to see you. You surprised us all, didn't you, Ophelia? I'm glad to have you back." A throaty response came from the cat, then she tucked her nose under Amanda's arm, apparently ready for another nap. Laughing, Amanda carried her into the house, closed the door with a bump of her backside and headed for the stairs.

She put Ophelia on the old quilt that was spread across the bed. "One miracle," Amanda said, stroking the feline's bridled fur. "Do I dare hope for another?" Adjusting her bustle, she laid on her side and crooked one arm behind

her head, the bedsprings creaking slightly with her weight
and movement. Slowly she ran her fingers along the gold
stitching. Ophelia moseyed over after a few moments of
washing and settled contentedly in the warm curve of
Amanda's body. Everything seemed right with the world.
The longing that had gripped her soul suddenly seemed
stronger. She felt it in her fingertips as they touched the
quilt. She felt it in her heart when she thought of Josiah's
quest for his brother.

This new objectivity elated her. "There will be a second
miracle," Amanda said with a sigh. "Tomorrow at the
quilting bee."

The supper hour drew near, and she left her notebook
and the sleeping cat to prepare dinner. She pulled her gingham apron off the peg in the kitchen and tied it about her
waist as she flipped the hook that latched the root cellar
door. Musty air flew up her nostrils, and the fine hairs on
her arms rose against the chill of the damp, earth-covered
room. Memories of the kiss she'd given Josiah floated
around in her head like an unrelenting melody. She absently
lit the kerosene lantern that sat with the box of matches on
the small shelf next to the door. An orange glow filled the
staircase and cast an eerie light down into the cellar. Shaking her wrist, Amanda extinguished the match and descended the narrow, sloping stairs.

Josiah. Josiah. Josiah. She couldn't get him out of her
head. Resting her shoulder against a timbered beam, she
wondered if he thought of her, thought about the kiss as
much as she did. She hoped so, hoped that was all he could
think about.

Lifting the edge of her apron to form a pouch, Amanda
picked four potatoes from the bin and had just dumped
them into the cloth when suddenly the room went dark. She
jumped and reflexively backed away from the stairs just as
the sound of boots hitting wood filled the air. Heart hammering in her chest, she let go of the apron edge and potatoes thudded to the dirt floor. With her hands behind her,
she groped for a weapon. Dried peppers to slap the intruder
silly? A bag of onions to knock him in the head?

Gulping spastically for air, Amanda ordered herself to

remain calm. It was getting harder and harder, for the footsteps were muffled now, telling her the intruder was down
the stairs and no doubt walking toward her. Fingers from
one hand closed around a bottle of ketchup and the others
reached back for the onion bag. The odor of tobacco
swirled around, sickeningly sweet. Something crunched in
front of her, and she swung the onions.

"Ouch! What the . . . Amanda, it's me!"

"Leon." Lowering the ketchup bottle, Amanda bristled.
"Why in heaven's name did you turn out the lantern?
You're lucky, because I was about to clobber you with a
glass bottle!"

Leon responded with a maniacal chuckle that seemed to
echo off the walls. It grated Amanda's nerves and made
her skin crawl.

"What are you doing here?" she asked. "Go get the
light."

"Your father invited me to supper. As for the second
question, I got the lantern right here." He tapped his finger
against the glass globe as proof. "And the matches, too. I
got them in my pocket, but I just don't know if I want light
yet. I kind of like the dark. Let me see if I can find you.
It'll be like a game."

Leon's voice sounded like it was slightly to her right. As
quietly as she could, Amanda sidestepped along the wall to
the left. The layout of the small cellar was ingrained in her
mind. If Leon continued on a straight path—and she hoped
he would—he'd no doubt trip over the empty squash bin.
She could make it to the stairs, but climbing them in the
dark could be treacherous. On the other hand, getting
caught by Leon could prove as dangerous. She trusted him
now about as much as she trusted a rattler.

"Come on, Amanda. Give me a little hint. Where are
you?"

The bile rose in her throat, and her appetite vanished.
Inching along the wall, ignoring the cobwebs and the furry
thing that her hand touched, she decided this was the last
straw. She'd make her father listen, make him understand
that Leon's actions were anything but acceptable.

"Am I going to have to light this blasted thing? You

aren't bein' much of a sport, now, are you?''

Amanda guessed her time had just about run out. She felt the stairway opening, saw only darkness and knew Leon had shut the door. Taking a deep breath, she started up the stairs. One, two . . .

"Ouch!" came Leon's cry. "What in the bloody blazes is that?"

Smiling now, Amanda hurried as much as she dared up the remaining steps. She flung open the door and sucked her lungs full of the fresh air.

The meager amount of light that shone into the cellar was enough to tip off Leon. Amanda heard him curse, and without thinking, she slammed the door and affixed the latch.

"What in the dickens are you doing? Amanda!"

Backing away, Amanda's eyes widened. The door vibrated under Leon's pounding. She didn't know what he'd do once she did open the door.

"I'll break it down. Amanda!"

"What in the blazes is going on?" Newlin's voice boomed as he entered the kitchen.

Amanda felt a rush of heat to her face. "Papa, I didn't hear you come in."

" 'Course not, with all that poundin'. What's Leon doin' locked in the root cellar?" Without waiting for an answer, Newlin pushed past Amanda and unlatched the door. Leon catapulted into the room. "Now," Newlin said, turning his gaze back to Amanda, "what's going on?"

"I locked him down there," she replied matter-of-factly. "I was getting potatoes, and he shut off the lantern and frightened me. When he wouldn't turn it back on, I sneaked up the stairs in the dark and shut the door."

"I was just funnin'. She knew that." He glared at Amanda.

Sighing in exasperation, Newlin raked his hand through his graying hair. "Leon, my boy," he said, draping his arm across Leon's shoulders, "the way to a woman's heart isn't by scaring the wits out of her. They're fragile, delicate creatures."

Rolling her eyes, Amanda clucked her tongue. "Please

don't patronize me by talking like I'm not even in the room. The way to a woman's heart is by earning her trust, not breaking it each time you're alone.''

"Huh?" Newlin's brows rumpled. "What're you talkin' 'bout?"

"Ask Leon. He can tell you his version of the story. I'll tell you mine when we're alone.'' Planting her hands on her hips, Amanda's lips twisted into a bleak, tight-lipped smile. "I didn't plan on company for dinner. There's a ham in the smokehouse. The potatoes are somewhere on the cellar floor with my appetite.''

Spinning on her heel, Amanda stalked from the kitchen.

It was well past midnight when she heard the floorboard outside her bedroom creak beneath her father's weight. Closing her eyes, she feigned sleep. Just as she expected, the door swung open and light from the hallway spilled into the room. She heard her father's quick intake of breath and guessed he'd spotted Ophelia curled at her side.

"Amanda?" he whispered hoarsely.

She didn't answer, didn't know if she wanted to hear anything he had to say. He sighed wearily and the sound triggered something deep inside her conscience. She didn't want to be like him, refusing to talk. Opening her eyes, she raised up on her elbows. "What is it?"

"Where in the devil did the cat come from? I thought she'd died.''

"Josiah took her to a friend of his. She was able to heal Ophelia. They saved her.''

He grunted. "Can save a blasted cat, but can't stick up for a member of his family?''

"I figured we'd get back around to this sometime. Papa, I'm not going to fight with you about Josiah.''

"Can I sit?" he asked suddenly.

Amanda patted the edge of the bed, depicting an ease she didn't feel.

"I don't want to fight, either," he said, dropping onto the bed. "And I don't want to talk 'bout them Amish.''

"All right." She cleared her throat, wishing she'd kept up the sleeping charade.

"You know Leon wants to marry you.''

The tight knot in Amanda's throat reappeared and begged for release. "You're kidding. You have to be. I don't love Leon, and I don't believe he loves me."

"Now, now, there's where I reckon you're wrong. I think he does love you. Like today, poor fella, he's . . . he's tryin' to be a little excitin', wantin' you to have fun."

"He's not fun. He's tried to kiss me and touch me when we're alone. I don't want to be anywhere near him." Rancor sharpened her tone. "Who knows what he would have tried down there in the cellar. I'm telling you, he doesn't act like a normal man."

"I reckon this is getting a mite out of hand. He's a young one and he's smitten with you. I told him weeks ago he needs to make you take notice of him."

"You instigated and encouraged this?" Her nostrils flared with fury. "How could you do that to me? I'd rather be a spinster than marry Leon Violette."

"Come now—"

"No," Amanda said. "I will marry for love. Nothing less."

"And I suppose it's that blasted Amishman you're in love with?"

"I don't know, but when I do know, you'll be the first I tell."

Newlin pushed to his feet. "I'd like you to stay away from him. All of them."

"Why? Not once has Josiah cornered me in a darkened room. I think he's safe enough. I admire him and everything he's trying to do for his brother. You could help them, you know, donate some of the profits from the store."

"What? After them people killed your ma, you expect me to give them my money—my hard-earned money? They killed her. I'll hate them people even after I'm in a pine box." He stormed to the door.

"Hate is so destructive," Amanda said in a hushed voice.

Her father let out a long, audible breath. "Yup, well, gullibility can be as well."

"Josiah didn't kill Mother. His family wasn't involved in that. The cholera killed her. The disease, not the Amish."

"You have your thoughts, I have mine. Go to sleep."

"Papa, wait. I'm invited to a quilting bee at the Millers tomorrow. I'm going."

With a stony expression in his face, Newlin stalked from her room.

∽

"WELL, MARY, WHAT DO you think?" It was a new day and Amanda was determined to concentrate on the quilt and not the disagreement with her father. She rested her hands on her hips and watched as her friend's gaze swept over and over the old quilt.

"I do not know," Mary said, shaking her head. "That area could mean many things. Crooked trees. I do not understand, but hopefully someone here will."

"A man certainly would know of a forest with leaning trees," Amanda mused.

"That is true, but the men will not be here. I do not think even Papa could make my brothers quilt." Mary laughed. "Quilting is women's work. Men do not have the patience for fine crafts." Tipping her head, eyes still twinkling with mirth, she whispered, "That would be some hen party, men gathered round with tiny thimbles stuck to their fingertips, all needle-working. Can you not imagine it, Amanda?"

Mary painted a humorous picture, and Amanda smiled. "We shouldn't laugh, you know. I'd bet the men have discussed just that sort of thing about the women. Could you imagine felling trees and constructing a house?"

"I think my female descendants may have done all that. When my people first settled here, I believe the women worked alongside the men. Perhaps," Mary giggled again, "that is why things have changed through the years. The women did not do a good enough job."

"Thank goodness," Amanda exclaimed, refolding the old quilt.

"Yes, I am glad, too," Mary agreed. "I would much rather quilt and prepare food for barn raisings than raise the wood. We are being ... what is your word? Loony." Smiling, Mary grabbed Amanda's arm. "We must go. You must take Grandmama's quilt to your wagon. Mama cannot know Josiah sold it to you."

"Hmm." Amanda's gaze darted around the room. "My coat. I'll put it under my coat and take it out now."

"Good. Please hurry. Mama's quilt is already pieced. The top and backing are secured, and I was asked to help put it in the frame. The boys have probably already carried it into the *Schtupp*."

"The what?"

"*Schtupp*. The room where our crafts and visiting is done. Today we will mark Mama's design and start the needlework."

They headed to the bedroom door, and suddenly Amanda felt panic set in. This was it. She had to get her information today. She chewed her lip, wondering what the next move would be if things didn't turn out like she expected.

"Mary, Mary, please," Amanda said, squeezing her friend's hand, "don't forget to help me. This could mean all the difference in Josiah's success. Just think, Elam could work alongside the men again."

"Your heart is like Josiah's," Mary replied in a gentle tone, "kind and giving. We will get your information."

Mary spoke with such conviction that Amanda felt her confidence returning. "Take me to your *Schtupp*, Mary."

Once down the stairs, Amanda slipped outside and put her coat and the quilt on the wagon seat. She rejoined Mary and was led through the kitchen and into a fairly spacious room opposite the fieldstone fireplace. The benches from the kitchen table, as well as three additional chairs, had been brought in and placed around a large square frame of wood. Mrs. Miller and several other Amish women already worked securing a black, purple and tan quilt to the frame. Mary immediately helped.

Amanda thought of the last quilt her mother had made before she'd died, the one hanging in the store behind the counter with the white background and the once-bright red-and-green rose wreaths and the vine border. Though now old and faded, it was soft and cheery-looking and would always be her favorite. The one Mrs. Miller had put together matched everything else in the somber house.

Amanda decided Amish quilt traditions hadn't changed much in the last fifty years. She was curious to see how the dark, almost doleful piece would look when it was finished.

Women of all ages filtered in, and the spacious room no longer seemed large enough to hold them all. Mary spoke in the dialect to some of the others, and a foreign, out-of-place feeling seeped into Amanda's bones. Though she wished she knew at least a few words of the Pennsylvania German language, she continued to smile, never forgetting the quilt and what its treasure could mean for Josiah and his brother.

"Let us begin," Mrs. Miller said in English, seizing Amanda's attention. "Mary." Nodding once to her daughter, Mrs. Miller took the single seat at the head of the quilt frame.

Mary walked to the seat to the right of her mother. "This is Amanda Glosser," she said, her chin held high. "She is my friend, and she is going to quilt with us today. If we could remember to use the English, then Amanda can understand us." Motioning to the bench seat to her right, Mary smiled archly. "You can sit here, Amanda. As we move around the frame you will meet all the others."

Amanda took the seat next to Mary, grateful for the smiles from the other women. Mary started around a wooden box containing a large pincushion, assorted thimbles and many, many spools of gold thread. Amanda chose a thimble and grabbed a needle and spool of thread. Suddenly Sarah bounded into the room carrying a bowl, her face smudged with dirt from playing outside.

"It is sometimes hard to include the younger children," Mary leaned over and whispered. "Today it is Sarah's turn to hold the bowl of starch."

Frowning, Amanda nudged Mary. "Why are we whispering?"

"We are always silent for the design-maker. Mama needs silence."

Amanda lowered her voice even more. "Sorry. I'll be quiet now. I just wondered about the starch."

Shaking her head, Mary grinned. "Watch."

Mrs. Miller stood up after rummaging through another small box. She held in her hands shiny pieces of tin. Amanda watched, fascinated, as Mary's mother dipped one of the pieces of tin in the starch bowl Sarah held, then pressed it to the uppermost corner square of the quilt. A tiny, six-sided star appeared in the purple square. Slowly and meticulously, Mrs. Miller moved the template, adding more stars to the quilt.

"What a wonderful idea," Amanda said, grabbing Mary's elbow. "I use chalk to trace my designs. Well, my mother taught me that, but this is so much easier."

Several pairs of eyes turned their gazes on Amanda. Releasing Mary's arm, Amanda clamped her hand over her mouth. "Oops. No talking. I'm sorry—I was so excited I forgot."

"It is all right. Mama is more experienced than some. I do not think she minds."

Amanda's amazement grew as Mrs. Miller exchanged tin pieces and next, beautiful, finely gridded wreaths appeared. Then, with the steady hands of an angel, she drew a pattern of double diamonds down the central bar pieces of the quilt. She repeated the running diamond pattern along the edges of the quilt, but also added a narrow row of scallops and feathers.

Amanda appreciated the gesture of silence for the design-maker, and thought about the times her mother had asked her as a child to be quiet until the design was done. Chalking a design in the back of a moving wagon had to have been quite a feat. Amanda's admiration for both her mother and Josiah's grew. She wished the two women could have gotten to know each other. She believed they would have had quite a lot in common.

A gale of laughter cut the stillness, snapping Amanda from her dreamy thoughts. Fingering the spool of thread she held in her hands, she envisioned gold stitches in place of the starch lines and pencil marks. A thoughtful smile curved her mouth. The dark colors would enhance the light, silky thread. The final result would be a statement of boldness and strength, colors befitting Josiah, his father, or probably any of the Amish men.

As soon as Mrs. Miller finished, the needles and mouths began to move. The women chattered, most remembering to speak in English; but a bit of the dialect could still be heard.

Taking a deep breath, Amanda tried to calm her nerves. So much was riding on the next few hours. With a prayer on her lips, she threaded her needle and began tiny, precise stitches on the scallops that lay in front of her.

"Such a face," Mary said, smiling. "So serious."

"I'm trying to remember to be quiet."

"Quiet time is over now, silly. You can speak as loudly and as much as you like."

"Yes, well, it's not me that needs to do the talking." Amanda sighed and lowered her voice once again. "I just hope these ladies are willing to talk to me about Sommerville."

"You worry for nothing." Mary pulled her needle through the fabric. "Give them a few moments to get warmed up. Then the tongues will flap like the wings on a flock of geese."

"I hope you're right." Swallowing hard, Amanda continued her stitching, not at all surprised to find her hands were shaking. She trusted Mary and told herself to relax, be patient and enjoy the quilting. The answers would come soon enough.

The warm sun poured in through the two windows of the room, providing plenty of light for the craft and casting a cheery ambiance. The room suddenly seemed alive with chatter. Amanda caught the buzz of two different conversations on the weather. She couldn't help but smile when Mary glanced her way, inclined her head and lifted her brows in a *see-what-I-mean* way.

A few minutes later, Amanda felt a kick to her foot. Mary pointedly cleared her throat. "Mama, I was thinking of Grandmama Miller. How far is Sommerville from here?"

"Miles and miles. I do not know exactly," Mrs. Miller answered. "Why do you ask?"

Mary grinned. "I was remembering that old quilt."

"Yes, your grandmama could not have been much younger than you."

"She was in Sommerville at the time the quilt was made, was she not?"

Nodding, Mrs. Miller tore the thread with her teeth. "Yes, she lived in Sommerville until she married your grandpapa. You know that. Oh, Amanda," Mrs. Miller smiled as she resumed her stitching, "you are a wonderful seamstress. You must be getting fourteen or fifteen stitches per inch."

Amanda's smile grew under Mrs. Miller's praise. It pleased her to think that they had so quickly gotten past the "merchant's daughter" stigma. "I started quilting as soon as I was old enough to thread and handle a needle safely. My mother made many quilts with such beautiful designs before she died. That was one of the special things she taught me. I've always enjoyed it."

"Making the designs is the most fun," Mary said, unwinding more thread from her spool. "Grandmama always got criticized for that first quilt she made. Who knows, maybe she was stitching her town."

Mrs. Miller tossed a sidelong glance in Mary's direction. "That quilt was an eyesore. I do not think it could have been Sommerville or any other town." With a wink at her daughter, she turned to the woman on the other side of her and said, "Maude, when will Jacob be baptized?"

Amanda chewed her bottom lip. Mary's mother had just politely dismissed the talk of Sommerville. Amanda had to keep the conversation about the old quilt going if she was to learn anything. She knew Mary was doing her best, but she wondered if it would be enough. More of the women needed to be drawn into the discussion.

"Mary," Amanda said, hoping to gain more information, "the quilt you're talking about—is that the one that—"

"I believe you have seen it," Mary said quickly. "It has the odd design. In the upper right-hand corner there is a spot of stitching that resembles crooked trees."

"What is that you say?" asked the old woman, Ruthann Keim, who was sitting two seats down from Amanda.

Amanda leaned forward. "We're talking about the quilt

Mary's grandmother made as a girl. I've seen it, and I think the stitching is a map. Were you ever in Sommerville, Mrs. Keim?''

''Yes, Fanny—it was not Miller then—Fanny and I used to play with our cornhusk dolls. Our papas' farms touched.'' Ruthann smiled and all the wrinkles around her mouth disappeared. ''Fanny was never good with a needle.''

Excitement brewed in Amanda's soul. She returned the old woman's smile. ''I'm curious. Is there a place in Sommerville where the trees are crooked?''

''Why, yes. A twister caused the unusual apparition. As children, we thought it was a wonderful place to play. Fanny especially liked it. There was another place not much farther, if I remember correctly, that I believe she liked even more. She planted daffodils there once, and would go back every spring to make certain they survived the winter. Yes, it was by a clump of trees. She seemed to love that spot.''

Hearing that information, Mary's mouth swung open like a faulty cupboard door. Amanda stifled a giggle.

''Are you certain about all that, Mrs. Keim?'' Mary asked.

''Yes. In fact,'' Ruthann mused, shaking her head, ''those childhood times were wonderful times. Fanny grew up to be quite a rebel, if you will, and marrying Moses Miller was the best thing for her.''

The quilting continued and three hours later, Sarah and Rebecca Miller brought around refreshments of sassafras tea and gingersnaps. Amanda realized she was hungry, but had just been too busy to think about food. Though the quilting party had changed places around the frame three times since they'd started, Amanda was careful not to move out of earshot of Ruthann Keim, for the woman continued to reminisce.

Amanda's head swam with all the mental notes she'd taken—the grassy hills Josiah's grandmother and Ruthann used to somersault down; the clump of birches with trunks as smooth as glass; and the spot where the daffodils were planted. She felt certain that spot was where the treasure was buried.

It suddenly hit her that throughout the entire afternoon she'd heard not a single word about a bank robbery or a stage holdup. All the daffodils in the world couldn't help Josiah and Elam if there wasn't a treasure of real monetary value. A sickening wave of nausea welled in her belly. Her positiveness evaporated. What if Fanny had simply loved flowers? What if Josiah had been right? What if his grandmother had simply quilted a map to her secret garden of flowers?

Amanda's skin grew clammy. There had to be a treasure. There just had to be.

16

AS AMANDA NIBBLED ON a cookie, she ordered herself
to calm down. She concentrated on the additional tales that
floated around the quilt frame, praying she'd hear some
tidbit that would confirm a treasure.

From the Amish teens' *rumspringa* to the discussion of
the Amish men and the brim widths of their hats, the chatter
continued with no further mention of days gone by.
Amanda's heart grew heavier with each inch she stitched.
Her gaze swept around the frame, landing on Mary.
Amanda stared, willing her friend to look up. Finally she
did. Amanda blinked owlishly and shook her head.

Mary frowned.

Peering self-consciously out of the corners of her eyes
at the women sitting near her, Amanda quickly mouthed,
"treasure." Much to her dismay, Mary's frown grew.
Amanda wasn't about to be dissuaded, and she silently
spoke the word again.

Mary studied her intently, the probing query never leaving her eyes. Suddenly the girl anchored her needle in the
quilt and bolted to her feet. Amanda met her halfway
around the frame.

"There's no treasure," Amanda said in a strangled tone. "I haven't heard a peep about a robbery or a holdup." Grasping her friend's hands, Amanda shook her head, feeling the blood drain from her face. "Mary, there has to have been money or gold. There has to have been an incident like that in order for there to be a treasure. I don't know what to do. Tell me what to do."

"I cannot just bring up this subject," Mary explained apologetically. "Most do not discuss the things you talk of." Her mouth dipped into an even deeper frown. "After what you have learned, do you still believe the design on Grandmama's quilt is a map?"

"Oh, yes, I'm sure of it. But maybe Josiah is right: maybe the treasure isn't monetary at all."

Exhaling audibly, Mary planted her hands on her hips. "Get your needle," she whispered. "You and I will trade places at the frame. Libby Wickersham is the oldest woman here and one who traveled from Sommerville. I cannot ask about a robbery. We would also raise suspicion if we were to ask the Hostetler sisters to move away from Ruthann Keim so that you could sit next to her again." Sighing, Mary rubbed her forehead as if it ached. "I do not know if Libby will tell you anything. She is not one to do much talking. Amanda, I am sorry, but you must be on your own for this."

"That's all right." Amanda squeezed Mary's arm and forced a smile. "You've done more than enough already."

"I hope there is a treasure," Mary said, setting her chin in a stubborn line, "for Josiah's sake." Turning on her heel, she hurried to Amanda's place at the frame.

Amanda, on the other hand, moved slowly toward Mary's spot on legs that felt like cooked noodles. Ignoring the several gazes that had curiously followed her path, she slid as gracefully as she could into the seat and reached for the needle sticking from the material. Libby Wickersham hummed and stitched at her right, neither conversing nor looking up from the quilt.

A dull ache gnawed at Amanda's soul. Time was running out. The sun had already dropped from its post in the sky, bathing the countryside in fiery reds. She needed her information and she needed it now.

From across the frame, Mary nodded, her eyes bright with encouragement. Taking a deep breath, Amanda cleared her throat. "Hello," she said to Libby. "Mrs. Wickersham, isn't that right?"

Libby glanced up for the briefest of moments, and Amanda wasn't even certain the woman planned to answer. She did, though, with a smile and a rather indecisive nod, never breaking the rhythm of her stitching.

"So, Mrs. Wickersham," Amanda hedged, "how long have you lived here in Prosper?"

"Years," came the simple reply in halting English.

Amanda stitched some more, panic rioting inside her. It appeared Mary was right—getting information from the elderly woman would be quite a task.

Chewing her bottom lip, Amanda gathered her thoughts and summoned her forgotten charm. Pinning on a smile, she forged ahead. "I understand you're originally from Sommerville, too. It's interesting that you, Ruthann Keim and Fanny all moved here to Prosper. Were there any other women?"

"None that are alive," Libby said, shearing the thread on her eyetooth. She pulled more from the spool, licked the end and narrowed her eyes until they were slits. Amanda blinked in surprise as the tiny gold tail poked through the needle's eye. More quickly than she'd ever seen before, Libby tied off the thread and continued her stitching.

Amanda's stomach was still clenched tight, but she mustered an outward calm. She needed to proceed with caution if she was to draw any information from Libby. "You know, Mrs. Wickersham," she said as casually as she could manage, "I find the tales of Sommerville very interesting. I heard the story about the tornado and how the crooked place came about. Is that true?"

"Yes, it is."

"I love history. There's nothing like a town with a secret. Doesn't sound like Sommerville has too many of those, though. Take *The Adventures of Huckleberry Finn*. Now, that was a town full of secrets."

Libby didn't look up, didn't even acknowledge that Amanda had spoken.

Amanda's painted on smile now held a touch of resignation and sadness. She had thought she was onto something, thought she'd sensed a spark in Libby. Now all she felt was more desolation and even guilt over trying to manipulate the woman into talking. Turning her gaze back to the quilt, she resumed stitching.

"I have read the Bible more than a dozen times," Libby piped up after some time. "I do not read the books you speak of. I like true stories about folks and their towns. Sommerville would make a great storybook."

Swallowing the welling optimism, Amanda girded herself for disappointment. Heaven only knew what the woman was referring to now. A strong possibility existed that this development would fizzle to another big zero.

"Why do you say that?" Amanda asked in a rush of words.

"It has the secrets you speak of."

"Secrets?" Swallowing hard, Amanda tried to keep her voice even. "What secrets?"

"Independence thrived in Sommerville. I do not know about the others, but that is why Milo and I relocated."

Uncontrollable elation surged through Amanda. "You have me intrigued, Mrs. Wickersham." Her voice rose an octave in her excitement. "What secrets does Sommerville have?"

The humming started again. Libby's capped head, with the sparse gray locks on both sides of the part, bobbed with the rhythm she'd set.

Though Amanda felt a strange sense of certainty that Libby Wickersham was the woman with the key to the treasure mystery, she clenched her jaw. She guessed that babbling and prodding would only serve to silence the woman. She'd have to wait for Libby to divulge the information on her own.

More minutes sped past, but Libby still did not utter another peep about the Sommerville secret she had referred to. Amanda's only consolation was in the fact that the woman had stopped the humming. She hoped that was a signal that Libby planned to talk again.

"Does that Finn book you spoke of have a robbery in it?" Libby asked at last.

"Yes, it does." Amanda's heart beat faster. "Grave robbers, actually. A young boy witnesses it."

Libby's eyes widened.

"But that's all fiction, taken from a man's imagination."

"It is not God's way to pass judgment," Libby said, leaning closer to Amanda, "but it was evil people, like in that book, who robbed the bank in Sommerville. I was a young girl of sorts, had just turned twenty-one. Like the tornado, I remember this incident clearly."

"What happened to the thieves?" Amanda asked, hoping she already knew the answer.

"They were never caught. The money was never recovered. Is that the way the Finn book ends?"

"No. No, the robbers were discovered."

"Sommerville's secret is still a secret." A faint light flickered in the depths of Libby's green eyes.

"Goodness. I had no idea. How long ago was this?" Amanda asked, holding her breath as she waited for Libby's answer.

For a long moment, Libby stared, impaling Amanda with her gaze. "It has been almost fifty years," she whispered at last. Blinking twice, she focused her gaze back on the material beneath her fingertips. The humming began again.

A smile spread across Amanda's face. Her spirits felt higher than the clouds in the sky. She glanced across at Mary who wore a very troubled expression. Purposely widening her eyes, Amanda nodded. Mary gaped, then finally a smile of understanding ruffled the corners of her mouth.

The rest of the afternoon flew by. The smell of sulfur filled Amanda's nostrils as Mrs. Miller lit the first oil lamp. Smoke spiraled up through the glass chimney, the orangy-yellow light casting distorted shadows across the quilt. Several women were done, and as Amanda took the last stitch in the double diamond she had been working on, Libby Wickersham revealed her great-grandmother's secret for making perfectly crimped piecrusts. Amanda smiled, for she felt the two of them had really hit it off. It seemed the elderly Amish woman had her own covert passion, secrets of all kinds.

Amanda breathed a silent prayer of thanks for Libby. Her information held the key to the treasure map. Josiah's dream would become a reality; Elam would have his legs. Amanda would see to that.

Two more women tied off their ends, and now only Mrs. Miller remained working. Her fingers and needle seemed to fly across the last bit of scallops on the outer edge of the top quilt. Even the poor lighting in the room didn't slow her stitching. It seemed like mere minutes passed before she took that last stitch, completing the quilt.

Amanda blinked with incredulity. The thread glittered against the dark fabrics like she imagined a real miner's riches would. Though she cherished the quilts from her mother, she knew she'd never seen a more regal one than this.

Mary had finished as well and after speaking to several of the women around her, she made her way to Amanda's side. "Amanda," she said, eyes dancing, "how did you get Libby to confide in you?"

"I think," Amanda replied, a flash of humor crossing her face, "we both share a zeal for mysteries and secrets."

"I am glad you are pleased. I hope the outcome is what you wish."

"Not what I wish," Amanda gently corrected, "what Josiah wants for Elam. This is for them, not me."

Smiling, Mary inclined her head toward Amanda's. "More secrets. The quilt and the treasure hunt is one that must be kept or trouble will be the result."

"Don't worry. The last thing I want is to make trouble. I'll keep mum."

"You are so full of goodness," Mary replied, squeezing Amanda's arm. "I must go to the springhouse and get supper ready. Mama and the elders will clean up. The boys will remove the frame."

Glancing to the window, Amanda knew she should take her leave. "I wish I could help you, but I should be going. I told my father I'd be home by dark."

Mary's face took on a stricken look. "You cannot go now, not by yourself. Mama," she called out, "Amanda wants to travel home now."

Mrs. Miller stopped her work at the quilt frame. "Can you not stay for supper? Josiah and Samuel will take you home afterward."

The panic returned. "Oh, no, really I shouldn't. I can't," Amanda squeaked. "I don't want to bother them, anyway. I know my way home."

Hands going to her hips in that motherly fashion Amanda was becoming used to, Mrs. Miller shook her head. "I do not like it. If you must go now, the boys will take you."

The buzzing in the room stopped. Amanda felt all gazes turn to her. She curled her toes in her high shoes. She didn't want to inconvenience any of the Millers, but by the look on Mrs. Miller's face, she knew she'd never be allowed to travel alone this time of day. But even more important, she didn't want to subject Josiah and Samuel to her father's suspicions or his sharp tongue. If she stayed a bit longer and joined the Millers for supper, there was the possibility that her father would be stretched out on the low-back sofa, like he usually was after dinner, snoozing. Then he'd never even see them. The problem would be solved. It was a big *if*, but the only hope she had that her father wouldn't cause an unpleasant scene.

"If you're sure it's not an imposition, I'll stay."

Mrs. Miller smiled and turned back to her work of removing the quilt from the frame.

"You can help me." Mary took Amanda's elbow again and led her outside.

The faint scent of woodsmoke danced through the air from one of the other houses whose owner already had a fire started. The dusky breeze blew through Amanda's hair like cool, invigorating fingers, caressing her scalp and skin.

"We must hurry," Mary said. "Papa and the boys will return from their work soon."

"What's this springhouse?"

"It is where we cool our food. It also has our summer kitchen. When the weather gets too hot, Mama and I do the cooking and the baking there so we do not heat up the main house. Since we quilted today, we will have a cold meal tonight. There will be ham and pickled eggs and beets. Papa loves Mama's tomato jelly so much that we usually have fresh bread with it every night. There are still stewed raisins and Mama's canned plums.''

Mary stopped abruptly, and Amanda nearly ran into her. ''I forgot the crates. I must go back to the house to get them so that we can carry the food. I will bring a lantern, too. The springhouse is just ahead.''

''What can I do to help?'' Amanda asked.

''I will only be a few minutes, then we can pull the ham and the crocks from the spring,'' Mary said over her shoulder as she dashed off.

''Well,'' Amanda sighed, ''I may just as well get things moving.'' She hurried to the clearing and, much to her dismay, saw two outbuildings. One was definitely larger than the other—large enough, in fact, that it looked similar to some of the smaller Amish houses. Amanda decided the smaller building located just behind the larger one had to be the springhouse Mary had spoken of.

As she approached the unlatched door that swayed gently in the breeze she heard a sloshing sound inside. ''Goodness,'' she muttered, ''I'll bet it's coons.'' Grabbing a small crooked stick from off the ground, Amanda ignored the voice in her head telling her to wait for Mary. Her palms grew clammy and she kept wiping them on her skirt. What harm could one small raccoon cause a person? The critter was probably after the ham and the other food the Millers planned to have for their dinner.

Reaching for the wooden door handle, she licked her dry lips. She hoped she had it in her to strike the small creature if need be. The sloshing sound started again. Raising the stick above her head, she slowly opened the door.

She froze at the sight in front of her, gaping in stunned silence. There was no raccoon in the springhouse. She wasn't even in the springhouse! She had entered some kind of bathhouse, and Josiah stood only several feet in front of her, stripped to the waist, washing his hair, face and upper body in the gurgling, fast-running water of the stream.

Her chest felt so heavy. She drew a labored breath, silently begging her feet to back her out the door. They just wouldn't listen. It was as if they had rooted to the ground.

Amanda watched helplessly as Josiah, by the glowing, cozy light of a lantern, rubbed soapy lather across the nape of his neck and back. His body glistened, the muscles bunching and then relaxing with his movements. Her heart throbbed, threatening at any moment to burst through her chest. She wavered, dropping the stick to the ground with a crack.

Josiah whirled around, lather flying. His homespun trousers were unfastened and hung low across his narrow hips, exposing a close-fitting undergarment. Amanda's gaze crept over every inch of his six-foot-plus frame, from the soapy whorls of hair on his chest to the dark, tapered line trailing a path down his belly and disappearing beneath the faded gray undergarment.

"*Ach,*" he groaned.

His silvery eyes were dark and hooded. Amanda didn't know what their look meant. She only knew she felt like a lump of ice setting out on a hot summer day. Her insides had melted and she couldn't seem to breathe normally, catching only short, quick puffs of air. She thought about apologizing for interrupting his bath, but she couldn't seem to make her mouth work. It was as if she was frozen in place.

The unlatched door flapped in the wind, producing a bizarre, arousing sort of rhythm. Josiah's gaze seemed locked to hers, consciously or unconsciously daring her to look away. She'd never seen a man so close to naked before, but there was no doubt in her mind that any others wouldn't have looked as perfect as him.

Droplets of water snaked down his collarbone, beseeching Amanda's gaze. She felt she was the loser, having looked away first, but the tightness and zealous stirring in her lower body strangely made her feel the winner.

A gust of wind crashed the door loudly into the frame, snapping Amanda from the reverie. She accepted it as her warning: if she didn't leave now both she and Josiah would be caught in a most compromising situation. Why did a lantern have to be lit? Things would have been much easier if she hadn't seen everything she had.

Drawing a deep, ragged breath, she fiddled with the folds in her skirt. "Um . . ." She swallowed hard, hoping something intelligent would quickly come to her foggy brain. "You missed a spot," rolled from her tongue before she could stop it. Josiah's eyebrows shot up in surprise, and she groaned inwardly, cursing herself with a few choice words she'd heard her father say.

"And where is this spot?" he asked in his teasing manner, but in a tone more throaty than she'd ever heard come from him before.

"Back there. . . ." She pointed to her own right shoulder blade, then felt foolish, for she doubted he could even see in the dim light. "It's . . . well . . . one of those spots that is just hard to get at. If I didn't have to take the ham and crocks from the spring for Mary, I'd probably be able to . . . to help you . . . reach it."

Good heavens! Where was all this gibberish coming from? The man was barely half-dressed, and she was offering to help wash his body. A flush heated her cheeks. Clearing her throat, she said, "Don't suppose there are crocks or hams down there in that water, are there?"

The edges of Josiah's mouth tipped in a lopsided grin. "Do you think you should check?"

Amanda backed toward the door, hands going out behind her, feeling for the escape. "No. No, I think I have the wrong outbuilding." She took another backward step, thankful she finally felt the doorjamb. "I'm such a loon. Food wouldn't be in the bathhouse. Just people . . . bathing would be."

Josiah slowly nodded his head, making no attempt to cover himself or to grab for the threadbare towel sitting on the old brick stove.

"Hope you get that spot," Amanda said, turning and plunging through the door to safety.

17

JOSIAH STARED AT THE spot where Amanda had stood, his body screaming for release. What was it about her that affected him so? *"Ach,"* he mumbled again, disgusted with himself for allowing her softness and curves and her innocent beguiling looks to drive him crazy. He groaned, his body irrationally responding to the light, flowery scent that still clung to the air.

Closing his eyes, he dropped his chin to his chest and circled his head around to left, then to the right. Every muscle in his body seemed tighter than an overwound spring. Every muscle. The drying soap itched. And that flowery scent—he couldn't get it, or her face, out of his mind. Dropping to his knees, he shoved his arms into the biting, swirling water. He splashed and rinsed himself until all traces of soap disappeared down the stream. It wasn't enough, though, to rinse English Amanda from his mind.

She haunted him and, in all honesty, had for quite some time. Shifting his weight, Josiah sat on the cool, damp ground. The wind filtered in through the cracks and crevices of the rustic outbuilding, but he didn't even notice the coldness against his wet skin. He thought only of Amanda.

Though he had been the one in the vulnerable position, and was stunned at first when he'd turned and seen her staring, he had done nothing befitting a gentleman. When her gaze had run slowly over every clothed and unclothed portion of his body like hot, searching fingers, his body overruled his mind and reacted to her like he'd never reacted to another woman before in his life. Just the bittersweet memories caused Josiah's manhood to rear shamefully again. He loathed the lack of control over his body. He didn't know how it happened, or when, but Amanda now seemed to have the control. With a guttural cry, he lunged and plopped himself in the icy water, boots and all.

As he sat there, his passion shriveling, a bit of humor shined through. Amanda's spirited humor. Grinning, he remembered the patch of dirt she had said he missed. He wondered if he had gotten it, or if it had ever even been there to begin with.

Suddenly the grin disappeared. What was Amanda doing at his house?

Josiah jumped to his feet and shook his wet head, water flying about the room. He fastened his trousers and snatched his dirty shirt and hat from the ground. Shoving his hat onto his head and his wet hands through the shirtsleeves, he grabbed the small towel off the stove and darted from the bathhouse.

He could barely see the springhouse, the trees and the hills almost completely nestling the descending sun. Purple and black shadows danced across the land. His father and brothers would be coming to wash soon. And Mary. Where was Mary? He needed to hurry so he could talk to Amanda alone. When he found her, he just hoped the apology came out the way he intended.

Before he even opened the door of the other outbuilding, he smelled her. The fresh, flowery scent teased his senses. His mouth crimped in annoyance. He needed to apologize, and he needed to do it without tripping over his own tongue. His brows knitted with determination as he pushed open the door.

Josiah heard Amanda's little gasp of surprise, or perhaps

it was alarm. The absence of windows in the springhouse made the interior very dark on spring nights like this, but the construction helped to keep the foods cool enough to retard spoilage in the summer months. He wished now he had grabbed the lantern.

"Mary?" Amanda quavered.

Josiah pulled tightly with both hands on the ends of the towel draped around his neck. How did a man apologize for not having the decency to cover himself in front of a woman?

"Who—Who's there?" Her voice sounded even more shrill. Here he was, fumbling for words, scaring the wits from her.

"It is Josiah," he said quickly.

Silence encompassed the room. He heard the faint swish of material as Amanda moved about somewhere in the obscurity.

"Don't tell me you got lost, too. I think your house is in the other direction."

The wariness in her voice had dissolved, and he thought he noticed a bit of humor. It warmed his soul. "I did not get lost. I came to apologize," he said with quiet emphasis.

"Apologize? For what?" She sounded surprised.

"I did not . . ." His body stiffened. He didn't know if he could even say the words. How could he apologize for something when he realized he'd do it the same all over again?

"Let me guess. You didn't wash behind your ears." She clucked her tongue. "Things could be worse. Take me, for instance, I walked in on a man bathing. And not even a relation. *That*, I believe, is what my mother would call scandalous and would definitely classify as needing an apology. Leave it to me to cause a scandal."

Amanda's chatter revealed her embarrassment and discomposure. Josiah's heart dove to his toes. He was the one who had acted without honor. "You do not—"

"Wait!" she interrupted, her voice sounding closer to Josiah than before. "Please, just let me say this. I'm sorry I walked in on you like that and didn't leave. I . . . I'm truly sorry. Tell Mary and your mother thank you for the wonderful afternoon, but I think I need to leave now.''

Josiah felt her more than saw her at his side. He reflexively reached toward her voice. "No," he said, grabbing her arm and swinging her around to stand in front of him. "You do not need to apologize. It is I who must." He felt the softness of her arms through her dress. She felt so warm beneath his cold fingers. He didn't want to let go, afraid she'd run. He breathed deeply, allowing himself the pleasure of her scent.

"I did not act like a gentleman. For that I am sorry."

"And how would a gentleman have acted?" she asked breathlessly.

A new surge of desire pumped through Josiah's body. Amanda had moved closer. But the door was in that direction. No matter. She was so close he could feel the heat from her body. He wanted to kiss her, taste her again like he had yesterday in the barn. Is that what she wanted? He didn't know, but wanted to find out.

Lowering his head toward hers, he whispered, "A gentleman would have covered certain areas." The words sounded insinuating. He realized he'd meant them to. What was he doing? Amanda Glosser was English! Was he so weak that he couldn't resist the slightest temptation?

"Amanda!" Mary called from outside. "Please open the door. My arms are full."

Josiah released his hold on Amanda and pulled open the door for his sister. Lantern light jumped into the structure as Mary entered. It cast eerie images against the timbered walls, distorting the features on each of their faces.

Amanda's was unreadable.

"Josiah, I didn't know you were out here." Mary smiled. "I am glad, though, because you can take this," she said, holding the lantern out as far as she dared without dropping the two wooden crates she held. "Then these, and then you can carry food in."

Josiah sloshed toward her, taking the lantern and a crate from her arms, puddling water as he went.

"Why are your clothes soaking?" Mary asked, her brows pleating in a deep frown. "Did you fall into the stream?"

The air in the small building seemed to thicken. Thankful for the dim lighting, Josiah only hoped it was dim enough so neither his sister nor Amanda saw the stain of embarrassment on his cheeks. He glanced back toward Amanda and saw a faint, clandestine smile curling her lips, fueling something deep inside him.

"You might say I was pushed into it. Is that not right, Amanda?"

"Ye—yes," Amanda replied, her smile fading. She turned her gaze to Mary. "I'm sorry, but I never did get the ham or crocks pulled like you asked."

"I will get them." Josiah ambled to the trough built into the stream, seized first the two bobbing yellow crocks and then the wrapped meat. He put the food in the crates Mary had brought and hefted both into his arms. "Take the lantern, Mary, and we shall go to the house and eat."

Josiah trudged in silence behind the two women. He tried to keep his gaze in front of them, focusing on the lantern swinging in Mary's hand instead of on Amanda's shapely, moonlit outline.

From what he could gather of their conversation, Amanda had come to quilt. He told himself in another hour supper would be over and the temptation gone. He could make it through that hour. After all, his parents and brothers and sisters would all be there. It wasn't as if he and Amanda would be alone like that again. Ever again. He'd make sure of that.

He changed his trousers and wiggled his feet back into his wet boots. Dinner would be quick and harmless, then Amanda would leave.

He couldn't have been more wrong. Dinner dragged. Josiah tried to listen to his father's ideas about repairing the one broken plow, but he couldn't concentrate. His gaze and thoughts stayed with Amanda. All of the children, and even, surprisingly, his mother, seemed fascinated with her and the funny stories she told of her traveling as a child across the Midwest in her father's peddler wagon. Amanda was enchanting, and he felt himself sinking, drowning under her worldly charms.

When a lull descended upon the discussion of the recipe

for pickled eggs, Josiah took advantage. Sliding his chair
back from the end of the table, he stood. "If you will excuse me now," he said more to his father than anyone else,
"I will go bed the animals."

"How long will you be?" his mother asked.

"I do not know." He shoved his hands into his pockets.
"Why?" he asked, suddenly reluctant to hear her response.

"You or Samuel need to take Amanda to her home. I
am sure her father is worried by now."

Josiah gritted his teeth. This couldn't be happening. Not
now—it was too soon, the memories still too vivid. He'd
let Samuel take her home. That was the only safe thing to
do. He glanced to his simpleminded, seventeen-year-old
brother who sat spearing stewed raisins with his fork. Samuel had been to town only twice that Josiah remembered,
and their father had worked the horses that time. It wouldn't
be safe for either Samuel or Amanda.

Wondering about his mother's motive, Josiah guessed
she had never had any intention of allowing Amanda to go
with his brother, but more likely had been baiting him,
knowing he'd step in and do the right thing. His gaze fell
to Amanda who now silently stared at her plate. "I will
take her," he said through his clenched teeth, "after I've
finished in the barn."

"You will take her when she is ready," his father replied
matter-of-factly. "Samuel and I will finish in the barn."

"This is ridiculous." Amanda scooted off the bench and
away from the table. "I don't want to put any of you out.
I know my way home."

Her eyes were wide with that deceptive look of inno-
cence Josiah now recognized. He regarded her quizzically,
knowing what a chore the trip to her home would be. Did
she not realize what she did to him? He suspected she
knew, and that made him feel all the more vulnerable.
"Perhaps you should not have stayed so long," he said,
not able to keep the edge of impatience from his voice.

"Perhaps you're right." Amanda's hands came to her
hips in a defensive sort of way. "Believe me, I had no
intention whatsoever of bothering you."

"But you quilt," Josiah retorted, pointing a finger at her.

"Surely you must know the hours put in to finishing one. How could you not?" A scarlet flush washed over Amanda's face, and Josiah steeled himself.

"Josiah!" Mr. Miller said sharply. " 'Judge not, and ye shall not be judged.' The matter is settled. You will take our guest home when she is ready."

Josiah knew he had been impolite, but he couldn't believe what was happening. He was going to end up alone with Amanda again. And it wouldn't be for only a few minutes this time. He wasn't angry with her, though he knew the brief interrogation—at least before his father stopped him—made him sound like he was. The simple fact was that he just didn't trust himself around her.

Bowing his head slightly, he said, "I am sorry for my rudeness. Whenever you are ready to go, I will be in the barn."

"I want to help here in the kitchen first—"

"That is all right, Amanda," Mary said. "Go now before it gets even later and your father is more worried. I want you to be able to come back. If he is angry, he may not allow it."

"Well," Amanda hedged, "only if you're sure."

Mrs. Miller nodded.

"Thank you again for supper and for everything. I had a wonderful time. Mary," Amanda smiled, "I'll talk to you soon. Thanks." She looked to Josiah, all expression gone from her face. "I'm ready whenever you are."

Hoping the air would serve to clear his head, Josiah hurried to the door. He yanked his patched work coat from the peg on the wall, picked up a lantern and swung open the door for Amanda. She breezed by him without a glance, back stiff and straight.

"Did you not bring a coat?" he asked, closing the door, gliding into step beside her.

"What do you care?" She was all businesslike as she headed for her buggy.

"Spring nights are cold. If you did not, you can take one of mine."

Amanda stopped walking and cast Josiah a sidelong glance. "I do have a coat; and even if I didn't, right now

I think I'd rather freeze than take anything of yours." Her chin jutted out in defiance.

Josiah grinned; Amanda glared. He didn't want to patronize her, but he couldn't stop himself from smiling. His heart thundered in his chest. He wanted to get control of his emotions, but there was just something about her that was so different from the Amish women he knew. She had this fire, this passion he was inexplicably drawn to. "Where is this coat of yours?" he asked as they came to the wagon.

Without waiting for his help, Amanda raised her skirt and climbed aboard. "It's right here beside my quilt," she said, picking up her coat and slipping it on. She rolled her eyes and shook her head. "Thankfully I didn't leave it at that bathhouse."

Adjusting her bustle, Amanda settled down on the wooden seat. Josiah's gaze seemed to have a mind of its own, for it followed her hands as they traveled across the tops and sides of her thighs, smoothing her skirt.

"So, Mr. Miller," she said brightly, "tell me, how do we do this? You take me home, and then you ride back on my father's horse, keeping it as payment?"

Was that a smile that played about the corners of Amanda's mouth? Josiah couldn't tell, but he sensed her lighthearted humor had returned. It filled him with apprehension. He knew he needed to distance himself now or be captured.

Looking toward the other Amish houses, wishing he were anyplace but here with Amanda, he said curtly, "I would not keep your horse. I will take Cinnamon along to ride back on."

"Oh, I see," she said, playfully. "You've done this sort of thing before with other ladies."

"No, I have not. Have you?" The accusatory tone had crept back into his voice, and Amanda frowned. Josiah didn't really expect an answer, didn't even know why he'd said that, other than possibly to get her irritated enough to stop talking. If she stopped talking, stopped the playful teasing, he thought he'd be able to get her home without incidence.

He swallowed hard, hoping she couldn't see the bob of

his Adam's apple, which revealed how constricted and dry his throat had become. Amanda's gaze bored into his. He felt it chipping holes into his facade of unaffectedness. He had already given too much. He stared back blankly, grasping for the determination not to care about her.

Amanda's eyes narrowed speculatively, then she shook her head again, as if tired of defending herself. "Guess you better go get your horse." She tossed her hair over her shoulder, sending waves of fragrance in his direction, then pretended to pick at something on the seat next to her.

Josiah tossed his coat to the seat of the buggy and sprinted to the barn. Samuel and his father weren't there yet, and for that, he was thankful. He did not want to talk to anyone. He especially did not want to discuss Amanda, and he figured any conversation with his family at this point would include her.

He entered the barn, his still-wet boots squishing slightly, but at the same time crunching the pieces of straw that had blown in from the barnyard or out from the stalls and landed in his path. Though it was dark, he knew his way around the interior of the structure like a mole in its underground home. For the moment Amanda's fresh scent left him, replaced by barnyard odors. He focused on the smell of wet straw—rotting straw, actually, because his family didn't have the room to store it all. He didn't think he'd find such things at Amanda's home.

He spoke softly as he approached Cinnamon. The horse nuzzled his shoulder and his neck, searching for a treat like she always did. Grabbing the worn harness, Josiah stroked the velvety nose of his four-legged friend. "No treats tonight," he whispered, "only temptation."

As he strode back toward the buckboard, the moon now generously lighting his way, he noticed the settlement had quickly stilled. Only a few friends remained outside, finishing up whatever it was that needed doing. Though the night and the moon were breathtaking, something to be shared and enjoyed, Josiah knew very few would see it. The awakening hour came early, and with it a full day's work.

He sometimes felt like the simple pleasures in life passed

him by. He never told anyone those feelings because no
one else ever seemed to have them. Not his father and not
even Elam, who was still recovering from the accident. The
feelings were selfish and wrong, and ignoring them was the
best thing. His life would be lived to help his brother. Josiah
wondered what Amanda would think of it all, the four
o'clock milkings, or the shoveling of manure that smelled
so bad at times he thought he would vomit if he didn't
catch a breath of fresh air.

He stopped walking momentarily, the buggy only a few
yards ahead. Amanda sat straight and proud, like a princess,
gazing heavenward, studying the stars. The differences in
their cultures grew before his very eyes.

English and Amish could not mix.

His horse nickered, breaking the silence.

"You took so long, I thought maybe you were bathing
again." Amanda glanced at him from over her shoulder, a
smile framing her face when she spotted Cinnamon. "Oh,"
she sighed, "she's even more beautiful by moonlight."

Nodding slightly to acknowledge her compliment, Josiah
tied the sorrel to the back of the buckboard.

"I suppose *beautiful* isn't a proper enough word to de-
scribe a horse, but to me that's what she is." Folding her
hands in her lap, she smiled. "You know we have that
stable behind the store. Actually," Amanda twisted in her
seat, her gaze again capturing Josiah's, "it's not really ours.
My father owns the building, and Leon—you know Leon—
he rents the space and owns all of the horses. My father
loves horses. He'd be smitten with Cinnamon."

Josiah said nothing as he climbed aboard. He took the
seat next to her, braced the lantern between his feet and
prodded her horse to movement.

The wagon bounced along, Amanda's thigh occasionally
bumping into his, unintentionally scorching his flesh. She
didn't even seem to notice. He wished the seat were larger,
wished she'd cover her legs with the old quilt that sat on
the seat beside her. Since all the wishing in the world
couldn't make it happen, he instead concentrated on the
sizzling noise coming from the lantern and the rhythmic

cadence of the horses' hooves. He thanked the Lord that Amanda kept quiet. He wanted the deed done, wanted to be home with his family where it was a bit easier to remember things like humility and sacred trusts.

An owl hooted from its hidden lookout along the trail.

"It's Josiah Miller and Amanda Glosser," Amanda whispered into the night. "May we travel your road?" She laughed. "Don't suppose you do anything loony like talking to wild creatures of the night, do you?"

Josiah felt her gaze on his face, felt his chest tighten so much he thought he'd smother.

" 'Course you don't," she said, shifting on the seat so that she could cross her legs. "That would be fun. I don't think you like having fun. How many smiles a day do you limit yourself to, anyway?"

Would she ever stop? Though he kept his head straight, out of the corner of his eye he saw the foot of her crossed leg dangling, her slender ankle showing as her skirt swished along with the up and down movement she was making.

"I think I counted four smiles on you today in just the short time we were together. And that last one—where you were teasing me about borrowing your coat—you did that all by yourself. I understand if you've reached some kind of quota, but you don't have to smile to be polite. Truly you don't. Take my father. He seldom smiles. Grimacing is more his thing, especially when it comes to me and my antics. But you know, with customers, most of the time his manners are impeccable."

Amanda sighed dramatically, and before Josiah could stop it, a smile stretched across his face. Remembering himself, he tightened his lips and the smile vanished. Still staring straight ahead, he retorted, "I do not believe I have seen that side of your father."

She seemed taken aback for a moment, for the chatter stopped. Then she gasped, startling him. "Oh, no, another smile! Now tomorrow your family will only get three!"

Finally he looked at her. She was laughing, eyes twinkling with spirit, daring him to join in. His smile returned and broadened until he thought his face would split.

"You," he said, cocking his head toward her, "are more playful than Sarah."

"It doesn't hurt to play sometimes. I'm always telling my father that. And you're right. He wasn't the best example of a polite person."

Licking her lips, Amanda pushed back several wayward locks of hair to rejoin the wealth of it flowing down her back. When she bent her leg slightly and turned even more in her seat to face him, Josiah felt helpless to look away.

"Josiah." She grinned and her brows arched mischievously. "I know I said I'd never bring this up to you again unless you asked, but I have to. I am so excited." Nudging him, she giggled. "You won't believe what I found out today. You just won't believe it. And now that you're chipper again, I want you to guess. Please."

Amanda grabbed Josiah's arm. The heat from her fingers scorched his skin and sent ripple upon ripple of desire through his body. If it was possible for a person to effervesce, she was doing it. The strength of her emotion was contagious, her eyes wide and imploring. He found himself falling deeply under her spell. "What did you discover?" he heard himself asking.

"Ta-da!" Snatching the quilt, she snapped it into the air, freeing it from the confining folds. "Elam's salvation," she sang happily.

It was hard to remain coherent so close to her. Jerking his head taut in the hope of clearing it, Josiah blinked. "Elam's salvation? What?"

"Treasure. There is a treasure. Libby Wickersham told me so. I know what you're thinking, but . . . Heavens!" Amanda screamed. "Josiah!"

18

JOSIAH HAD SEEN THE look of horror on Amanda's face a split second before her shrill screams had ripped through the night. His head snapped back toward the trail just as the doe darted into the path of the buckboard. The hackney whinnied as the deer collided with it. There was a ghastly thud and the snapping of bone as the wood and merciless iron wheels of the wagon took control.

The frenzied horse reared. The wagon lurched even more sharply as the helpless doe was dragged beneath it. Amanda catapulted against Josiah, and the edge of the old quilt dipped into the flames from the lantern still squeezed between his boots.

She cried out and he dropped the reins, grabbing frantically for his coat. Slapping at the flames, again and again, all the while trying to hold onto Amanda, Josiah prayed. Accepting God's will was supposed to be the Amish way, but as with Elam's accident, he knew he would not be able to accept something happening to her because of him.

Much to Josiah's surprise, he extinguished the fire quickly, but the crazed horse reared a second time. The reins were nowhere to be found, and the buckboard pitched, out of control, like a tiny ship tossed on a stormy sea. The wood seemed alive, cracking and groaning in protest as it tipped. His only thought was Amanda's safety. Yanking her into his arms, he jumped.

∽

JOSIAH'S HEAD ACHED LIKE an axe had been buried in the base of his skull. He could hardly breathe. He just wanted to go back to sleep. All was quiet except for the familiar nickering of Cinnamon and an odd thrashing sound. Something forced his eyes open. He saw that Amanda lay half sprawled on top of him, her beautiful face, only inches from his, now pale and lifeless. His brain seemed numb. Why . . . Why was she . . .

The accident and the fire flooded his memory. He gently nudged Amanda's shoulder, fearful his living nightmare had become a reality. When she moaned and stirred slightly, he released the breath he hadn't even been aware of holding.

"Amanda," he called out softly. "Amanda, are you all right? Please, talk to me."

She moved off him, groaning some more. Suddenly her eyes opened. They fluttered as she focused on Josiah's face. "You're not smiling," she said weakly. "Are we dead?"

Emotion welled inside Josiah. Reaching out, he tenderly drew her into his embrace. "No, thank the Lord, you are not. Are you all right?"

"Oh! The horses! And that poor deer." She pushed from his arms and together they helped each other up.

Amanda froze, then Josiah saw what she saw, the light of the moon making the horrible scene before them even worse. The hackney fought, valiantly trying to stand on what appeared to be his crushed hindquarters, the broken buckboard holding him, making his struggle all the more painful. Cinnamon, miraculously unscathed, stood grazing nearby, the worn leather reins that had attached him to the back of the buckboard having apparently snapped from the bit at some point during the accident. The innocent, mangled doe lay a few yards back. Dead.

"No!" Amanda cried, slapping her hand to her mouth. "Goodwin! Oh, dear, Goodwin!" She ran to the hackney and began pulling pieces of the damaged buckboard off the horse.

Josiah hurried after her. "Amanda, it is no use. He is suffering. We must—"

"Stop! Jus—just stop it. Help. Help me get this off him."

Ignoring the throbbing of his head and the pain in his back, Josiah went to work, futilely freeing the horse of the debris.

Amanda dropped to her knees and lovingly stroked the animal's forelock. She wiped the flecks of blood around the muzzle with her skirt. "You're going to be all right, Goodwin. You're going to make it, baby."

Kneeling beside her, Josiah draped his arm around her shoulder. "He suffers, Amanda. It is time to end his misery."

Shrugging off his arm, she stiffened. "No. I can't."

"Yes, you can. You must not think of yourself. Think of the animal."

"That's easy for you," she said, sniffing, running the back of her hand across her nose. "Cinnamon's right there. Unhurt. This is my father's. He loves this horse. I can't just . . . just kill it."

The hackney labored for breath. More blood oozed from the flaring nostrils. Amanda wiped it away again as tears poured down her face.

"Do you believe in God?" Josiah asked softly.

"Yes," she retorted through her gnashed teeth, "but I can't do it."

"I will do it for you. 'Faith is the substance of things hoped for, the evidence of things not seen.' I am sorry this happened."

Pushing to his feet, Josiah pulled Amanda up beside him. He gazed at her tear-streaked face, feeling that same guilt he'd felt after Elam's accident. "Lead Cinnamon down the trail around the next bend. I will not be long."

He stood there, watching her dodder down the path, fading slowly from his view. It took only a moment to find a large fieldstone. He'd never had to do anything like this before. The bile rose in his throat as he ended the horse's suffering.

Though he had done the right thing, it didn't make him feel any better. He wiped his hands on his thighs, wishing he could scrub them with soap and water, but knowing even that wouldn't wash away the feelings he had.

Pushing all thoughts from his mind, he headed down the trail after Amanda. He found her sitting on a stump, staring blankly into space. "Are you hurt?" His stomach knotted at the possibility.

"No. I'll be fine."

"Are you sure?"

"Yes. Truly."

"I am sorry this happened. I will bury your father's horse tomorrow when there is light."

"And we have a shovel." Amanda raked her top teeth across her bottom lip with a big sigh. "It's sad, but it was an accident. You don't have to feel sorry, you know. It wasn't anyone's fault." She gazed up at him, an earnest expression on her face that made Josiah feel uncomfortable. "You saved me. I would have either caught fire— Oh!" Her hands flew back to her mouth. "My quilt. Where's the quilt? We have to go back. Josiah, we need that quilt to get the treasure for Elam."

"Do not worry about that quilt. There is no treasure," he said through gritted teeth.

"There is, I tell you." Jumping to her feet, Amanda shot Josiah a withering glare. "I'm going back to get that quilt. I don't care that you don't believe me. I know what I know." Planting her hands on her hips, she stalked back in the direction from which they'd come.

Throwing his hands into the air, Josiah frowned in exasperation. "Amanda! Amanda, wait."

She continued to walk, and he ran after her. Grabbing her arm, he stopped her and turned her around to face him. "You are the most stubborn woman I have ever met."

Her wild sapphire eyes mellowed slightly in the moonlight. "Thank you. Now let me go."

"I will get the quilt. You will wait here."

"Orders?" Amanda rocked back on her heels. "I don't take well to orders."

"I do not want to subject you to what is left at the buckboard. Please, wait here with Cinnamon."

Her eyebrows flickered a little, as if she was contemplating what he'd said. "All right." Turning, she walked with stiff dignity back toward the grazing Cinnamon.

Though he felt like a child, Josiah couldn't stop the lump that formed in his throat when he came back upon the dead animals. Swallowing hard, he dipped his head to avoid the continuous vision of death. He searched through the wreckage for the quilt, wanting only to be away from the scene. He finally found his jacket, and underneath it, the coverlet. Quickly he tugged both free and started back on his way. The clouds seemed to have cleared an even larger path for the moon, and for that he was thankful. The night with its chaos was already far too dark.

AMANDA CLASPED AND UNCLASPED her hands as she waited for Josiah. "It has to be all right," she said, pacing beside the horse. "Oh, Cinnamon, my quilt can't be ruined."

The pacing continued until she heard the snapping of twigs and underbrush. Her lips formed a mute O when she saw Josiah with the quilt hanging over his arm. Heart soaring, she ran to him.

"Thank goodness. Oh, thank goodness. Let me see," she said, grabbing it from Josiah's arm. Holding the corners, she snapped it high into the air. It fluttered, then landed on the dewy ground like a weary butterfly. Ignoring the aches already possessing her body, Amanda arranged her now-deformed bustle and dropped to her knees on the old coverlet.

Muscle quivering at her jaw, her gaze darted nervously back and forth across the quilt. She blinked, suddenly feeling giddy. "Josiah." He stood directly at her side. "Josiah, look," she whispered, reaching, stretching for his arm.

He sank to the ground beside her, and she returned her

gaze to the quilt. "We're lucky," she said, closing her hand over his, smiling when he didn't flinch. "It's here. It's all still here." She squeezed gently. "Only a small portion of the crooked place burnt. But that's fine. We don't need it. I was so scared it would all be gone."

Amanda turned toward Josiah, wanting him to understand the importance of the quilt. His handsome face was reserved and somber, but an almost hopeful glint shone in his silvery eyes. Her heart tripped over itself. She still held his hand, reveled in its strength, loved the way his flesh felt beneath her fingertips. Taking a deep breath, she ran the tip of her tongue across her dry lips. She wished she was brave enough to lean closer and kiss him again. A flush crept across her cheeks at the thought. She wanted to, but didn't know if it was what he wanted.

Clearing her throat, Amanda let go of his hand. "When do we leave? Once we get to Sommerville and find the property your grandmother grew up on, we can find the treasure. The sooner we go, the sooner Elam gets his leg."

Josiah's eyes changed right before her own. An unspoken pain was alive and burning in them. It confused her. "What's the matter?"

"Do you not understand?" His voice sounded strained. "Treasures are in storybooks. Treasures are not—"

"You weren't there. I talked to Ruthann Keim and Libby Wickersham. They grew up with your grandmother Fanny. Every spot stitched on this quilt is a place in Sommerville. They told me."

Flat, passionless orbs bored into her. "It is nonsense, I tell you. I cannot waste my time on stories fabricated at a quilting bee. Hidden wealth does not exist."

Amanda felt her cheeks color again. Squaring her shoulders, she raised an eyebrow in amused contempt. "There was a robbery almost fifty years ago in Sommerville. About the same time that Fanny made this quilt. Libby Wickersham told me the gold was never recovered. I know where it is. If you're smart, you'll accept what's hitting you over the head."

Josiah's face creased into a sudden smile, which instantly

softened his features. "If *I* am being struck, then you are already unconscious. We must go now."

He pushed himself to a standing position and his powerful hands yanked Amanda to her feet. A clean, musky scent wafted from him and hovered around her, muddling her senses. She had to remind herself of her stand in the odd situation. "What did that comment mean?"

"You are forgetting one important piece of this treasure puzzle. How would my grandmama have gotten this gold?" Josiah stuffed his hands into his pockets, staring at Amanda. "I will never believe she was the robber. That is what your theory suggests. It is time to go."

Amanda felt her embarrassment deepen to shame. She had thought about the implications. She curled and uncurled her toes in her high shoes, cursing herself for not realizing how profoundly this would affect Josiah. Maybe she had been thoughtless on that account. She didn't believe Fanny had been the thief, either, but maybe more the witness, the innocent party in it all.

Picking the damp quilt up from the ground, Amanda tucked her thoughts away. By the time she reached Josiah and Cinnamon, she knew what she would do.

"So," she said, affectionately slapping the horse's hindquarters, "who gets to ride Cinnamon?"

"You do, of course," Josiah answered. He led the sorrel to a clear spot on the trail, steepled his fingers and then turned his palms up, inviting Amanda to mount.

"Oh, goodness," Amanda said, making a theatrical gesture, "my carriage awaits me." She stepped onto his hand and up to the horse's back.

An amicable silence enveloped them as they started back down the road. To save time, they bypassed Prosper and cut through a small woodland. The denseness of the spruce and pines allowed only scant amounts of light to filter in, but Josiah carefully picked their way through the underbrush, as if he had some uncanny nocturnal ability. Having nothing beneath her except the horse's bare back was something Amanda hadn't experienced in years. Though she felt a mite uncomfortable, she didn't complain. In fact, she breathed deeply, loving the pine scent and the serenity that surrounded them. Even the occasional pair of glowing eyes that seemed to be following them didn't bother her. She felt safe with Josiah. It was as if the entire world had gone away and all that remained was them. She loved the feeling.

All too soon, they made it through the forest and to the clearing. In less than a quarter of an hour she'd be home. Amanda ran her fingers over the quilt draped across Cinnamon's neck, wishing she could go anywhere but where her father was. She wasn't looking forward to telling him all that had happened.

"Thanks for the ride," she said, breaking the silence with her thready-sounding voice. "You can let me off here. It's not much farther."

"I will take you to your door and explain to your father about your lateness and the accident."

"No. Oh, no, you don't have to do that. This spot here is fine."

As if he hadn't even heard her, Josiah kept walking.

"Excuse me," she said more loudly. "I said to stop."

Still, he continued on. Amanda felt a sudden pang of anxiety in her belly. Her father was going to be furious about the time, there would be no getting around that, but when he found out about Goodwin and the buckboard . . . Her stomach knotted, and she fiddled with the edge of the quilt. He'd never listen to reason, especially if the explanation came from Josiah. An icy shiver traveled the length of her spine. Her father would think he had a reason for more hate. She couldn't let Josiah take her all the way to the house. She just couldn't, but how did one go about stopping an apparently stubborn Amishman?

"Josiah Miller, have you suddenly gone deaf? This isn't funny. I want you to stop this horse, or I'll jump. Truly, I will."

Josiah cast her a sidelong glance. "Jump if you must."

Amanda wrinkled her nose. "If I jump, I'll get hurt."

"Then do not jump."

"You don't understand," she said, her voice growing more shrill. "I have to be the one to explain everything that happened. It'd be best if you weren't there."

"I feel the need to explain the accident to your father as well."

"No, you don't have to. I will."

One of Josiah's shoulders rose in an indolent shrug. "We will do it together."

"Please, Josiah, just stop for a minute." Much to her surprise, he listened.

"What is it I do not understand?"

"My father!" Wringing her hands, Amanda searched for the words to make him understand without hurting his feelings. "My father's this ... proud man. He ... he hides everything inside, or hides behind it. He's bitter and angry. He's been that way ever since my mother died. He thinks ..." She let her voice trail off, knowing there was no way to spare Josiah the truth and be fair at the same time. "He believes my mother contracted cholera at your Amish settlement. She was helping deliver a baby there." Swallowing hard, Amanda dug her nails into her palms. "It was one of those things, like tonight, but he's always been one to place blame." Exhaling with a whoosh, she said in a hushed voice, "Now you understand."

Nodding, Josiah made a clicking noise with his tongue and prodded the horse forward.

"Wait! What are you doing?"

"You can walk if you wish, but I am still going to the house. You may as well ride."

"But you just said you understood."

"That is right. I understand now why it is especially important that I explain to your father."

"Oh, wonderful. You're making a huge mistake." She wished Josiah would turn and look at her. He didn't. All she saw was his back, broad shoulders set straight and head held high. He exuded confidence, and oh, how she needed some of that right now.

The house loomed ahead. As they approached it, she half expected gunshots to whiz through the air. The hour was late. Amanda knew all her father would focus on was Josiah's dark clothing and his intimidating, almost threatening form.

They were almost at the porch. Amanda couldn't see it,

but from somewhere nearby a rifle cocked. "Papa!" Beads
of perspiration broke out along her hairline. "Papa, don't
shoot. It's me!"

"Amanda?"

His voice came from the clump of birches shadowed by
the house. She couldn't see him, but she heard his relief.

"Who in blazes . . . Miller." Newlin lurked out from behind the shadows, the rifle poised at Josiah. "What in tarnation are you doin' with my daughter?"

Josiah stopped the horse and Amanda gulped, feeling her
stomach contract into an even tighter ball. She wanted—
needed—to be the one to explain to her father why Josiah
was with her. Reaching for the quilt, she slid from the
horse's back, stumbling as she landed.

"Josiah," she pleaded, grabbing his arm, "let me talk
first."

"Jiminy." Newlin growled. "First it's his given name,
and now you're touchin' him. What's goin' on?"

"Calm down, Papa. We should all go into the house so
we can talk civilly, and you can put that rifle away."

"Civilly? Hell, no! Do you know what time it is? Do
you? Where the dickens you been? Didn't you think I might
be worried? Where's the buckboard? And Goodwin? Leon
said Rogers harnessed Goodwin for you. Blast that Rogers.
He should've never got that wagon ready without checking
with me or Leon first."

"There was an accident, Mr. Glosser," Josiah said
calmly. "A deer ran into the path of the wagon. Your horse
was hurt badly. I ended his suffering."

"You what? You killed my hackney? You killed Goodwin?"

"Papa." Amanda rushed to him and tried to pull the rifle
from its ready position. He elbowed her away, eyes bulging
from their sockets.

"I want you," he said to Amanda, though his gaze was
pinned on Josiah through the rifle's sight, "to tell me what
in the devil happened today. And don't you be leavin'
nothin' out."

"No," Amanda said through clamped teeth. "I won't do
that until you put that gun down." She matched the glare

her father turned on her with one of her own. She knew he was an ornery, unreasonable cuss, but he wasn't a murderer.

"Mr. Glosser, Amanda—"

"Josiah, be quiet. This is between my father and me. Not you," she said in a softer tone. "Papa, what's it going to be? Can't we please go in the house and talk like rational people?"

Newlin scowled and lowered the rifle. "I ain't puttin' it away yet." Turning his back on Amanda and Josiah, he stalked into the house.

Josiah stepped toward her. "This is not—"

"Stop." Amanda waved an arm, quilt swinging, as though warding off a flock of swooping birds. "I know you probably have some truly wonderful biblical saying that fits this instance, but right now I don't want to hear it. My father is not like your father. This family, *my* family, is not a thing like yours. Let me handle this."

She stormed after her father, a corner of the quilt tracing a path in the dirt as she walked. "Just tether your horse on one of the trees," she called over her shoulder.

She found her father in the sitting room, perched on the edge of the navy-blue upholstered, balloon-back chair, chest puffed out and back rigid as if it were attached to a pole like that of a scarecrow. An inappropriate giggle welled inside of her and she quickly squashed it. There was nothing funny about this situation. The rifle still lay across his lap, his index finger still crooked around the trigger.

"Where's the Amishman? The spawn of murders. That's how I think of him. Dressed all in black like they do, because they cause death."

Taking a deep breath, Amanda counted to ten. "This isn't about Josiah and his being Amish. This is about me. You're angry with me, so don't take it out on him."

The front door Amanda had left open clicked closed. "Josiah," she called out, collapsing onto the low-backed sofa, the quilt in her lap, "we're in here."

Josiah entered the sitting room, seeming to fill the entire doorway, his black hat in his hands. Amanda saw her father straighten in his chair even more, and she felt a pang of sympathy for him. He was such a bitter, unhappy man.

Though furious with him right now, she couldn't stop her heart from aching for him. He wouldn't use the gun—she felt certain of it—but she guessed that having it made him feel in control.

"Sit down, Josiah," Amanda said softly.

He didn't sit next to her as she had hoped. Instead, he chose the spindle-backed rocker opposite her father. And like her father, Josiah sat on the edge of the seat, but in contrast, had rested his hat on his knee and folded his hands as if in prayer.

"I went to the quilting bee like I told you," Amanda began, concentrating on keeping her own hands on top of the coverlet and still, so as not to reveal her anxiety to her father. "We worked until sundown."

Eyes narrowing, Newlin grunted.

Amanda didn't know what the sound meant—disapproval, distrust? Indignation sparked in her. "I'm sorry I worried you, Papa, but you did know where I was. I accepted the Millers' supper invitation. Maybe I shouldn't have, but I did. Since it was so late, Josiah took me home." She gave Josiah a smile. "Then the accident happened. The deer was . . . just . . . there. There was nothing anyone could do. Truth be known, Josiah saved my life. The lantern tipped and the quilt caught fire. We had to jump from the buckboard."

"Are you in pain, honey?" Newlin asked, all harshness gone from his tone and a pensive look on his face.

"No, not really. Just bumps and bruises."

"I think we'd best get you upstairs." Newlin pushed down on the sofa cushion and stood. He took hold of Amanda's elbow. "Mr. Miller," he said, the coolness returning, transforming him into the man he'd been before, "wait here and we'll discuss this further. Seems bad luck, or should I be saying trouble, follows you people everywhere. You're going to pay me for this."

Pulling her arm from her father's grip, Amanda stared at him, saucer-eyed, the meaning of his words all too horribly clear. "Were you listening? Did you hear anything at all?" She wanted to stomp out her frustration. "Josiah saved my life. If that's not worth the buckboard and a horse to you . . .'' Swallowing hard, feeling a hurt deep in her soul, she blinked back the tears that stung her eyes.

"Your father is right," Josiah said. "I failed in my service to you. You should not have been harmed."

"What?" Amanda whirled to face Josiah. "You're not my keeper. You're more loony than he is," she retorted, jabbing a thumb in her father's direction. "If anyone should pay you, Papa, it should be me."

"You like blood bays, is that not correct?" Josiah asked Newlin.

"Yup." Newlin regarded Josiah with cold speculation. "I like bays, all right."

Amanda knew where the conversation was leading. "Oh, no you don't. Josiah, don't. Don't do this."

Ignoring her pleas, Josiah rose from the chair and set his hat back on his head. "My horse, you admired it before."

"No!" Amanda cried.

"Oh, shush up now," Newlin snapped. "Yes, I like that horse."

"I believe I can repair your wagon," Josiah said. "Cinn . . . My horse will replace your horse."

Newlin rubbed his chin, seemingly contemplating Josiah's solution.

"You can't take his horse." Amanda grabbed her father's arm, begging him with her eyes and her heart. "Please don't take his horse."

"Why not?"

He spoke with such detachment that Amanda cringed. It was ironic, really, for she guessed her father's prejudice to be the sole reason for him even considering Josiah's offer. Had it been Leon or Doc Rollins bringing her home after the same events had occurred, things would be different. She felt such contempt she thought she'd be sick from it. "I'm asking you to please . . . not take Josiah's horse."

She saw her father's lip curl. She thought they'd made such progress in their relationship over the last few weeks, but now, as he stood there looking at her like she was a misbehaving child, she felt she didn't know him at all.

"This is business, daughter. I make the business decisions in this family."

"This is not business. And family?" Her voice cracked. "I'm ashamed to be part of this family."

"It is all right, Amanda," Josiah said, his eyes intense with understanding. "Your father has done nothing but accept what I offered. 'The fear of the Lord is the instruction of wisdom; and before honor is humility.' "

A fleeting smile crossed Josiah's lips, and Amanda knew it was for her.

Turning to her father, Josiah said, "I will bring the horse back tomorrow, and I will repair your wagon."

19

NEWLIN MOVED TO THE window, pulled back the edge of the curtain and peeked out at Josiah. "He won't be back. I'm out a blasted horse and buckboard."

"I wish that was so," Amanda replied, words dripping spite, "but you aren't. Josiah'll be back tomorrow morning with Cinnamon just like he said. And he'll fix your buckboard. He keeps his word."

Her father's gaze flew to hers, and she boldly met his eyes. Time seemed to stand still as they stared at each other, neither wanting to give in. Finally it dawned on Amanda that in this instance she was indeed her father's daughter. She shuddered, suddenly feeling tired and weak, every bump and bruise now painfully noticeable. Needing the solace of her room, she turned from him and ventured toward the doorway. Any other time, she knew she somehow would have felt the loser, but she didn't now. With her chin held high, she moved with unhurried purpose on achy legs that felt as wobbly as what she imagined those of a newly foaled colt would feel.

"Jiminy, you are hurt. Let me help you." Her father hurried over and took her arm.

Fixing one last level stare at him, Amanda spoke with grave deliberation, "I don't want your help. Until you change, I don't want anything from you."

Brow wrinkling in vexation, Newlin dropped his hold on her and stepped away. "What bee's up under your bonnet, girl?"

She blinked with incredulity. Was it possible her father really didn't understand? "You've no business taking that horse. You're swindling Josiah."

"I ain't doin' no such thing. He was supposed to have brought you home. Safely. Said it himself."

"An accident is an unintentional, unfortunate mishap," Amanda said through gnashed teeth. "That's exactly what this was. It wasn't his fault."

"I know what an accident is, so don't be quotin' me the dictionary. Most accidents can be prevented, this one included."

Shaking her head, Amanda clucked her tongue, hurried from the room and started up the staircase.

"I know you think I'm wrong on this," her father shouted after her, "but I ain't. You'll—"

She couldn't close her door fast enough. Leaning against it, staring into darkness, she dropped the quilt and covered her ears. What was it Josiah had said about honor and humility? Amanda couldn't remember. Nothing seemed clear except what she felt in her heart. Her father could take Josiah's horse and speak critically of him, but he couldn't change the feelings she had for the Amishman.

A soft gasp escaped her as she slowly lowered her hands from her ears. She suddenly realized that she loved Josiah. She didn't know the exact moment it had happened— maybe it had been years ago. But that wasn't important; her feelings were all that was important. The shock of this discovery hit her full force, and her jaw dropped. She loved Josiah Miller! She truly did. And she'd do anything in her power to make him happy.

Feeling for the switch, Amanda turned on the gaslight, bathing her room with brightness. Ophelia jumped from the bed as she stooped to retrieve the quilt. "Ouch," she exclaimed as a corset stay poked into her abdomen. "Darn these things, anyway. Maybe the Amish are right about vanity, Ophelia.''

With a smile on her face, Amanda patted the purring cat. Then, hiking her skirt, she removed her bustle and petticoats. She took a deep, much freer breath and decided that maybe tomorrow she'd forgo the corset, too. Sometime during the last few months she'd changed. She liked the woman she'd become. Seizing the coverlet and Ophelia, she happily jumped onto the bed. Though her father still hollered downstairs, her spirits soared. She'd never done anything like this before. She'd make her plans, and tomorrow, with or without Josiah, she'd leave on the treasure hunt.

∞

JOSIAH SHUFFLED THROUGH THE barn with Cinnamon on his heels. The horse's hooves made a dull clomping sound on the hardened dirt floor. He had walked the horse the last half mile, no longer able to bear riding, knowing that come daylight Cinnamon would no longer be his. His heart ached and nausea mercilessly twisted his insides. He didn't blame Newlin Glosser. He didn't blame anyone but himself.

Banishing all thoughts of what the morrow would bring, Josiah maneuvered his way through the barn, the moonlight revealing the familiar path to the oat barrel. He shoved his hands deep into the container, the millions of tiny, smooth seeds devouring his limbs. Cupping his hands, he scooped up some of the feed and pampered his beloved friend with a treat. ''A going away present,'' he said, stroking Cinnamon's biscuit-colored forelock.

Josiah was no longer certain if the moon's luminance was a help or a hindrance, for as he gazed at the munching horse, a huge, painful lump forced its way up into his throat. Stepping closer, he draped an arm around the animal's neck and rested his pounding forehead against the velvety muzzle. Staring at the ground, he clenched and unclenched his free hand. Amanda's father had said trouble followed him. That seemed an understatement. The ''God's will'' theory his parents and the other Amish in his community believed just didn't fit. It felt more like a black cloud. And now—Josiah closed his eyes against the guilt—he'd pulled Amanda under it with him. He wished he'd never taken the quilts to her, wished he'd never set foot in the Prosper General Store.

He straightened his body with a deep breath. That wasn't true. He couldn't imagine not ever knowing Amanda, never experiencing the sweetness of her kiss. How was it that he couldn't even be truthful to himself?

Swallowing hard, he patted Cinnamon's nose one last time, then trudged from the barn.

A lone lantern light flickered behind the window coverings of Elam's bedroom, capturing Josiah's attention with its sad, eerie glow. He knew his brother and sister-in-law weren't making love in their tiny house like a young newlywed couple should be doing, but more likely than not, were in the midst of changing bandages, or perhaps, tearing more.

Commiseration welled in his heart. Shoving his hands into his pockets, Josiah ducked his head and hurried into his own house.

Darkness, silence and the odor of woodsmoke enveloped him as he closed the door. The smell used to bring comfort, but tonight it stifled him. Resting his back against the timbered walls, he yanked off his boots and set them next to the door. His jacket and hat came next, hung upon a wooden peg beside his father's, like he'd done an infinite number of times before. He felt like a puppet, always going through the proper motions, never acknowledging the fact that the strings had long ago frayed and snapped.

Josiah raked his hands through his hair, yearning for a way to end the ceaseless thoughts that crowded his mind. Amanda. Elam. The quilt. Amanda, Elam and the quilt. Like debris in a tornado, faster and faster ideas swirled in his head until he thought his throbbing temples would pop. He needed a respite, if only for a short time. He took the stairs two at a time, hoping sleep would bring a bit of peace.

In the hallway outside the room he shared with his brothers, Josiah shrugged out of his suspenders and unfastened his trousers to the sound of snores filtering through the silent house. The last thing he wanted was to wake someone and be bombarded with questions regarding his lateness. Quietly turning the knob, he pushed open the door and crept into his room.

Suddenly a shadowy figure bolted upright in his bed, and Josiah started.

"Where have you been?" Mary demanded in a hushed whisper.

Releasing an audible breath of relief, he moved to the bed and plopped beside his sister. "I took Amanda home as Ma instructed," he whispered back. "There was an accident. The Glossers' horse had to be put out of its misery."

He heard Mary's gasp, and he could imagine the shock on her face, though he couldn't see it clearly.

"Goodness, Josiah." She took both his hands in her own, her touch full of warmth and empathy. "Were you or Amanda hurt?"

"No," he replied, pulling his hands away, feeling as though he didn't deserve Mary's sympathy.

"What happened? What kind of accident?" She shifted on the bed, and Josiah guessed she'd tucked her legs beneath her.

"Well?" she persisted.

"It is too late for questions. You should be asleep. Dawn nears."

"You should be asleep, too," Mary muttered, her voice full of authority. "Tell me. I will not leave until you tell me everything."

Josiah flopped back on the mattress, feeling drained and lifeless. "It happened on the way to Amanda's home." He stared upward, the memories more pure and vivid than the obscure ceiling above. "I do not know why, but a deer darted onto our path. It collided with the buckboard. Their hackney was injured."

"It is a miracle you and Amanda were not injured as well."

"Yes, well, I do believe Mr. Glosser would have preferred my demise." Josiah swallowed a bitter chuckle. "That man despises me. Us, really—all of us."

"Do not pass judgment, Josiah Miller. You forget yourself.'' Mary's words were quiet but coolly disapproving.

"I am not forgotten, but lost forever," he replied softly, almost mockingly, as he rubbed his burning eyes. "I will repair the Englishman's wagon and turn over Cinnamon as repayment for his horse. When I am ridiculed by him, I will bite my tongue and turn my cheek, as I must. With only you, Mary, will I speak the truth as my heart feels it."

Silence dropped around them, broken only occasionally by the breathing of the sleeping boys in the room.

"I do not know what to say," Mary murmured at last. "I am sorry about Cinnamon. I know how much he means to you. Wait!" Leaning closer, she tugged Josiah to a sitting position. "The quilt," she whispered eagerly. "Once you find the treasure, you can buy another horse to replace Mr. Glosser's. You will not have to give Cinnamon away."

"Not you, too? There is no treasure," Josiah said through gritted teeth. "Amanda has made *you* forget yourself, dear sister. It is time for sleep."

Mary clucked her tongue. "Unlike you," she said, raising to her feet, "I believe in God's will. I also believe he works in mysterious ways. There is a treasure. Your convictions to help Elam are strong; and just as strong are Amanda's and my convictions that there is a treasure meant for you to do just that."

She headed to the door like a floating apparition. "Sleep well tonight, for tomorrow your dreams may be haunted."

"What is that supposed to mean?" Exasperation laced Josiah's tone. Weariness claimed every muscle in his body, and all he wanted was to end the conversation.

"With or without you, Amanda plans to find the treasure. You know as well as I, she is stubborn as Papa's ox. Good night, Josiah."

Mary's words affected him like an icy hand squeezing his heart. He knew that had been her intention. Tossing and turning in his narrow bed, he wondered if Amanda would really set out on her own to find the fabled treasure. He knew she wasn't stupid, but worried that her willfulness would cloud her good sense. He'd repair the wagon at first light, take it to the Glossers' place and talk Amanda out of any crazy notion she might have of a treasure hunt.

Exhaustion overtook him, and finally he slept.

∞

AMANDA BUSTLED ABOUT IN the kitchen, dreading the time when her father would be down to eat breakfast. She wasn't up to another argument, fearful she'd somehow let her plans slip. Tossing the hot muffins into a linen-lined basket, she tried again to calm herself by shoving all thoughts of Josiah from her mind. She needed to get through this last meal.

She had just poured two cups of coffee when the sound of whistling came into the room, cueing her to the inevitable. "Help me keep my temper," she mumbled to herself. "Help me keep my temper." The chant did little to soothe her nerves, and she repeatedly wiped her hands on her apron as she waited for her father's entrance.

"Morning," Newlin said as he pushed through the swinging door.

"Good morning, Papa," Amanda replied, bringing the two steaming cups to the table.

"Oh, jiminy." His gaze roamed the table. "Suppose you'll be huffed all over 'gain if I take my breakfast with me."

"No. I haven't even made the eggs yet. Didn't know how you'd want yours." Shrugging, she said, "I can wrap the muffins and sausage easily enough."

"That'd be mighty fine. I want to get to the store early. I expect to be seein' your Amish friend."

Amanda bit her lip to stop the retort from flying out of her mouth. Hurrying to the pantry, she rummaged around on the shelves until she located the small wickerwork hamper. The fact that her father was leaving early was a wonderful omen. Things would go according to plan, if only she could continue holding her tongue.

Taking a deep breath, she returned to the kitchen with the hamper hanging in the crook of her arm. She quickly wrapped three of the muffins and a half-dozen links of the sausage in another napkin and dropped them into the container. "What else can I get you?" she asked, hands going to her hips, basket swaying with the movement.

"That right there'll be dandy." Eyeing her curiously, Newlin reached for the basket.

Amanda swallowed hard, hoping he couldn't read the excitement in her eyes.

"Well, ain't you goin' t'say anything 'bout last night?"

"I think enough was said," she reflected with some bitterness. "Unless you want to start your day with an argument, we'd better move onto a different subject."

As if he were contemplating some earthshaking matter, Newlin continued to gaze at her, stroking his chin with his thumb and forefinger. A flicker of anxiety coursed through Amanda. She told herself her fears were premature, that there was no way her father could suspect anything. Still, her heart thumped madly.

"What are you staring at?" She clenched her hands until her nails dug into her palms. "Have I a fennel seed stuck between my front teeth?"

The edges of Newlin's eyes crinkled with humor. " 'Course not. I was just thinkin' 'bout what Leon told me. I know you don't want to hear this, but reckon you need to, seein' as how that Amishman's turned your head so."

Amanda curled her lip. "Leon's opinion of Josiah is the last thing I want to hear."

"You need to, though. Seems that Amishman is intent on capturin' your fancy at any cost. I don't trust him and I wouldn't be surprised to find that accident last night was no accident. Reckon he planned it."

Her father's eyes poked at her from under his craggy brows. Amanda couldn't help herself, and she burst out laughing. She'd never seen a frown so big. His entire idea that Josiah was conniving enough to stage something of that magnitude was utterly ridiculous.

"What in the blazes is so funny? This ain't funny."

"I'm sorry, but I think it is. Do you know what you're saying? Do you honestly think Josiah would risk his life," she swallowed another giggle, "and give up a horse he loves, to impress me?" Covering her face with her hands, Amanda shook her head. "Tell me," she said, sliding her hands down her cheeks, "how could he have staged that deer running out onto the path?"

Newlin's eyes were now hard and flat. "I don't know. Point is, Leon and I don't trust him."

"And I don't trust Leon anymore." She shrugged matter-of-factly. "That argument is brewing, Papa. Maybe it'd be best if you leave while we're still speaking to each other."

"You're too blasted stubborn for your own good."

A sour smile turned the edges of Amanda's mouth and she wagged her finger. "It's ironic you should say that. Just last night I was telling myself I'm definitely my father's daughter. I'm not certain I like it."

Cursing under his breath, Newlin stalked from the kitchen. Closing her eyes, Amanda waited for the slamming of the door. It never came. Finally her lids popped up and she ran to the window. Off in the distance she saw the black speck of her father's mount and a lingering cloud of dust. A strange sense of contentment filled her. He hadn't slammed the door. If that wasn't progress, she didn't know what was.

A new strength surged through her. She didn't need anyone's help. She felt confident in her ability to follow the map on the quilt. All she needed now was a wagon. As much as she hated to admit it, she needed Leon's help.

Pulling the letter she'd written for her father from her apron pocket, she stood it against the basket of leftover muffins setting on the table. When her father came home, he'd see it. Though she hoped he'd understand, she knew deep inside that that would take a miracle. She prayed he would at least find it in his heart to care for Ophelia as she'd requested. When it was all over and Josiah had what he so desperately wanted for Elam, she'd concentrate on making proper amends with her father. Right now, she needed to act, for precious time was wasting.

Amanda hurried to the cellar, untying her apron as she went. It fell to the floor as she grabbed the carpetbag of her necessities and the quilt she'd stashed on the stairway. Though the late May sun showered radiant presummer glory, she yanked her cloak from the peg and laid it on top of the coverlet draped over her arm. One never knew what temperatures the night would bring. Good preparation was a must. With long purposeful strides, she made her way out the front door to the bush by the barn where she'd decided to hide her supplies until she returned with a wagon. Hope was in her heart as she rushed off, on foot, to see Leon.

Puffing like a train's smokestack, Amanda stopped behind the tall oak at the top of the last hill before town. She took a deep breath, relishing the sweet floral scents wafting on the warm breeze. Leaning one shoulder against the rough-textured bark, she lifted the damp hair off her neck and closed her eyes, willing her heartbeat to return to normal. She didn't want Leon being suspicious, so she rehearsed in her mind the story she planned to tell. He could be the one obstacle to prevent her from her quest. Hugging her arms to her body, her lips moved quickly in prayer. Then keeping to the trees, she started down the hill toward town.

The streets of Prosper were beginning to awaken. Amanda kept her head down, hoping she didn't run into anyone who would mention her presence in town to her father. Staying clear of the main road, she darted through the pasture to the lane in back of the stable and her father's storage barn, keeping to the shadows of the buildings like a sneaking scoundrel. The back door of the stable loomed ahead. With a bravado she didn't quite feel, she opened the door and went inside.

Dank air and the odor of manure assailed her. Two buggies and a buckboard sat off to one side, as did saddles, harnesses and a wide selection of brushes and curry combs. Leon's love for horses was something Amanda never doubted. Appealing to that love was something she counted on now.

"Leon?" She swallowed dryly, barely recognizing the thready-sounding voice as her own. "Leon, are you here?"

As if answering her call, a horse whinnied from somewhere in the big barn. Suddenly the tiny hairs on the back of Amanda's neck stirred, and she guessed Leon was near, probably watching. Her stomach roiled in anxiety, and she struggled to calm herself. Taking a deep breath, she reminded herself what was at stake. She regrouped her wits and summoned her feminine wiles. She realized she needed to use every means available, honest or not, to pull this off.

Licking her lips, Amanda purposely twisted her hands. "Oh, dear, Leon," she said loudly, now thankful for the shakiness in her voice. "Where are you? I need your help." She mustered her best helpless sigh and started for the door.

"My, my, my," Leon said as he walked around a wooden partition, shirt unfastened to the waist and sleeves rolled to the elbows. "What has got my beautiful Amanda so distraught?"

Amanda stiffened slightly at the possessive *my*, but let it pass without comment. Knowing she'd spoil the ruse by laughing, she concentrated on keeping her gaze averted from Leon's chest. It was a difficult task, since the sparse sprinkling of ebony hairs there made it look like he'd been splattered with shoe polish. She wondered if he had truly been in the stage of dressing, or if he had deliberately unfastened his shirt to try to impress her. Though she longed to reiterate what she'd already told him—that she wasn't interested—she bit her tongue.

"Oh, Leon," she said, moving to stand in front of him, "you didn't hear about the accident, did you?" She placed her hand on his forearm and shook her head in dismay.

"What accident? What in the dickens you talkin' 'bout?"

"Goodness." Amanda clutched at her heart and allowed her eyes to flutter. All the while she hoped her theatrics were believable. "Goodwin had to be put out of his misery. I could have been killed."

"What? When did this happen?"

"Last night. Coming home from the quilting bee. Josiah was taking me home . . ." She shuddered. "There was an accident. It was just horrible."

"Damn that Amishman. I told you he's nothin' but a half-wit. Did you get hurt?"

"No. Thank the Lord, I'm fine. Papa's angry. He's taking Josiah's horse as repayment for Goodwin."

"That so? Which horse?"

Leon's voice held a rasp of excitement that made the

acid well in Amanda's stomach. "I believe the sorrel," she replied through marble lips.

Chuckling, he dropped an arm firmly around her waist. "Maybe this is all for the best. Hope you can see you're much better off with me, darlin'."

He pulled her into his hardness and kissed the top of her nose before she had time to think. Fighting her revulsion, Amanda cast her gaze downward so that he couldn't see it in her eyes. She moved her hands to his chest, his skin feeling damp and sweaty beneath her palms. She didn't want to make him angry, but neither could she stand being pressed intimately against him.

"Leon, please," she said, pushing gently. "You're hurting me. I'm full of bumps and bruises from last night."

"Sorry, darlin'. I wasn't thinkin'. I just go crazy when I'm near you."

Stepping back away from him, Amanda chewed her bottom lip. "I'm here because I have a favor to ask you."

Leon's eyes smoldered with interest. "I do collect repayment on my favors," he said huskily. "As long as you agree to the terms, I'll do whatever I can for you. How does that sound?"

Anxiety stabbed Amanda's gut when he stretched out his hand. He was serious about the repayment. She could only imagine what he'd want, and those possibilities made her knees tremble. She was in up to her neck. But he was her only choice.

Slowly, she placed her hand in his.

20

LEON SQUEEZED UNTIL SHE thought every bone in her hand would snap. The uncalled-for bullying behavior confirmed the suspicions she harbored regarding his depravity. Pursing her lips with suppressed fury, she yanked from his grasp. "You know," she said, shooting him a warning look, "I don't think too highly of bullies. Is that the category you want me to put you back in, Leon?"

"Don't reckon you're in the position to be threatin' me."

Amanda felt her face grow hot. Muscles tensing, she turned a cold eye on him. "I think I came to the wrong person. I needed a man who cares enough to help me, not hurt me."

"I was just kiddin' you. You know how I kid. Like the other day in the cellar. I was kiddin'." Leon made a feeble, placatory gesture. "Forgive me?" he asked, clasping his hands as if in prayer.

"I don't know."

"Come on. What was it you wanted? Name it. Anything."

Amanda felt suddenly invigorated. The little incident would be a factor in helping her to sway Leon. Turning her back on him, she sniffed and dabbed at her eyes.

"Amanda? Darlin', I was kiddin'. I'd never hurt you. Tell me what you want. I'll even make them repayment terms looser than loose. What do you say?"

Her ire flared at the mention of repayment, but she turned back toward him and with one last exaggerated sniff, pushed her lips into a slight smile. "All right. What I need is to borrow your buckboard."

"My buckboard? That's it?"

"Yes. I'd like to use it until ours is repaired. I'll need a horse, too, of course."

" 'Course. I can do that. Just one thing." Leon scratched his head. "How come your Pa didn't stop by to get it? Not too often you set foot in here."

"Oh, well, Papa rode this morning. And I . . . I'm stopping by . . . Widow Marly's. I told Papa I'd come by for it since I'm the one that needs it."

Leon looked at her uncertainly, his brows tilting together. "The widow's, you say?"

Amanda cursed herself. Why had she said Widow Marly? Could Leon know the old woman hadn't returned from her visit south?

Avoiding his gaze, Amanda hedged with a sigh and pretended to pick a piece of lint off her skirt. "Goodness, I must get going. I have oodles to do today. Could you get it ready now, Leon?" She practically sang his name, and to be safe, offered a smile that she hoped sent his lurid pulses racing.

"Little smooch right here first." He pointed to his mouth where the edges were already lifted in a lecherous grin.

Her skin crawled. She hated coercion, but she'd instigated it. Since her options appeared nil, it seemed a harmless enough thing to do to clinch the deal. Trying to keep her mouth from curling in revulsion, she shuffled her seemingly rooted feet forward. Nostrils flaring, she rose on tiptoe and lightly brushed her lips against his.

Much to her surprise, Leon didn't grab her. He simply stood there.

A warped sense of gratitude filled Amanda. Scooting away, she quickly dismissed it. "I—"

"Don't have to say nothin'. I already know you want to go." Spinning on his heel, Leon marched to the nearest stall and led a small but hardy-looking horse from the compartment. "This is Will. He's a mustang. He's strong and don't ever seem to get tired. That's how he got his name. He's pulled the wagon quite a few times."

The tenderness in Leon's expression as he gazed at the horse was similar to what she'd seen in Josiah's eyes when he looked at Cinnamon. The discovery that Leon and Josiah had something in common shocked her. A tiny, tiny part of her somewhere deep inside wondered if she hadn't misjudged Leon.

In less than fifteen minutes, the mustang was hitched to the buckboard, and the double doors to the stable opened. Amanda climbed aboard.

"Keep Will and the wagon as long as you need 'em." Shoving his hands into his pockets, Leon rocked back on his heels, a smirk on his face. "Might take that half-wit Amishman a long time to repair your wagon."

Amanda's antipathy quickly resurfaced. Not wanting any further delays, she squelched her retort. "As soon as I'm able, I'll return this."

"And don't forget," his eyebrows-arched suggestively, "you do owe me."

"Don't you forget your promise of loose terms." Clucking her tongue, Amanda prodded Will from the stable. When she got to the street, all thoughts of Leon vanished from her mind. She glanced in both directions, hoping with everything in her she wouldn't run into anyone who wanted to stop and chitchat. Luck appeared to be on her side, and she prompted the horse to a faster gait.

The farther away from the store she traveled, the easier it became to breathe. As her defenses somewhat subsided, she realized how tense she'd been. All had gone well. Even the slip about Widow Marly had been insignificant, for Leon had appeared none the wiser.

The buckboard bounced across the terrain and Amanda felt an indefinable feeling of rightness. The sun bathed her with promises, and even the birds along the route joined in her glory and sang their song of triumph. The closer to home she got, the more her excitement grew. "This time tomorrow, Will," she said with a sigh, "we could be in Sommerville."

∞

JOSIAH POUNDED ON THE door again. Still, no answer. Shifting his weight from one foot to the other, he glanced over his shoulder to the far side of the barn where he'd left the buckboard and Cinnamon. The repairs to the Glosser wagon hadn't taken nearly as long as he'd anticipated. Since it was still fairly early, he'd expected to catch Newlin Glosser before the man left for the store. Josiah had even prepared a speech of rhetoric on the ride over. It didn't matter now. As much as he wished it were otherwise, it appeared the store would be the place where he'd end up repaying his debt to Amanda's father.

Walking to the edge of the porch, he sank to the top step, rested his elbows on his knees and steepled his fingers. The prediction Mary had made last night about Amanda and the treasure plagued him. And as soon as he'd risen, a nagging sensation of dread had encompassed him. Maybe that, too, was an unconscious factor in his expeditious repair job. He needed to see Amanda with his own eyes to assure himself that she was safe and not planning anything foolish. Her absence now did nothing to alleviate his anxiety.

With a snort of agitation he slapped the wooden planks of the porch with his palms. "Where are you, Amanda? Where are you?"

Suddenly a faint jingling carried through the air. Josiah sat straighter on the step, listening. That sound meant only one thing. A wagon approached.

Only a minute or two passed when a buckboard topped the knoll to the north of the Glosser property. Josiah stayed on the step, knowing he was hidden by the thick cranberry bushes surrounding the porch. The wagon came closer. A smiling Amanda pulled back on the reins of a horse he had never seen her use before. The buckboard was unfamiliar, too, for that matter. Moving a few fragrant branches so that he could see better, he watched as she jumped from the wagon and scurried to an overgrown evergreen shrub.

Though he'd never in his life done anything as low as spying on another person, he couldn't move, couldn't seem to locate his tongue to call out a greeting.

Dropping to her knees, Amanda rummaged through the bush, looking as though she were about to be consumed by it. She extracted her cloak, and tossed it to the ground; and then a carpetbag. She leaned even farther into the shrubbery, and Josiah's heart plummeted to his toes when she pulled the old quilt from the depths of the green boughs. Jerking to his feet, he ran to her.

Surprise showed in her face and in her large, liquid eyes. She rose to her feet, the coverlet hugged against her. "Josiah!" She wiggled a hand from under the material and placed it on her breast. Breathing deeply, she exclaimed, "You startled me. What are you doing here?"

"I have brought Cinnamon and the repaired buckboard. What are you doing hiding such items in the bushes?"

"You're done fixing that? Already? Oh," Amanda groaned, pushing back the several locks of hair that had caught on the shrub and had been teased into a golden cobweb about her face. "I truly wish I'd have known it wasn't going to take that long to repair." With a wrinkle of her nose and a big sigh, she proclaimed, "Guess I can't change what's already done."

Josiah didn't know what she was talking about. All he cared about was the escapade he knew she planned. "What are you doing with those items?" he asked again.

"I'm going away."

"Where?"

"Questions?" She looked at him with amused wonder. "I thought the Amish weren't allowed to be nosy bodies. That's what you're being, you know. Tsk, tsk, tsk," she teased, shaking her finger at him.

Josiah's mind told him to resist her beauty and her charm and walk away from this craziness, but his body refused. "Amanda." He reached out, grabbed her hand and pulled her closer. Feeling the heat from her body, he swallowed hard, his Adam's apple bobbing. Cupping her chin with his hand, he gazed into her eyes, imploring her to listen. "You jest over a matter that is very serious. I know what you plan to do. I am here to stop your foolishness.''

Stiffening, Amanda haughtily swung her head away from his touch. "We've had this conversation before. You're not my keeper. You don't own me. You certainly can't tell me what to do.''

"The treasure is a fable," Josiah said more sharply than he had intended.

"Fine." She threw her hands up in mock resignation. "I guess I'll find that out for myself then, won't I?''

"I want to buy the quilt back.''

Her brows shot upward. "You what?''

"The quilt. I need to buy it back," he said reaching for it.

"Uh-uh." Backing away from him, she clutched it more tightly to her body. I'm sorry, but that's out of the question. Now, if you'll excuse me. I truly don't have time to finish this argument.'' She spun and darted for the buckboard.

Josiah caught her about the waist before she was able to climb aboard. "You cannot go alone. It is dangerous. I will not allow you to do that.''

"You can't stop me," she said, pushing his arm away in a sort of unspoken challenge. "If you're so worried about me, the only thing you can do is come with me.''

There was an almost-imperceptible note of pleading in her voice. Josiah felt a gamut of perplexing emotions like he'd never felt before. If he went with her, it would probably mean leaving his faith . . . forever. Going on a treasure hunt with an English woman would definitely be a cause for ostracization. He'd never be baptized like the other Amish men. Maybe it wasn't meant to be. Maybe that's why he hadn't joined the church already as an adult. Taking off his hat, he raked his hand through his hair and paced a small path in front of the buckboard. If there was indeed a treasure—he shook his head at his own ridiculous conjecture—he could right the wrong he'd done Elam. Whatever the cost, that would be worth it.

"Josiah, please. I want to leave now.''

Amanda's voice tipped the scales. Stuffing his hat back on his head, Josiah joined her at the buckboard. "I will go with you, but I am not prepared. I have neither food nor water. And Cinnamon must be unhitched from the buckboard.''

Smiling, she said, ''You take care of your horse. Put him in the pasture in back of the barn.'' She tossed the quilt into the wagon and headed for the house. ''Don't worry,'' she called out over her shoulder. ''I'll take care of everything else.''

She rushed up the stairs to her father's room. Yanking open a drawer to his bureau, she pulled out two pairs of dark trousers. Though Josiah was taller than her father, she decided pants that were too short were better than not having a change of pants at all. Feeling the same about the shirts, she grabbed three and an overcoat from the closet.

''Ophelia, sleepyhead, good-bye one last time,'' she said, poking her head back into her bedroom. The feline looked up as though she'd been horribly disturbed, then snuggled her nose back under the tip of her tail. Laughing, Amanda retraced her steps to the hallway and put the clothes down.

''Wonder how long we'll be gone?'' She chewed her lip, debating whether or not to grab more food than the dried beef she'd stuck in her bag. ''I'd better,'' she said as she rushed off to the smokehouse. She grabbed a small wooden crate and dropped a half-ham and a slab of bacon into a gunnysack. Back in the kitchen, her gaze swept the room like a hungry predator searching for prey. She added the leftover muffins to the sack, careful not to disturb the note still resting against the basket. An iron skillet and coffeepot pulled from the cupboard were haphazardly added to the crate. Lastly she raided the pantry of lard, coffee and the last five cans of beans. Two place setting from the sideboard topped the lot. Then, carrying her supplies, she scrambled back to the front door.

Draping all the clothes for Josiah across her load, she made her way back to the wagon.

The repaired buckboard sat where Josiah had left it, absent Cinnamon. Amanda moved as quickly as she dared toward Leon's buckboard, her precious china cargo clinking into the cans of beans. With a grunt, she hefted the wooden box onto the platform in the back next to her carpetbag and cloak.

Anxiousness to get started coursed through her body. "Josiah," she shouted as she lifted her skirt and climbed aboard, "I'm ready whenever you are."

Amanda scooted over so that Josiah had better access to the reins. Suddenly the blood in her veins turned to ice. The quilt was gone!

Dropping to the footboard, she looked frantically under the seat. She didn't really think the quilt had somehow crawled out of view, but the only other explanation was something she couldn't face. Cradling her face in her hands, she fought the tears spilling from her eyes. She'd trusted him.

"Are you looking for something?"

Amanda's hands flew down to her sides. Josiah leaned over her, the quilt draped across his shoulders. He'd palmed the seat and the floorboard, capturing her between his arms and intimately putting their faces and lips mere inches apart. Though still angry, a ribbon of sensation unfurled deep within the recesses of her body.

"You are crying." A frown creased his brow. "Why?"

His breath fanned her cheeks, drying her tears. "You stole my quilt," she snapped. "How could you do that?"

"I did not steal it." There was a faint tremor in his voice, as if some emotion had touched him. "I—as you would say—was teasing. I did not mean for you to become so upset."

Amanda's anger and despair dissolved on the spot. Josiah's firm, sensual lips were so close to her own. She couldn't stop looking at them. Touches of humor appeared around the corners and his dimples suddenly poked out at her. She slid her gaze upward, capturing his, wondering how she could ever have doubted him.

Almost instantly, the lines of Josiah's mouth tightened. The smile faded, and the dimples disappeared. He quickly moved away from her. An odd sort of bereavement filled Amanda. She suspected her eyes had revealed what she felt in her heart. The knowledge obviously upset him.

"Enough playfulness," he growled. "It is time to go."

Though he extended his hand to help her, he pulled away from her touch as soon as Amanda had risen to her feet. Silently he swung up to the buckboard.

The wagon dipped slightly under his weight, and she moved over on the seat as much as she could. She wished she could just speak her mind and tell Josiah she loved him, but she didn't think that was what he wanted to hear. She didn't know what he wanted to hear, but she couldn't take the brooding silence.

"I'd like to be the navigator and hold the map." Tilting her head, she smiled. "If we get separated, I know I'll keep going."

"And you believe I will not?"

"Oh, it's not that I don't trust you, even after the stunt you just pulled, it's just that I'm the only one who understands the design." Flipping her hair jauntily over her shoulder, she held out her hands. "You couldn't do this without me. I'm indispensable on this hunt. The quilt, please."

Josiah handed it over and Amanda noticed the faint mischievousness in his eyes again. She realized for the first time that his ever-changing moods seemed to have something to do with her. The more compromising the situation, the more he appeared to withdraw. She viewed him with abrupt but exhilarating clarity. Now that she knew what she was dealing with, she'd turn the tables and make them work to her advantage.

A smirk curling his lips, Josiah continued to gaze at her, making no move to prod the horse to motion.

"Oh," Amanda slapped her palms to her cheeks. "Do I as navigator have to say *go* or something?"

"You have the map and *know* its markings. Which way do we go?"

"Well, let's see." Hands trembling with eagerness, she flapped the quilt into the air as she'd done so many times before. She stared at it until her vision blurred. Snapping her fingers, she said, "My notes. I'll get my notes." Shoving the quilt to Josiah, she turned in the seat, opened the carpetbag and removed three sheets of paper. "To . . . to . . . the west. We need to travel to the west."

"You are sure?" Josiah's brows were high and rounded. "Which marking has told you Sommerville is to the west?"

Amanda's stomach shriveled. Squeezing her eyes, she wagged her head and crumpled the notes to her chest. "Oh, no. No. Josiah," she moaned, opening her eyes again, "I didn't write it down. I don't even remember Libby or Ruth-ann saying which direction Sommerville was. This is ter-rible. Libby said by now it could be a ghost town. We'll never find it if we don't travel in the right direction."

Hesitantly Josiah reached out and pushed back some locks of hair that had fallen into Amanda's eyes. Tingles traveled through her entire body, and she wanted nothing more than to lean into his hand.

All too soon, he stopped and dropped his hand to rest back on his thigh. "Seems we are both indispensable." He treated her to a devastating smile. "Put your notes away, navigator. I happen to know Sommerville is to the east."

Amanda trembled inside. She loved Josiah's moods, loved it when he teased her, like now. Oh, and to look at him! He had unlocked her very heart and soul. How could he not know it?

Her mouth and lips felt like dried-out wood. Running her tongue across them, she turned to replace her notes in the carpetbag. All the while, she felt his gaze following her every move. It would be a miracle if she made it through this trip without throwing herself at him.

As she righted herself in the seat, he smiled again. "I assume you have packed a tiny, tiny shovel, an axe to chop firewood and a lantern with matches in that carpetbag of yours?"

Sinking in her seat, Amanda felt a blush scorch her cheeks. "See what a good thing it is that you're coming with me? Of course I didn't pack a shovel. I love to dig with my hands. And the blacker the night, the better to dig." She groaned. "My father has both in the barn. I'll be just a minute." She stepped from the wagon with as much dignity as she could muster. She felt Josiah's fiery gaze on her as she walked.

The items were finally loaded, and he helped her back

up to the bench. Then with a flick of his wrist, he snapped the leather reins and the mustang started off.

They hadn't gone more than fifty yards when an eerie prickling traveled Amanda's spine. She glanced over her shoulder, expecting to see her father and that they'd been caught. She saw no one, however, nothing out of the ordinary. Discounting it as nervous excitement, she settled herself for the trip to Sommerville.

Mile stretched into mile and the morning soon turned to late afternoon. The silence that enveloped them felt comfortable, and a part of Amanda wished the trip would never have to end.

From the corner of her eye, she stole another look at Josiah. Though his profile spoke of power and strength, she knew the sensitivity that lay beneath the surface. His heart was bigger than most people's and full of selflessness. With a little contented sigh, her gaze moved from his face to his upper arms, the muscles there bunching beneath his work shirt. She took in his rolled-back sleeves, liking how the tawny hair on his arms curled around the homespun fabric. He was the epitome of the perfect man.

Smiling, Amanda looked back to the trail. The terrain had changed slightly, the gently rolling hills giving way to steeper slopes and valleys. Long prairie grasses swayed around them, looking like a wavy ocean of rich greens and deep blues. Her stomach broke the stillness and grumbled its displeasure, having long ago digested the muffin she'd eaten for breakfast.

Josiah cast her an amused sidelong glance. "I believe it is up to the navigator to decide when to stop to eat."

"Of course it is." Pointing to a small grove of trees off in the distance, she said, "Seeing as how you're hungry, we'll stop there."

"Me? We are stopping because I am hungry?"

"Why, yes." Her entire face spread into a smile. "Everything I do, I do for you. Don't you know that yet?"

A deep crimson stained Josiah's cheeks. He looked back to the path, just as Amanda knew he would. His mouth was tight and grim again. He definitely had retreated behind his wall, and unknowingly confirmed her earlier suspicion.

Maybe it was the warm sun, or the clean fresh scent that seemed to clear her head. Whatever it was, Amanda felt braver than brave. Turning in the seat to face him, she tapped his shoulder. "What is it that keeps you from being honest with me?"

Josiah drew a quick intake of air, and she knew she'd surprised him with the question. Staring at him, she waited. "It's rude, you know, to ignore someone pointedly." Her tone dared an answer.

Tugging on the reins, he stopped the buckboard and turned his fiery, silver gaze on her. "Then I must beg forgiveness."

"Don't beg," she said, rolling her eyes, "just ask. You don't even have to do that because I forgive you already."

"Thank you, I guess." He clucked his tongue and the horse started again.

"You're quite an ingratiating evader, aren't you?"

Shaking his head, he chuckled. "You speak words I do not understand."

"Do I? Ingratiating means charming. An evader is someone who deliberately dodges something. In your case, my question."

"You do not know what you ask."

"Yes, I do. I ask for truth. You even had a quote about truth. What was it?" She wrinkled her face. "It was something like, Truth is mighty and great above all."

An easy smile played about the corners of his mouth. "That is close enough."

"Well, come on, then," she said, rubbing her hands together in an exaggerated gesture. "It's truth time."

"Truth is great, but truth can also bring pain." Josiah's expression stilled and grew serious. "You are English. I am Amish. That is truth. You are accustomed to adornments, fancy and outlandish clothing. I wear homespuns that have been patched and mended too many times to count. I work the land so that it will provide for me, you purchase what you need and you sell it to others."

"So," she replied defensively. "What's wrong with that? And outlandish? My clothes aren't outlandish."

"To my culture they are foreign. *Outlandish* can mean foreign, can it not?"

"Not only can you quote the Bible, but you can quote a dictionary, too." Amanda slouched in the seat and wiped her palms on her skirt. "You're one up on me. I'm not good with the Bible."

"It was not my intention to pass judgment." He spoke in an odd yet gentle tone. "I only wanted you to see some of the truths I see."

"You've opened my eyes. Just stop the wagon. I want to eat now," she lied.

The silence returned, but it was not comfortable like it had been before. She wished she'd never started the honesty bit. The wedge between their cultures seemed larger than ever, and her heart simply ached because of it.

21

THEY DIDN'T STOP LONG, taking time to eat only a piece of ham and a muffin. Amanda felt even more inadequate when Josiah asked for a drink, and she realized she'd forgotten to bring water.

"I thought I could do this. What a fiasco," she said once they'd started again. "And I always thought I was an organized person."

He drew in his lips thoughtfully. "We will do what our ancestors did. We will find our own water. We will survive."

Exhaling with her own agitation, Amanda slumped back against the seat. She crossed her arms over her bosom. "Well, the horse is on his own, too. I forgot about him. I didn't bring a lick of feed."

"It does not matter. Since the beginning of time, creatures of the land have made do with what God has provided. This horse is no different."

She regarded him speculatively. "You always say stuff like that. Sometimes it's . . . so hypocritical."

Chuckling, he glanced at her, then back to the trail. "What have I said that makes me a hypocrite?"

"What you just said. You can't have things be God's will only when it suits you."

When he frowned, she threw up her hands matter-of-factly and said, "It's clear, really. You believe it selectively."

"I do not."

"Yes, you do. I think that's more an English trait than an Amish one. Maybe you aren't as Amish as you think." Her gaze clung to his face, analyzing his reaction to her half-teasing remarks. Though Josiah kept silent and judiciously watched the road, his jaw shifted back and forth. Amanda knew she'd touched a nerve. Her hope and courage returned, and she quickly continued on. "What you're trying to do for Elam, it's not something a typical Amish person would do. From what I know of your culture, the majority would have accepted what happened and left it alone. But you can't. I think we're more alike than you care to admit."

"You talk too much," Josiah growled, shooting her a blazing look. "That also is an English trait."

Her lips trembled with the need to smile. She'd said enough, for now.

∞

AMANDA SCOOTED CLOSER TO the blazing fire. Pulling the old quilt more tightly around her body, she watched the tiny embers as they popped free from the wood, then floated up into the stars. "I can't believe Sommerville isn't Sommerville anymore. It's sad."

"We were fortunate even to have located the man who knew of it. Fifty years is a long time. The land and people change."

"But for a town to be just gone forever . . ." She shook her head. "That is strange."

"Perhaps. You must realize that tomorrow when we start, we may find the landmarks stitched by my grandmother are gone as well."

"No. They won't be. We'll find the grove of oaks and the crooked place and all of it." Adjusting her dress,

Amanda hugged her knees with her arms. "I refuse to believe that it's not going to work after how all this came about, how you brought this quilt to me and how everything unfolded. It won't fizzle out. It can't. We'll find that treasure."

"Supposed treasure," Josiah corrected gently, stirring the fire.

Amanda rolled her eyes. "Supposed to you. I know it's there." She breathed deeply, the crisp odors of their campfire now richly mingling with the dewy fresh scents of the night. "Haven't you ever just . . . known something? Even though all the odds are against it, you still believe it with your heart and your soul?"

He continued to poke at the fire, eyes downcast. "Josiah," she said softly, "did you hear me?"

"Yes."

"Well, have you?"

"I have already answered. Yes," he said again in a resigned voice that shocked her.

She rested her chin on her knees, studying him. The glow of the fire cast shadows across his face that she knew masked his feelings. Suddenly their gazes met and held. Emotions surged through her and her pulse skittered alarmingly. How she loved him! She had to tell him, had to throw away all doubts and let whatever was supposed to happen, happen.

As if reading her thoughts and wanting no part of them, Josiah looked away. Though desolation filled Amanda, she vowed to herself to confess her feelings before they returned to Prosper.

"Dawn will come soon," he said curtly. "We must sleep." Without giving Amanda even the smallest of glances, he sank to the ground beside the fieldstone he had sat upon earlier. Adjusting it behind his back and neck, he leaned against it as though it were a feather pillow. Crossing his legs at the ankles, he pulled his hat over his eyes, then folded his arms over his chest.

She knew she'd been dismissed, and it bothered her. She wondered if his eyes were closed, or if he watched from under the brim of his hat. With an angry sniff she lifted her chin and pasted on a smile, just in case he watched.

Pushing to her feet, Amanda moseyed toward the thick expanse of trees that surrounded them on one side. She had no intention of going for a stroll in there this time of night, but was merely testing Josiah. Creeping closer to the forest's edge, she fully expected him to call out and stop her, at least ask where she was going. He didn't. Pausing briefly, she wrinkled her nose, suspecting he was testing her as well.

"A battle of the minds, is it?" she murmured. "Fine." With a bravado she all but felt, she walked into the raven blanket that loomed ahead.

The crackling of the fire instantly disappeared, swallowed by the trees. She pushed her feet forward another yard or so and felt like she'd been consumed as well. Tipping her head every which way, she tried to spot Josiah and the camp. It was too dark. Shuffling back a couple of steps, she finally caught a glimpse of him still lying next to the fire. It didn't look as if he planned on making any moves to come find her. If she moved into the copse any further, she'd be in pitch darkness, and then would probably truly need finding.

Pursing her lips, Amanda reminded herself that pride and stupidity weren't a good match. She needed to forget the little vagary she'd instigated, swallow her pride and go back.

Before she had time even to take a step, something in the forest behind her snapped. She felt gooseflesh rise on her arms. It felt like a spider had crawled up her spine. Heart thundering, she shot from the trees.

She stopped when she came to the buckboard, anticipating Josiah's laughter. He still hadn't moved. Glancing over her shoulder to the trees, she saw nothing, and wondered if her imagination had just run wild. She grabbed the two coats still on the wagon seat and the axe from the back. Though she felt a bit safer with a weapon in hand, she only half turned her back as she walked away from the ominous trees and the secrets they held.

She didn't waste any time retrieving the old quilt and the carpetbag before returning to Josiah's side. The even rise

and fall of his chest told her he slept. She instantly decided
against using the bed he'd made for her out of leaves and
pine needles. It was too far away from him and just too
close to the forest.

After unloading her arms of the axe, coats, carpetbag
and· quilt, Amanda added two more logs to the greedy fire
and stirred it up the way she'd seen Josiah do. Embers and
sparks danced into the air. The wood hissed in protest as the
yellow and orange flames rolled across. Fires were supposed
to keep animals, like wolves, at bay. Satisfied that no beast
would attempt to come close, she draped Josiah with her father's coat. Sinking to the ground beside him, she covered up
with her cloak and spread the old quilt across them both.

Weariness settled around her, and Amanda realized how
safe she felt with Josiah. It had nothing to do with the axe
lying beside her; it was him. She scooted closer, as close
as she dared, knowing that that feeling of security came
from loving someone.

An owl hooted from somewhere, bidding her good night.
A sleepy smile curled her lips. That was what she had heard
in the trees. It had only been an owl.

∞

A POPPING AND SIZZLING sound pulled Amanda from
the depths of her slumber to semiconsciousness. The smell
of bacon and coffee wafted up to her, rousing her more
fully. Pushing herself up on one elbow, she shoved her
disheveled hair away from her face with her free hand.

Josiah had started another fire. Bacon crackled in the
skillet set up on fieldstones. The coffeepot sat off to the
side of the flames on its own stand made of rocks. He stood
at the buckboard a few yards away, his bare back to her
and his trousers drooping slightly around his narrow hips
as if unfastened. Memories of that night not so long ago in
the bathhouse flooded her mind. The core of her body
stirred. Helpless to do anything else, she watched as he
shook the water from his hair and pulled one of her father's
shirts from the wagon. The muscles of his shoulders and

back flexed and extended as he donned the garment.

Closing her eyes briefly, Amanda memorized all his body's contours. She didn't know what would happen once they found the treasure; she only knew she never wanted to forget even the minutest of details.

When he slid his hands into his pants and began to tuck in his shirt, a groan escaped from deep in her throat. Josiah spun around, their gazes momentarily locking. He looked away and quickly tried to fasten his trousers. The stain of crimson on his cheeks, and the way he fumbled twice before achieving success, made him all the more endearing to her.

"Something's burning," she said sheepishly.

His gaze flew back to hers, his mouth twisting wryly.

"No. Really." Laughing, she pointed toward the smoke that hovered around the iron skillet.

Stuffing his hat on his head, Josiah dashed to the fire. Using the blade of the axe, he slid the pan out of flames' reach and onto the ground. "That was breakfast."

"I like my bacon crisp."

"Good, because that is what we have." Planting his hands on his hips, he studied her thoughtfully for a moment. "We will eat, then we will start. I believe it would be best if we go on foot."

Amanda scrambled from her bed. "Do you truly think that old man was right? You think we're that close? To go on foot, I mean?"

"Yes, to all of your questions." Her reaction seemed to amuse him, and he smiled. "If you would like to wash or change, do it now while I take care of the horse and the fire."

Grabbing her carpetbag and a strip of the bacon, she chewed as she hurried off in the direction of the stream they'd used the night before. She finished eating and quickly washed and changed into a gingham skirt and blouse. Though her dresses hung loosely and without any shape, the comfort she felt without the corset and bustle were worth it. Freedom of movement was of the utmost importance, especially now with the treasure hunt about to begin.

When she returned, Josiah had already put out the fire and rolled their coats together into a pack. Two plates with blackened strips of bacon and muffins sat on the ground next to two steaming cups of coffee. Setting down her carpetbag, she picked up one of the coffees and blew lightly, sending steam swirling about her face. From over the edge of the cup, she watched him as he rigged a long tether from the reins and the lead. His skills impressed her. Several times now she'd seen him make something out of next to nothing. She smiled when he attached the tether to the buckboard and led Leon's horse to a lush grassy spot. The animal could now graze leisurely but not wander off.

Amanda lifted her carpetbag and walked slowly toward the wagon, sipping her coffee. She wondered if there was anything Josiah couldn't do.

"I will get that for you," he said when he saw her. His fingers innocently brushed the inside of her forearm and palm as he took the bag from her. Amanda's toes curled and a wistful smile tipped her mouth. She was so helplessly in love, and he seemed so unaffected. He returned the piece of luggage to the rear of the buckboard as if he hadn't even been aware of touching her skin.

"Let us eat." He grinned and inclined his head toward where the food lay.

Nodding dumbly, Amanda followed him like a pup would follow its master. They ate in silence, in the same spots in which they'd slept. She felt glad to have the chance to regroup her own thoughts before they started off. The treasure was paramount in Josiah's mind. She knew that and scolded herself for letting romantic notions get in the way. Popping the last bite of a muffin into her mouth, she snatched the quilt and pushed herself to a standing position.

Josiah took her cue. Unfolding his legs, he also rose to his feet. Once the dishes and the rest of the supplies were packed away, he grabbed the spade and the gunnysack with the ham in it. A lazy smile stretched his mouth as he slung their coats and the bag of food across his shoulder.

Winking conspiratorially at Amanda, he said, "Is my navigator ready to search for treasure?"

"Oh, yes." She loved the possessive way he'd said *my*.

Excitement bubbled inside her as they started out for the open field.

The sun shined like a supreme beacon. Stillness surrounded them, and other than the soft rustle of their clothing and the occasional crackling of the brush they traipsed through, it was as if the entire world had disappeared.

The confident set of Josiah's shoulders told Amanda that, even though to this point he'd been a nonbeliever, his heart was in this quest now. She had no doubts. This time tomorrow, Josiah would have all the money he'd need for his brother.

"What is the first landmark?" he asked suddenly.

"Oak trees. We need to look for oak trees."

"No. I do not believe so."

"Yes, we do. It's a grove of oaks." She stopped and gazed down at the left-hand corner of the quilt. "It's right here."

Stroking his chin, Josiah glanced to the quilt, then back to where they'd camped. "What is the second thing we are to look for?"

"Pine trees and a huge rock. What are you thinking?" Amanda fingered her lip. "Josiah, come on. Tell me what you're thinking."

"I believe we slept next to oaks."

Looking back to the forest, she frowned. "You really think so?"

"Fifty years is a long time. A small grove of oaks left alone would now be very large. The pines you speak of are up ahead."

Shading her eyes from the sun, Amanda gazed at the horizon. Her breath caught in her throat, for off in the distance loomed tall, emerald evergreens. "Oh, my!" She hugged the quilt as though it were a long-lost friend. "I've been looking for oaks and they were right under our noses. Josiah," she exclaimed, grabbing his arm, "we're going to reach that treasure in no time."

For the first time his smile matched hers in liveliness. "I hope you are right." Taking her hand, he said, "Come on."

They ran awkwardly toward the pines, laughing with each step. Along with the underbrush, the supplies they carried between them hampered all hopes of any speed. Amanda didn't think she'd ever seen Josiah so lighthearted before. The dimples that peeked at her from behind his day-old growth of beard made her heart trip over itself. She prayed he wouldn't be disappointed.

"This is right! We're following the quilt," she squealed. "I just know it!" She could imagine Josiah's grandmother so many years ago taking this same route.

They cleared the evergreens in minutes, and when they forged past a mammoth fieldstone, Amanda thought she'd burst from the excitement. She pulled Josiah to a stop. "Look! Oh!" She put her hand to her chest and drew a couple of reviving breaths. "Josiah," she said, squeezing his arm, "aren't those grassy hills the most beautiful sight you've ever seen?"

"That they are." Shoving the blade of the spade into the ground, he rested his arm on the handle and took a deep breath. His eyes glinted with pleasure. "What is next, after the hills?"

"The crooked place. Hey," Amanda said with a smile, brows flickering, "race you to the hills." She darted off, Josiah's laughing protest like music to her ears.

She ran as fast as she could, the underbrush tugging at her legs, hindering her flight. He easily closed the distance and caught her around the waist. Dropping the coats and shovel, he picked her up and twirled her around. "You are a cheat," he said, laughing.

Amanda tried to throttle the current racing through her. It was futile. The hard expanse of Josiah's abdomen and chest were smashed into her hips. She felt his arms, like ropes of steel, about her waist. Their playful antics had crossed over and, to her, had become something much, much more. She needed to get away from him before she was so consumed she lost perspective again.

"Put me down," she said sharply. "Now."

The spinning stopped along with his laughter. A frown rumpled his brow as he set her on her feet. They were still so close, she could feel the heat from him. The sweetly intoxicating musk of his body overwhelmed her. Her insides felt like hot, flowing honey, and she backed away.

Swallowing the lump that pushed up into her throat, she reminded herself over and over to stay focused. She had to, for him. "I . . . I just want to find that treasure. That's all I want. Can we go now?"

His eyes took on a wounded look. "Yes, your treasure," he said, yanking the spade from the ground with a force that made clods of dirt fly and Amanda cringe. Seizing the coats, he stormed off toward the grassy hills. She hurried along behind, hoping she'd done the right thing.

The crooked place was not only easy to find, but the phenomenon was simply amazing. Loamy-scented air greeted them and the little creek that twisted through the trees gurgled a welcome. Josiah was all business. He didn't make any comments and he didn't offer any replies to the ones she made. Amanda decided it was all for the better. It would be easier when they returned home if she could somehow fall a little out of love with him.

"Where do I dig?" Josiah asked coldly when they'd stopped.

"Not here, but by a clump of birches." Looking all around, she pulled her bottom lip between her teeth. His gaze bored holes into her confidence.

"There are at least twenty clumps of birches here." He leaned against one of the smooth-surfaced trees and exhaled with an exasperation she knew had everything to do with her. "Which one, *navigator*, does the quilt tell you it is?"

His mocking tone irritated her, and though she knew he was still angry and confused by her reaction earlier, she wadded the coverlet as much as she could and hurled it at him. He ducked and it landed a few yards away next to another set of trees.

"You said yourself fifty years is a long time. Your grandmother didn't take that into account when she stitched that quilt." Lifting her chin a notch, Amanda crossed her arms over her bosom. "All I know is that the treasure is buried at the base of a clump that looks like fingers and a wrist. And I know daffodils were originally planted on the spot." She moved past Josiah toward the discarded quilt, her jaw tightening.

Wondering what to do next, she bent to pick it up. The

sun caught her eyes, shining gloriously through the branches several trees away. Her heart skipped a beat when she saw the brownish, straw-colored wisps littering the ground. "Josiah!" she shouted, scrambling to her feet. She rushed to the spot. "This is it. This is where the treasure is."

Shrugging, he said, "I suppose it is as good a spot as any."

"No, this is *the* place."

"You are certain?

She nodded.

"Then I will dig."

Amanda relieved Josiah of the coats and the ham, and he went to work. She held her breath with each shovelful of dirt he removed from the ground. As the mound grew, her hope diminished.

"I . . . had this feeling. I really thought this was the spot. Oh, heavens," she said, shaking her head, pacing a few steps. "We're so close. We can't not find it."

Josiah paused for a moment and wiped the sweat from his brow. "Your feeling was right. I believe it is here, too."

Her jaw dropped in astonishment. He'd never said anything as positive as that. He resumed digging, and hope surged through Amanda. Closing her eyes, she said in a voice more softly than a whisper, "Help us, Fanny."

Josiah's gales of laughter made her eyes open. "I have found something. Something is here." Laughing some more, he dropped to his knees and dug with his hands. The broadest smile Amanda had ever seen spread across his face as he pulled a dirty gunnysack from the hole.

"Oh!" She sank to the ground beside him. "Oh, goodness," she said as he held the bag out to her. "No. No." Shaking her head, she covered her face with her hands. "I can't look. You look."

Silence descended on them. Amanda waited, trembling, wondering why Josiah didn't say anything. Suddenly, she felt him gently pulling her hands away. Tears glistened in his eyes, and she knew.

"Thank you," he murmured against her lips.

Amanda quivered at the sweet tenderness of the kiss. She

never wanted it to end. Finally, their mouths parted, but a promise lingered. She felt herself getting lost in the way he was looking at her. Her heart fluttered wildly in her breast, and she couldn't stand it any longer. "I love you," she blurted. "I know you couldn't possibly love me, but—"

Her words were smothered by Josiah's lips. He hungrily devoured her softness. She felt his tongue, exploring and searching, timidly at first. Then more boldly, he tasted the inner recesses of her mouth. Just when Amanda thought she'd surely die, or at the very least swoon, the kisses stopped.

He dragged his lips from hers and drew a labored breath. His eyes were like silver lightning, and resting his palms on his thighs, he looked at her with a gaze as wonderful as an intimate caress. "I did not mean for this to happen, but I am helpless to do anything but love you."

He took her hands in his, mindless of the dirt until it sprinkled to her lap. "I am sorry," he said sheepishly, releasing her. "A man who works the land does not always notice the dirt on his palms or beneath his nails. I believe that is Amish."

Laughing from sheer joy, Amanda shoved her hands into the dirt, then lifted them into the air so that it sifted through her fingers. The laughter and delight turned sensual when their gazes locked. "The woman who loves the man doesn't notice the dirt, either."

Leaning closer to Josiah, she straightened to her knees and brushed her lips against his brow, whispering, "All she cares about is the man she loves."

She felt his gaze as though it were almost a tangible force. It dropped from her eyes to her shoulders to her breasts. Her heartbeat throbbed in her ears. She wanted him to touch her, didn't think she could bear it if he didn't. Though this was all new, she sensed the rightness of it. And like the first time she'd quilted, she knew she'd make mistakes. They'd make them together.

"Josiah . . ." She swallowed hard, barely recognizing the throaty voice as her own. A little simple flirting she could handle, but how exactly did one go about asking a man to make love?

"Your eyes tell me your thoughts, but I do not know—"

"You talk too much," Amanda said as her hands explored the strong tendons of his back. She moved closer so that her breasts were almost touching his face. She didn't know what other invitation she could give short of placing his hands where she wanted them. Suddenly it struck her. It was almost the 1890s, and she was her own woman. Pushing off Josiah's shoulders, she rose to her feet and stepped out of her skirt. "This is an English trait I hope you like," she said as she began unfastening her blouse. Her hands shook with each button she slid from the hole. Laughing nervously, she paused and crooked her finger at him. "You can jump up and help anytime."

With a deep and guttural moan, Josiah shook his head. "I like this English characteristic the way that it is." His stare was bold as he shifted from his knees to his buttocks. When the last button was undone, he grabbed for her with a powerful, demanding grip and hauled her to the ground beside him.

Leaning across her, he took her mouth with a fierce intensity. The kiss was as challenging as it was rewarding. Amanda matched the movements of his tongue, then stroked and teased with some thought-up ones of her own. She loved how his body felt against hers, and she eagerly raised her arms above her head to help him remove her underclothes. It didn't matter that is was closing in on noon and the sun drenched them in brilliant beams of light. It didn't matter that she lay on dirt and grass. The only thing that mattered was their love.

Their kisses contained a dreamy intimacy now. When Josiah's hand outlined the circle of her breast, shivers of deliciousness rocked within her. Reaching between their bodies to unfasten his trousers, Amanda felt a tiny, somewhat solid, pointy object. "Josiah?" she said in a strangled voice.

He pulled his head from her breasts, a devilish smile curling his lips. "Yes?"

"What is . . . I . . . thought . . ." She gulped. She'd never in her life seen a naked man, but she had read, had seen pictures, and considered herself knowledgeable on their anatomy. This was something none of the books mentioned.

"Is something wrong?" he asked, humor dancing in his passion-filled eyes.

"No," she assured him. "No, I just—"

"Would you like to see it?"

Before Amanda could find her tongue again, Josiah propped himself on an elbow and shoved his free hand into his trouser pocket. He pulled out a small sugar beet. "This was a treat for Cinnamon, not you." Chuckling, he slipped it into the pocket of his shirt. "Now," he breathed into her ear, desire thickening his tone, "you are free to search for the real me."

22

MAKING LOVE WITH JOSIAH had been everything Amanda dreamed it would be. As they approached their makeshift camp, a delightful shiver of longing ran through her. She wanted to love him again. And again.

"Josiah," she said, insides tingling, "I know that sugar beet is somewhere in your pocket. I think I'd like to . . . *find* it again. That poor horse does deserve a treat."

The smile in Josiah's eyes burned with a sensuous flame. "Yes, good work and good behavior deserve reward. I believe I owe you a reward," his deep voice simmered with a barely checked passion. The implication sent waves of excitement rolling through her.

They'd stopped walking, and though Josiah still had his arms full, Amanda instinctively arched her body against his. "Goodness," she murmured breathlessly. "What did you have in mind?"

"Only this." Lowering his head, his lips parted hers in a tantalizing massage.

"Aren't you two somethin' else?"

Amanda gasped at the sound of Leon Violette's voice coming from the trees. She stiffened in Josiah's arms.

"Go on," Leon said, "finish your blasted kiss. It'll be the last time any part of him touches you."

Moving in front of Amanda, Josiah met the other man's angry glare. "What are you doing here?" he asked through gritted teeth.

"What am I doin' here?" Leon made an exaggerated gesture, flashing a small gun he held in his hand. "What do think I'm doin' here, you half-wit." He stalked from the trees and stopped a few feet in front of Josiah. "Let me see. Amanda didn't tell you who she borrowed the buckboard and horse from, did she?" Tapping the side of the barrel of the gun against his temple, he winked at Amanda. "I knew you were up to no good as soon as you stepped foot in the stable. You hate that place. And I reckon me, too."

"No, no, I don't, Leon." Amanda pushed past Josiah. "I like—"

"Shut up! You're a liar."

"No, I—I only lied because I didn't want to worry you. I figured, the kind of man you are, you'd stop me or come looking for me."

Cocking an eyebrow, Leon shook his head. "You're lying now. You're nothin' but a liar. And a tease. Yup, you're quite the tease. Didn't I tell you it'd blow up on you?"

"What do you want?" Josiah asked, again placing his body protectively between Amanda and Leon.

"Widow Marly," Leon said, clucking his tongue, ignoring Josiah's question. "Didn't think I knew the old dame was gone, huh, Amanda?"

The way Leon spat Amanda's name, Josiah knew a burning anger fueled him. Thoughts of how to get out of this mess alive whipped through his mind. Until he determined exactly what Leon had planned, he decided to bite his tongue and not provoke the man any further.

Slapping the gun barrel in his palm, Leon slowly meandered around them, stopping beside Amanda.

She swallowed drily, and though Josiah wanted nothing more than to take her into his arms, the gleam of hatred in Leon's eyes told him that was the worst thing he could do.

"So," Leon leaned toward Amanda until his nose almost touched hers, "did you find it?"

"Wh-what?"

"The treasure, my dear. Did you find it?"

"Yes," Josiah replied before she could speak. He swung the gunnysack from his shoulder and outstretched his arm. "It is here. Take it."

"No!" Amanda shouted, locking a surprisingly strong grip on his arm. "That's for your brother." She shoved his hand away. Taking a deep breath, she turned to face the enemy.

Josiah knew she'd have that imploring look in her blue eyes, but he didn't think it would be enough to change a heart of stone.

"Leon, Josiah's brother needs this," she pleaded. "He needs to walk again, be a whole man." Grabbing Leon's arm, she whispered, "Please. You can understand that, can't you?"

"Please?" He snorted. "You askin' me for another favor when you haven't paid for the first?"

"You don't under—"

"Stop it." Leon ordered, raising his hand as if he were going to slap her.

Fury raged rampantly through Josiah, and he bunched his fists at his sides. "Leave her alone."

"Oh! You gonna . . . *fight*, Amishman?" Chuckling, Leon rocked back on his heels. "We all know you won't strike another. Lucky for me, I reckon, that that's one of them half-wit quirks. You are a mite bigger. No matter. I got me all the help I need right here," he said kissing the butt of the gun. "Now, the treasure."

As Josiah handed the gunnysack to Leon, he knew he'd have to continue with the submissiveness. That would be their only hope of escape.

"You won't get away with this, Leon." Amanda looked down her nose at him. "I left a detailed note for my father."

"Oh, mercy! Whatever will I do?" Leon shrieked in a feigned, high-pitched voice. "You talkin' 'bout this little note here?'' Face hardening, he withdrew a piece of paper from his trouser pocket.

Amanda's eyes widened. "How could you? He won't know where I am."

"I'm not a monster. I left another. Explained to Newlin how the Amishman here abducted you. By now, everyone thinks the half-wit's unstable. Crazy, even."

"It was you," she hissed. "Every time my skin crawled, it was because of you. You followed us when we left. You were in the forest last night, too."

"Yup, yup, yup. Wasn't until I walked in your house and saw the note that I knew what was going on. A treasure. Never guessed that. I could use some extra money just like the next fella."

"Well," Amanda said, nostrils flaring, "there's one thing you didn't think of that contradicts what you told my father. The buckboard. Josiah repaired it already and brought it and his horse as repayment. My father'll see them both and it'll raise questions. He'll wonder why Josiah did it all if his plan was to abduct me."

"Reckon you're on to somethin' there. You see, though, we're both a mite smarter than he is," Leon said, flicking his thumb toward Josiah. "And I'm a bit smarter than you, my dear. That's why I brought this." His face lit with bitter triumph as he tramped to the forest again and returned leading Cinnamon.

Josiah's face flushed with indignation, and he started for Leon.

Pointing the gun at Josiah's chest, Leon growled, "Close enough." Arms akimbo, he shook his head. "I'm tryin' to finish a story here. Where are your manners? In case you were wondering," he laughed wickedly, "I also took an axe to the buckboard you repaired, Miller. It's in pieces now. Papa won't be too happy with the Amishman after all, right, Amanda darlin'?"

"You're sick, Leon. You truly are. Let's go back, just you and me, and we'll talk to Doc Rollins."

"You're stupider than Miller if you think I'm going back to confess everything. Way it is now, the half-wit here is the outlaw. No matter what you say, even your father isn't

gonna believe anything different. Now," he said, shifting
the bag of gold to the hand that held the gun, "there's the
little matter of what you owe me. Since you gave so freely
to the Amishman, I'm expecting big things from you,
Amanda."

Sticking her chin out defiantly, she said, "I don't know
what you're talking about."

"You have blood on your skirt. Unless I missed you
skinning an animal somewhere along on this little trip, I'd
say you ain't a virgin anymore."

Amanda regarded him with a mixture of hatred and contempt. "You have the gun. Josiah and I are at your mercy.
Do what you want with me. I don't care because you can't
change what's in here," she said, placing both hands over
her heart. "I love and respect Josiah. You, Leon, I pity."

A sickening wave welled in Josiah's belly. Leon's eyes
bulged from their sockets at Amanda's words. When he
pulled a rope from Cinnamon's neck, pure terror seized
Josiah. He wondered if he hadn't gone about this all wrong.
Maybe he should have tried to overpower the madman from
the start. If Leon hurt Amanda in any way, Josiah knew
he'd kill him.

"Come on," Leon ordered, waving his gun. "Over here
by the trees, Miller. I'll even be a nice guy and tie you by
your horse. Oops," he leered, "it's not yours anymore.
When I bring Amanda back safely from the crazy Amishman, I reckon Newlin'll give it to me. Reckon he'll give
me whatever I want."

"You are a loon," Amanda said, shaking her head, her
voice high and hysterical. "Listen to yourself."

"Shut up," Leon ordered, pointing the gun at her. "Just
shut up. All I ever wanted was for you to love me. But no,
it was Miller here that took you away." Leon squinted and
blinked as though his head or eyes hurt. "Drop all that
stuff, especially the shovel, and get over here, Miller," he
said, tapping a tree with the gun.

Josiah dumped the pack and shovel. He crossed the short
distance to Amanda and caressed her cheek with the back
of his hand. "It is not over," he said to her, willing her to
believe in him.

"Damn you!" Leon sprang, smashing the gun butt into the back of Josiah's head.

A snarl of agony flew from Josiah's lips. His skull felt like it had been split. He heard Amanda's screams. They seemed so far away. Though he struggled against the blackness that hovered, he was helpless to fend off Leon. He felt himself being dragged by the ankles across the sticks and brush to the trees. He thought he heard Cinnamon nickering, too, as if in protest.

Suddenly it hit him. As the trees blurred overhead, he fought harder to stay conscious. He needed just a little more time with Leon's back turned to implement this escape plan. He prayed it worked.

When Leon tied his hands and feet together, Josiah lolled his head, pretending to be barely conscious. Leon pulled a kicking, screaming Amanda into the forest.

Though the base of his skull ached, Josiah shook his head, hoping to clear some of the fogginess. He couldn't believe his good fortune. From where he'd been tied, Cinnamon was not more than a yard away. "Come here, girl. Come on," Josiah coaxed, finagling the sugar beet from his palm where he'd hidden it to between the rope and his wrists. The horse nickered again, and he knew he had the animal's attention. "Want a treat? Come get it," he whispered harshly, wiggling his fingers, while visions of Amanda and Leon flashed in his mind.

Cinnamon trudged over, shaking her tawny mane. Josiah wiggled his fingers some more and the horse lowered her head. Warm bursts of air from her nostrils hit his wrists as she sniffed. It felt like heaven. "It's there, baby. Come on, girl. Work for it."

A gasp of relief broke from Josiah's lips as soft, moist lips brushed the skin of his inner wrists. He felt the gnawing of the horse's teeth against the ropes. Within minutes he was free, and Cinnamon munched the sugar beet. Glancing upward, he whispered, "Thank you." Then, swallowing hard, he murmured, "Please forgive me for what I may do."

Seizing the discarded shovel, he snuck into the woods to find Amanda.

"Confound it all," he heard Leon growl. "Your bitin' was bad enough. Stop your scratchin', or I'll tie you yet." The sound of flesh striking flesh cut through the still forest air.

Josiah crashed through the trees, swung the shovel and connected with Leon's head. Leon crumpled across Amanda without making a sound.

Dropping to his knees beside her, Josiah untied her gag and rolled Leon's body off her. He drew Amanda into his arms, and for a few moments they simply rocked each other.

"Did he hurt you?" Josiah asked, fearful of her answer.

"No. How in the world did you get loose?"

"That sugar beet. Cinnamon will chew through anything to get at one."

Amanda laughed, and the sound was like music. Then she quieted, and asked timidly, "Did we kill him?"

"He still breathes. That is why we cannot stay. We must leave for home."

"Yes." She scrambled to her feet, tugging Josiah along with her. "We'll take everything and leave after we've tied him to a tree. It'll serve him right."

Gathering her into his arms, Josiah held her snugly and kissed the top of her head. "That is not my Amanda talking," he said gently. "We will leave Leon the possessions that are rightfully his—the horse and the buckboard."

"Whatever for?" She pushed from his arms, a deep frown pleating her brows. "He'll come back to Prosper and continue with his lies."

"We will arrive first and disprove his story. Truth always prevails over hatred and lies."

Contempt still glazed her eyes, but with a sigh she said, "All right. You know more about that religious stuff than I do. Just to be safe, though. . . ." She knelt next to Leon's still form. With a gulp and a face wrinkled with disgust, she shoved her hand into the pocket of Leon's trousers, withdrawing the letter she'd originally written. Smiling, she said, "In case God's a little busy."

Except for the gunnysack of gold, the letter, quilt, their coats and the last piece of ham, they left everything behind.

Amanda felt comfortable on Cinnamon's bare back this time. She loved how the wind hit her face and blew back her hair, but even more, she loved the feel of Josiah's body pressed so intimately against hers.

Though they hadn't talked about what had happened between them, she had no qualms. Her heart sang, and she felt fully alive. When her father saw how happy she was, he'd accept Josiah. He had to.

An annoying, outspoken voice inside her head told her he didn't have to. And that given the history between them, he most likely wouldn't. Shutting out the voice, Amanda swallowed at the lump that pushed into her throat. She snuggled closer against Josiah and blinked back the tears that burned her eyes.

They rode until it became too dark and dangerous to continue. As soon as they were off the horse's back, Amanda felt a tangible difference in their relationship. Josiah seemed cool and reserved as he went right to work rubbing down Cinnamon's sweaty hide. Sitting on a log nearby, she fought the nausea churning her insides.

"When will we be home?" she asked finally, breaking the awkward silence.

"By noon tomorrow. Possibly before that."

"Josiah . . ." She fingered the quilt sitting in her lap, wishing she could see his face. "About us. I know my father hasn't always been . . . nice to you. He'll come around."

"There cannot be an *us*. I have been a fool," he said in a strangled voice. "I do not have an excuse for what I have done to you. It will never happen again. That is a prom—"

"Don't make a promise you'll regret." Anguish seared Amanda's heart. "Nothing happened that I didn't want. You love me. I know you do."

"Stop!" Josiah demanded. "What we did was a mistake. You will see that. You do not love me."

"How dare you tell me what to do or how to feel? You said back there that good always prevails. Was that another of your hypocritical statements?"

Exhaling with a whoosh, he stormed toward her. "You

do not understand. When I return tomorrow, I will belong nowhere. I will be cast from my community for searching for the treasure, and I will be no better a man in the eyes of your father. I will not let you lose your family for me. That," he said through clenched teeth, "is not good. I would die before doing that."

"But I love you. That is good." Amanda felt a wretchedness of mind she'd never known before.

"It is time to sleep," Josiah said sharply, thrusting her coat at her, then walking away.

Tears she could no longer control found their way down her cheeks. After some time, she moved from her seat on the top of the log to the ground, resting her back against the rough wood. Even the crickets chirped a woeful serenade. Hugging her knees to her body, she ignored the dew that seeped into her clothing and chilled her bones. Staring into the night, she waited for the dawn.

∞

"AMANDA. BREAKFAST."

Amanda heard Josiah, felt him gently shaking her shoulder. A dense fog clouded around her brain and she forced her eyes open. Though it took several seconds for them to adjust, she was certain she saw a smile on Josiah's face before he turned into the sullen-faced man again.

"Here is the last of the ham. I want us to leave soon."

"Yes, sir." She took the meat and gave him a mock salute. "I'm surprised you want to go back. What are your plans then, Mr. Man Without a Place in the World?"

Josiah straightened to his full height and crossed his arms over his massive chest. "You jest," he said, looking down at her, "but to me it is not funny."

"You're right. I'm sorry. I thought you had this all figured out before. You knew anything you did to raise money for Elam would sentence you to being an outcast. I don't think anything's changed, other than the fact that you've admitted you love me. I've never known you to give up so easily." Setting the food aside, she jerked to her feet. "I'm not hungry. I'm ready to go home."

She'd contemplated the situation most of the night, and as much as it dismayed her, she finally saw the truth in the words he'd spoken yesterday. To tell him, though, would seem as if she was discounting and giving up their love. She couldn't not have hope that somehow everything would work out, that they could be together and not lose their families in the process.

As Josiah swung her up in the saddle behind him, Amanda made a wish on the last star fading into the morning light. She didn't know if wishes during the day worked, but she figured it couldn't hurt. She didn't want to have to make a choice between two men that she loved, but if forced, she would.

It seemed the closer they got to Prosper, the grayer the sky and the cooler the air became. By the time they reached her father's property, Amanda was shivering, for the wind had picked up considerably, bending saplings and swaying majestic old hardwoods. Cinnamon's pace slowed, too, as she fought to move forward in the wind. Amanda usually liked to give credence to omens. Nothing good could possibly come out of this weather.

They finally reached the barn, and Amanda slid off the horse's back. After landing on the ground in a heap, she stood up. "Just go," she shouted to Josiah. "I need to find and talk to my father."

"I will wait. If he is not here, I will take you to town. I must return Cinnamon to him."

Throwing her hands up in exasperation, Amanda ignored the buckboard that still sat where Leon had demolished it. She headed to the barn where the heavy double doors banged ominously as if they were weightless. Peeking inside, she saw that the chestnut mare was not in her stall, which could only mean her father was not at home. She hoped he wasn't out looking for her in this weather. Stomach churning, she retraced her steps, latched the doors and fought the wind walking back to Josiah.

"They'll know in town where he is," she shouted through the wind. "I need to find him."

23

DESPITE HAVING DONNED HER coat before they'd left, Amanda still felt the eerie chill in the air. Lightning zigzagged across the dusky sky, and she debated whether they'd make it to town before Mother Nature unleashed her fury.

The five-minute mark came quickly. Cinnamon responded to Josiah's prodding and spiritedly fought the wind, increasing her speed to nearly a full gallop. Her thundering hooves turned clods of earth that were instantly blown away, and white puffs of air shot from her flaring nostrils. Despite the cool temperature, her velvety hide glistened with sweat. Amanda's heart went out to the overworked horse.

At last they topped the remaining hill, and Prosper came into view.

Through the dust that whipped around them, Amanda saw a throng of people gathered near the jail. Several were dressed in the telltale darks of the Amish. Josiah's body stiffened beneath her circled arms, and she knew his dread matched her own.

When they reached the gathering, he yanked on the reins,

startling Cinnamon to an abrupt stop and nearly sending
Amanda sliding to the ground.

As the faces of those gathered turned toward them, nau-
seating spurts of adrenaline coursed through Amanda. Mr.
and Mrs. Miller and Mary were there, relief muting the
concern etched on their faces. Some other Amish people
that Amanda had never seen before were beside them. She
easily spotted her father, his face swollen and scarlet, the
veins in his neck standing in livid ridges.

As Josiah dismounted, a loud curse flew from her father's
lips. Reality pommeled her hopes. The little voice from
before had been right.

"Get your blasted hands off my daughter," Newlin de-
manded over the whirring of the wind. "I'll help her down.
I don't want you anywhere near her. You'll be arrested if
I have my way."

"No, Papa!" Amanda shouted. "You don't understand."

"Shut up." His angry fingers bit into her waist as he
seized her and set her roughly on her heels. "Arrest him,
sheriff," Newlin ordered, shaking his fists. "What in the
bloody hell you waitin' for? That man abducted my daughter!"

The Millers now stood emotionless, but tears streamed
down Mary's pale cheeks.

"Stop it. Stop it, Papa!" Shaking her head, Amanda
faced the sheriff. "Josiah didn't do anything. He only came
with me because he didn't want me to get hurt."

"Aww, jiminy. Don't you be lyin'. I saw the note from
Leon. He's out looking for you right now."

"Leon tried to kill Josiah. Papa, listen to me. Leon is
not the man you think. He tried to rape me. If Josiah hadn't
gotten free, he would have."

"You're lyin'!"

"Calm down, now. I think we'd best move this discussion inside the jail, Newlin," the sheriff said.

The blustery wind swirled Amanda's loose skirt with
such force she thought for a fleeting moment it would be
torn from her body. Bizarre lightning danced almost con-
tinuously in the sky. The smell of rain and something evil

wafted through the air. Many of those gathered looked toward the heavens.

"Sheriff's right," someone said. "This storm's gonna be a bad one. Maybe we'd better be takin' some shelter."

More bystanders left until only a handful remained.

"Papa, listen to me for once. I'm not lying. I have nothing to lie about." She gouged her fingernails into her palms. "If my word isn't good enough, I'll give you proof. Please get my letter, Josiah."

"What letter?" Newlin's brows knitted together.

Josiah slid the gunnysack of gold from Cinnamon's neck. Opening the sack, he pulled out the wrinkled paper and handed it to Amanda.

"This is the real letter, the letter I left for you," she said, passing it to her father. "I went to Leon to borrow a horse and buckboard. He was suspicious and followed me back to the house. After Josiah and I left, he snuck in and found the note. It wasn't until he learned about the treasure that he decided to follow us and try to take it for himself. That's why he left you a fake note. He wanted to incriminate Josiah and make himself the hero in your eyes. Oh, Papa, everything Leon did, he did to make you dislike Josiah more."

While Amanda prattled on so valiantly in his defense, Josiah's gaze swept across those around him. Unlike Mary, whose eyes were filled with compassion and acceptance, his parents and the other Amish were loaded with suspicions and disappointment. No matter what Amanda said, he saw it wouldn't make a difference in the face of his community. Newlin seemed unaffected as well, for his mouth crimped so tightly with resentment his lips were tinged blue.

Everything was at stake for Amanda. Josiah wasn't about to let her ruin her relationship with her father. "This is not Amanda's fault." He shouted to be heard above the roar of the wind. Squaring his shoulders, ready to be cast from his family and from Amanda's life, he said, "I am to blame."

Amanda whirled around to face him. "What are you trying to do? Just stop it. What happened," she said slowly, shooting him a warning look, "happened because of me. I wanted to help Josiah help Elam. We followed the stitched map on that old quilt, and we found the treasure. There should be more than enough money for Elam's new leg."

Newlin's head popped up in surprise. "Treasure? What in blazes are you babbling about? There really was a treasure?"

"Treasure ain't gonna matter if it gets blown away," the sheriff interrupted. "Something's brewing here. You people best get to the shelter in the jail. I'm gonna go to the school. Them kids ain't out for the summer yet."

Glancing to the sky, Newlin shook his head. "All right, all right, we're comin'."

"I tried to tell you about the treasure, Papa, but you thought I was being loony."

"Can't hear you," Newlin hollered back at her.

"I love Josiah!" Amanda shouted more loudly. "This was the only way I could help him. I love him!"

"What?" Newlin exploded, face redder than an autumn apple.

"You heard me." Amanda met her father's withering glare, then turned and approached the Millers and the other Amish. "And in case you didn't hear me, I love Josiah."

"Amanda . . ."

Josiah reached for her arm, but she pulled away. "Be quiet, Josiah! Let me finish this." Swallowing hard, Amanda took a deep breath, sand and dust inching up her nose and into her eyes from the relentless wind. "I know enough about your culture to know you think something like this is wrong." Though she shouted at the top of her lungs, her voice sounded weak and soft against the elements. "If you can't see the good in what your son is doing," she hollered, "then I think I'm glad he's not completely like you."

A barely noticeable smile that Amanda knew was meant for her curled Mary's lips. In the next instant, Josiah's sister screamed.

All gazes seemed to fly to the blackened sky at the same time. An enormous funnel cloud not too far in the distance skipped across the heavens, bringing with it the blasting sound of tens of freight trains.

"Get to the jail!" Newlin hollered.

Suddenly Leon appeared from nowhere on horseback. "My horses! The damned thing is gonna get my stable. I have to get over there to set my horses free, or they'll never make it!"

"There is no time!" Josiah ran at him and tried to capture the reins as Leon's frantic horse sped by.

Newlin ran, too, and grabbed Josiah's arm, dust and wood particles swirling around them, covering them like a blanket. "It's too late. We have to let him go. Get Amanda and your people to that shelter," he shouted into Josiah's ear. "The sheriff hasn't come with those young'uns yet. I'm gonna help him."

"I will go." Josiah shrugged from Newlin's forceful grip. "You will not make it. I am faster."

"Dammit, Miller!" Newlin grabbed at him again, their faces so close that their breaths mingled. Josiah blinked, startled to find himself staring into the same imploring blue eyes as Amanda's.

"Do this for me. Get my daughter to that shelter! Please, Miller. Take care of her."

A tacit understanding passed between them. Josiah ran then, searching for Amanda and his family in the turbulent dust cloud. He found them and pulled them into the jail. "Get into the shelter," he ordered, thrusting a lantern and matches at his father and the gunnysack with the treasure at Amanda.

Dashing back to the street, he shaded his eyes to try to locate any people left out in the storm. Two women next to the bank stood frozen, as if somehow mesmerized by the tornado's long black body and all it had stolen as it bounced along the ground. He ran to them and dragged them to the jail, then returned once more to the chaos.

The tornado closed in on the town, springing about in an erratic path. Josiah knew there were only seconds left. Clutching the support beam of the overhang, his gaze sifted through the flying debris for any signs of the sheriff, Newlin or the children.

With a heavy heart, he raced for safety.

He closed the door and dropped into place the thick piece of wood that served as the latch.

Amanda screamed and flung her arms at him wildly, but he couldn't hear her since the sound above the ground was now deafening. Squirming past him, she reached for the latch. Capturing her about the waist, he roughly yanked her from the door. A heart-stopping roar filled the tiny space. The door shook and rattled violently as if the devil himself were fighting to get in.

Within a matter of minutes, the shelter and the world grew silent.

Peering about wild-eyed, Amanda muttered, "It's over. It's over." She shoved away from Josiah's arms and darted the short distance to the door. "Papa. I have to find him."

"Wait," Josiah pulled her back again. "Let me see if it is safe."

"Safe?" Her tone was edged with steel, and she glared at him. "You locked my father from safety. I saw you two fighting. I saw it all. You were right when you said before there can be no us." Gulping, she forced her lips into a sardonic smile. "I would have chosen you over him, too." Shaking her head, she whispered brokenly, "I thought I knew you." She straightened her shoulders with a deep breath. "Now, get your hands off me. I need to find . . . what's left of my father."

Josiah felt like he'd been punched in the stomach. He released her, heaving as he breathed. He could imagine how the scene between Newlin and himself had looked to her. His heart cried out, ordering him to wrap her in his arms and make her see the truth. His soul, though it wept, told him this outcome was the best thing for Amanda.

With her head held high, she swung open the door. "Make sure Elam gets his leg," she said as stepped from the shelter.

∽

"WHAT DO YOU THINK, Doc Rollins?" Amanda chewed a fingernail.

"Well, there's no broken bones. That there is a miracle in itself the way them walls blew in. Time is what your father needs now. He's a strong, ornery cuss. Reckon he'll wake when he's good and ready and not before. Just watch for fever. Let me know if he shows any signs of one." Doc Rollins smiled. "We're all lucky. Things could have been so much worse. The schoolhouse and the store, those are just buildings with items that are replaceable." Pursing his thin lips, he shook his balding head. "Leon, now that's a tragedy. Them horses were like his family, though. In his eyes, he had to try and save 'em."

"I think they were really all he did care about," Amanda said softly.

"You could be right." The doctor picked up his bag and smiled again. "Sure is something about your pa saving them schoolkids. Take care of that hero. I'll leave you my buggy for transportation. Get a message to me, my dear, if you need anything. I'll show myself out."

Doc Rollins left the room and Amanda paced the woven rug, finally leaning beside the window. The doctor emerged from the house, crossed the yard to his horse and rode from sight.

As far as she could see, things looked normal. It seemed strange that only a few miles away lay utter destruction. The doctor was right, though. The damaged buildings would in time be rebuilt. Life would go on for everyone in Prosper, everyone but Leon.

Returning to her father's bedside, Amanda sank wearily to the upholstered armchair. Ophelia padded in and rubbed her back against Amanda's leg, purring, but even her feline friend couldn't lessen the ache in her heart. The discord inside her was like nothing she'd ever felt before.

One day turned into four and still her father slept. "What do you think now?" Amanda asked when Doc Rollins returned to check on the patient. "I'm worried." She wiped her palms on the front of her skirt. "Have you ever seen sleep like this?"

"It's not at all uncommon with a head injury. His pulse rate is good. There's no fever. I know how frustrating this is, Amanda, but there isn't anything more we can do. I have confidence that Newlin'll wake soon. We must keep the faith and wait.''

She crossed her arms over her bosom. "I'm not good at either.''

The doctor's eyebrows raised into a straight line across his forehead. "That's not what Josiah tells me. I've heard the entire story about that quilt. Your faith was unwavering. What you did for Elam Miller was a wonderful thing.''

An unexpected surge of elation filled Amanda. She quickly squashed it, reminding herself how Josiah had locked her father from the shelter to die in the tornado. She berated herself. She was the despicable one for still caring, but the harder she tried to bury her feelings for Josiah, the more they persisted.

"I'm glad Elam is going to get his artificial leg," she said curtly. "Let's talk about something else now, please.''

" 'Course,'' Doc Rollins said, eyeing her curiously. He gathered his stethoscope and dropped it into his black leather bag. "Just one more thing about the Millers. I didn't say that Elam is getting his leg. I said what you did on his behalf was wonderful.''

As the doctor packed the rest of his instruments, his words echoed in Amanda's head. She had to know what was going on. "Why wouldn't Elam get his leg? Wasn't there enough money?''

"I reckon there was more than enough, but no one has made the arrangements. Josiah's been shunned by the community. He can't go back there. I insisted he stay with me until he decides what to do. Fact is, he's been single-handedly rebuilding your father's store.''

"What?'' Amanda asked in a suffocated whisper.

"The store. Day after it happened, he was out there cleaning up. He's working like a mule. Was gone before dawn yesterday, too. He's determined to fix that store. I feel bad for the boy. He's hurting inside. Won't talk about it, though. That sister of his . . .'' The doctor scratched his head.

"Mary,'' Amanda supplied for him.

"Yes, that's the one. She's been by once.''

"That's good.''

"Yes, but I don't know if she can make a difference in a culture that's been the same for so many years. I've got to go, my dear." With a wink, Doc Rollins disappeared from the room.

"Oh, goodness," Amanda muttered, pacing the rug again, the lonely silence weighing heavily upon her shoulders. She bit her lip until it throbbed like her pulse. Grief and despair tore at her heart until she thought she could no longer stand it. "I don't know what to do." Tears blinded her eyes and choked her voice. "Oh, God, I don't know what to do."

"I ain't him," came her father's weak voice, "but maybe I could help?"

"Papa!" Amanda ran to his bed and threw her arms about him. "Oh!" she shrieked, bolting upright again. "I'm sorry. You have no broken bones, but I'm certain you must be sore. I wasn't thinking."

"Naw. I'm all right. How long I been in this godforsaken bed?"

"Four days. Do you remember what happened?"

"Yup. I remember the blasted twister. Remember goin' for them kids. Got that last little freckle-faced gal in the cellar of the store and, jiminy, the walls blew in on me. I was thinkin' I was gonna be with your ma again." He licked his lips.

"Let me get you some water." She rushed to the bureau and poured a glass of water from the pitcher. "Here you go," she said, cradling his head and bringing the glass to his lips.

"Ah, that's good," he exclaimed as Amanda gently laid him back on the pillow. "Throat feels like sandpaper."

Though purple shadows accented his sunken eyes, there was a spark of something there that she didn't recognize. It worried her. "Maybe you should rest now. We can talk later."

"Mercy, girl. Been sleepin' for days and you want me to rest some more?" He chuckled and some of the pallor seemed to vanish before her eyes. "Like I was sayin', I thought that was the end. I saw your ma, but she wouldn't let me stay. Wasn't my time," he said in a casual, jesting way. "She told me I had some fences to mend first. I see that I do."

"Oh, Papa," Amanda said, perching on the edge of his bed. "I have my own fences to mend. I'm sorry about everything that's happened here lately. I just—"

"You fell in love, that's what you did."

He closed his eyes, and she thought maybe he'd fallen asleep. As soon as she rose from the bed, he opened them. They were misty and wistful. She'd never seen her father like this before.

"Papa, what's wrong?"

"Nothin'. Everything's gonna be right. Now," he said as he wiped his hands across his face, "I ain't never been a good listener, you've told me that yourself, but I'm gonna be. I'm gonna be everything I never was. Where's Miller?"

"I—I guess at the store. Doc says he's been clearing debris and rebuilding."

"That right? What do you say about all of it?"

"I don't know what you mean."

"You and Miller. What do you say? What are your plans?"

Nodding her head, Amanda said, "I see what you're doing. All right, I'll say it. You were right about him being no good. You've been right all along. I was wrong." She sighed in exasperation. "Enough talk. You rest, and I'll go warm some soup."

"Whoa, whoa just a minute there, Amanda." Newlin clutched her hand. "What's this right and wrong nonsense?"

"Josiah. He locked you from the storm shelter. He wouldn't let me find you. You almost died because of him. He isn't the man I thought he was."

"Good for him." Newlin's grin turned into a chuckle. "He listened."

"What?" she asked, dropping back on the bed. She so badly wanted the pieces of this puzzle to fit together.

"I told him to get you to safety. He argued at first, wanted to go for them kids. I insisted. I figured if he loved you as much as his eyes said, he'd die himself tryin' to keep you safe. I couldn't bear to lose you. If he's part of the shipment, then I best accept it.''

Tears of pleasure found their way to Amanda's eyes. ''Do you mean it?''

''I ain't gonna start wearin' black, though, I'll tell you that right now.''

She embraced her father, laughing and crying at the same time.

''Reckon there's someone you need to be seein'.''

''Yes, but your food. You must be hungry.''

''Couple hours ain't gonna matter none. Bring Miller back with you. I want to see about gettin' that brother of his that leg.''

''Oh, Papa. I will.'' Amanda's lips trembled as she smiled. ''I was terrible to him. Wish me luck.''

''It's gonna be all right. I feel it in here.'' Newlin placed his hands over his heart and smiled.

During the ride to town, Amanda rehearsed her apology, wishing she felt her father's confidence and praying what was in her heart would be enough for Josiah to forgive her.

From the last hilltop she saw what looked like havoc below. Many of the townsfolk were gathered about, and it looked as if many Amish had assembled as well. Horrible thoughts crowded her mind. Her stomach shriveled. What else was included in the shunning practice?

She stopped the buggy just outside town in front of a big oak that had been unearthed and now blocked the road. Jumping from the wagon, she ran. Beads of sweat dotted her forehead as she dodged the debris still left from the storm. As she neared the people, something clicked in her mind. She spotted the smithy clearing rubble, and Doc Rollins's smiling face was among those there as well.

Side by side, Amish and English worked together. Finally Amanda's gaze landed on Josiah. He and his father were embracing. That certainly couldn't be part of the shunning process. A cry of relief broke from her lips, snaring Josiah's attention. His eyes were gentle, understanding. Amanda threaded her way through the people.

''I am so sorry,'' she whispered through her tears. ''My father's awake. He's going to be all right. He told me what happened. He wants us to be all right, too. He told me so. He's changed. Oh, Josiah, can you ever forgive me?"

"Forgiveness is all around," he said, eyes brimming with tears. "In your family and in mine. Mary and my parents petitioned the elders. I am no longer Amish, but I still have my family. And I hope you."

"Yes. Yes, you do! I love you." Burying her face in his neck, she breathed a kiss there. "I love you."

"Do you know what I think?" Josiah asked, brushing his lips against hers. "I think it is your quilt. It has revealed to all of us the many treasures of the heart."

A Quilting Romance

Patterns of Love
by Christine Holden

When Lord Grayling Dunston appears on Baines Marshall's doorstep asking for her only quilt, she sends him on his way. But Baines discovers that Mary's Fortune is no ordinary quilt—its pattern reveals the map to a treasure Gray desperately needs to pay off his debts. When the quilt suddenly disappears from her home the two embark on a journey that deepens their attraction and changes their lives...

❏ 0-515-12481-8/$5.99

Friends Romance

Can a man come between friends?

☐ A TASTE OF HONEY
by DeWanna Pace   0-515-12387-0

☐ WHERE THE HEART IS
by Sheridon Smythe   0-515-12412-5

☐ LONG WAY HOME
by Wendy Corsi Staub   0-515-12440-0

All books $5.99